The Tale of
Khun Chang Khun Phaen

ABRIDGED

TRANSLATED AND EDITED BY

Chris Baker and Pasuk Phongpaichit

Silkworm Books

ISBN: 978-616-215-084-5
© 2015 Silkworm Books
All rights reserved

First published in 2015 by
Silkworm Books
6 Sukkasem Road, T. Suthep
Chiang Mai 50200 Thailand
info@silkwormbooks.com
www.silkwormbooks.com

Illustrations and cover art by Muangsing Janchai. Covers show detail from two of his mural paintings of the Khun Chang Khun Phaen tale at Wat Palelai, Suphanburi.
Cover design by Lisa Carta

Typeset in Minion Pro 11 pt. by Silk Type
Printed and bound in Thailand by O.S. Printing House, Bangkok

5 4 3 2 1

CONTENTS

Preface   *v*

Principal characters   *ix*

Three births   *1*

The deaths of the fathers   *9*

Phlai Kaeo is ordained   *25*

Phlai Kaeo meets Phim in a cotton field   *37*

Khun Chang asks for Phim's hand   *53*

Phlai Kaeo goes into Saithong's room   *62*

Phlai Kaeo marries Phim   *76*

Phlai Kaeo goes to war   *85*

Laothong is given to Phlai Kaeo   *100*

Phim changes her name to Wanthong   *109*

Siprajan gives Wanthong to Khun Chang   *120*

Khun Phaen and Wanthong quarrel   *129*

Khun Phaen states his case   *141*

Khun Phaen is parted from Laothong   *151*

Khun Phaen forges a sword   *158*

Khun Phaen enters Khun Chang's house   *163*

Khun Phaen flees with Wanthong   *177*

Khun Chang follows Wanthong   *185*

Khun Chang accuses Khun Phaen   *196*

Khun Phaen gives himself up   *207*

Khun Phaen is jailed   *215*

The birth of Phlai Ngam   *227*

Phlai Ngam volunteers   *242*

Phlai Ngam romances Simala   *259*

Khun Phaen rescues Phra Thainam   *278*

The capture of the King of Chiang Mai   *294*

The army returns home   *304*

The princesses are presented   *319*

The marriage of Phra Wai   *329*

Khun Chang is found guilty   *341*

Khun Chang petitions the king   *350*

The death of Wanthong   *360*

Glossary   377
List of Illustrations   380

PREFACE

Khun Chang Khun Phaen is the great classic of Thai literature. The plot is a love story set against a background of war and ending in high tragedy.

The tale is set in Siam, the old name for Thailand, in the era when Ayutthaya was the capital, or prior to 1767. Exactly when the tale is set and when it was created are unknown. We believe it emerged around 1600, but that is no more than an informed guess, and others have different theories.

The tale was originally recited by storytellers for local entertainment and passed on by word of mouth, becoming very popular. Starting probably in the eighteenth century, the court took up the tale and started writing it down. In the early nineteenth century, court poets, including two kings of Siam, revised many chapters. The first printed edition appeared in 1872, and the standard edition was edited and published in 1917–18 by Prince Damrong Rajanubhab, a half-brother of King Chulalongkorn (Rama V).

In 2010 we published the first-ever English translation of the tale, based on Prince Damrong's edition with over a hundred passages restored from other versions, and with over two thousand footnotes to explain many unfamiliar things, from dress and weapons to flora and magic.

The aim in this abridged edition is to tell the full story and leave out no scene, incident, or significant speech. We have reduced the length by shedding detail, repetition, and poetical flourishes. The one exception is at the start of the Chiang Mai campaign, where the original has two and a half chapters about regional diplomacy in which none of the main characters of the tale appear. We have summarized this passage into a couple of paragraphs.

We also present the text without the distraction of footnotes, and with the number of unfamiliar words reduced to a minimum (and explained in a glossary at the back). For background, look up the Wikipedia entry for *Khun Chang Khun Phaen.*

Much of the action takes place in two towns to the west of Bangkok. Suphan (now Suphanburi) is a very old town that was important as a strategic and religious center. Kanburi (which has been shifted and renamed Kanchanaburi) was a frontier outpost defending the route between Siam and Burma.

The storytellers of the original tale often used flowers and trees as metaphors. To retain the flavor of the metaphors, we have invented several new names for these flowers and trees, including hiddenlover, secretscent, and pupil tree.

"Khun" is one of the lowest titles in the old Siamese official nobility. Khun Phaen is named Phlai Kaeo at birth and receives his title after winning a military victory. Khun Chang probably had a birth name but it does not appear in the text. "Chang" means elephant. His father was a local keeper of the king's elephants and the name Khun Chang was probably a local nickname passed on to his son.

"Chaophraya" and "Phraya" were the two highest titles in the old Siamese nobility, held by ministers and governors of major provinces. "Phra" and "Luang" were slightly lower titles.

At the time of the story, Lanna, with its capital at Chiang Mai, was a separate country. Today "Lao" is the term for the people of Laos and the speakers of its language. At the time of the story, the Siamese court used the term "Lao" to refer both to the people of Lanchang (the old name of Laos) and to those of Lanna.

In Buddhist ethics, people acquire merit by doing good deeds and acquire demerit by doing bad deeds. The balance, often called karma, determines what happens to a person after dying and becoming a spirit, including how that spirit may be reborn for a future life and what might befall him or her there.

The original Thai version of the tale is in a verse form called *klon* with a complex scheme of linked rhymes that crosses chapter boundaries. The very last paragraph of this abridged translation is rendered in an English approximation of the rhyming scheme that is used throughout the story.

The illustrations are by Muangsing Janchai, who has also painted a series of murals on the tale in Wat Palelai, Suphanburi.

PRINCIPAL CHARACTERS

Suphan

Khun Krai Phonlaphai, a soldier

Thong Prasi, his wife

Phlai Kaeo, son of Krai and Thong Prasi; later **Khun Phaen**; later Phra Kanburi

Phlai Ngam, son of Khun Phaen and Wanthong, later **Phra Wai** Woranat

Phlai Chumphon, son of Khun Phaen and Kaeo Kiriya

Khun Siwichai, a local official in charge of elephants

Thepthong, his wife

Khun Chang, son of Siwichai and Thepthong

Phan Sonyotha, a trader

Siprajan, his wife

Phim Philalai, daughter of Sonyotha and Siprajan; later **Wanthong**

Saithong, foster-sister of Phim

Ayutthaya

King Phanwasa, ruler of Ayutthaya

Chaophraya Jakri, minister of the north

Phraya Yommarat, minister of the capital

Phra Thainam, a military chief

Phramuen Si, one of the four heads of the royal pages

Chiang Mai

King of Chiang Mai

Apson Sumali, his queen

Soifa, their daughter
Saentri Phetkla, a military chief

Chomthong

Laothong, daughter of the headman of Chomthong village; wife of Khun Phaen

Sukhothai

Kaeo Kiriya, daughter of the governor; wife of Khun Phaen

Lanchang

King of Lanchang
Keson, his queen
Soithong, their daughter

Phichit

Phra Phichit, governor
Busaba, his wife
Simala, their daughter
Moei, Simala's servant

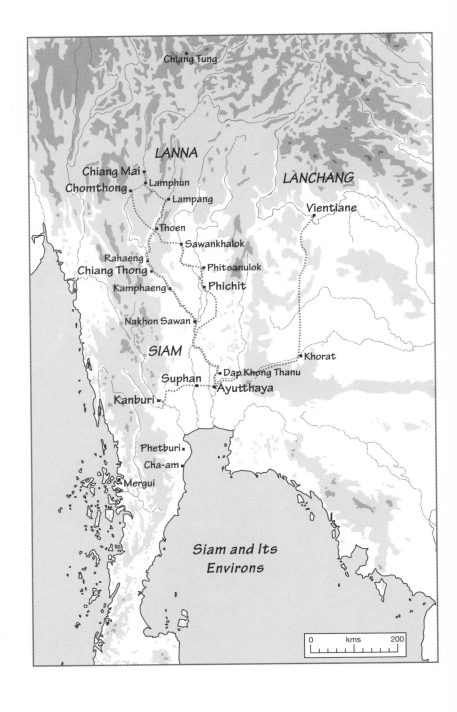

Chiang Tung

LANNA

LANCHANG

Chiang Mai
Chomthong
Lamphun
Lampang

Vientiane

Thoen

Sawankhalok

Rahaeng
Chiang Thong
Phitsanulok

Kamphaeng
Phichit

Nakhon Sawan

SIAM

Khorat

Suphan
Dap Khong Thanu
Ayutthaya

Kanburi

Phetburi

Cha-am

Mergui

Siam and Its
Environs

0   kms   200

THREE BIRTHS

This is the story of Khun Phaen, Khun Chang, and the fair Wanthong. Their parents were subjects of King Phanwasa of Ayutthaya. Let us begin with the births of these three characters.

At night, a wicked spirit at the top of a tree fashions human bodies by molding and remolding, adding this and that to make them complete, in fits of laughter. When beings who have suffered in hell for their bad karma are released from torment, the spirit catches them, shapes them as humans, and slips each into a womb.

Khun Siwichai, a provincial official in charge of elephants, was a rich man with masses of wealth and many servants. Together with his wife, Thepthong, he lived at Ten Cowries Landing in Suphan.

In her sleep, Thepthong dreamed that a bull elephant died and rolled down a steep bank where its head became swollen and putrefied. A baldheaded adjutant stork flew over from the forest, picked up the elephant in its beak, and set it down in the hall where she slept. She called to the bird, "Come over here, bald lord" and cradled both stork and elephant to sleep.

Waking up, she retched at the foul smell lingering on her chest, roused her husband, and begged him to massage her neck. When she had recovered and related the dream, Khun Siwichai interpreted it. "Well, you'll be pregnant! Nothing to worry about. Our child will be a boy. Our blessings are complete, my love, but this child will be bald from birth. He'll bring shame on us, yet will be rich with cartloads of money."

Thepthong did not want this kind of blessing. "By mother's clan! Why should I raise a bald baby?"

When Thepthong's belly grew huge, she was constantly fidgeting in discomfort. She craved liquor and raw meat salad, dribbled spittle like a hungry ghost, and complained to her husband. "I feel that a spirit has taken over my body. The more I eat, the more I want to eat."

She shoveled eels, chickens, turtles, lizards, giant spiders, and paddy frogs into her mouth in great handfuls but was never satisfied. Liquor jars emptied faster than they could be bought. For many months, she was aching, queasy, and uncomfortable.

After nine months, the child kicked. Nearing delivery, the pain grew worse. Thepthong writhed and screamed uncontrollably. Her husband, parents, and all the servants rushed up into her room. Some cast auspicious mantras on broken rice, or prayed while cramming cowry shells between the wall planks. The midwife straddled her belly and warned that the child was crosswise. Someone sat behind Thepthong to support her back, and others by her side. Khun Siwichai clutched her hair and blew on her forehead.

Thepthong's mother helped to press, but nothing happened. The midwife said, "It's straight now. Push again!" The baby wailed and the mother opened her eyes. She turned the baby boy over, back and front. "For shame! The spirit molded him like this—bald from the womb like the round moon. He looks shameful, like a suffering ghost with those two pitiful patches of straggly hair." With her left foot she booted him down onto the floor of the room. "What a waste of effort carrying him around. By mother's clan! Why raise a mangy puppy to be a laughingstock for the neighbors? Which side of the family does that head come from?"

Finished with cursing, she went to lie by a fire. Wet nurses and servants looked after the baby—washing him, feeding him, rocking his cradle, and singing lullabies every day.

Because of the merit brought by this baby, the family's wealth expanded from the day of his birth. The grandparents on both sides were pleased, and gave him an auspicious name. "At the time he emerged from the womb, a white elephant was presented to King Phanwasa. Let our beloved grandchild be named Khun Chang in commemoration of this event."

They had silver and gold made into a necklace, lots of bracelets for both hands, strings of beads for both arms, and silver anklets so big that he walked with legs splayed apart. Around his waist he wore a soft chain, dangling with chili-shaped charms that tinkled as they swung to and fro.

He jumped around laughing loudly with his mouth open wide. Thepthong shouted at him, "Hey, you beggar, you goggle your eyes like a dumb cat eating fish and dance up and down like a clown in the mask play, like a big unruly monkey that can't stand still. What uncouth spirit molded you? Why don't you die of cholera?" She cursed him day in and day out.

When Khun Chang was three and went off to play, other children took fright at the sight of him. "What's that over there, Mummy? It's got a face like a big tomcat, a humpback, a hairy chin, gaping mouth, hair all over its body, big feet and hands, and rows of odd things round its neck."

Their mothers told them not to be afraid. "That's Khun Chang, son of the rich man from Big Wall Village. Don't get in his way."

Khun Krai Phonlaphai, a man of property from Ban Phlap, and Thong Prasi from Wat Takrai had become a couple, dismantled their house, and brought it to build anew in Suphan. Khun Krai was a skilled and sturdy soldier in command of seven hundred of the king's men. No matter how many enemies he faced, he stood his ground and never fled the field. His royal appointment made him a dignitary in Suphan. From experience, officials knew never to cross him.

In her sleep, Thong Prasi dreamed that the god Indra flew down and offered her a ring with a great diamond. When the diamond's gleam flashed in her eyes, she started awake, flailing her arms, and roused her husband.

On hearing the dream, he said, "A special ring with a beautiful glittering diamond from Indra is very auspicious. You'll be pregnant with a boy! He'll be like one of Vishnu's warriors—strong, brave, and daring, with the power to conquer all three worlds. He'll become a great soldier with high rank and many retainers, a favorite of the king." Thong Prasi raised her clasped hands to receive this blessing from her husband.

As she approached her time, her skin was as radiant as if burnished with gold, her face like the full moon, and her breasts full to bursting. She glowed with health and was a delight for the eye. She followed the Buddhist precepts, prayed regularly, and made offerings of lotus flowers.

At nine months, the child's head turned down towards the opening. Pains made her cry aloud. Crowds of relatives and servants arrived. The midwife fussed around getting things ready. At an auspicious time, Thong Prasi gave birth with ease to a wailing boy. He was rubbed with turmeric, rocked in a winnowing basket, and laid on a little mattress covered with a blanket. All the grandparents happily admired his cute tuft of hair like a lotus seedpod.

His mother slept by a fire to be warmed all through, and came away after a month without a blemish. The parents consulted the grandparents on naming their grandson. The maternal grandfather, who was an astrologer, cast a horoscope for him. "His birth time is three by the shadow on Tuesday in the fifth month of a year of the tiger. The Chinese emperor has presented glittering crystal to the King of Ayutthaya to be placed on the pinnacle of the great stupa, built since the wars with Burma, called Wat Chaophraya Thai in the past. Give him the name Phlai Kaeo, the brilliant."

A soul-calling ceremony was promptly arranged. They decked him with beaded bracelets, splendid golden bangles, gilt wristlets on both arms, a jewel-inlaid necklace made with a whole bar of gold, anklets, and a soft chain around his waist, inlaid with bright emeralds and dangling with golden chilies.

All the clan was present. They lit candles and incense, cheered three times, and chanted for the child's soul.

"On this sacred and auspicious day
We call on the soul of Phlai Kaeo not to stray
Oh soul, stay with this body for joy and health
Enjoy elephants, horses, servants, and wealth
Don't go hunting and wandering aimlessly
Oh soul, enjoy this abundance happily."

They extinguished the candles, wafted the smoke towards the infant, and daubed scented powder on his forehead. "May you live over ten thousand years, win victories, and be prosperous!"

By the time he was five years old, Phlai Kaeo could speak fluently and cleverly.

Phan Sonyotha and his wife, Siprajan, a rich and handsome lady of good lineage, lived at Maids Landing in Suphan. One night, Siprajan dreamed that Viswakarma, the craftsman of the gods, flew across the sky, slid an ornate ring onto her finger, and returned to his golden palace. She awoke at dawn, roused her husband, and blurted out the dream. "Does this mean I'll fall sick? Tell me how bad it'll be."

Phan Sonyotha laughed merrily. "You're going to be pregnant! The ornate ring means the child will be a girl, and because the ring came from Viswakarma, she'll be really beautiful, very special."

Siprajan laughed merrily. "May it be as you say! If I have a child to treasure, I won't have to carry other people's children around, causing a lot of gossip."

When her belly was huge, Siprajan was cheerful and merry. At the completion of nine months, the baby stirred and kicked to be born. Siprajan tossed and turned, her cries echoing around the house. The parents, grandparents, a midwife, spirit medium, other relatives, and servants all came in haste. Some threw cowries as offerings, made wishes, and mumbled frantically.

The old spirit medium swigged liquor, chewed betel, and got up to dance, bobbing up and down, clapping, and swaying drunkenly to the four directions. "A great spirit has come to protect us. Nothing bad will happen." She took off her clothes. Siprajan had a contraction, doubled over, and cried out. The midwife squatted down and pressed, kneading busily until the mother gave birth.

The infant was a girl, pretty and adorable. She lay on her back, wriggling her arms and legs. She was bathed, rubbed with turmeric, given milk to drink, and put in a cradle. Wet nurses and servants took care of feeding her and keeping her happy all the time. The grandparents and elders came to hold a soul ceremony, and adorned her with numerous gold rings. She was given the name Phim Philalai.

By late in her fifth year, her figure was slender, elegant, and as peerlessly lovely as if sculpted. Her hair was beautiful, black, and glossy. Among girls of her age, no other matched her skill at needlework and embroidery.

Phlai Kaeo and Khun Chang went out to play along with their servants. Phlai Kaeo said amiably, "Let's go and buy liquor."

Khun Chang gulped the liquor until his head swam, then poured some into a bowl to swear comradeship. Taking Phlai Kaeo's hand to touch the bowl, he swore, "We will be faithful to each other until death. If either is traitor to his buddy, may the swords of the guardians of the four directions not spare his neck, and may he be separated from his mother for five hundred eras."

They dipped fingers in the liquor, and drew them across their necks. Phlai Kaeo took a gulp. Khun Chang swigged, rolling his eyes. Phim was bent over with laughter. "Serves you right, you outcaste."

She played at cooking rice and curry, building a house from sand, making merit and giving alms. "Let's invite the abbots. Khun Chang can be a Mon abbot—no need for him to shave his head—and Phlai Kaeo can be a Thai abbot."

After the sermon was over and the monks fed, Phlai Kaeo made a funny suggestion, "Let's play at husband and wife."

Khun Chang cried, "I'd like that!"

Phim said, "You bald-headed misfit! I won't play."

Phlai Kaeo said, "Let's do it. Khun Chang can be the husband. I'll creep in and steal you from his side."

The two boys begged her to join in, and gathered leaves to make a bed. Phim swept sand to make a house. She lay down on the ground and Khun Chang lay beside her, pretending to sleep. Phlai Kaeo jumped in between them, hitting Khun Chang's bald skull.

Khun Chang hollered, "A thief has stolen my wife!" He stood up and shouted to his gang. Children appeared in a noisy crowd, and the two gangs fell to blows. Noses were smashed. Mouths split. Blood flowed. Some ran off shaking with tears, calling out to their mothers and fathers.

Phim cursed Khun Chang. "Damn you! I don't want to play with you. You bald leper, you villain!" She took her gaggle of servants off in a rush.

Children's play is strange but not wrong. Should it come true, well, the envoy of the gods makes it happen. This story comes down from ancient times, and there is a text in Suphan.

Khun Siwichai and his wife decided the time had come to present Khun Chang at the court of King Phanwasa. They instructed servants to bathe him, wash his hair, rub him with turmeric, and dress him up. Father and son traveled on a bull elephant with servants in a jumble behind. They dismounted at the riverbank and crossed by the official ferry into the capital city of Ayutthaya.

When local people caught sight of Khun Chang, they cried out, "Oh, what a shame! What kind of child has such a totally bare head?"

"Was it some kind of monkey in a rush to be reborn?"

"What wayward spirit molded that?"

Nobles waiting to attend on the king burst out laughing as soon as they saw him. Khun Chang got flustered and crouched behind his father's back.

At a little after four, the king was bathed, anointed with scents, and gloriously attired. Holding a regal sword with a lifelike face of a naga serpent, he appeared at the front courtyard and sat on an exquisite throne to the sound of horns, conches, gongs, and drums.

Khun Siwichai crawled forward, raised a salver with incense, candles, and flowers, and placed it in front of him. Khun Chang prostrated close behind his father, shaking almost to death in fear.

The king mused, "A shiny head with no hair on the pate, dark-skinned, and fat as a barrel drum. What a disaster! His forehead bulges very oddly."

He spoke. "Heigh! Khun Siwichai, whose child have you brought here? His head looks pitiful. Whose lineage is he from? Are you bringing him to present to me?"

Khun Siwichai prostrated and said, "My liege, Your Gracious Majesty, my life is under the royal foot. Khun Chang is my own son. Please allow me to present him to be a soldier and seek the bo-tree shelter of the accumulated merit of your victorious lordship. Since the birth of this son, money, valuables, cattle, elephants, horses, and servants have appeared as never before."

The king laughed merrily. "That's curious. At present, he's still a child. Wait until he grows up and then bring him to present again." He ordered attendants to arrange royal gifts including cloth. Father and child prostrated three times, happy at the king's grace.

THE DEATHS OF THE FATHERS

The king recalled being told there were many wild buffaloes in Suphan. He ordered Khun Siwichai, "Go quickly to Suphan. Five days from now, I'll leave to stay in the forest and round up wild buffaloes. Tell Khun Krai to have his men find a broad upland near a stream to set up a camp and a royal lodge. Arrange for five hundred troops to chase the buffalo herd in to me."

Chaophraya Jakri, minister of the north, summoned recruitment officers to bring the registry rolls. "Call up elephants, horses, and men. Clear away the undergrowth to make a level path eight fathoms wide. Be ready without fail within five days."

Khun Siwichai rode an elephant across the fields towards Suphan as the sun's rays sank behind the forest. Once home, he sent a message to Khun Krai, who ordered unit heads to round up men forthwith.

That night Khun Krai's house echoed with ominous sounds of spiders beating their chests, scaring everyone so their scalps crawled and their hearts were chilled. Thong Prasi started awake in fright, and aroused her husband to interpret her terrible dream. "A tooth broke and flew out of my mouth. I don't think this is good. Please tell me what this dream means."

Khun Krai knew it meant something bad would happen, but he was reluctant to tell her for fear she would try to stop him leaving.

He said, "This isn't a bad dream. Don't get worried, believe me." But in his heart he thought, "This time I'll die because of the wild buffaloes."

At break of dawn, he washed his face, picked up Phlai Kaeo, and kissed him tenderly. The child opened his eyes and flung his arms around his father's neck. "Papa, tell me where you're going. Why are you up so early? It's like you're running away from me."

Khun Krai hugged him tightly with a sigh. "Papa doesn't want to go away but the king has commanded it. Probably I'll be gone from now on. Things are strange and not to my liking."

Then he turned to Thong Prasi. "This is our only child. He's still little. Take good care of him. Raise him well. If he's naughty, set him right, but don't distress him so much that he runs away. Make sure to teach him whatever there is to be learned so he can carry on this military line."

Thong Prasi sensed that her husband's instructions and the way he hugged the child were different from anything in the past. She embraced her husband's feet and raised them onto her head, with fires licking at her heart. Khun Krai quickly got dressed, and picked up his sword. As he left the house, he turned back to see Phlai Kaeo. "Father's pet, my heart is almost breaking." Tears welled in his eyes, and he felt very afraid.

Just as the sun was setting, he led his men out of Suphan town to Phra Hill and gave orders to keep watch as they awaited the king.

At dawn, officials of the Department of Elephants prepared several royal mounts with saddle pads, harnesses decorated with stars, yak-hair tassels on each ear, and forehead cloths checkered in gold. The mahouts wore patterned lowercloths, shirts instilled with powerful lore, and belts cinched on top.

At the first light of the sun, the king was bathed in a spray of fragrant rosewater, anointed with majestically aromatic unguents, and fanned by throngs of consorts. Those in charge of the royal garments and headgear entered prostrate, bringing the appropriate raiment to dress the king for entering the forest according to the planetary disposition for that day: britches with curved ends and double cuffs; a brocade lowercloth with a gold stripe; a royal helmet decorated with yellow topaz against a black background; and a regal sword.

He walked to a gilded mounting platform and sat on the royal elephant. Horns, gongs, and flutes sounded, signaling the troops to move out in columns. Flags and banners fluttered overhead. The troops rolled out in a rowdy, hectic, rumbling tumult that shook the earth enough to break apart. As they headed for the forest, herds of animals took fright. Parrots flew off in fear, swooping this way and that through the woods, squawking loudly.

The king traveled through the hills, admiring the peaks with overhanging rocks and curving cliffs, and the streams flowing down, glinting like diamond or black sapphire. Trees bloomed in lovely sprays of flowers, and fragrant pollen wafted on the wind. Fruit lay everywhere on the ground, pecked by flocks of birds, and scrapped over by troops of monkeys. A tiger crouched, stalking deer. Rabbit, porcupine, and bear lurked. Langur, lemur, monkey, and gibbon whooped, howled, gamboled, swung, and leapt away in fright.

Reaching a broad upland, the column halted, and a royal lodge was erected for the king to spend the night. He summoned Khun Krai. "Tomorrow you will drive the buffaloes in."

Luang Ritthanon, who was deputed to make a stockade, assigned men to clear bushes, level dense forest, and lop away thick brambles. They shaped stakes, dug holes, drove in the posts to form a stockade, and fetched creepers to bind the stakes. Some ached and collapsed with exhaustion, but overseers beat them back to work. When a heavy rain fell on the forest, men collapsed and lay shaking, or crept away into the trees to sleep. At sunset, work stopped and things cheered up. Men went off to gather vegetables, collect firewood, and catch ducks and chickens. They cooked rice and fell asleep around the stoves, bathed in sweat, and snoring from exhaustion.

At dawn, Khun Krai led his five hundred men out to seek buffaloes. They slipped along paths through the forest, whooping and yelling. When they set an arc of fire, murky smoke spread through the trees.

Deer, tiger, bear, boar, and rabbit took flight. Monkey and langur swung away from tree to tree.

The forest was in uproar with men shouting, fire crackling, and a racket of gongs, clappers, and drums. Great numbers of wild buffaloes were seized with panic, plunging around in all directions, battering and buffeting one another in a clamor of clashing horns.

Looking out from his pavilion at the hordes of buffalo, King Phanwasa called out, "Heigh! Khun Krai, why aren't you driving them into the stockade? Do you trust the men to chase them while you stand around doing nothing? Useless."

Khun Krai leapt up, grabbed a spear, and rushed out to the front. The men roared loudly, making the animals ever more confused. A buffalo with curved horns charged forward, butting people wildly. Khun Krai rushed out to face the beast, leaping, kicking, and stabbing like a windmill, his spear swishing and slashing. Buffaloes dropped dead to the tune of around one hundred beasts. The remaining herd broke away in panic and charged off into the forest in all directions, leaving only the dead strewn everywhere.

The king was inflamed with rage, as if a black vapor had blown across his heart. He bellowed like a thunderclap. "What are you up to, Khun Krai, spearing so many buffaloes? Do you mean to offend me? I saw it with my own eyes! Because of your fooling around, the buffaloes have all fled into the forest. Heigh! Heigh! Bring the executioners immediately. Off with his head! Stick it up on a pole and raise it high! Seize his property and his servants at once!"

The fearsome executioners strode up and dragged Khun Krai away. They tied his hands behind his back, brought him to a stake driven into the ground, and told him to bow his head. Khun Krai felt shattered to dust. His body trembled with fear, and the blood drained from his face.

"Oh, pity, pity! Why did this have to happen? On the day before coming here, I had a premonition—those ominous noises in the house. And my jewel, Thong Prasi, had a bad dream. I pretended to interpret it wrongly, but my bad karma has caught up with me, darling housemate. If you count the days waiting for me, they'll stretch into years. I'll never come back to love you. Will my little son know his father came to such disaster?"

He turned to plead with the executioners. "Now that I'm about to die, show me some consideration. Please inform Thong Prasi so she understands that my time was up, and the king ordered my execution. Tell her to look out and fear the worst. What bad did I do that I have to come and die in a forest where my corpse will be prey for vultures and crows?"

He called his friend Ritthanon over. "Please tell my wife."

Luang Ritthanon could not contain his own tears. "Dear friend, why be so upset? When the time comes, it comes. Who lives to prop up the sky, year in, year out? Even Lord Siva, Lord Indra, and the moon must be destroyed, and descend from the heavens. Nothing born can escape death."

Khun Krai gathered himself and controlled his grief. He put his hands together and concentrated on prayer. He thought of the virtue of the Buddha and his teaching. He paid respect to monks who upheld the precepts. He honored his father and mother who brought him into this world and raised him. "Let it be known throughout heaven and earth that I, Khun Krai, made a mistake and paid for it with my life, yet died with integrity in the manner of one from a line of valiant and victorious warriors." He closed his eyes, composed his mind, stifled his fear, and signaled with a finger for the chop.

With one blow of the executioner's razor-sharp sword, the heart of Khun Krai stopped beating, and his life turned to dust. The jailers took the body away to impale on a stake.

After witnessing his friend's death, Luang Ritthanon quickly wrote a secret letter, and gave instructions to a soldier. "Hurry to Suphan. Tell Thong Prasi that the king has commanded she be seized. Tell the dear lady not to treat this lightly."

The soldier acknowledged the order and took his leave. He found a sidebag, grasped a big pike, strapped a knife on his back, and shambled off. Arriving at the house of Thong Prasi, he told her with tears welling up in his eyes, "I'm here on Luang Ritthanon's instruction. It's all here in this letter."

The letter informed Thong Prasi, "Your husband and my good friend, Khun Krai, was condemned to death by the king, and stuck on a post in front of the buffalo camp. The king has given orders to seize his property, wife, and child. Don't stay at home. Flee from Suphan!"

Thong Prasi beat her breast with both hands and flailed around. "Oh husband, how can you have been chopped to death? You were invulnerable, and nobody could defeat you, but now your power has gone. On that night when I had a dream, you said the meaning was good. Never before had you made such a mistake. Our property will be seized. Who can we turn to for help? Where will your wife and son find a place to sleep? We're done for."

She turned to look at Phlai Kaeo. "Your father is no more, my jewel. Karma has caught up with us. The house will be cold as a graveyard. The servants will be scattered to the winds. Officials will trample all over us. We can't stay here any longer."

Hearing Thong Prasi, the servants could not hold back their own tears. They lamented loudly over the loss of Khun Krai.

"He never got angry or held a grudge."

"We servants could always depend on him."

"Wherever we went, nobody dared bully us, because everyone feared Khun Krai, but now they'll all come and push us around."

That evening, around a hundred Ayutthaya officials and members of the local guard surrounded the fence of Khun Krai's house. The governor of Suphan said, "It's sunset already. Light fires and post guards all around to prevent anyone getting away overnight. We'll draw up the inventory of goods tomorrow."

Thong Prasi saw them surrounding the house. In a panic, she picked up Phlai Kaeo, grabbed a basket and two bags of money, jumped down from the house, and hid in the shadows of the house pillars. Bending down, she squeezed through a hole in the fence, grabbed her son's hand, and ran off by the light of the moon.

Meeting an old neighbor, she begged, "Oh please, I'm all out of rice and fish. The whole house has been seized and we've got nothing to eat." The neighbor was kind enough to share what she had. Outside the village, they climbed a tree, looking for somewhere to sleep. She tried to comfort her son so he would not cry.

"Oh my dear Phlai Kaeo, you've never slept in the forest. Now we're in terrible trouble. That golden peacock sounds like the spirit of Khun Krai. Oh Father, please look after us tonight. Don't let a tiger, bear, or other animal chance upon us."

Sitting on a branch in the darkness, she had a hollow feeling of fear in her throat. Worried that her son would fall out of the tree and die, she tied one end of her cloth around his waist and fastened the other to a branch. She caressed her son to sleep, but he was too upset. His life seemed torn into a hundred shreds. Red ants scurried over every inch of his body. Midges and mosquitoes buzzed around. He yawned, "I'm so tired but I can't go to sleep. My bottom is so itchy, Mama. I'm being eaten alive by big bully ants. Come and slap them for me. As soon as it's light in the morning, let's get away from here."

Thong Prasi wept in pity. "Dear child, this is karma. What can we do? There, I've chased the ants away, my jewel." Stretched out on the branch of the banyan tree, they soon nodded off from exhaustion, and slept through the night.

Promptly at dawn, the officials went into Thong Prasi's house and impounded the cattle, buffaloes, elephants, and horses. The housekeeper was seized, beaten, and questioned until she blurted out that the mistress had fled. Officials went up into Khun Krai's apartment and carried everything out to the terrace. Pikes, swords, tooled sabers, nielloware bowls, silk, carpets, felt, velvet, nickelware, brassware, crockery, and anything else of value was written down on an inventory. Five thousand in cash was put in a chest and bound with a thread and large seal. Two trunks of money were locked by key, and carried out to load onto elephants. Looms for cotton and silk were put into carts. Mortars and pestles, pottery jars, and bowls were placed on rafts, taken for inspection at the provincial office, and then loaded onto elephants.

Within one night, the officials reached Ayutthaya and reported to their superiors, "Handing over the goods seized from Khun Krai!"

"Put them in the warehouse according to the inventory."

By break of dawn, Thong Prasi had resolved to take Phlai Kaeo to Kanburi. She quickly dropped down from the tree, balanced the basket on her waist, and led her son by the hand. They skirted the edge of the forest, looking for paths, then pushed a way through the trees. Phlai Kaeo caught sight of papaya and wild olive scattered all over the ground. "Mama, look over there—wild fruit! I really, really want to eat them all." She gathered them up for him.

They reached a lake and stopped to rest. She took out the cold rice left over from the previous evening. Phlai Kaeo broke off some with his hands and popped it in his mouth, but it was so dry and chewy that he lay down on the ground and cried. "Where's the curry, Mama? Give me something to taste. The rice gets stuck in my throat." He screwed up his eyes, "I won't eat it."

"Where can I find curry, dear Phlai Kaeo? We're on the run. The only thing left is some fish."

"Cold rice and dry fish! How will we have any strength, Mama? If there's no curry, then just give me some fermented fish mixed in a bit of water."

Thong Prasi hugged the child and wept. "Your mother doesn't know where to get it. Darling son, we're in bad trouble—so bad I'm at my wits' end."

They set off along a path through the forest. Seeing her son so hot under the glaring sun, she wrapped a cloth around his head. Phlai Kaeo walked behind, clinging onto her waist, with a face grim from hunger and thirst, and his feet burning from walking on pebbles and sand. "Mama, I've had enough. I'm fit to drop. My throat is so dry I don't want to go another step. Walk slower, Mama. If I try to take long strides, I'll fall over. My feet are aching and swollen. The ground is as hot as a furnace."

She lifted him up and dangled him on her waist. When she got too tired, she hoisted him onto her back and raised the basket out front as shade. Then she got stiff, and lifted him up onto her shoulder, holding his legs with one hand. Her feet swelled up with blisters, making her hobble slowly. When her attention wavered, she tripped and fell, sending the child tumbling along the forest floor.

Phlai picked himself up in a daze. "I almost died! My legs hurt. From here on, don't carry me, Mama!"

They reached Kanburi. "Son, there are people I know well in this town." Khun Krai had once told her that he had relatives owning land at Cockfight Hill. They walked around asking for information until they found them. Without any delay, the relatives built a house for her.

Bit by bit, she began to earn a living and to acquire some money and property. She redeemed some slaves and men so they could farm. She bought land, elephants, horses, cattle, and buffaloes. She made money through trading. People looked up to her with respect. She gradually established herself and settled down there with her son for many years.

Janson of Red Saltlick Village was bold, invulnerable, and brave as a lion. His expertise was banditry. He would burst in somewhere, make an uproar, and plunder everything. He attacked boats from north or south and got worthwhile takings. He made allies with thieves in Kamphaeng. They feasted together, got staggering drunk, and then played unruly games, slashing and stabbing one another, or blasting away with guns, with no cause for fear because of their invulnerability.

Janson said, "Hey, gang, I've got an idea. Today we'll go and raid Khun Siwichai at Big Wall Village in Suphan. He's a very rich man. A moneybags like that has lots of men, but our gang can overpower them."

They dressed to look as fierce and fearless as possible, armed with pikes, swords, flintlock guns, powder horns, fuses, and spears. "Bring up the elephants now. Hey, don't hang about!" When Janson had climbed halfway onto his elephant, a mate drove a pike point into his rump and shoved him up into the howdah. The elephant trundled off.

They arrived near Suphan, and left the elephants among the trees. Janson made an eye-level shrine with a white cloth as a canopy. All the gang brought their bandeaus, sacred threads, pikes, and swords to place on the shrine along with offerings of liquor, rice, food, sweets, incense, candles, powder, and fragrant oil. Janson raised his clasped hands in prayer. "I call on the gods from all eight directions, Lord Siva, Lord Vishnu, Lord Brahma, Gautama, powerful yogis and rishis, teachers with expertise, the moon, the sun, and other powers, the guardians of the four directions, the gods of travel, the earth goddess, and the chief overseer of the spirits, please empower the weapons on the shrine!"

Dark clouds and mists shrouded the earth. As each took a drink of the enchanted liquor, hearts flashed, ears burned, flesh thickened. They tied bandeaus around their heads and hitched up their lowercloths to make themselves look awesome. Janson led the way off, with five hundred robbers arrayed behind. At Big Wall Village, they chopped at the gate with axes until it splintered and fell with a loud thump, then rushed in, whooping, pounding loudly on the house, and firing off their guns.

While Thepthong and Khun Chang still slept, Khun Siwichai woke up with a start and jumped out of the house with no clothes on. Robbers chased after him, beating left, thrashing right, throwing spear after spear, and waving torches.

At the sound of gunfire, other members of the household awoke and ran off in all directions, breaking down fences, crashing into buildings, stumbling around in fright and confusion, picking up their children and grandchildren and taking to their heels, carrying baskets, bags, sidebags, and whatever they could.

The robber gang swarmed all over the place, searching everything, tapping the house walls, breaking water pitchers and storage jars, yelling and hollering. They caught the mother and son and tied them up by their necks. "Fear me, you hag. Had enough yet?"

Khun Chang was so frightened that his body trembled and his eyes bulged. Thepthong begged them to punish her alone. The robber gang hauled them to the center of the house. "Is this baldy your husband?" Thepthong cried, "This is my son. My husband abandoned me and fled."

The robbers brought fire to burn her bottom. "Can you stand this, or will you tell us where the money and valuables are kept?" They tied her arms behind her back, arching her body. "Don't tell us lies."

Thepthong cried out, "I'm done for!"

When the robbers brought gunpowder, Khun Chang fell to his knees and begged them, "Spare my mother. The money and valuables are in a chest. I'll show you." Whooping in glee, the robbers broke open the big chest and brought out more treasure than they could carry, dropping stuff on the ground all over the place.

Janson said, "Gang, bring the women over here. Get them to sing chicken-flapping songs." Janson sat on an upended mortar. The servants danced and jigged around energetically. "Hey, mother and child, get up and dance. If you stay still, I'll belt you on the mouth!"

Thepthong said, "We can't dance without a flute and drum."

All the robber gang chanted a rhythm, and tootled like flutes. Mother and son clomped around clumsily.

"The boy is jiggling okay, but the mother is hopeless."

"Her waist is stiff as a board."

Thepthong jiggled and wiggled in all four directions, swaying her shoulders and bottom around to the rhythm, waving her arms clumsily so her droopy breasts swung and slapped against her body. Khun Chang jumped up and down frenetically like a big monkey.

Meanwhile Khun Siwichai had rounded up two hundred villagers. Carrying guns, crossbows, pikes, staves, swords, and spears, they waited, hidden in ambush.

Janson shouted to his gang, "Pick up the loads now. Let's get moving!" He led the way, followed by Thepthong and Khun Chang, roped by the neck. They made her shout, "Anyone there, don't follow us, or they'll kill us." The robbers fired off their guns threateningly, and hollered loudly.

Khun Siwichai's band watched the robbers approach, then they too whooped, hollered, fired their guns, and rushed towards them.

Khun Chang and his mother slipped free. The robbers dropped their loads in surprise, then roared back at the villagers and leapt into the fray, slicing, slashing, and hacking. Blades clanged and clashed. Guns boomed and banged. But the villagers' thrusts were useless, not piercing the robbers' bodies but enraging them to hack harder. Villagers fell dead in heaps. The injured, covered in blood, cried out pitifully.

Khun Siwichai came upon Janson. The pair plunged into combat, thrusting and feinting with pikes, whirling around like windmills, pulling back to measure up their opponent then charging into the battle, eyeball to eyeball. Both were powerful and fearless fighters. Reaching the end of their strength, they grappled at close quarters, wrestling each other down rolling on the ground.

The robber gang gathered round and grabbed Khun Siwichai. They tried to cut off his head with a sword but the blade did not enter. They tied his neck and chopped it like a log but the blade bounced off. They hacked at his shoulders but the sword crumpled and broke off at the hilt.

The robbers said, "This guy is good!"

"Look what he's done to these weapons!"

They tied his feet together like a roasting pig, shot and stabbed him, but still nothing penetrated. The robbers were getting frustrated. "Hey! What to do?"

"Ah! I've got it!"

They took a stave and pierced his anus. Khun Siwichai's life was snuffed out. He died in the forest, eyes closed tight.

The robbers celebrated by firing guns and whooping through the woods, dropping lots of booty without bothering to pick it up. The villagers crept into the forest to hide and sleep.

At break of day, Thepthong asked her people to look for her husband. When they found him, she beat her chest so hard her sagging breasts slapped against her stomach. "My friend in hardship, you've gone and left your wife and child all alone. Truly, what karma made you die such a violent death, naked on the ground in the middle of a forest? Maybe in a previous life you skewered a fish, and so in this life you've been skewered to death too. You look pitiful, dreadful. Someone please pull that stave out of him."

Khun Chang hugged the corpse, whimpering, rocking back and forth in sorrow. The servants ran up in a great mass, crying floods of tears.

"Our master came to the end of his merit!"

"We've lost our protector!"

They carried the corpse back and buried it at a graveyard, then returned to the forest to gather up all the goods abandoned by the robbers.

Phan Sonyotha went to trade with the Lawa and returned with a fever. Siprajan exhausted herself nursing him, but the fever abated only to return more gravely each time. A spirit had possessed his body, making him crave pork, beef, spicy sausage, and spicy raw salad that he swallowed in huge mouthfuls, lolling his tongue, rolling his eyes, nearing death. Siprajan went to summon the abbot but it was too late. Phan Sonyotha breathed his last.

Siprajan collapsed to the ground, beating her breasts. "Oh my lord! You gave no thought to young Phim. Poor, forlorn little child, your father has left his wife and daughter all alone. Oh Father, in the past you went off everywhere but you managed to stay alive. This time you've been careless and we won't see you ever again."

Phim hugged her father's corpse in grief. "Dear Papa, when you had a fever, I would grind your medicine, but now you're dead and gone to the land of the spirits. This evening, the house will be as cold as a graveyard. I won't need to lay out your mattress, mat, and coverlet."

The relatives of the clan wept and wailed too. The corpse was bathed, daubed with turmeric, wrapped in white cloth, bound tightly in the prescribed way, and placed in a wooden coffin in the main room. Prayers were chanted every evening for many days.

Siprajan and Thepthong came to an agreement. "Our husbands have met their deaths. We should have the bodies cremated in the best way possible so we don't make trouble for their spirits."

They promptly asked Abbot Som to arrange a cremation at Wat Khao. Craftsmen carved wood, wove bamboo, and made frames and panels for a grand crematory pavilion decorated with English gold, inlaid with glittering white and green glass, and embellished with flowers waving on wire stems. On the front was fashioned a brilliant image of Lord Indra riding a three-headed elephant. Cooks were summoned to prepare food with nothing stinted.

When the work was finished, the two bodies were brought in procession and placed on the pyre while flute and drum played a dirge. At evening, fireworks were lit. Bangers exploded. Rockets whizzed in the air. Strings of crackers popped and banged. Firewheels were tossed, spinning and bobbling on the water.

To the beating of gong and drum, the monk clowning began. Monks performed in pairs, dressed up as people of different languages. First came a pair of monks playing Vietnamese with white teeth and tousled beards like forest langur.

"*Khoan khoan khoan ho khoan, khoan ho khoan.*
To the stars, no attention pay.
It'll happen anyway!
Jump up, dingle dangle dong,
End of the Vietnamese song!"

The next pair of monks were decked out as Chinese with beards like goats. One clacked claves, and the other chinked cymbals in reply. They wailed to the rhythm through twisted mouths.

"The Vietnamese monk has a secret weapon to scare me,
Six-six, dee-dee, three-four-two!
But the Vietnamese girl and I can still become lovers.
For a couple of coins, one time can do!"

A pair playing as Lao opened their mouths wide and sang,

"Di-dum, di-dum, smart or dumb, it's all the same,
You're dead and I'm sorry, but that's the game.
Without whittling, a thorn is sharp.
Without shaping, a lime is round.
We all end up like you, even me.
A-hey-diddle-diddle, diddle-diddle-dee!"

A pair dressed as Khaek with bearded chins gurgled on a hookah and chanted,

"With all support denied,
You closed your eyes and died.
Parents and all your kin
Fought death but did not win.
In the end you join them!"

Up came two monks decked out as Westerners. They rolled their eyes, bashed their bottoms together, fondled themselves for the audience to see, and sang,

"This fellow's captain is shorter than me.
I know how to solder constructively,
so mine is better than his!"

He took a swig of liquor, rang a bell, and the captain stood up and swayed to the music. He pulled down his trousers for the Khaek monk to see.

The Khaek monk's mouth dropped open, and he spat. "What are you showing me this tiddler for?" He waved a fan and tried to hit the Westerner, who dodged, picked up a fan, and raised it to fight back. They went at each other crazily, one drunk on liquor, the other smashed on ganja. The crowd roared in appreciation.

"Every one of these pairs is superb."

The hosts of the event hastily intervened. "Damn you! Liking these monks sounding off and rolling their heads! Where did this evil pair come from? Peeling off their clothes for all to see. Disgraceful!"

As the golden light of dawn brightened the sky, the monks stepped down from the platform. A mask play and puppet performance were still going on merrily. Food, alms, and robes were offered to the monks.

After three days, the bodies were cremated in the presence of crowds of kinsfolk who paid respect to the remains, gave hampers of offerings to the abbot, and returned to their homes.

PHLAI KAEO IS ORDAINED

Phlai Kaeo and Thong Prasi lived in Kanburi until he was fifteen. He never stopped thinking of his late father, Khun Krai, and wanted to follow in his footsteps as a valiant soldier. He begged his mother, "I'd like to gain knowledge. Please take me to a learned monk and ask him to ordain me as a novice and become my teacher."

Thong Prasi had no objection at all. "If you want a teacher skilled in the inner ways, Abbot Bun of Wat Som Yai is good. You're thinking well, mother's jewel. Once you learn about the military arts and invulnerability, you can carry on the line of your father."

She gave orders to the servants. "My most beloved son is going to be ordained. Go and get some good-quality cloth to make his robes, and the right sort of sidebag and almsbowl."

Servants went off to fetch betelnut, pan, and banana leaves. They all helped to peel betelnut, coil and bind pan leaves, and roll wax candles. White cloth was measured, cut, and sewed into monk's robes. They made a shoulder cloth from soft chicken-skin silk, and sewed on silk toggle buttonholes. All sat round in a circle, making lots of noise but working busily with devotion.

Turmeric was pounded to dye the cloth. "Oh, have you never done this before? The color's too light. Pour some vinegar in. That'll make it deeper and brighter." A clothesline was tied for drying the dyed cloth, and then the triple robes were placed on a salver.

A team of the very best cooks steamed and boiled busily, their faces burned black from the stove. They cleaned rice and put it in pans, curried river snails, mixed spicy salads, made sweets, arranged fruit for offerings, and set everything on many rows of trays.

Thong Prasi shouted at the servants. "Why are you so slow? Take the big bowl and fill it with water. What have you done with the turmeric and powder? Yesterday I put them in the crock."

She bathed her son, rubbed him with turmeric, powdered his face, and combed his hair. He was dressed in a brocade lowercloth with a pleated front like folded leaves, a light robe with gold embroidery, a conical hat with waving flowers, an embroidered belt, and a diamond ring with a glittering stone. He was given incense, candles, and lotus flowers to hold in a pouch. Strapping Nai Dam was summoned to carry him on his shoulders with an umbrella overhead. Thong Prasi walked along beside.

At Wat Som Yai, the offerings were placed in the front hall. Thong Prasi took Phlai Kaeo to pay respect to the abbot. "Your Lordship, I've brought my son to be ordained. Please teach him to be something of substance so he may make merit and share it with his late father. Also, teach him to read and write so he can learn young."

Abbot Bun sighed heavily. "Such a pity Khun Krai passed away. His son is very much like him. I'll take care of him, don't worry."

He turned to give instructions to a novice. "Call the monks downstairs. Lay mats and arrange the seating. Shave Phlai's head." When the monks had gathered, Abbot Bun initiated Phlai Kaeo as a novice.

All the monks' bowls were lined up and pots of rice were carried in. Everyone helped place food into the monks' bowls and present the usual offerings. After eating, the monks chanted an offertory blessing. Novice Phlai and Thong Prasi poured water on the ground.

The novice studied to read and write. With diligence, he soon mastered Khmer, Thai, arithmetic, the main scriptures, and calculations of the sun and moon. The teachers were intimidated by his cleverness. Among all the many elders and novices there, none could match him. Within less than one year, he had things by heart, could write perfectly, and could translate texts.

The abbot said, "That's all I know, my dear Novice Phlai. There's only the big volume with all the mantras I've been collecting since I was a youth. Until now, I haven't shared it with anyone. Because I'm fond of you, I'll pass it on. There are mantras for invulnerability, robbery, raising spirits—something for every occasion."

Novice Phlai absorbed the master's volume but still wanted to study more. He went to pay respect and beg leave to go to Suphan. His teacher was pleased. "The abbot of Wat Palelai is very able. He and Thong Prasi know each other."

Novice Phlai took his leave and went to tell his mother. "My studies there are finished. The abbot told me that Wat Palelai is very good. He said you've known the abbot there for ages. Please take me and put me under his care."

Thong Prasi laughed with pleasure. "That's right. As I recall, in Suphan there are two monks good at the inner ways—Abbot Mi of Wat Palelai and the master at Wat Khae. I used to send food over there. He and Khun Krai loved each other greatly. It's no problem to place you under his care."

She immediately instructed the servants to prepare elephants along with food for the journey and for offerings. In three days they reached Suphan and went straight to see Abbot Mi in Wat Palelai. "I haven't seen you for a long time."

The abbot laughed merrily. "I haven't seen your face for many years. Whose son is this novice? I don't know him."

"He's my own son. Since Khun Krai passed away, I've been a widow on my own. I had my son ordained so he could study and make something of himself. He's now a gangling lad and I'm far away, so

I want to put him under your care. Please teach him. If he's lazy and doesn't study, punish him with the cane."

"Don't be impatient. If he doesn't listen to my instruction, why should I look after him? But I'm not the sort of person to use threats. I'll teach him what his own mind can take. If the child is good, he alone gets the praise; if he's bad, they blame the teacher. He has a respectable name and pedigree. I don't think he'll disgrace the lineage."

Thong Prasi chuckled at the abbot's words. "Dear Novice Phlai, remember this well." She returned home to Cockfight Hill.

Novice Phlai had an agile mind and was diligent without being told. After three months of practice, he had sermons down by heart. He spoke beautifully with a peerless choice of words, and a voice as charming as a cicada. Wherever he gave a sermon, people loved to come and listen. Monks would skip the forenoon meal and sit waiting to beg for some recitation.

In the evenings he took instruction from the abbot: how to make a sword for war, transform a thorny branch into a buffalo charm, enchant dummy soldiers, and charm a woman so that once their eyes had met, her heart would be captivated forever.

The abbot laughed. "I know you're interested in the lover stuff. Don't cause trouble for people's wives but old maids and widows—take them! I'll teach you everything about sacred formulas. You'll be a real gem."

He spat out the betel he was chewing, made Novice Phlai eat the remains, then hit his skull with a pestle. "There! It didn't crack or bruise. Like bashing stone." The abbot rolled about with laughter. He taught the novice until his mind was quick and his confidence grew by the day.

At Songkran, the new year, all of Suphan came to Wat Palelai to make merit by building sand stupas around the grounds. In the afternoon, the monks chanted prayers. In the evening, every house was up until late preparing food for almsgiving on the following day.

At dawn, everyone crowded noisily into the wat. Among them were Phim, her mother, and their servants carrying food to put in the almsbowls and salvers with incense, candles, and flowers for offerings. The monks came down to the main hall, and sat in order. The faithful paid respect. Each monk was presented with a salver of medicines. After Abbot Mi gave the precepts and the monks paid respect to the Buddha, the women scurried to prepare trays of food for offering to the monks in order of seniority.

Phim brought a large tray with bananas, sweets, oranges, and a bowl of rice. She walked gracefully to give to the seniors and then down the line. Coming to Novice Phlai, she glanced at him and hesitated, remembering something from the past. "This novice and I seem to know each other." She ladled a heap of fried pork, dried fish, halved boiled eggs, sausages, dried fish, watermelon, and a bowlful of curry.

Novice Phlai had his head bowed. Seeing so much food, he thought, "Is someone teasing me?" Lifting his head, he saw Phim's face, smiling with her eyes averted. "You're giving me so much my bowl is overflowing. How can I eat it? There's too much, but you haven't given me what I really like."

Phim broke into a smile. "Oh novice, when I saw the empty bowl, I thought it was an old mendicant, so I heaped it in. You accuse me of teasing. Would you rather have me lose merit? In Suphan it's hard to get good stuff like this, and expensive."

Phlai Kaeo thought for a moment with his heart thumping. "I remember. She used to play with me. Her name is Phim Philalai. She's grown up so beautiful she makes my eyes hurt."

The monks finished eating. The abbot gave the offertory blessing, repeated by the other monks. The lay faithful poured water on the ground. Everybody merrily bustled off home.

In the tenth month, the Buddhist faithful in Suphan decided to stage a recitation of the Mahachat, the great jataka story, at Wat Palelai on the next holy day. The lay elders held a meeting at the wat. Volunteers came forward to sponsor the decorations and offerings for most of the thirteen episodes that would be recited over a single day.

"Who should we have for the big episode? That's more expensive. It's not easy for just anyone to sponsor."

"*The Children*? Yes, that's true. Give it to the bald fellow from Big Wall Village. Nai Bun, you know him well. Pop over there."

Nai Bun went to Khun Chang's house. "Sir, would you not like to show your devotion and make some merit? Siprajan and Phim have the *Matsi* episode. There's still no taker for *The Children*."

Khun Chang laughed with pleasure. "I'd be happy to have the great, great episode! Don't spare a thought about the expense. Even if it costs me four hundred baht I won't mind. I'll be born rich in my next life. I'm only too willing to make merit in such a way."

Monks distributed handbills. People began making preparations.

Khun Chang was still as bald as an adjutant stork, while his chin and chest were a mess of whiskers and hair. He had fallen for a neighbor's daughter and they had married, but after a year she had fallen sick with a fever. He had called a doctor, who said, "The illness has passed into a fatal stage. Treatment would be useless. Why didn't you send for me at the beginning?" Before long, she died. Khun Chang had arranged a noisy cremation and frequently made merit for her.

In preparing for the recitation, Khun Chang was expansive to the point of extravagance. "Servants! Go and fetch wood and don't take too long about it. You, weave some hampers in preparation. And you, take this cash and buy all the everyday stuff to offer to the monks. Find some good quality cloth to make triple robes. You women, go and find the offerings for the episode. You pound the rice and sift the flour to make wheel sweets. And don't stint. I want hundreds of everything. Don't worry about using lots of oil. Just go and buy some more. And every type of orange and fruit. The cost is not a problem. Don't be stingy and create gossip. I'm considered gentlefolk."

At Phim's house, Siprajan shouted at the servants, "Get in here and lend a hand at once." They mixed sweets, coated them in flour, and fried them in sputtering oil.

"Hey, this fire is too hot!"

"Pull some firewood out."

"Done to a turn!"

Rice crackers and biscuits were tossed in Phetburi sugar and placed alongside. Young rice mixed with flour was deep fried and filled with egg, coconut, and sweet palm sugar. "When they're done, pierce them on sticks."

The crowd of servants milled around, helping one another with this and that, and making a racket like a mask play. Siprajan harried them, "Pass them over carefully! Don't throw those or they'll break!"

The sponsor of the first episode got up before the cock and rushed over to Wat Palelai as dawn broke. He laid out his offerings in the preaching hall, and lit incense and candles as offering to the Buddha. A monk chanted the precepts. The first four episodes were soon over.

Khun Chang woke late in a panic. "Come here everybody! I've forgotten the main offering. I've been a widower for many years, and there's nobody to do these things. Shaping animals from papaya has me stumped. Is there anybody here who can help?"

A servant spoke up, "Me. I can give it a try. I'll soon get the hang of it."

They purchased a basket of papaya, and in no time she carved them into shapes—an abbot riding on an elder, novices in the middle, and then vultures eating a corpse. It all looked very odd. Khun Chang was delighted. In reward, he gave the carver a brass ring.

He ordered the servants to carry the offerings along the road so people would see. "Be careful! If you drop or lose anything, I'll kick you along like a ball." The servants carried everything to Wat Palelai, yodeling as they went.

Phim's household carved papayas into many shapes—a majestic lion with a full face; Lord Brahma in a votive pose; Lord Indra soaring through the air holding a crystal; and Lord Narai mounted on Garuda, swooping across the sky. They added color to make the figures bright and attractive, and set up the whole display as a mountain range.

When the servants put them on display at the wat, people crowded around to look. "Oh, they did everything so beautifully!"

"All that hard work was certainly not wasted!"

"The animals all look so real."

Khun Chang ordered his servants to fill a big tub to the brim with water, scrub him clean, and rub his body all over with turmeric. Still his skin looked as green as water hyacinth.

"Quick, the *Great Forest* episode is almost finished!"

He patted powder over his body. Scooping up pomade, he shaped his hair like a wing and swept it across to hide his bald pate, but the middle was still as bare as a buffalo's water-hole.

"My head's a disaster! I'm so ashamed."

He put on expensive clothes. "Today, I'll dress to the hilt to show off to Phim." On his fingers, he put a snake ring, wasp-nest ring, diamond ring, and another decorated with rubies. "This set of rings with five jewels belonged to my father. The people of Suphan will quail before such a rich man! Like this, Phim is almost mine!"

He crept over to look at himself in a big mirror. "Ugh! My head is as horrid as a shithole. Yet a ghastly head can still belong to a gentleman. Servants! Come here, ten of you, and take the mats. Follow my arse and don't go off anywhere. You, carry the flask and the betel tray, and don't give yourself airs and graces."

He strutted along with his head in the air, nodding in greeting to bystanders. Before long he was bathed in sweat like a butting buffalo. At the front of the main preaching hall, the lay elders made way for him to enter. His servants laid a reed mat, and he sat down, striking a dignified pose.

A group of friends came over to greet him. "Oh, why are you sweating like this?"

Khun Chang was offended and snapped his face away. "People should not pass remarks."

He called orders to his servants, "Hey you, pile up the main offerings—all the taro, potato, white sugarcane, red sugarcane, watermelon, pomelo, red sticky rice, touchstone sweets, clam sweets, and big melons. Don't muddle things up! Bring in the monks' robes and bowls, the mats, mattresses, seats, and cushions! And don't hide away the main offering! Place it out in front of the salver with the triple robes!"

A monk made the recitation. The lay elders and faithful lit incense and votive candles and offered flowers in worship.

Phim said, "It's almost time for our episode. Let's get going, Mother."

She bathed, briskly rubbed turmeric all over her body, shaped her hairline, put oil on her hair, powdered her face, and polished her teeth so they glinted shiny jet black in the mirror. She put on a shimmering red lowercloth, a soft inner breastcloth in pink, overlaid by an elegant ruby-colored cloth with gold stripes and brilliant embroidered flowers, bound to delight the men. She added a diamond ring decorated with rubies and a snake ring with a moving tongue on her little finger.

Siprajan said, "I'm already grey-haired and past it. Why should I get dressed up? Anything will do."

"Mother dear, aren't you ashamed you'll seem out of place?"

"Karma, karma!" She changed into something grander.

At the wat, Siprajan and Phim laid out their mats, sat down, and paid their respect. The monk finished the previous recitation, and Khun Chang presented his offerings while a music ensemble played. Siprajan had their servants carry in their offerings—almsbowls, sidebags, articles for everyday use, salvers, triple robes, oranges, many other fruits, and various sweets. Everything was set out in rows with the main offering in front.

In the monks' quarters, the abbot summoned Novice Phlai. "I've been sick for several days, and I'm not up to it. You give the *Matsi* recitation instead of me."

Novice Phlai rushed off in a flap, grabbed the text of *Matsi*, and began reading. He memorized the words and practiced reciting in the style of his teacher. Then he called another novice to carry the text for him, and he went to change into a robe in open style clinging tightly to his body. After paying respect to the abbot, he rubbed beeswax on his lips, walked to the hall with the text carried in front, and sat below the monks, composing himself.

His eyes slid sideways and saw Phim's soft face. She glanced up and their eyes met. Shyly, she bowed her head and kept still. Novice Phlai repeated a Beguiler mantra several times to join their hearts and eyes by special power. The force of the mantra drew her gaze irresistibly to his. As their eyes met, he nodded to her with love and desire welling in his heart.

"Please come closer. The abbot is sick, so he had me give the recitation. As patron of this episode, what do you say?"

"Whoever does it, it's the same to me. As long as it follows the Pali."

She smiled and met his eyes, then pushed a betel tray towards her maid, Saithong, who knelt and placed it as an offering.

The novice went up to the pulpit, picked up the text, cradled it carefully in his hands, and read faultlessly up to the passage where Matsi is searching for her lost children. A lion and two tigers block her path. She reaches the hermitage, and is chilled not to find them. Sobbing with grief, she sets out to search further. The sound of "*Sathu!*" rose from the audience in unison as all were inspired to devotion.

Phim took off her ruby uppercloth, folded it, paid respect three times, and laid it on the salver. "I salute the almighty power. I offer alms. May I have rank and servants into the future, and be rich and joyful in every way."

Khun Chang watched her. "Oho! Even a woman can do that! If I sit here quietly, I'll lose face by comparison. People will gossip."

Casting a smile at Phim, he took off his embroidered uppercloth, folded it, raised it above his head, and made a prayer. "I salute the almighty power with a heart of loving kindness. Please grant fulfillment to my mood of love quickly, as my heart desires, by this evening without fail."

He placed his cloth beside the ruby one. "May I have Phim as my wife to entwine our hearts before too long, by the evening of this day."

Phim felt gravely offended. She clicked her tongue and ordered servants to pick up the salver. They passed it over the head of Khun Chang, who stared angrily into their eyes. Saithong cried out to a servant, "Hey, Phrom! The end of the cloth brushed the gentleman's head. Your manners are so wretched! Let's go, Phim."

Phim strode out. "I'm so ashamed. Really and truly. Oh dear me. He's worse than a farmer's son but knows no better!" She returned straight home, cursing Khun Chang.

After she left, Novice Phlai was love-struck and in turmoil. He skipped through the rest of the recitation and came straight down from the pulpit. The next episode began promptly and soon all thirteen were complete. The lay faithful poured water onto the ground, expressed their appreciation of the abbot, and left before midnight.

Deep in the night, a gentle wind blew and a brilliant moon shone. In the quiet stillness of Wat Palelai, the novice could not get Phim out of his troubled mind.

"Oh my soft, fair Phim, after you left, did you think of me at all? Or did you forget me without any feeling? I love you so much I want to swallow you. Millions of other women don't interest me at all. If we can share a pillow, I'll sweep you up and enjoy you so there's no single night without love. What must I do, precious Phim, to talk a word or two with you? I don't even know where you live. That accursed Khun Chang messed things up. You went off home in a boiling rage, and I blundered through the reading. Even if you're hidden away in some hill or valley, I'll find you wherever you are."

He hugged Phim's ruby cloth, kissing it, stroking it, and inhaling its fragrance to bathe his heart, falling ever deeper into turmoil until the first streaks of the sun.

Near dawn, Phim began to dream. She and Saithong were swimming across water; in the shallows at the shore, her feet touched and she stood up; Saithong handed her a golden lotus flower; she inhaled its fragrance, awash with joy, wrapped it in her uppercloth, and made her way back across the water. As the dream ended, she woke up and groped around for the lotus. "Oh! It's gone."

She promptly shook Saithong awake and told her the dream. "What's going to happen? Tell me, please!"

Saithong knew the meaning without a shadow of doubt. "I've been noticing things for some time. Don't be worried, eye's jewel. Dreaming about having a lotus means you'll gain a partner in love. It seems this man isn't far away and may turn up very soon. The fact that I handed you the lotus probably means you'll depend on me in the time ahead. If you get what you desire, please let me have some benefit too."

"Oh Saithong! Why do you come up with this interpretation? Where did you see any hint of such a thing? Have you ever seen me all restless and irritable? I don't accept this means a man for me. In the dream it was you who picked the lotus. If the man goes straight for you, I'll laugh. Please give an interpretation more to my liking and I'll reward you."

Khun Chang tossed and turned, pined and longed. "Oh my Phim Philalai! When you shouted at me, it sounded so mellow, so crystal clear. Among thousands of girls, there's none other the same. Your arm is shapely, your slender waist so elegant, and your bottom enchanting. What must I do to fondle and caress you all day long? I'll place food in your mouth to eat, provide you with an elephant to ride, surround you with perfumes while you sleep, and make you a shower spray to bathe. I love you as much as my own life but I worry my hopes will come to nothing. I fear you'll hate my ugly body. Even if you loved me, you'd worry about your reputation. Stop thinking about it! Why fret now? I'll find some way to plead my case."

He opened his mosquito net. "Is it dawn yet? Oh, the moon's still high in the sky. This is a sign that I'll get my beautiful lover for sure!"

PHLAI KAEO MEETS PHIM
IN A COTTON FIELD

As golden rays lit the sky, Novice Phlai thought longingly of gentle, lovely Phim. He washed his face, put on his robe, picked up his almsbowl, and went out. He searched every lane, alley, and bush. Before long, he arrived at Maids Landing in Suphan town. Seeing a bench set out for almsgiving, he paused and stood composing himself.

Phim was inside with Saithong preparing food for almsgiving. She opened a window and saw a novice standing with eyes lowered. The ochre color of his close-fitting robe made his skin glow like moonlight. She picked up the food and started down the stairs with Saithong. Novice Phlai raised his face. Phim glanced long enough for their eyes to meet then ducked and hid behind Saithong. "Oh! Seeing his face makes me shy." She passed her bowl of rice to Saithong, and hid behind a wall.

Novice Phlai blew a Great Beguiler mantra onto her, making her tremble with passion, hardly able to restrain herself from rushing down.

Saithong raised her hands to wai the novice. He unhitched the almsbowl from his shoulder. "I'm late because I've come a long way. At yesterday's recitation, the sponsor of the episode dashed off. Maybe she's angry with me. I'd like a chance to explain. I'd also like to talk to you."

Saithong placed food in his almsbowl, invited him to come to the river after the midday meal, and returned up the stairs. Novice Phlai went outside the fence and hid. Phim looked out and saw him. He hugged his bowl close as if it were something else. Phim smiled, hid her face, and disappeared. He walked off with a spring in his step, looking back over his shoulder again and again. At Wat Palelai, he offered food from the almsbowl to the abbot and waited attentively on him. After eating, he went back to his sleeping quarters and moped.

When Saithong returned upstairs, Phim beckoned her into the bedroom. "What took you so long down there? I saw your mouth chattering away with him."

"Nothing. Let's eat. Afterwards we can spin some cotton and then go to bathe."

"Food isn't going to pacify me. I saw you standing there, all smiles, speaking together for a long time. Why won't you tell me?"

"There's nothing. Do you want me to make something up? He just said that he'd come a long way to get here."

"Right. Don't tell me. I'll probably find out in time because these things don't stay hidden." She left the room in a huff and did not eat with Saithong. Afterwards, she sat spinning cotton with a group of servants. When Saithong came to collect her for bathing, Phim said, "I don't want to go."

"Let's go to the landing, I've something to tell you."

"Don't kid me. Why would you tell me anything? You're determined to keep it all to yourself."

"What am I determined to keep to myself? Is that Novice Phlai making a pass at me?"

"I'm not going. Don't insist."

Saithong walked slowly and gracefully out of the room and went to the bathing spot on the river with several servants.

At Wat Palelai, Novice Phlai could not get Phim out of his mind. Knowing from Saithong that they would go to bathe, he crept down the stairway, went to the landing, and spied from the bushes. "These people are all servants. I don't understand."

Seeing Saithong washing herself on the riverbank, he threw some earth and coughed to get her attention. Saithong quickly came over, and they stole away to hide in the shade of a big heartache tree with sprays of flowers blooming overhead.

"Please forgive me. Don't think I'm being too forward. I've fallen in love and into utter confusion. I can't concentrate. I can't relax. I want to put my life in your hands. I'm like a rabbit stuck on the ground pining for the rabbit in the moon. Only Lord Indra can put him out of his misery by letting him romp with the heavenly rabbit. Little Phim is like that rabbit and you are like Indra. I'm counting on you. Maybe two rabbits can taste the joys of heaven together. If you're kind, I'll be grateful for as long as I live. Please get me out of this darkness and gloom. Bring me back to life. Save me from dashing to an early death. I'll support you from today until you die."

Saithong turned her face away. "I'm not listening to this. I've never acted as a go-between before. If we put a foot wrong, the scandal will be as loud as the troops in a mask play. If I plead your case but she doesn't soften up, I'll get my back caned, while you'll be dancing outside the curtain. All that stuff about her being like a rabbit in heaven is very clever. But I've never seen *two* rabbits in the moon. If Indra went to the aid of a miserable rabbit, he'd be mocked all over the world, and the moon would be tarnished by the romping. I'm too scared, novice. I won't get the meat to eat or the skin to sit on, only the bones hung around my neck. This is not something you nibble. One bite and you die."

"What a pity you have no sympathy. Every day I do nothing but pine and pray. If you do me a favor, and I then come to live in your house, the favor won't have been for nothing. I'll share everything with you on par with the fair and lovely Phim. Money, food, and everything else. Be kind to me, Saithong. Please persuade her. When I've got Phim, I'll bring you a reward. This evening, you must talk to her. I'll wait to hear at almsround tomorrow."

"Are you really in love? I'm afraid that once you have her, this reward will vanish, and no amount of shouting will have any effect. You have to pay up on delivery. Tomorrow, come for the news."

After sunset, a white, haloed moon floated across the heavens. Saithong said to Phim, "Tonight the moon is dazzling as pure silver. Why does the moon care so much for the rabbit that it keeps her imprisoned up there? She's like us, without a partner. She stays in the sky without going anywhere, but the rabbit in the forest gazes at her all the time. I've loved you and brought you up. Because your parents redeemed me from slavery, I'm like both a relative and a slave. It's a pity to go through a whole life without knowing what it is to have a husband and children. I can accept the hardship because I love you. If I didn't, I'd probably have gone off roaming all over the place, maybe got myself arrested or killed. I have to continue looking after you because you don't have your own household yet. The fate of parents is to get older every day. I'm worried what will happen if Mother Siprajan passes away. Young men will sneer that this girl has no father or mother. I think about this day and night, and it sorrows me. If you get married while your mother is still alive, then she'll see the wealthy line continue unbroken. What do you think about this?"

"I don't think about it at all, Saithong. A mother makes every effort to bring up her daughter with the aim of setting her up in a household. We're said to be gentlefolk. Doing something hasty without Mother's consent would be disobedient, and it would bring shame on her. If Mother dies before I'm married, that's fortune. It's not as if I don't have men to pursue me. If you're ugly, cancerous, leprous, or just no match for your friends, there won't be any suitors. But if you're good-looking and have money, they queue up. Fruits are raw before they become ripe. It's better to avoid the sourness and wait to enjoy them sweet. If I had a craving like hunger, your words would be fitting. Admiring the moon together is relaxing, but your talk is unsettling me. I don't like it."

"Now, who's harassing you to have a husband? I'm thinking of you, not acting as a go-between. Have I said anything about this before? You're yawning. Go to sleep. I'll sing you a lullaby.

Oh have pity on the poor young boy
why does he roam like a vagabond
trying to forget that he fell in love
now far from home, from everything fond

wasting away with love's dire grief
how long must he suffer enough to die
Oh gentle Phim, go to sleep, go to sleep
La la, la la la, dear Novice Phlai."

"Oh Saithong, you put the novice into my lullaby. When you went down to give alms, did you fall for him? When I asked you this morning, you wouldn't reply. I didn't get it then but now it's clear. You met him again when you went bathing, and hit it off. Did you come back later than usual because you floated downstream? Don't sleep near me. You'll scare me by talking in your sleep and hugging me."

"Lightning strike! How come it turned out this way? Now I'll tell you the whole story. When I went to bathe today, Novice Phlai came and hid in the bushes at the back. I told him off. He said, 'She won't talk to me. Maybe it's because I'm poor and down on my luck. When we were both tiny, we were playmates, but because of troubles, I had to leave Suphan. My home was a long way from her, a night's travel, but I couldn't stay away like a cock evading a trap. I made the effort because of love. Was it right for her not to acknowledge me? I can't bear it so I'm counting on you.' Even if you don't accept this business of love, he begged to see your face and talk just once. On the day of the recitation, he thought he saw a sign. He felt he could fly in the air, walk on the clouds, pick up the stars and swallow them. He woke up with his mouth still full of them. He thought this meant his wish would be fulfilled. So he blundered off on almsround at first light, desperate to find how things would turn out. I tried to put him off several times but he kept on at me to persuade you. I didn't know what to think, but after some reflection, it made sense. If he were fooling around, why would he trek from Kanburi to Suphan? Maybe you could be a happy couple."

As she listened, Phim was falling into the trap. Since her eyes had met those of Novice Phlai, her mind had been bent on love with no wish to escape. Yet feminine instinct made her dissemble. She put on a sullen face, and left a long pause before turning to reply.

"I thank you from the bottom of my heart, dear Saithong. You have always loved me and protected me. I can put my life in your hands. But why are you offering me the novice on a plate? You and he have hit it off, haven't you? What you two get up to doesn't bother me, but why are you leading me to dream? It's not as if every other man in the world has died. People will sneer and gossip about me all over Suphan. I won't know where to hide my face. You're in love with him so let it be you alone. I'll help you cover it up."

"Oh Phim, you're really thumping me around. I feel bruised all over. You've never made fun of me like this before. Dear me, with this lad, younger than me, really? Am I a slave who wants to be on par with her mistress? I know my place. Do you think the novice doesn't know it too? I'm poor and my body is all wrinkles. I'm like this lead ring— no use as the setting for a diamond. I'm fired up over this because I love you. Remember your dream? You got a golden lotus because of me. If I don't help you, let's see if this doesn't end in tears. I'll leave you in torture for a bit, until swallowing rice is like taking medicine—it brings tears to your eyes."

"Ha, ha! Really funny. Now, how much money has he offered as reward for you to stick your neck out and be so insistent? Should I risk being spoiled just because I fear you'll be angry? If he goes back on his word and abandons me, what can I do? He must ask for my hand. If he just wants to be my lover, I fear it'll end badly. We're born for only one life. If I make a careless mistake, I'm done for."

"Oh Phim, if he weren't good, would I drag you into spoiling yourself and being tarnished? I think he's a perfect match for you.

You're both lovely, young, and bright-faced, like the sun nestling beside the moon. If you marry, I'll earn merit. My job will be to furnish and decorate your home. Mattresses and pillows kept neatly on a bed. A fine, silky-looking mosquito net trimmed with gold and hung with flower tassels and garlands. I'll depend on your merit and sleep happily without a care. Why would I lie to you? If things turned out badly, you'd beat me and send me off to the kitchen to pound rice and carry water, day in, day out. At dawn, Novice Phlai will come to beg alms. I'll make arrangements with him to meet you in the fields. You can listen to him and make up your own mind—accept his love or put your nose in the air and take fright at any man's approach, then the burden will fall on me again, and see if I don't complain. Now go to sleep, my eye's jewel."

At dawn, Novice Phlai rose early, hastened to Phim's house, and intoned a mantra in his mind in the hope it would make her come down.

Phim and Saithong were in the house preparing food, tobacco, betelnut, pan leaf, and medicine to place in the novice's almsbowl. "Why is Novice Phlai slower than the other day?" Phim opened the window and saw him. She hid and nudged Saithong. "Look. The little novice is as composed as an old monk. I'm not going. I'm scared."

Saithong prompted her to go down. Phim cradled the bowl, hid behind Saithong's back, and timidly stepped down the stairway. She crouched down and paid her respect, unable to look at his face, so nervous she almost upset her bowl. She put tobacco, fish, betelnut, and pan leaf into his almsbowl, all mixed up. With face bowed and heart thumping, she went back up the stairway and hid behind a door.

Saithong glanced around to check there was nobody nearby before whispering, "After the forenoon meal, I'll bring Phim to the cotton field. Where is it, novice? Give me the money."

"I haven't forgotten the agreement. If the cotton field is a success, I'll reward you. If I don't, you can create an uproar at my wat. I observe the precepts and I won't go against my word." He went back to Wat Palelai.

After lunch, Phim went to see her mother. "I'm going to the north field. The cotton bolls have burst and are all scattered around. I don't trust the servants. They steal the cotton to buy food and gamble."

Siprajan scolded the servants and all their forebears. "If you catch them, beat them with a big stick so they cry out like a Chinese pork vendor. It has come to my ears many times that those tricksters not only steal but gossip about me too."

Phim and Saithong went to the field with a throng of servants carrying baskets, and sat down under a big bushy tree. "You lot go off. Don't laze around and play about. Do a proper job, and come back here at four o'clock." Once far from their mistress's eyes, the servants sang songs while picking the cotton.

After the forenoon meal, Novice Phlai slipped away downstairs, slung some clothes in a bundle, and went to speak with a monk in the preaching hall. "I'm running away from the abbot. Please allow me to disrobe, and re-ordain me when I come back."

"Off you go. Bring me back some betelnut and tobacco."

Novice Phlai disrobed, put on his lay clothes, and rushed to the cotton field. Saithong intercepted him. "If you'd arrived just a bit later, we'd have missed one another. You can't stay here by the path. Go and hide under that tree with the low-hanging leaves. I'll bring her."

He crept through a gap in the thick foliage and saw Phim sitting plaiting a flower garland. Her whole body seemed to bloom. Love surged in his chest, but he was nervous because he had never done this before. Thinking what to say made his mouth tremble and his heart shrink.

Love triumphed over fear. He approached and greeted her with a smile. She started, and her body stiffened with shyness.

"It's a pity you have to come for picking cotton. You have masses of servants. You must be stiff and weary from walking. I fear the strong wind and fierce sun will spoil your fair face. How good of you to make all this effort. I followed you here because I love you. Did Saithong tell you that? Since the day of the recitation, I lie awake all night long. I feel a fire is licking after me, and I can't escape. I'm sick with desolation and yearning. How is it with you?"

Phim's chest shook with consternation. She had never had such a conversation. She turned her face aside and shifted farther away. Her face trembled. She glanced this way and that without meeting his eyes or speaking a single word.

"What's this, my eye's jewel? Have you forgotten the past? When we were little children, we played together and loved each other very much. Remember playing 'bridal house' with Khun Chang? Why are you shy with me now? Please say just a couple of words. It's hopeless to think Saithong could convey my message to you. Why are you afraid? I won't do anything rough, believe me."

Phim knew that Phlai Kaeo's words about the past were all true. She turned to look at his face. Her fear receded and her trembling heart calmed.

"Honestly, I'd forgotten you, though I recognized you on the day of the recitation. But I'm a woman. I couldn't greet you first. That doesn't mean I dislike you, I'm just worried that people will gossip. I know you complained to Saithong. Were you so angry that now you want to complain to my face? Why have you disrobed? What brings you through the forest to our field? Have you finished your study and disrobed to go home? Or have you fallen in love with Saithong? Look for her by the big tree over there."

"I came here because I knew you'd be here. If the abbot finds out, I'm not afraid of being punished. Let me tell you the whole story. Something made me think of you, and then I couldn't stay with my mother. I was unhappy, incredibly unhappy. I had the idea of being ordained. As quick as I could, I moved to Suphan. I had to make the long journey on my own. I met you but no smile, no greeting. I became even more unhappy. I ran into Saithong and that gave me a channel, so I sent a message. We came face to face when you gave alms, but you still wouldn't greet me. Today we meet with nobody around. I want to offer my love. I'm not spinning a story to get my way. My mind's made up a million times over. Let me be your partner and cherish you. This isn't a passion that will pass once we part."

"It's a pity you talk like all the others. You see the face of an old playmate, and seem to imagine we've been in love forever. It's not proper and I forbid it, Phlai Kaeo. We've been sitting too long. The servants will come back. I'll say goodbye." She stood up.

"Please don't rush off. I'm not making things up to seduce you. I'm deeply in love and terribly miserable. I feel there's a great mountain weighing on my chest. I've prayed to Brahma, Indra, the moon, the whole lot of them, everything in the heavens. If they don't turn to give me some help, I'll surely die."

"Very eloquent. If I were naive, I'd be carried away. You thought out what you were going to say here, didn't you? This is just the beginning of love, and you can already die for it. You braved the forest because of love. You live in constant melancholy. You'll never desert me until your dying day. Human beings are too full of greed. Like with food. We always want something else, salty or sour, raw or cooked, boiled, curried, fried, or grilled. We get tired of anything we eat too often. When a love is brand new, it's thrilling. Like getting a brand new cloth that you can wear and show off. But what happens once that cloth becomes old? It gets used for bathing. Wash and wash, whack and whack, until it becomes shreds, rags for wiping, nothing left. A man and a woman say they'll die together, but how long does that feeling last? Tongue and teeth are together all the time but sometimes they get in each other's way. I think I do care for you a little so I won't reject your feelings completely. Go to my mother and ask for my hand. If she consents, I'll be happy to have you as husband. But chasing after me to be your lover frightens me. People will gossip. When it suits you, on whatever day, come and ask for my hand in the proper way. Now evening is coming and the servants may see us so please return to the wat or I'll be shamed."

"Why rush to chase me away? What if your mother doesn't consent? With days passing and so many other diversions, you'll forget me. If you've definitely decided to love me, don't run away from it. You say we always hunger for different kinds of food. Yes, that's the nature of people in general. But take the example of rice. It's always there—like passion's turmoil. You talk about cloth that gets washed again and again until it's threadbare and torn. But think of a cloth that beautiful and special, that's taken a lot of money and effort to make. We store it carefully in a fragrant chest and take it out to be admired on special occasions, like a big festival. Even though we have many other new cloths, we don't treat them with the same care."

He kissed the end of her uppercloth. "Let me enjoy this a bit. It's very pretty and suits your fair complexion. Did you weave it yourself or buy it somewhere?"

She tugged the cloth away from him. "Don't waste your praise. Mother gave it to me. You're acting like a bully. Because we're in the middle of nowhere, are you going to force yourself on me? If you get your satisfaction by making me miserable, then you won't find love. It's like being so hungry that you eat uncooked rice even though it's still hard and not tasty at all. You're in too much of a hurry."

"Gentle Phim, have a care. You're cutting off my love at the first try. Please calm down and stop accusing me." He kissed her. "Don't take offense, precious. I love you honestly. I'm not forcing myself on you." With passion rising at the thought of parting, he pushed her hand away and pulled the end of her uppercloth. "Stop punishing me. Your breast curves beautifully like molten silver." He lifted her onto his lap. "Why are you trying to slip away?" He tried to peel away her uppercloth but she hung on with a firm grip.

"Are you going to kill me here in this field? Making love to me in the open will make people talk. It's wrong because we're not married. You should make it official, arrange a bridal house for me, then I'll consent. My body is not something that's for sale, something to be laid out in the middle of nowhere. Go home. You die from no food, you don't die from no lovemaking." She lowered her face onto her knees and pleaded to be let down.

He tenderly kissed and stroked her hair. "You're so lovely. Your skin is so fair, so soft. Please give me a little smile, heartmate. I love you too much to let you go. Lugging my love away from here will be torture." He picked up her hand and pressed it to his chest. "See, my heart is bursting. In the evening I'll come to the house to find you." He lifted her chin, kissed her, and hugged her tightly to his body, feeling her full, firm breasts budding against him. He took her hand and looked at her fingers. "So beautiful, these ten fingers, so lovely." She bent her face over her lap and said nothing.

With the sun dropping and the light fading, the servants returned from picking cotton with baskets well stuffed, singing songs as they came. Saithong cried out to warn the couple, "Let's go, let's go! It's almost evening!"

Phim pleaded with Phlai Kaeo. "They're coming! They'll see us. Have mercy and go quickly!"

Phlai Kaeo embraced her on his lap, still reluctant to let her down. But as the sound of the servants came close, he slipped away among the trees. Phim stood up at once. "How are the cotton bolls, you girls? The sun is setting so it's time we went." She left the bushes and walked off.

Saithong fell in beside her, nudged her, and whispered teasingly, "What happened today? Your back and shoulders are soiled."

"Don't speak so loud that others can hear. I'm happy enough to fly. But don't say anything. Nothing happened. Just a little speck of dirt."

Saithong smiled quietly. Phim flashed her a sidelong glance with fiery eyes. By the time they reached home and stored the cotton bolls, darkness had fallen. Saithong led Phim into the bedroom where they lay whispering on the pillows. "Now fair Phim, how was it today? Don't hide anything."

Phim rolled over onto her side. She was in turmoil. She pinched Saithong and said, "Because you'd advised him what to do, after a couple of words he jumped all over me. We went two rounds with me bent double and him trying to raise my head and pull the clothes off me. I'd rather die than go on living. I'll take a knife and stab myself to death to erase the shame. Luckily, in the thick of it, the servants came. Any later, one thing would have led to another. You complained that I wasn't being cooperative and showed no gratitude for your efforts. But all he wanted to do was to impale me on his sharp sword. He even wants to prolong matters. He says he'll come back at midnight tonight."

She slammed the door shut, closed the windows, barred them with battens, and sat rigid, gripping a knife, looking angry enough for blood to drip from her eyes. "Leave the room. Don't tell anyone. Tonight, I'll wait through to dawn without sleeping."

Saithong soothed her. "Don't be so angry. Examine your heart first. Love and longing make the heart feel hot, tight, bursting. Phlai Kaeo is a young man and very virile. He can't restrain his love. He's carried away because he's never met a woman before. Men have very little shyness. But a woman, even when stirred up with lust, still has her feminine instinct. Don't rush to think all this is unseemly. Phlai Kaeo is a virgin, of that there's no doubt. You're a virgin too, and beautiful. Since you came of age, nobody has touched you. You've only just met Phlai Kaeo but already you want to drive him away. Suppose someone else romances you, and then you run into the old flame. You won't know where to put your face. Don't snap this off too hastily. Stop worrying for now. If you don't go to sleep, you'll wake late tomorrow and Mother will be concerned. Phlai Kaeo wouldn't dare come." Saithong walked to her own room and went to sleep.

Phim continued to mope and moan. "Oh Phlai Kaeo, have you forgotten me already? Are you so furious you'll fling me away and leave me lonely? Now that you've made me moody and miserable, will you drop me? I remember you promising to come tonight. It's late already and my heart feels empty."

As Phim lay pining, the moon sank out of sight, and she fell asleep.

Phlai Kaeo had arrived back at the wat but not been re-ordained. He made calculations and found an auspicious time around midnight. As the moon slid across a star-spangled sky, he stood gazing at the shining clouds and the glitter of the Milky Way. He made calculations for the Iron Spear and Great Spirit to determine the direction to set off, and was heartened to find a time that was a conjunction of great success. He examined the breath through his nostrils and strode off on the side where the breath was stronger.

At Phim's house, he scattered enchanted rice to make everyone sleep, used a Loosener mantra to unlock the doors and spring the bolts, and climbed up into the house. Tiptoeing quietly, he made straight for Phim's room.

By lantern light, he eased his way past her betel box, bowl, beautiful cosmetic set, elegantly carved half-moon seat, looking glass with two side mirrors, and handsome gold ornaments. A curtain strung across the room was embroidered with a story of two lovers.

"My darling, your skill is excellent!" He carefully drew the curtain, opened a mosquito net, and saw her sleeping face.

"Lovely smiling cheeks inviting me to share your pillow. Beautiful eyes that seem to know I'm admiring you. Slender neck and sweet little chin. Fingernails long and polished to look beautiful. Breasts full and firm. Faultless."

He gently touched her breasts and blew a charm to undo the sleeping mantra.

Phim started awake. "What? You got in here even though the door's locked! Now, this really is forcing yourself on me. You got no satisfaction in the field so now you practice housebreaking. In the field you jumped on me, got itchy cotton fiber all over my body, and almost shamed me in front of others. Tugging at my clothing with your heavy hands is so rude. Having such a fine fellow as a husband, I'd be afraid of being in the same house. Just teasing, you leave lots of scratches. Please go away at once. I don't care for you."

"Oh my beauty, my utmost love, please don't chase me away. I'm ready to fight to the death without a care for my own life. I'm not rough. My fingernail grazed you accidentally when you swiped me away. I'm sorry. If some cloth's been torn, I'll sew it back together. Let me kiss and caress where it hurts."

"The wounded can look after themselves. If you don't leave this room, I'll scream out loud for the neighbors to hear."

"Go on, cry out loud and clear. Make a racket so your mother catches us. Fetch a knife and slash me. Don't think I'm afraid to die. I want to hug you, be close to you—whatever kindness my heartstring will allow. Don't squirm. You can't get away. Both your cheeks are smiling happily. May I kiss one? Please have mercy."

"Lightning strike! You're playing with me as if I'm your war slave. You don't listen to me at all. However much I pinch, you don't hurt. Ow! Don't touch me there. Aren't you ashamed to batter me?"

He hugged her to his chest, pushed her down on the pillow, put his face against hers, and rocked her to and fro. Dark clouds gathered in the sky above. Storm winds hummed and howled. Great clouds, glutted with rain, swirled and swung around the sky. When a first gust of rain broke from the heavens, nothing endured throughout the three worlds.

Phim was thrilled with love, her heart churning with passion. They lay close together on her bed with faces touching. She did not want to move from his side. She fanned him, hugged him, mopped his sweat with her delicate cloth, and mixed fragrant water to cool him. She begged him to eat some sweets. She set up tables on both sides of the bed, and gave him betel and tobacco. They whispered sweet talk, back and forth, on fire with love's ten thousand passions. Neither was interested in sleep.

Cockcrows echoed around. Flowers bloomed on the touch of dew. Phlai Kaeo's heart lurched. "Leaving lovely Phim is terrible. Parting is like dying. When evening comes, I'll be back. Stay well. Let me say goodbye. My heart will break any minute."

She sighed and sobbed, listless with great yearning. "You came here to make my heart ache. I deserve to be miserable for my stupidity. I love myself but I don't love my own well-being enough. From now on I'll be miserable from morning to night. When will this agony end? You love me, I love you, Phlai Kaeo. But this is planting a tree of love and then cutting it down, leaving us in torture. Will this love break because we're far apart? Will Mother beat me and Saithong scold?

Please come back this evening. Seeing your face every night will lift my heart."

"I love you. I don't want to be apart and unhappy. But the cock is crowing and I must get away. Don't worry. At sunset I'll escape to come here and caress away your sorrows. Parting from Phim is like being shot by a gun."

He tenderly lifted her up and carried her to the door, his face pale and streaked with tears. The sky was already turning golden but he could not bring himself to leave. He sat down, racked with longing. They kissed and hugged in a daze.

"Go inside and close the door, my love." He got up and moved off, his love multiplying a hundredfold. The more he looked back, the more he yearned. Phim forlornly closed the door. Phlai Kaeo steeled his heart and walked away from the house. At the wat, he evaded the abbot and went to ask a monk to re-ordain him.

KHUN CHANG ASKS FOR PHIM'S HAND

Khun Chang was smitten. From the day of the recitation, he dreamed of Phim, babbling drunkenly. When he got up from sleep he felt groggy and had no appetite for food. His heart thumped in distress. He did not hear what people said to him. He was obsessed with Phim.

One day before sunrise, he imagined he could dimly hear her voice. He went to open the door, but saw nobody so returned to his bed and moaned, "Oh Phim, your soft skin shines like moonlight!"

A servant, Krim, who thought he was calling her, answered him and crawled up to the mosquito net.

Khun Chang was overjoyed to hear a sweet voice in reply. "My darling, why did you come just before dawn?" He hugged her, kissed her, and caressed her belly. Krim was happy that the master loved her. She lay still and let him have his way. In ecstasy, he squeezed her breasts, surprised to find they hung so very long and pointy.

"Who's come here under false pretences?"

"It's me, Krim, master. You called me, and I was afraid you'd beat me if I didn't obey."

Khun Chang froze, dumbstruck. "Well, one good thing, you got here in no time. He grabbed her and caressed her feverishly. Wonders burst into a river. A boat pitched and yawed. Spume broke over the gunwales, splashed against the housing, and streamed down from the upper decking over the sides.

When dawn broke, Khun Chang went to wash his face at a window. Krim brought him a betel tray. His mood darkened. He put betel in his mouth and stood with jaw open and chin resting on his chest, completely engrossed in thoughts of *her*.

He went to see his mother. Thepthong sensed he was in an unusual mood. "You seem out of sorts. Your face is as black as a sooty pot. What's up? Don't hide things from your mother."

Khun Chang sobbed out loud. "I'm enormously miserable. I feel my chest is infected and swollen with pus, or a bo tree was felled across my body, shattering my bones. I'll ache for a hundred years without relief. If things get worse, I may die. Only you can save me. Since my dear wife passed away, I've been a miserable widower for more than a year. I have heaps of money but no one to look after it. There are millions of women but I can't find one suitable to be mistress of the house—except Phim. We've been in love for a long time. Every day she begs me to ask for her hand in marriage. If she gets pregnant, there'll be shame in front of the neighbors. Please ask for her hand. If her mother doesn't consent, I'll abduct Phim from their house. The first waxing day of this month is an auspicious day. Today would be a fine time to go."

Thepthong did not believe a word. "Young Phim is more beautiful than anyone else in our town. You're like a field turtle on the ground wanting the moon far away in the heavens. It'd be a waste of my time. You have heaps of money so why not use it to redeem a slave. Go to the city of Ayutthaya and choose a pretty thing who suits you. Why go begging after someone who doesn't want you? Even when you were children, she made fun of your bald head."

"Kids play like kids, and I'm not bothered about what happened then. Now that we're grown up, manners matter. If we live together, love and fear will prevail. I've promised her that we'll be married within three nights. She said she'll hang herself if I don't ask for her hand. If she dies, don't imagine I'll want to carry on living. I'll split my head open with a cleaver and chop my whole body into pieces. If you're not kind to me, Mother, I don't know who else to turn to."

"You're like a naughty schoolchild who won't listen to the teacher. Take a look at yourself. You're like an unlovely basket of kapok. I don't see how anyone will go for you. And Phim is a beauty. Is she going to couple with a pig-dog and make the neighbors gossip? I don't want to get a headache and sore feet walking over there for nothing."

Khun Chang went into his room and threw himself down on the bed. "I've never loved anyone like I love Phim. She's so beautiful, so graceful, so perfect. My head looks like a herd of elephants trampled across it! I'm no good at courting. I'm built for wrestling and that's all. But I don't have to stay here with my face buried in the bed, torturing myself. Phim will soon go to bathe. I'll take my retinue and go down there. I should be able to bribe someone. Seven or eight hundred baht, who cares! Invest a little to achieve success."

He looked up at the sky. "Damn! It's rather late." He grabbed a bag, put in four hundred baht of cash, threw on some clothes, and doused himself in sandal oil. He cinched his waist with a belt but his belly bulged out like a balloon. He marched down from the house with a gaggle of servants following behind. At the landing, they hid in the trees and waited.

Phim and Saithong arrived and went down to bathe. Their crowd of servants played a rowdy game of chase. Khok lunged at Rak, grabbing the end of her cloth. The pair plunged under the water wrapped together, and came up with eyes bulging. Rak spewed out enough water to fill a big bowl. "Horrors! I almost drowned." She lay on the ground with no lowercloth. Hong clapped his hands. "Oh, it's huge, mistress! It looks like the mouth of a horse fish. Horrible!" He threw back his head and guffawed.

On the riverbank, Saithong and Phim shook with helpless laughter. Phim's cloth slipped from under her armpits. Khun Chang saw her round, sculpted breasts. He half-squatted down, grasped his shins, and rocked up and down like a house lizard. "Oh Mother, today I die!"

Saithong called the servants, "Let's go. The sun is dropping." Khun Chang emerged from the trees, caught up with Phim on the path, and walked beside her with a broad smile on his face. Saithong and Phim stepped off the path and let him walk on ahead. He pretended to recite a love poem within their hearing.

"Oh, heavenly magnolita by the flowing brook . . ."

A servant continued his master's verse.

" . . . I saw your breasts and took them for a sweet,
Whopping palm fruit in syrup for me to eat. . ."

Phim burst out angrily, "Your mother! You old baldy!" She rushed home.

Khun Chang followed more slowly. At the gate, he told a servant, "Please be kind enough to inform Siprajan that we are here." Siprajan came to a window and saw Khun Chang, his forehead damp and shiny with sweat. Her heart sank.

She invited him up. "You're drenched in sweat. Have a wash." She bustled around shouting at the servants. Khun Chang entered the main apartment on his knees, sat on a mat, and raised his hands to wai Siprajan.

She reciprocated and invited him to take betel. "Why did you come in the hot sun?"

Khun Chang coughed and spluttered, lowered his face and sat there, saying nothing.

Siprajan prompted him. "What's up? No need to be hesitant. We're not formal here. Why have you come?"

"My dear lady, this is all beyond me. My wife died many months ago. I have heaps of money but it gets stolen. One pair of eyes is not enough to watch over it. Today they broke the locks on my chests in broad daylight. Cloth also gets taken from time to time. I need someone to help look after my property. Someone like Phim."

Greed rose in Siprajan's breast. She could not stop herself bursting out, "A man like you can easily find a suitable match, someone equal in social rank, who knows how to sew and embroider. But around Suphan, I don't see anyone. In truth, young Phim is almost an adult but her status is no more than middling, comfortable, not like some in Ayutthaya."

Khun Chang's face brightened into a smile. "Finding someone else like Phim would be impossible. I think constantly of having her as my partner. But my mother doesn't agree. Because Phim and I used to play together like brother and sister, she thinks it's improper. She's afraid you won't consent so she hasn't paid you a visit. May I invite some elders to talk with you? I'll hand over cattle, buffaloes, paddy lands, money, cloth, and everything."

Phim was listening with Saithong in the next room. "What a liberty!"

She opened a window and pretended to call a servant. "Phon! Where have you got to? Come here, you evil hairy-chested baldy. There's work to do."

Baldheaded Phon came out of a hut with his head gleaming, and strode up the stairs.

Khun Chang felt embarrassed. He quickly took leave of Siprajan and stumbled down from the house, passing Phon on the stairway. Through bared teeth, he hissed, "We meet again after a long time."

Phon shakily raised his hands to wai. "This sin is the result of a cockfight in the past." Khun Chang ignored him, and lurched off with an angry face.

After sunset, the world was bathed in the light of a sublimely beautiful haloed moon. Phim was missing Phlai Kaeo. For many days there had been no sign of him. She went to consult Saithong.

"He made promises but things are not turning out as he said. I can't blame you alone. I must blame my own heart for being too careless. I was taken in by his good looks and eloquent words, and now I've wasted my love. Khun Chang had the nerve to ask Mother for my hand, and I fear she'll consent because she's totally bowled over by his wealth. Saithong, please tell me what to do."

Saithong lifted Phim's chin and wiped away her tears. "Phlai Kaeo means to love you till his dying day. He's not just trying to lure you as a plaything. Perhaps he's sick, or too tired, or is tied up by important matters. Perhaps word has got to the abbot. Tomorrow I'll find him and bring him here." She fanned Phim to sleep.

Next morning, Saithong woke early and went to Siprajan. "Last night Phim had a very strange dream. She was asleep in some other house when it caught fire and she was burned and blistered by the flames. I'm going to Wat Palelai to consult the abbot."

"Go quickly. Take along some betelnut and pan. Oh, dear Phim! And lots of sweets and fruit as offerings."

Saithong arrived at the wat, sent the servants to pick flowers, and went to offer food to the abbot. When he had finished eating, she slipped into Phlai Kaeo's room and spoke to him in a rush.

"Phim has been waiting for you many days. She's desolate with worry. This evening, she orders you to go to her. It looks as if you seduced her for your enjoyment, then abandoned her to misery. Yesterday when we went to bathe that vile Khun Chang acted very coarsely. Phim lost her temper and poured all sorts of abuse on him. But then he came to see Siprajan and dared to ask for Phim's hand. He thinks everything will fall into his lap. Phim says I acted as a go-between, persuaded her to give herself to you, and now she's heartbroken. She's worried she's done wrong, you seem to be easing away, and the bad news will spread far and wide. Are you going to face up to this or just save yourself? I'm close to her so it's me that gets beaten."

Novice Phlai smiled to reassure her. "Phim and you are the two nearest and dearest to me. My heart is pledged and my love will never fade. Let's talk this through slowly, Saithong. Keep the matter quiet, and don't let it reach the ears of others. The problem is the abbot. He makes me study and practice recitation from breakfast until dark. The night I went to see Phim, he tied me up and beat me. You got flayed because of me, but you undertook this task so please see it through. I'll repay you, don't worry. Please plead my case with Phim. The day I can escape the eye of the abbot, I'll come straightaway."

He blew a love mantra onto a betelnut, and offered it to Saithong. The love charm made her hair bristle and nerves tingle with desire. She said, "A poor person has to put up with nothing but hardship. I'm like a banana leaf for wrapping sweets—discarded without a care after the sweets are eaten."

"Make merit and you'll see the results later, Saithong. First things first, tell her I'm a good person. And don't be angry at me. Where did you get beaten? Open your uppercloth so I can see."

"What is this, pulling at my clothes to peek at my breasts?"

At that moment, an old monk who was returning from the toilet heard a muffled female voice, and spied through a gap in the wall.

"A curvy waist and big breasts like balloons! Damnit, she's a meal for the novice. In broad daylight, not afraid of anyone! This is improper behavior in the monks' quarters. I'll tell the abbot."

But he watched for a long time before walking away, shouting, "Oh Lord Abbot, Novice Phlai is with a woman. They're tugging at each other's clothes!"

The abbot gnashed his gums, seized a walking stick, strode shakily over, and opened the door with a crash. Just in time, Novice Phlai and Saithong ducked behind a water jar. The abbot loped around, thrashing about with his stick. Saithong slid down a trapdoor and hid. The novice jumped out of an open window and galloped away, his robe streaming behind him. The abbot ransacked the room, finding nobody. "Ugh! That dog-faced novice and his ghost woman have defiled our quarters." He sat down to pound some betelnut but the pestle remained motionless while he ranted until he felt satisfied.

Saithong scurried away. Novice Phlai was nowhere to be seen. She stopped in the middle of the wat, straightened herself out, and called the servants to hurry back home. Siprajan saw her arrive. "Why did you take so long? Did the abbot interpret the dream as good or bad?"

"The abbot went off on almsround for ages, and then we had to wait while he had his meal. He thinks this is a very bad omen for Phim. She must be very wary for the next three days."

She went inside and huddled whispering with Phim. "Novice Phlai says his promises are all sincere. He'll find a way to disrobe and come. Even if there's a sword waiting to cut his throat, he won't retreat."

Novice Phlai could not return to Wat Palelai. "I've been studying a long time but I'm not yet expert in various branches of knowledge. My mother told me to seek out Abbot Khong at Wat Khae, who was a close friend of my late father. Yet I'm also concerned about Phim to the depths of my heart. She'll complain I broke my promise and ran away. But if I disrobe now, my knowledge won't yet be powerful. Though I value being true to my word, I must stifle my longing for her."

He crossed fields and found a path through a thicket of trees. At an elephant enclosure, he made inquires and was pointed the way. A lone elder sweeping the wat told him to look for Abbot Khong in the scripture hall. Novice Phlai rushed across just as the abbot came out to a terrace. "Where have you come from, young novice?"

"I'm the son of the late Khun Krai. My name is Phlai Kaeo. My mother is Thong Prasi. She told me to seek you out as a teacher so I came to Suphan."

"Oh right! I used to be a good friend of Khun Krai. I'm still disappointed that he died without putting up a fight. He'd lost his knowledge. Why didn't he come to see me? Even if they raised an army of ten thousand from all over the land, they'd flee before one night had passed, waving white flags, and abandoning thoughts of victory! I miss him every day."

He turned to examine Phlai Kaeo. "You're a puny thing, not tough looking at all, yet you made it through the forest from Kanburi to find me. Is Thong Prasi well? We're all scattered in different places. Stay with me. I have a duty to Khun Krai. You're exactly like him. I'll teach you, and not let you get killed as he was."

"Father did not try to escape because he had drunk the water of allegiance and was not tainted by thought of revolt. In order not to dishonor his oath, he renounced his superior powers so that all his lore was lost. That's why they could easily slash him to dust. As for my mother, she's getting older and older but she's not ailing and hasn't lost her memory."

"She's getting on, is she? I haven't seen her face for about ten years. I'll teach you the military arts. In the future, don't boast about keeping your word, and don't risk being slashed to dust. Go stay in the quarters next to the central hall."

Novice Phlai went to a room where there was a bed, mattress, and pillow. His thoughts turned to fair gentle Phim, and he grew miserable. In the evening, his longing worsened. At the last rays of the sun, he went to ingratiate himself with the abbot by fanning him. The abbot began to give him instruction straightaway: putting an army to sleep and capturing its men; summoning spirits; making dummy soldiers; concealment; invulnerability; undoing locks and chains; calculating auspicious times; enchanting tamarind leaves to become wasps; the Great Beguiler mantra to induce strong love; stunning people; withdrawing protective powers from others; and keeping spirits to act as spies. He studied all branches of knowledge, reciting to commit everything to memory.

He thought of Phim but did not go to her because he had fallen in love with gaining knowledge.

PHLAI KAEO GOES
INTO SAITHONG'S ROOM

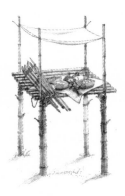

Khun Chang pined for Phim. He did not eat or sleep but stayed in his room, sighing and simpering. "Tomorrow I'll ingratiate myself with her mother and plead for her hand, using money and all the tricks at my disposal. Even if I look awful with my bald head, she should be considerate."

In the morning, he dressed smartly and went to Siprajan's house. She welcomed him, and they chatted like neighbors. "What have you come for? Speak freely. Is your mother well?"

Khun Chang grasped the opportunity to reply. "Please let this son be your humble servant to serve you like a pair of shoes. I'm sincerely in love with gentle Phim. Please settle her with me, my dear lady. If she is mine, I'll cover her body with gold. Even moonlight will not be allowed to touch her. Why live in fear of poverty and hardship? Please accept me as your son."

Siprajan listened with a beaming smile. She would be very happy to have a rich son-in-law. "My dear Chang, whatever merit and karma decree, whether the horoscopes match or not."

She called out, "Phim, where are you? Why don't you come and get to know each other?"

Phim had seen Khun Chang arrive and had hidden behind a screen to listen. She was furious. She called back to her mother, "I'm not coming however much you call me."

She pretended to abuse a servant. "Hey, Phon! Where have you got to, you baldy? You're so puffed up, boasting about money, and thinking you're a great lover! Ugh! All that powder and sandalwood oil and your hair parted on two sides like pigtails! A dog was due to be born but you arrived in its place. With a face like that, who'd marry you, you dog-licked mango? You're like a dragonfly boasting you can race Garuda across the ocean, a little rock that thinks it's mighty Mount Meru, a forest firefly that wants to rival the sun."

Knowing this abuse was meant for him, Khun Chang felt ashamed in front of the servants. He took leave of Siprajan, and quickly went down from the house.

Now Siprajan was furious. She got up, grabbed a stick, and chased after Phim. "You're uncouth, terrible, too much! If you're like this, who'll have you?"

She beat Phim until her back was soaked in blood and her face bathed in tears. Phim fled into the kitchen, shot the bolt, and sank down on the floor, whimpering. "Where have you got to, Saithong? I've been beaten almost to death. Please help me."

Saithong found the door closed and bolted so spoke through the wall, "What did you call me for?"

"Mother is going to give me to that half-headed fellow. Let's run away to the wat right now. I'll tell the novice and see what he thinks." She opened the door, made sure the coast was clear, then crept away with Saithong to Wat Palelai. "As I remember, the novice's room was that one." Saithong crept up and saw that it was empty. Their hearts sank further.

She whispered to some other novices there, "Is Novice Phlai still here or has he gone elsewhere?"

"The abbot beat him. He ran away to stay at Wat Khae."

"Karma, karma! Bad news multiplies. Sorrow piled upon heartbreak."

They went to Wat Khae. Heads poked out of windows and doors. "There, over there. Women. Come and look!" The monks crowded around and stared. "Are you court ladies?"

Novice Phlai was studying. Hearing the noise, he looked out and called them over. Seeing Phim's swollen eyes, he was taken aback. "Why this sad face? What brought you here?" At the sight of him, Phim managed to break into a smile. She came up the steps with Saithong, and sat down close to him.

"What is this, novice? You seduce me, then you skip off. I want to think you have a good heart, but what about your promises to ask for my hand? Now, something has intervened. Khun Chang has asked for my hand and my mother has consented. I objected and she beat me until my back nearly caved in. What do you have to say? Speak up, right now. Or else I'll curse you until I feel satisfied."

Phlai Kaeo stroked her hand soothingly and wiped away her tears. "That Chang is a terrible troublemaker. You've been striped with a stick because of him. Lightning strike! Even your little finger is scored. After the abbot beat me, I went to my mother. She doesn't want me to leave the monkhood, and I don't have any money for getting married so I don't dare disrobe. My love and longing for you is unbroken. Don't be so miserable. My heart doesn't forget my promises."

"How come you're so slow? Why can't you get some money? I'm afraid it means you don't really love me. Oh, this is my karma! Why was I born a woman? I fell for your sweet words, and now it looks as if I've really fallen. This evening, please come to the house. I'll find some money to give you. On second thoughts, maybe I shouldn't go back home. I fear Mother will beat me again. If I stay here at the wat with you, what would happen?"

"Oh eye's jewel, you can't. This evening I'll ask the abbot to let me disrobe. If he refuses, I'll run away."

He shifted so his body touched hers. "Your skin is soft, silky soft. You look so beautiful, like something made in a mold, like a lotus bud bursting out behind a leaf. Raise your face and give me a little kiss, Phim. I'm only a novice, it's not against the rules."

"What is this! Soon you'll be chased out of here like that other wat. If anyone sees, we'll have to jump out of the window but this one is too high. I have to go. If Mother finds out, things will get blown up. Disrobe and come this evening. No more lies and evasion."

She strode out and returned home with Saithong.

At dusk, the forest came alive with the calls of animals. Tigers roared and elephants trumpeted. Deer cowered in fright.

Unable to find any peace of mind, Novice Phlai went to see the abbot. "I'm greatly troubled. I feel there's a bonfire raging in my breast. Because of past sins, I have no merit to be in the monkhood. The yellow robe is too hot for me to wear. I beg you to allow me to leave. Without your blessing, I'll be burned to death in this blaze."

The abbot was disappointed. "I was hoping you'd look after my cremation. Now you want to run away without any feeling left for me. As a lay person, life will be tough. Do you want to disrobe and get yourself tattooed for corvée? Once your wrist is marked, it's all hard times—carrying packbaskets on your shoulder until you collapse. If the overseer likes you, things are a bit easier. He can find work that's not too heavy. But if he hates you, he'll use you until you ache—sawing wood, dragging big logs—heave ho! With a body like yours, slender as a sculpture, do you think you can manage that? Listen to me. Don't rush to disrobe."

"You're right. I can't argue. But I no longer wish to be here. Please look for an auspicious time."

The abbot saw he was beyond restraint. He picked up his slate and checked the date by the lunar calendar. He wrote in the day, month, and year of Novice Phlai's birth, and made calculations according to the astrology manual.

"Your fate is to be a soldier, my son. But I can also divine that you've been lying to me. I understand now why you're in such turmoil—a love affair. Listen to my words and remember them well. After disrobing, you'll marry as you intend and set up house together, but it won't last. You'll be separated and she'll have a new husband. When you reach the critical age of twenty-five, a misfortune will occur. You'll be clapped in irons and locked away. At the age of forty, you'll do well."

Abbot Khong's words made Novice Phlai's heart lurch. He knelt to pay his respect and left, shaking with fright and stifling his sorrow. He returned to his quarters, prostrated three times, and disrobed.

He strung a subduing charm and a mercury amulet round his neck, and inserted a kris with a crow's head handle in his belt. He prepared a set of offerings, cast a powerful mantra over rice, and set off with candles in his hand. The sky glittered with stars. The moon shone with an aura like a royal parasol.

He hastened to a graveyard and built an eye-level shrine with a white cloth as a canopy. He lit candles, made a protective circle with sacred thread, sat cross-legged inside the circle, and summoned the spirits. In every direction, the lofty forest trembled. A storm wind thrashed through the bushes. Trees bowed over and came crashing down. Lightning flashed and thunderbolts exploded like the thumps of a giant pestle. The ground under him quaked as if being shaken apart. A swarm of spirits rose up and ran towards him, their bodies transforming into different shapes.

Once they came close, they were overawed by Phlai Kaeo's lore and could do him no harm. They all bowed and beseeched him, "Lord, what do you desire here?"

The leader of the spirits found this intolerable. He extended his body upwards with stretching noises, rolled his flashing eyes, waved a club, and screeched, "If you don't get out of here, I'll beat you to dust!"

Phlai Kaeo yelled loudly and threw rice. The spirit reeled backwards and shrank as small as a bee sting. Phlai Kaeo asked, "Are you the boss in this graveyard?"

The spirit quailed and wanted to disappear into the ground. "I'm master of this graveyard, the demon in chief. The god Wesawan, guardian of the north, granted me this territory a long time ago. What business brings you here?"

Phlai Kaeo slashed at the spirit with a nettle vine. "A big matter. Will you come along to help? Answer quickly!" The spirit prostrated and consented. Phlai Kaeo placed a cloth with a Three Lions yantra over the spirit's head and jumped up onto its shoulders. They glided away as if borne by a strong wind, aiming straight into Suphan town. As they landed in Siprajan's flower garden, the wind wafted a fragrance of pollen. Phlai Kaeo got down from the spirit's shoulders. "Stay here until I return." He walked quickly to the stairway.

Inside the house, Phim was fretting that there was still no sign of Phlai Kaeo. "I think he's tricked me. If he doesn't turn up tonight, I'll hang myself."

Saithong chattered away in an attempt to cheer her up. "He's despicable, this Novice Phlai. Maybe he's lurking around outside for fear someone will see him. I'll go out to look."

She soon came upon him. "Now, my rich fellow, why have you been dawdling? Phim is waiting. And I want the reward you promised me."

Phlai Kaeo smiled back. "Please let me postpone a little. Take me to her for one more night. Tomorrow I'll give it to you. Honestly."

Saithong spread her uppercloth to hide him as they walked up into the house. Pretending it was accidental, he touched her breast. When she did not react, he grasped with his full hand. Saithong pushed him away. "Hey, that's my breast! You're not worth helping."

"I only touched it a little. Forgive me. I thought it was Phim—soft, nice and soft. May I have a kiss?"

"Hey! Has there been anyone who thinks so much of himself? If you create a scandal here you won't get what you want." She snatched back her uppercloth, tossed her head, and flashed him an angry look. "That's her room. Creep in yourself. I don't want to see her."

Phlai Kaeo went straight to the bedroom, found the door open, and went in. Parting the curtains and mosquito net, he saw her sitting with head bowed. In the glow of a lamp, her complexion shimmered as fair as the moon. Her parted hair fell prettily, framing her sad face. He could barely restrain his desire to embrace her.

Instead, he teased her by clearing his throat, "Ahem!" Phim looked up and came forward with her eyes still lowered. Her cheek collided with his nose, and his hand with her breast. She jumped away, stumbled, and uttered a squeal of shock.

"Oh! You've come. What are you skulking around for? I thought it was a ghost. Haven't you had enough of fooling around?"

Phlai Kaeo doubled over laughing. He hugged her and guided her into the room. They sat on the bed side by side, fondling. "Eh, were you waiting for me?"

"So what if I was waiting? If you didn't come tonight, I was going to say farewell to Saithong and hang myself."

"Oh Phim, how could you abandon me so easily? I'd have to stay in the monkhood until death, with no one else from now on, praying and telling beads to make merit for you. I was delayed by the abbot. I told him all sorts of lies but a real teacher can see the truth. He made lots of objections. That's why I'm late."

He caressed her, kissed her left cheek, then the right one, hugged her tight to his chest, and gently guided her down on the bed. Hearts thumped. Passions multiplied. Chaos approached. On the ocean, winds whipped up waves that crashed on the shoreline, recoiled, and crashed, over and over again. A Hainanese junk sailed into a small canal. The sky shivered with thunder, and rain sluiced down. The captain lost his way and turned the helm. The ship faltered, grounded on the shallows, and broke apart.

Phlai Kaeo sat up and said, "My love, it's very hot. Let's go and bathe." She took his hand and led him out to the terrace. As they crept along, floorboards creaked.

Siprajan called out, "Who's there?"

Phlai Kaeo nudged Phim to reply. "Just me. I'm going to bathe."

They sat on a low bench and Phim released water from a lead nozzle. He tugged at her uppercloth.

"Hey, don't play around. I'm shy about my breasts and I've never bathed with nothing on. People will see. Don't embarrass me, please."

"There's nobody else to see us, dear Phim. Bathing with your clothes on is not as cooling."

He peeled the cloth away. In the light of the moon floating through a hollow sky, her breasts shone full and fair. Water splashed on them like a shower of diamonds.

"Darling Phim, they rise and shine at the touch of moonlight. Let me wash you. I won't be rough on your skin—soft as a spider's web."

She stretched out her arms. Phlai Kaeo hugged her tightly to him and caressed her gently with his hand.

"Hey! Didn't you have enough just now? I'm very ticklish and you're annoying me. You're really too much."

"Forgive me. I was a bit lost. It's chilly. That's enough bathing."

They got up and dressed.

"Turn your face here. Your right cheek has to be powdered just so."

"Don't fuss over my cheeks. They're not worth it."

"Oh Phim, you keep finding fault about everything." He guided her gently back onto the bed where they fooled and fondled.

Phlai Kaeo began to think about Saithong asking for her reward. "I could find the money for her somehow but that would be a waste of my talents as a lover. There's an old saying that hits the nail on the head: If a thorn pricks, use another thorn to pry it out. Money is not what she's after."

He turned to Phim. "Suppose I come to ask for your hand but your mother refuses. I'll die of a broken heart."

"If our horoscopes don't match, I'll probably run off with you. Whether it's for better or worse, I'll think about that later. What I'm really afraid of is that you won't ask for me."

"Why do you say that? You pick at me about everything. But tell me, what's your birth year? Then if I'm asked, I can tell them a year that's a good match. Don't believe that stuff about predicting whether we'll be good or bad for each other. There are lots of people who elope without bothering about their horoscopes."

"Me? I'm the year of the rat. This year, I'm sixteen, just blooming."

"Younger than me by two years, tender Phim. How about Saithong? What year is she?"

"She's the year of the horse, twenty-two, as I remember. Why are you asking for her year? Are you hoping to marry her too?"

"Oh Phim, what a shameful idea. You're always having a dig at me."

He hugged her tightly to his body, feeling her breasts taut and proud enough to burst. He caressed her to sleep in no time. He had in mind to go and offer his love to Saithong. "She's neither old or young but youthful enough and good-looking. Her breasts I felt just now are still nice and firm. She's only four years older than me. I'll sneak over to her. Even if she doesn't like it, she dare not make a row because she herself let me into the house."

He stepped down from the bed and tiptoed away. At the sound of his footfalls, Phim turned over. He edged back to her side, and rocked her back and forth. "Don't you want to nap, Phim? Though we did it until the sweat flowed, still you don't sleep."

He opened a sandalwood fan and fanned her. Under his caresses, she lapsed into slumber. He left her room, crept directly to Saithong's, and blew a Great Loosener mantra, making the bolts spring and slide out. He sat down beside Saithong on the bed, kissed her cheek, and nuzzled her breasts that lay round, proud, large, and exposed. He blew a love mantra and nudged her awake.

Saithong came to her senses, and turned to see Phlai Kaeo. Her heart felt full of a craving for love. Under the mantra, she trembled with excitement and confusion but her female modesty prevailed. "Who is this?"

"Please don't cry out. I've come to find you because I couldn't swallow the love that's weighing down my heart. Don't think of yourself as Phim's elder sister. You're not many days older than me. Making love together isn't wrong. Please don't stop me and leave me yearning."

"This is embarrassing. You're like a kid standing on tiptoe to court a grown-up. You're too used to getting your own way. If Phim finds out, it won't be pretty. She'll think I made a date for you to come here. You may end up not tasting the cream. Think carefully. Please leave this room."

"My heart felt you loved me so I dared to come. Even if Phim finds out, don't worry. I'll patch things up so you don't get any of the blame. Don't complain and make a loud fuss now I've fondled you this much already."

"Do you want to create a scandal all over the house? Here, I'll scratch you so it hurts! Oh, who would want to be in my place? All this pinching and teasing is uncouth and shameful. I thought you were a good fellow not a wicked one. Please leave the room or else I'll scream, Mother will come, and you'll get what you deserve."

Phlai Kaeo chanted a mantra, and blew it onto her body, arousing her to passion. "Have pity, Saithong. If you aren't kind, I'll probably hang myself." He picked up a cloth, tied it over a beam in the wall, and wrapped the end around his neck.

"Don't do it, Phlai Kaeo! Are you mad enough to kill yourself so easily? It's very difficult to be born a man. Won't you miss Phim? She's young and she's got the figure of an angel. I'm old already and my figure is not beautiful."

"You're like Phim in every way. Your body and your breasts are just right. I've seen the lot. Being a bit older, you must have more skill, more tricks, all the various games. That can't be bad." He touched her breast lightly, kissed her head very gently, and hugged her tightly against his chest.

"Don't be rough with me. I'll let you stay. I'm just worried that you'll couple with me then throw me away. Give me your word that you really love me, then I'll lie back and let you do what you want."

"It's a pity you need my word, but I don't object. I swear that I won't lie to you, let lightning strike me down."

He blew another formula onto her breast. Saithong's eyes drooped, and she lapsed into a drowsy stupor. Raindrops pattered, lightning flashed, thunder rumbled, wind howled. Waves battered a junk that heeled over, and sought refuge by slipping along the riverbank. In the heavy storm, the sail was reefed to half mast, yet the ship still pitched and yawed, wallowed and rolled. Several times it had to throw anchor and heave to for a while. Making love with Phim was like being in the shallows at a river's edge with only some splashing ripples. With Saithong it was like being hit by a kite storm. As soon as the ship left the bight, it sank to the bottom.

Back in her room, Phim awoke and sleepily reached out for Phlai Kaeo. He'd gone. Her heart sank. She sat up and saw the door standing open. "Where has my love run off to? Maybe he's playing a joke on me." She parted the curtains and looked around. "Why didn't he tell me where he was going? Maybe he's angry at me for something but I don't see I've done anything wrong. Maybe he has left word with Saithong." She crept to Saithong's room and heard the muffled sound of conversation inside.

Saithong was feeling listless and full of uncertainty. "Because you're strong, you tend to be a bully. Now that I'm tainted, you have to look after me. If you neglect me, I'll be shamed. If Phim finds out, she'll bully me too. I'll be the minor wife and I won't be able to avoid paying respect to her."

"I'll love you equally and not put one above the other. Remember when you came to talk about the reward for persuading Phim? Because I loved you, I acted the part. If I'd tried to court you then, I was worried you wouldn't talk to me. But I love you more by five to one."

Unable to stand any more, Phim pushed the door open with a bang, and stamped up to the bed. Opening the mosquito net, she peered in to find them in each other's arms.

"He forced me, Mistress Phim! I tried to fend him off but he wouldn't budge. If I made any noise, I worried I'd get you into trouble. Because I love you, I accept what comes, bitter or sweet. Do you take me at my word? I didn't know this Phlai Kaeo of yours would be like this." She put on a show of modesty, lowered her face, and burst into tears.

Phim spoke with acid sarcasm. "I thank you for having such a good heart. You're kind and considerate in every way—straight, really, straighter than a chariot's curving shaft. It's all of *us* who are crooked."

Then she turned on Phlai Kaeo. "Why did you come and bully her? She's older than you and she raised me from childhood. You're just out for what you can get—like an over-exuberant little monkey, like a pushy Chinese who's bent on riding an elephant. Good thing I came in time, otherwise you'd probably have speared her again. It's like when Rahu swallows the moon. Only when people ring bells does he shit it out."

"It's not like that. Please calm down. Creating a row will only bring scandal and shame. I came to ask Saithong if I could postpone paying the reward that I'd promised her. Really. That's all. It's a pity you're so angry."

"I'm more hurt than you can imagine. I heard it all. You're not telling but I saw the truth. Not just a reward, you tossed her the full ding-dong bar of gold!"

Saithong was too hurt by the sarcasm to hold herself back. "We all know what's going on here. It's you who has all the gold, enough to fill a chest. This is already the thinking of a wife. You coached him to go back on his promise to me, didn't you? You don't want him to give me the reward money so you can have it yourself. This is the first man you've fallen for, and now you won't have any use for me until the sky caves in. I worked hard at bringing you up. Is this how you repay me, beloved?"

"You're not bad yourself, Saithong. You string words like a braided necklace. They sound wonderful. But laughable, ha-ha! You worked hard at getting him to fall in love with you. And why shouldn't he be smitten? Loved to stupefaction. I can't compete—inferior by five to one, because I can't match your pace and style. I thank you for bringing me up. There's an old saying: Sisters from the same womb are like each other's hands and feet."

"Your tongue is sharp so keep scolding and I'll knock you down. I may be small but I can be fearsome."

"Go on, hit me. I think of him as my lord and husband. You're the minor wife taking liberties and not knowing your place. I'll grab your hair and bash you with a coconut shell!"

"What a speech! I'll have to beat this sharp-tongued girl."

"Don't you dare hit me, Saithong!"

Phlai Kaeo jumped between them. "Don't, Phim! Noise will only create trouble. Saithong, you're throwing more fuel on the fire."

Siprajan started awake. "What's that racket? What are you all doing at this late hour?"

Saithong called straight back, "Phim's reprimanding me. I went to sleep and let a dog eat the fat."

Phim smiled and contributed to the lie. "If I hadn't come to chase the dog away, the whole jar of fat would be gone." She glared at them angrily and went back into her room.

Phlai Kaeo followed her and tried to make things up with kisses and caresses. Phim shoved him away. "Don't come and sleep in this room, my dear sir. Why touch me? It's a waste of your hands. I'm not fragrant, not like Saithong. Is it true, you've fallen for her?"

"Oh, dear Phim, you get at me for everything you can. I'm weighed down by problems that you don't see. What if I come to ask for your hand but your mother doesn't consent? I went to talk this matter through with Saithong. I hadn't even chewed the betel into bits when you burst into the room. There wasn't enough time to get mixed up with her. You're concerned about nothing."

"Lightning strike! You're quite something. I was hiding there listening for a long time. If things are like this, will we love each other in the future? You say you'll ask for my hand but I'm still waiting. It's second nature for you to lie about everything. I've fallen in love but it's all one-sided. I didn't listen to the sayings they teach us—that really smart men have about thirty-two tricks. By comparison, you have at least sixty-four! You speak as beautifully as a gong circle playing but you don't love. I won't believe in promises from now on."

The cry of a coel announced it was close to dawn. He opened a window and saw the early glimmers. The thought of leaving made his heart churn. Phim clung on to him not to go, her heart falling apart at losing her love. "Late in the night I'll be thinking of how you came to me. My bed will be cold at that chilly hour. Will you make it to Kanburi? The wild animals will give you terrible trouble. Walking on your own will be lonely. Your poor fragile feet will ache. When the sun is high, the heat will be unbearable. In the evening you'll hear only the gibbons. When they swing around and whoop-wheet, it sounds so lonely and desolate, like the cries of the spirits. Oh beloved, I'm desolate too."

She got up with her eyes full of tears, opened a chest, and took out four hundred baht wrapped in a ruby colored cloth. "Pay for an elephant to ride there. Pay whatever they ask. Don't walk."

Phlai Kaeo took the money, rested his chin on her shoulder, and whispered, "Stay in your room. Don't even poke your head out of a window. Don't go down to the ground. If I could divide myself in two, I'd leave one half here to keep you company. But that's beyond me. I don't have the powers of Lord Vishnu."

Almost at dawn, the sound of monks tolling a bell and a coel's haunting cry in the forest made the heartbreak seem infinite. Tears welled in his eyes and spattered onto Phim's shoulder. He stood up and moved to a window. "Wait for me, my gentle darling. Within seven days, I'll come to ask for your hand."

He stood on the window ledge and called to the spirit. Stepping onto its shoulders, he tied the money round its neck, and turned back for a final aching farewell. "My heart stays here but I have to say goodbye."

Phim raised her hands to wai him. So pent-up she could scarcely speak, she sobbed out, "Safe journey." The spirit whisked him away. She stayed looking until he slipped from sight then closed the window and collapsed on the bed, softly sobbing herself into a stupor. "Oh my Phlai Kaeo! When will you come back to lie on this pillow?"

PHLAI KAEO MARRIES PHIM

The spirit sped across forest and grasslands to Kanburi, and disappeared promptly as the light came up. Phlai Kaeo walked into the house and embraced his mother's feet. "Oh son, why did you disrobe? Why can't you stop crying? Where did you get this money?"

"Mother, I'm going through a very bad time. Worse than bad—unbearable. Phim and I are in love. She gave me the money so I can ask Siprajan for her hand. If she won't consent, Phim will follow me anyway. Please help. Phim is miserable waiting for me. Pity her for having to eat only tears."

"Karma comes, karma goes! Oh eye's jewel, don't take a wife yet. Let your mother admire you in the robe. Make some merit for your late father first by being a monk for just two seasons then I'll make you the son-in-law of a lord! Forget all this. Phim isn't suitable. There are many more beautiful than she is. If you want an attractive palace lady, I'll offer a silver and gold plate to the king."

"I have no desire for some heavenly maiden. Their only good point is their manners. Nobody in Suphan can rival Phim's beauty. And she's sharp and witty too. There's no bar on entering the monkhood after marriage. Please don't raise these objections. If I can't follow my heart, I'll surely die."

Thong Prasi was very cross, but she had sympathy too. "If you won't listen to me, then I'll fall in with your wishes. If I ask for Phim's hand, Siprajan can't refuse because we're old neighbors. Stop crying. You'll have Phim as your wife. Have something to eat."

That cheered Phlai Kaeo up. He went down to the jetty to bathe, and then had his meal.

Thong Prasi called the servants, "Take this money and go to the timber wharf. Buy what's needed for building a new house—the posts and everything for five rooms." She sent others to buy sugar, savories, sweets, betel, and coconut. By sunset, ten carts were loaded and ready.

Phlai Kaeo went to his room. His thoughts turned to Phim, and he embraced a side pillow in a fit of passion before falling asleep.

At sunrise, Phlai Kaeo mounted a cart and led the way off into the forest, all creaking noisily along. In the heat of the sun, they rested the buffaloes. From evening until dawn, they forged ahead. After three nights in the forest, they reached Suphan and halted the buffaloes just beyond Siprajan's garden. The servants cut wood, drove in posts, hung floor beams, fastened ridgepoles, raised rafters, cut reeds for the walls, and thatched the roofs of five houses.

In the evening, Phlai Kaeo set off to find Phim. A bright shining moon floated across a star-spangled sky. Wild animals called out of the surrounding silence. He cast a Loosener mantra, springing the bolts, and clambered in through an open window. Everyone in the house was fast asleep. Finding Phim's door bolted, he chanted a Loosener to slide the bolt out. Quietly drawing the curtains apart, he lay beside her, and hugged her awake.

Phim awoke with a start and screamed, fearing that a thief had got in. Phlai Kaeo held tightly onto her hand. "I'm here, eye's jewel. Don't be alarmed. Since the day we parted, I've been buried by worry over whether you'd wait. As soon as I got home, I pleaded with my mother to come. She was cross but I cried and cried, and then she gave in. We arrived here today."

Phim smiled brightly and leaned against his chest. "If your mother hadn't been kind, I'd die. If you weren't sincere in your words, I couldn't have lived with the shame."

He caressed her gently. "I love you. Don't doubt my heart is true. If I could, I'd cut open my chest to let you see, but that's beyond my power. Though my body was far away, my heart was still here. I was worried about Khun Chang so I've wasted no time. Tomorrow my mother will come to your house and ask for your hand in the ancient way."

He peeled away her shoulder cloth and lifted her onto his lap. They wrapped around each other with passions surging. A storm wind arose, strong enough to destroy an era, howling and booming as if it would erase the world. Thunder rumbled. Oceans churned. Forests shuddered. Mountains heeled over, cracking apart. Sun and moon were obscured by chaos. Trees came crashing down, trunk and branch. Only when rain fell did the storm subside.

A cock flapped its wings and crowed loudly. The piercing cry of a coel announced the approach of the sun. He said, "I must go. Please come to see me off at the stairway." She led him by the wrist past the sleeping servants onto the terrace. At the gate, he turned back for a last, reluctant goodbye, and hurried down the stairs as the moon faded from sight.

Early that morning, Thong Prasi called on two pairs of elderly neighbors and asked them to accompany her to visit Siprajan. Everyone dressed smartly. Phlai Kaeo enchanted beeswax for the elders to rub on their lips. At Siprajan's house, they called out for someone to take care of the dogs. Siprajan shouted at her servants, who tumbled down the stairs to escort the guests up into the house. Mats were laid and a tray of betel and pan hastily prepared. They all sat around in a circle, and Siprajan opened the conversation.

"I've been thinking and thinking of you, Thong Prasi. We meet again after eleven years. You look thinner and paler than before. Your hair is white and many teeth are broken. Things must have been hard.

When the king had your husband executed, where did you and your son disappear to? How are things now? What brings you to my house?"

"You must have heard about our troubles. All our property was seized—cattle, buffaloes, paddy fields, home, everything. I had to flee with my dear son. We staggered around the forest for over a month until we found some friends who welcomed us, gave us a house to live in, and were all so kind. Times were hard beyond belief. Now I've blazed a path here through the elephant grass, holding my face high. I ask you for seeds of squash, marrow, cucumber, and bottle gourd to plant in my field. As we're poor and short of cash, I've come to sell you young Phlai so you may use his services. Think of him like a pair of leather shoes. If you don't trust me, I'll find guarantors. After the toil and trouble of coming to your house, don't turn me away."

Siprajan laughed. "So you've come here to go through these motions! We were neighbors for a long time. Why should I be possessive about my daughter? Even if your son's poor, it doesn't matter. As long as he comes with a big knife slung on his back, I'll give her to him. He can work to make a living. The money given by parents soon vanishes if someone doesn't know how to look after it. Let me ask the elders about this son of yours. Does he gamble, drink liquor, smoke opium, or get giddy on ganja? Is he tall or short, dark or fair? So far I haven't seen him with my own eyes. Tell me the truth."

The elders spoke up. "In the future you'll be able to rely on him."

"This son of Thong Prasi is a very good lad."

"He's clever, easy to teach."

"Smart and handsome."

"A nice well-mannered young boy."

"There's not one bad thing about him!"

"When he was a novice, he recited *Matsi* so eloquently. Last year, you yourself were sponsor of the episode. Phim liked it so much that she took off her cloth as an offering. It created an incident because Khun Chang took off his cloth and put it down over Phim's. Don't you recall?"

"I do remember now. We felt annoyed for a long time. Because Phim's my only child, I want to see her married. I'm getting old, and I tend to get sick. How long will I live? I'm not so rich but I'll provide as well as I can. I'll give my daughter twelve hundred baht. I'm not fussy about the size of the dowry. One set of cloth for offering is about right. The bridal house should have five rooms and timber walls. Please give some thought to Saturday the ninth waxing day of the twelfth month as the date."

Thong Prasi accepted immediately. "Up to your judgment. I've no objection. It's time for us to take our leave." She left to tell her son the outcome.

Siprajan boarded a large boat and went to Wat Khae. The abbot was sitting with his back turned, enjoying a game of chess. He picked up a bishop and banged it down. "Lured into checkmate, right in the middle square!"

Siprajan called, "Your Lordship, I came to invite . . ."

"It's not mate. The king can escape!"

"I wish to make merit . . ."

"The rook attacks. Checkmate!" He turned to see Siprajan, tried not to laugh, and asked her to repeat why she had come.

"I wish to ask for ten or so monks to chant prayers. Phim is getting married. The date is fixed so don't muddle it up."

The abbot said, "Is she old enough to have a husband? Seems only last year I saw her coming to bathe, taking off her cloth, eyes red from crying, running around the wat wearing a child's charm. Those kids dash around and break the trees. Every day I curse them and chase after them with my walking stick. I haven't seen her face for a couple of years and now she's to have a husband! You and I have to think about ourselves. We're both growing older."

"You and I are the same, Abbot. In old age, health is never really certain. In a little while, we'll all be dead. The appointment is fixed. Please remember it. I'll take my leave."

Nearer to the appointed time, Phlai Kaeo organized his male friends to build a bridal house beside Siprajan's. All the materials for the construction were brought and left at the site. Holes were dug for the posts. At an auspicious time just before dawn, they held a soul ceremony for the posts, finishing in seven minutes. To the banging of gongs and hollering, the posts were raised and put in place. The floor beams and roof beams were shaped to fit snugly and fixed with nails. Hammer beams were set to support the purloins, and kingposts placed to bear the central roof ridgepole. Rafters were nailed on, thatch busily passed up, gable ends raised, and the walls fixed in. The task was completed in one day. Siprajan called servants to feed all the workmen.

When dawn broke on the auspicious day, Thong Prasi arranged a large canopy boat with a music ensemble for carrying the dowry. An attractive woman was chosen to carry the first dowry tray. When they moored at Siprajan's landing, old Phon came down with a big stick to block their way, and money had to be paid before they could carry the dowry up the stairway. Inside the house, elders checked the cash and cloth against the promised amounts. The dowry party was fed and then returned home.

In the afternoon, Phlai Kaeo fetched jars of liquor and told a servant, "Go quickly and find Khun Chang. Tell him I'm inviting him to be part of the groom's party."

Khun Chang was sitting relaxing when the servant arrived and announced, "Phlai Kaeo has asked for the hand of Phim Philalai in marriage. He's short of people for the groom's party. He sent me to pay respect in friendship and beg you to go over today."

Khun Chang felt someone had split open his head with a sword. Tears flowed down in anguish over Phim, and he turned to the wall to hide them. "Things haven't turned out as I hoped, but I won't give up trying, regardless."

He dressed grandly and walked to Siprajan's house with a gaggle of servants behind. Members of the groom's party had already gathered and were sitting around eating, drinking liquor, and chatting in a tipsy hubbub.

Phlai Kaeo said, "My friend, don't hold it against me that I love Phim. Please leave her to me."

Khun Chang felt uncomfortable. "If you weren't my buddy, I wouldn't agree. If you don't love her, I'll take her." He knocked back liquor and got merrily drunk.

Late in the afternoon, the groom's party went by boat to Siprajan's house, where monks were waiting to chant. The bridal party came out of an apartment, huddled around Phim. The couple sat in front of the abbot, who placed a sacred thread on their heads.

Khun Chang watched dolefully. He picked up a piece of betel but missed his mouth and put it in his ear. He chewed and chewed, wondering why he had only leaf. Others in the groom's party burst out laughing.

Monks chanted prayers and sprinkled water. Tea was offered to the monks, who then took their leave. Siprajan had sweets and savories brought to feed the groom's party. Nielloware jars plated with gold and leaf baskets of fermented tea were set out in rows to be given to everyone as mementoes. As the light faded and evening came, Khun Chang left to return home.

Phlai Kaeo went to see Thong Prasi. "Now that the marriage is over, why should you stay here? There's nobody looking after the elephants, horses, cattle, and lands at home."

"There's no hurry. Everyone's tired from working hard. I'll go by and by, maybe in about five days. You go over to stay in Siprajan's house."

In late afternoon, Phlai Kaeo dressed smartly and walked to the house of Siprajan. He climbed the stairway into the bridal house, and went to sleep there, pining for Phim through the prescribed period.

After three days, Siprajan talked to her daughter about being a wife. "He's your partner from previous lives. Hundreds and thousands of other people did not inspire you, only this Phlai Kaeo. Now you're grown up and leaving my bosom, I'm worried how you'll look after a husband. You must make no mistake that moves the man to malice. A cool head is mistress of the house. In whatever situation, be careful to pay him respect and heed his words. Don't get jealous and make accusations that cause a scandal. May you be blessed with constant happiness. Now, Phlai Kaeo is waiting for you."

She led Phim over to the bridal house. Hearing a footfall, Phlai Kaeo got down from the bed. Phim hid behind her mother, peeping out. Her fair face seemed to float in the lamplight. When their eyes met, she lowered her face demurely.

Siprajan said, "I'm bringing Phim to you. Please live in harmony and look after each other forever until the end of your lives. Whatever mistakes are made, talk it over first. Don't shout and fight. Stay here, my dear. Your mother is taking leave."

Phim hung on and would not release her hand. "Is Mother abandoning me here?" They pushed and pulled until Siprajan persuaded Phim to drop her hand, opened the door of the room, and walked out.

Phlai Kaeo went to sit close beside Phim. "Precious, please join me on the pillows inside the mosquito net. Are you hot? I'll fan you to sleep. I've been here three days waiting for you." He put his arms round her, squeezed, stroked, and kissed. "Let's go and lie down together."

She squirmed and giggled. "Hey, don't play around like that. I can't stand all this pinching and tickling. Go to bed if you want. I'm not sleepy yet."

He got up and went inside the net. "Lots of mosquitoes! Light a candle and bring it in here."

She unbolted the door. "It's too hot. I'm going to sit in the cool."

He grabbed the end of her cloth.

"Lightning strike! You're always pestering me. I'm not running away but you're so rough and pushy. Are you hungry, like you're starving for rice, sir? It's so hot and sweaty, I'm wilting. I'm going to freshen up with fragrant water."

"Oh good, let's do it together. When you're nice and cool, you'll feel better." He pulled the cloth off her breasts, round and full like lotuses in bloom. Even in the dim light, they shone.

"If you're looking for the powder, why are you tugging at my uppercloth. What is this? Is dawn coming up already?" She tossed her head and ran across the room to open a pot of scented water.

He followed and said, "I'll powder you. Turn your face here. I'll make you even fairer." He picked up a fan and fanned the powder dry. "You look as fair as the sheen on a gourd shaded by a leaf from the sun." He powdered her breasts, making her heart jump.

"For pity's sake, you're too much. I can't even sit and powder myself. What's wrong with wanting to cool down? It's irritating to be bathed in sweat."

"The sweat is not the problem, is it? You're really a big tease. Let's go and lie down. Don't make me beg so long." He hugged her to his breast and kissed her very softly.

Phim smiled but shot him a sharp look. "Hey, your sweat has smeared my cheek."

"What sweat? Look in the mirror. There's nothing. The net is full of mosquitoes. Let's go and see to it, or we won't be able to sleep." He swept her up in his arms, and pressed her close to his bursting heart. Phim continued to twist and squirm until they entered the curtains, when she prostrated to him.

Phlai Kaeo nuzzled her breasts and kissed her hair. Hugging and stroking, he told a tale. Lord Ram followed Sida into the depths of the forest, crossed the ocean to Lanka island, and devastated a whole clan of giant demons. He suffered countless hardships for his beautiful lady, and only fourteen years later brought her back to the city. At the end of the story they fell asleep together.

PHLAI KAEO GOES TO WAR

A missive arrived at Ayutthaya with news that Chiang Thong, a city in the north which sent tribute to Ayutthaya, had been attacked by an army from Chiang Mai. The senior officials immediately went to the audience hall in an angry mood. The king came to sit on a jeweled throne, and the missive was read to him.

"A Chiang Mai army besieged Chiang Thong. The city's ruler submitted without a fight and agreed to drink the water of allegiance. He appears to be in revolt. Hearing this matter, the governors of the neighboring territories of Thoen, Rahaeng, and Kamphaeng have promptly dispatched this message by fast boat downriver."

The king was enraged. "Discuss this matter among yourselves today. Should we send a major army? Who will volunteer to command it? Return here tomorrow to report."

The senior officials discussed the matter but nobody volunteered and the meeting broke up without any agreement. The army chiefs went home feeling very apprehensive.

At audience on the following morning, the king bellowed, "Officers of all ranks! I am enraged because Chiang Mai has acted in an insolent and contemptuous manner. Will we sit and take this quietly? No! They will exult and become yet more insubordinate. They will believe I fear their power, as if we had no soldiers in Ayutthaya. When such things happened in the past, we sent Khun Krai who has now been dead and gone for many years. This time, who will go? Did Khun Krai have children?"

A military officer prostrated and spoke without delay. "My liege, at the time Khun Krai lost his life, he had one son aged almost five years. Thong Prasi fled from Suphan with the little child and disappeared. I do not know whether they are alive or dead but I heard they are in Kanburi."

The king immediately asked Khun Chang, "Your home is in Suphan. You should know about Thong Prasi. Is her son still alive?"

Khun Chang had been a page at court since childhood and was fluent at talking with royalty. He saw a way to possess Phim by making sure the king sent Phlai Kaeo off to war.

"My life is under the royal foot. The son of the late Khun Krai is called Phlai Kaeo. His mother is in Kanburi but he and his wife live in Suphan. He is brave, skilled in lore, and knows everything about raising spirits. He is about seventeen years old."

"Go and fetch him here. Guards will accompany you."

They left Ayutthaya and arrived in Suphan at dusk. Khun Chang went up into his house to bathe, then walked to the house of Siprajan and called for someone there to light a torch. Saithong invited them up into the house. The guard officer told her, "His Majesty wishes to attack Chiang Thong. He is looking for an able person with knowledge. Khun Chang said that Phlai Kaeo is suitable so we have to fetch him to the palace."

Siprajan trembled at these words. She went straight to her daughter's bridal house and collapsed sprawling against the couple. "Oh, my dear children!"

Phlai Kaeo and Phim did not know what all this weeping was about.

"Has someone dropped dead?"

"One of our relatives?"

"Khun Chang told the king that you, Phlai Kaeo, are clever and equipped with knowledge, so the king has ordered you to war. What do you know about such things? Your waist is as slim and elegant as a painting. Just a flick would snap it. Where would you have got knowledge!"

Phim angrily cursed Khun Chang, "The villain! The interfering, uncouth troublemaker! How can he do this with no fear of sin and karma? Because he's frustrated in love, he wants to separate us and send you off to suffer in the forest. In a few days, you'll be gone, my jewel!"

Phlai Kaeo spoke calmly. "Why get worked up when it's no use? This is about royal service, army work. It's been like this since my father's time. We should be able to take Chiang Thong. The guards have come all the way to our house. Calm down and make some food. If they don't have anything to eat, they'll say hurtful things."

He ushered the guard officer and Khun Chang up to Phim's bridal house. The three dropped their bottoms on a mat, and Phlai Kaeo called for a betel tray. Phim was so angry she pushed it through the door without showing her face. Khun Chang gazed at her little finger with a snake ring. Though a mosquito bit him, he did not brush it away.

When food was ready, Phim called baldheaded old Phon to carry the trays over. Khun Chang stared with his mind seething. "Not this accursed fellow again."

Phlai Kaeo smiled innocently and invited them to eat. "This is all we have, sirs. It's dark now, too late to do anything." After eating, they chatted together until late.

"I'll truss up the Lao and bring them back. Make a name for myself."

Khun Chang saw he was serious and made agreeable noises. When they yawned, mattresses and pillows were arranged for the visitors. Phlai Kaeo went into his bedroom and hugged Phim tenderly with his heart breaking into fragments. Khun Chang shifted to lie close to the wall, craned his neck, and heard the sound of boards creaking. He clapped his hands to his face and kicked his feet in the air. Sweat ran down his face.

Phlai Kaeo hugged her tightly. "When I'm gone, you'll be gloomy. We won't pleasure each other for many days."

Phim's tears fell on his chest. "I fear you'll fall fighting the Lao."

"Don't fret." He caressed her breasts tenderly, and kissed them passionately.

Khun Chang heard the kiss and rolled over face down. "A spirit has possessed me! Oh Buddha! The spirits of this house are very fierce! I'm new here and they haven't possessed me before!"

By next afternoon they reached Ayutthaya, and went straight to the official hall. Phlai Kaeo paid respect to the nobles there. They saw he was good-looking with round, black eyes befitting a soldier. "If you succeed in this war, it should be good for you. You'll be able to enter royal service."

At audience next morning, a military commander addressed the king. "We have Phlai Kaeo, the son of the late Khun Krai. He will volunteer. He seems an able person with knowledge who speaks boldly and fears nobody."

The king said, "Bring him here quickly." A palace guard summoned Phlai Kaeo to crawl in and pay respect. The king examined him for a while. "Appealing. His appearance is appropriately good-looking. Eyes round and bright."

He called out, "Heigh! Phlai Kaeo, you were born to a line of soldiers. Do not dishonor your deceased kin. Perform royal service in succession to your father. If you gain victory over Chiang Thong, I'll bestow on you money and cloth. Ponder carefully and be certain. Can you do it or not?"

"My liege, lord over my head, my life is beneath the royal foot. I beg to volunteer, sire, and fulfill Your Majesty's wish without fail. As long as I live, I will not shrink from battle."

The king slapped his thigh. "Ha! Crush them to dust! Don't let the arrogant Lao come to attack the Thai!" He gave orders for rapid conscription of an army, then bestowed cash and clothing on Phlai Kaeo to encourage his martial spirit.

"Your humble servant will return home first to enchant the equipment."

"Good! Go home but don't stay long." Phlai Kaeo prostrated to take leave. Servants wrapped the cash and followed him out.

A senior official sat in the main official hall to make arrangements. "Issue call-up notices for royal conscripts. Send orders to round up both those on and those off this month's rota. If any hide or abscond, reprimand their parents and overseers. The sick must hire a replacement for cash. Find many elephants and horses. Requisition guns and other weaponry. Prepare food supplies. In three days the troops leave for Chiang Thong."

Arriving home, Phlai Kaeo walked straight into the house without even a smile for Phim. She followed him headlong into the room. Phlai Kaeo rushed into her arms.

"King Phanwasa is sending me to war because Chiang Thong is in revolt. If I disobey the king's order, my back will be crushed, so I volunteered. The king was told that I'm invulnerable and strong on lore so the enemy will be pulverized in the blink of an eye. I'm not so anxious about the fighting but I'm worried about missing you. Every night I'll be far from my love. It'll be a year until I return. When you think of me, you'll have only the side pillows to clutch close. To tell your troubles, you'll have only Saithong. At night, you'll lie and mope. At meal times, food will be tasteless and hard to swallow. Every night will leave another trace of wrinkle. Your hair won't know the tweezers. A hundred days won't see mirror or comb. The fragrant powder will turn dry in its pot. Turmeric will go unused and your face will lose its sheen. Your heart will imagine all sorts of disaster. Pining so much will make your proud breasts droop. I'm worried about you."

Phim too was distraught. She doubled over on her chest, tears splashing down. "Can you walk to Chiang Thong? Your soft feet will blister from sole to heel. Who'll help pry out thorns in your flesh? If I went along, I could pull them. Your tender skin is used to a soft mattress, not the hard earth. The dust in the woods will make your body itch. Who'll help scratch your back? You don't eat like other people, just a little fish and vegetables. Even with three full meals a day you don't put on any weight. Now all you'll have will be plain and tasteless, just wild yams. In the dawn chill, when the gibbons whoop, you'll think it's my voice. The blazing sun and brute wind will batter your body. In fatigue, you'll sleep soaked in sweat. You'll bathe in stream water so cold you shiver all through. Who'll put on the fragrant powder, whose scent will refresh you? You're not used to being far from love. You came to lie with me in the bridal house twice a day, not letting me stray from the pillow, fanning me when I was hot, whispering sweet nothings, running your fingers through my hair, without a break all through to dawn without sleeping, too blissfully in love to lie apart, never rolling over with your face turned away, or ever saying you were a little tired. When you're gone, who'll hug me to sleep? When eating, you always waited for me to sit with you. If I took nothing, you'd plead, knead the rice, and place it in my mouth. I've seen many other couples but none loving each other like you loving me. How will I survive sleeping alone? Husband, lord, and master, your wife will die."

"Don't be so sad. Nothing can be done about a troubled karma. If it were possible, I'd take you along to see the forest in bloom. We could pluck the flowers you love, bathe happily in the streams, and ride horses through the trees. If a Lao army mounted an attack, we'd dress you as a man, with a tight shirt to flatten your chest, and a Western-style hat to hide your hair under the brim. You'd ride carrying a sword with magnificent power and a kris tucked in your waist. I'd enchant herbs to make you invulnerable to all weapons, and I'd slash the Lao down into dust. But it's beyond my power to imagine getting away with it. I can't stay here to hug you to sleep either."

At a cock's crow, he opened a window to glimpse golden rays lighting the sky. "Dawn is here already, my jewel. Kiss me again to give me heart." They crept out of the mosquito net, still locked in each other's arms, and walked out of the room leaning together, cheek to tearful cheek.

Siprajan asked, "Eye's jewel, what's the matter? After you came back from court last evening, you didn't explain things to me clearly, only that Khun Chang knifed you with the king. Are you going off to war? Look, this is very tedious. Both of you are smothered in tears."

Phlai Kaeo told her the news. "My fate is bad—only three days in the bridal house! I leave early tomorrow morning and go away to suffer in the wilds. Don't count the days because they'll surely stretch into months. I'm furious at Khun Chang. He's been in love with Phim forever. He dug up a story to tell the king, hoping I'll go and probably die. He's clever, crafty, and silver-tongued. Look after Phim until I return. If anyone says I've died, don't believe them easily. Make inquiries in the capital to be sure. Even if anyone comes to talk with gold in their mouth, don't be carried away and comply."

"Don't worry about Phim. I've looked after my daughter for a long time, not letting even a beetle or spider touch her. Don't treat royal service lightly. Don't stick your neck out when you shouldn't. Don't be too sure of yourself and get lured into a trap. Hang back, play clever. At night don't think of sleep. Sit guard. Set lights. Have gongs ready. Keep a company hidden and waiting. May you win victory. Try to bring back cattle and buffaloes for plowing. Servants! Come here quick! At dawn tomorrow, young Phlai is leaving. Mill rice and tie it up in sacks. Grind chili and salt. Make all kinds of sweets. Where's Saithong disappeared to? May the wretch be mauled by a tiger! When something's urgent, she wanders off somewhere to hide. The betelnut, pan, and lime paste are not ready." While Siprajan badgered the servants, Phim and Phlai Kaeo went sadly back to their apartment.

The servants pounded chili like the thunder of horses' hooves, then added galangal, ginger, chili, and salt, and mixed until it was ground fine and well blended. Others took baskets to measure rice from the granary for milling. Giant snakehead fish were grilled with onion and garlic, and packed away. Sugarcane juice and cake sugar were prepared. Caramel was made with coconut milk, flour, and sugar. At first the mixture was runny and easy to whisk but with heat and stirring it thickened.

"What's up? Is your shoulder tired?"

"My arm's stiff enough to die!"

"Here, it's sticking to the pan and getting messy."

"Use a paddle to scoop it onto a banana leaf."

"You taste it from the edge of the pan. I'll taste it too."

"Mmm, good, sweet, and nutty—yummy."

When the edge had gone, they scooped tastes from the middle. "Half the pan's disappeared!"

Siprajan said, "Phim, why are you sitting doing nothing? You haven't arranged the betel, pan, or tobacco. How long is the princess going to keep on crying? You're not paying attention to his clothes either. Is this what you call loving your husband, just hanging your head and weeping? If I wasn't here to take care of things, he'd have nothing but salt to crunch his teeth on. I'm making all the effort as if I were the minor wife, not the mother-in-law."

Phim felt too pent up to lend a hand but her mother's scolding got to her. She began to peel the betelnut and tie rolls of pan leaf. When she glanced over at Phlai Kaeo, her chest felt cramped and her head spun. She tried to roll the pan leaves but failed. A ball of cotton lay forgotten in her hand.

Phlai Kaeo moved to sit beside her and wipe away her tears. "Don't cry so much, my darling. Please roll the pan so I can have some in the forest. Here, I'll help put in the lime paste."

He kept on stroking, fondling, and teasing her playfully, "There, Phim, your chest is so bruised it's swollen."

"Don't say bruised. It's completely collapsed." She quickly gathered up all the betelnut and pan into a betel box, and put the leftover in a cloth bag with a drawstring.

"Husband, lord, and master, come back to me before these pan leaves dry out and wilt, while the Phetchabun tobacco is still pungent, and the banana leaves still green."

She folded his clothes into neat little pleats, and put them into a chest. When she picked up his pillow and little mattress, the sadness returned. "Oh, you'll be far from my bed, sleeping alone."

As Phlai Kaeo's wedding had only just taken place, his mother was still in Suphan and would see her son off to war. She arranged the loading of a boat and asked Siprajan if she was coming too.

"The house needs looking after. You take Phim to see him off."

Phlai Kaeo arranged a rendezvous. "You go off by boat first, Mother. Look out for the mosquitoes at night. Tomorrow I'll go overland to the capital to take leave of the king. We'll meet at Bang Lang on the day after."

Thong Prasi and Phim boarded a canopy boat. The oarsmen paddled away from the landing, slapping their oars and crying out the time. The helmsman was not practiced and turned too sharply. "Hey, paddle a bit at the bows!"

They could not correct in time. The prow hit a bank. The stem post collided with a wasp nest. Some people fell in the water. Thong Prasi picked up a mat and covered herself in fright. Phim crawled into a sack far enough to hide her head. Water poured in where the boat was holed. An oarsman dived into the river, scooped up mud, and pasted it over the hole. Everyone shouted at everyone else.

By dawn, they were near Bang Lang.

After his mother and wife had left, Phlai Kaeo readied his gear and medicines for warding off weapons. On arrival at Ayutthaya, he lodged overnight and went to royal audience after sunrise.

Seeing Phlai Kaeo, the king's face brightened. "Grind the Lao into fine dust! I present you with this sword. The hilt contains a spirit." The king also gave him a fine lowercloth, britches, a brilliant sash, and a fringed helmet.

At the official hall, he received his orders with an official seal. At an auspicious time to march, the massed hordes of elephants, horses, and troops marched out of the capital, bristling with weapons of all types, echoing with the sound of gongs and war cries. At the mouth of the Bang Lang Canal, they stopped to rest and eat. Phlai Kaeo ordered the troops to march on ahead. "Wait for me at Wat Pa Fai." The troops saluted their chief and moved off.

Phlai Kaeo looked around and saw the boat with Phim and his mother at a mooring. The three agreed to plant three bo trees to serve as an omen. They searched around for saplings and dug them up, taking care not to snap the roots and to keep a nice clump of soil. They crossed the river by boat and chose a site marked by a big tree. After making offerings to the deities that resided in that spot, each of them dug a hole, planted one of the saplings, and made a prayer.

Thong Prasi went first. "If I pass away, may this bo tree of mine die. If I'm sick, may the bo tree sicken in the same way. If I'm hale and hearty, may this bo tree be leafy, lush, and shady for all to see." She lifted the sapling into the first hole.

Phlai Kaeo followed. "I'm going off to war. If I die, may this bo tree die too. If I gain victory over the enemy, may it be beautifully green, leafy, and lush." He lifted the bo tree into the hole, pushed in soil, and tamped it firm.

Phim's tears spattered down as she raised her hands. "Oh lords, gods of great power, I pray that, if my life be snuffed out, may this golden bo tree likewise sicken and die. As long as I remain alive, may it grow happily to be so lush and shady that even the nectar of the gods bears no comparison. Should my body sicken, wilt, and waste away, may the leaves of the bo tree wither unnaturally."

They heaped earth around the three holes and poured water. Each took off their uppercloth and wrapped it around a tree. "We call on the gods that the cloth tied on each bo tree is a sign that we three will meet again after this long parting. Should any one of us die, may that person go happily to heaven above, to be born again in the next life. May we meet together for hundreds of ages and thousands of eras until attaining nirvana."

They boarded the boat and paddled to Wat Pa Fai. Phlai Kaeo gave orders for loading goods onto elephants. Thong Prasi gave him a blessing. "May the future be auspicious and prosperous."

Phim sobbed out, "Safe journey."

Phlai Kaeo replied, "Save your heart, save your love, wait for me." Husband and wife craned their necks to look at each other, trying to hold back the tears until they were out of each other's sight. Along the way home, the servants joked merrily among themselves but Phim sat with face lowered, unable to speak.

The troops set off. Baskets and panniers swayed to and fro. Fish heads poked out with open mouths like bamboo bracts. Boxes of chili and crates of ginger bounced and clattered together. Some men dragged their feet with fatigue, sat down to smoke ganja, closed their eyes with a drowsy yawn, and fell asleep until wakened by their clothes burning.

After passing Nakhon Sawan, they entered the great forest where trees grew thickly together. Bark on trunks had split and peeled away. A green snake slithered to the tip of a branch. Fallen trees stood propped up with their roots exposed in a messy, dead tangle. Overhead the shoots of rattan canes intertwined like a canopy. Below was dank and marshy, a tangled, dilapidated mass of decomposition and decay. Trees were polished naked and shiny where herds of elephants had stripped the bark. Monkeys and langurs leapt along the way, breaking off small branches as they swung ahead. Creepers hung as if deliberately intertwined.

They entered a gorge. Looking up, their eyes were dazzled by sunlight sparkling off striations of red and green, misty purple quartz, red rocks shining like rubies in an exotic and elegant bracelet, black gleaming like jet fashioned into the shape of luxuriant foliage, and white sparkling like diamonds. Water surged and splashed, throwing up a dancing spray that smashed against the cliffs.

Phlai Kaeo thought constantly of Phim. "If you'd come with me, you'd be sitting plaiting garlands to hang around the howdah as fresh, fragrant braids."

At Kamphaeng, Rahaeng, and Thoen, he presented his orders to the governors, who organized troops from each city, and held a big, rowdy feast. They left at an auspicious time for victory and soon crossed the boundary of the Chiang Thong region. Now they rushed into villages, shouting wildly, creating chaos, slashing people dead in piles, and seizing property. Men and women ran off but were captured by the soldiers who danced up and down in glee. "Who stabbed you? There's still a hole." A soldier seized a girl, and lifted her cloth to look at the bush. She bent over and cried out, "Please have pity on me. It hurts to death." Others dragged off silver in sacks. The villagers were stripped of everything but their buffaloes, and ran off in fright.

Since Chiang Thong had not put up a fight, the Chiang Mai troops had become careless and overconfident. Men had gone off to court country girls, forage for fish and vegetables, or swagger around, singing, dancing, and getting boisterously drunk. They could not organize their defenses in time, and the Thai stabbed them to death in large numbers. When the Chiang Mai officers realized an enemy had arrived, they frantically called their troops to return to camps around the city moat. Seeing that their confusion meant a Thai army had come, the Chiang Thong people closed their gates immediately.

The ruler of Chiang Thong rejoiced. "I'll chop off the heads of these Chiang Mai men! Have the head monk go to explain to the Thai army that we didn't rebel against their king."

The patriarch left from the rear of the city, accompanied by two other monks. Seeing they were holy men, the Chiang Mai soldiers let them pass. At the Ayutthayan camp, the Thai troops took them prisoner and brought them before their officers. The governors were suspicious that the monks were spying, but Phlai Kaeo hushed them and asked, "Who told you to come?"

The patriarch replied, "The ruler of Chiang Thong sent me. Our city was besieged by a very large force. Food supplies were exhausted, and it was impossible to go out foraging, so we pretended to side with Chiang Mai. We wanted to send word to Ayutthaya but the enemy guarded the city tightly. Today we're happy to see you have come. I've been sent to say that we'll help you surprise them with a joint attack from front and rear. Do not doubt our sincerity. If we harbor thoughts of deception or revolt, then kill us all—man, woman, and child, even infants no larger than a cotton bud."

Phlai Kaeo smiled at the patriarch's words. "Even if Chiang Thong treacherously turns against us, we'll still crush this Chiang Mai army.

Because you're monks, we find you credible. Please return to the city, and inform your ruler that tomorrow afternoon we'll destroy this Chiang Mai army. He must get his troops organized and be ready at the auspicious time."

The patriarch hastened back inside the city walls, and relayed the message. At dusk, guns were hauled up to the ramparts, and weapons of all kinds were made ready. Gongs and drums were beaten loudly all over the city.

The Chiang Mai officers discussed the situation. "Now that the Thai have come, the ruler of Chiang Thong has recovered his courage. But why should we fear them? However many thousands have come, we'll scatter them into the foothills! As for that arrogant ruler of Chiang Thong, we'll truss up his wife and children and put them to the sword!"

The army commander, Phraya Falan, gave orders to two deputies, "You two defend the city side against Chiang Thong. We two will attack the Thai. They have only a few handfuls of soldiers. The fighting need last no longer than one blink of an eye."

The Chiang Mai cavalrymen enchanted their equipment with herbal medicine. Gunners in cross-belts read powerful mantras over their kit. At an auspicious time, the troops poured out of the camp in columns and advanced close to the Thai camp where they planted their flag.

After enchanting oil for the three governors and troops to rub on themselves, Phlai Kaeo advanced the troops in a great uproar, hollering, yodeling, banging gongs, and firing volleys of shot.

Hearing the Thai army launch its attack, the Chiang Thong troops opened the gates and poured out of the city. The army alone counted around five thousand, and more city people came out to join the battle. They wrenched up the defensive spikes in the ground, hauled away the guns, and torched the enemy camps, leaving a pall of smoke.

The Chiang Mai forces responded with volleys of gunshot, then plunged into close combat with spears and sharpened bamboos. Legs were severed and scattered around. People fell dead in droves. The uproar of battle echoed through the forest but neither side yet had victory.

The Chiang Mai commanders noticed a handsome figure on a high-spirited horse driving the Thai army forward. To trick him into revealing how good his knowledge was, they shouted out, "Hey, little Thai! You're still a child, not even old enough to be ordained."

"We think you must have studied only the devices of love and just a little bit of army lore. It seems inappropriate for you to be in a battle. Maybe your friends provoked you to volunteer and blunder up here."

"What's your name? How come the Thai king puts such faith in you? Our king sent us to capture and kill this Chiang Thong rebel. It's no business of the King of Ayutthaya."

Phlai Kaeo smiled and shouted back, "Who am I? I'm the principal soldier of Ayutthaya! My name is Phlai Kaeo. I volunteered because I'm skilled. Chiang Thong tricked you into believing they had surrendered, but now they've come out to fight on our side and you'll be destroyed for sure. Don't underestimate the Thai. If we weren't good, why would we have come? What's your name? You talk big and boast a lot, but in one blink of an eye, you'll die. Nobody will be left to return. I'm telling you this to earn merit and peace of mind. Please submit to the Thai and survive."

Phraya Falan clapped his hands and laughed. "Dammit! You're a good talker. But if you act too big for your boots, I don't think you'll survive. My name is Phraya Falan. Watch out!"

The two armies engaged, hurling bombs, loosing volleys of gunfire, slashing and stabbing with pikes and swords. Soldiers daubed with protective medicine war-danced bravely into battle. The rear cavalry swarmed over the battlefield, whips urging their steeds into the attack. Pikes were hurled, flashing in the sun. Men grappled at close quarters, cloaked in noise and dust. Some fell dead on their backs with necks broken.

Gripping the war sword presented him by the king, Phlai Kaeo spurred his horse straight towards the enemy's deputy commander. He slashed but the enemy turned the blow with the end of his spear and lunged back. Phlai Kaeo dodged away nimbly and the commander toppled forward. Phlai Kaeo slashed at him with a loud thwack, cutting him open from shoulder to waist.

Falan spurred his horse into the fray. Phlai Kaeo slashed Falan, who shat himself as his severed head fell and his body dropped from the horse to the ground. Seeing their leaders killed, the Chiang Mai troops broke into flight, running in all directions, abandoning elephants, horses, and weapons.

The Thai army camped overnight then advanced towards Chiang Mai, looting along the way. At Chomthong village, they halted and harmed no one. Many soldiers found a wife, old or young according to fate. While waiting to return to Ayutthaya, they enjoyed themselves the whole time.

LAOTHONG IS GIVEN TO PHLAI KAEO

The headman of Chomthong and his wife had a daughter, Laothong, now at the end of her fifteenth year and as radiant as a lotus in bloom. Having never felt the harsh sun, her face was without mole, freckle, or other blemish. Her shoulders were wide and her waist slim. No man had touched her because her two proficient nursemaids, Wiang and Wan, kept her hidden away.

As the warring had now subsided, Phlai Kaeo would soon return to Ayutthaya. The headman and his wife pondered the prospects. "Hundreds of villages and thousands of cities felt his wrath. Many fled, some died, others were captured. Only our village was happily spared. Now that he's going to return to the southern city, he might sweep all of Chomthong away with him as war prisoners. That would mean ruin for every household. Though Laothong is very dear to us, we must give her to him. If he takes her as his wife, our kinsfolk won't be scattered to the winds."

The two summoned their daughter and her nursemaids.

"Now, our darling Laothong, you're a pure and attractive girl. Soldiers have come from north and south to fight around here. Rice, betelnut, and everything else are running scarce. Soon the army will return to the Thai capital, and we expect them to round up people to take along—husband separated from wife, and wife from husband, with not a stitch on their backs. Up to now, their army commander looked after us and stopped his men from chopping us down, but I'm worried now that he's leaving. We must deal with this thorn before it pricks us, not allow ourselves to be trodden underfoot like grass. Your old father and mother feel we're in a dark thorny forest and can't see a way out, but there's one ray of light, and that's your radiant beauty. When you were tiny, you depended on your parents. Now that your parents are old, they must depend on you. We'll give you to the commander to love. My dear child, don't be upset. He's a skilled fighter. He should doubtless do well, and you'll be able to depend on him in the future. Chiang Mai and Ayutthaya will probably be at war for some time yet. People will come from this way and that to trample all over us, and very likely you'll be hauled off as someone's wife. This way nothing bad will happen to you. Wan and Wiang will go along to look after you until death."

Laothong raised her hands above her head and burst out crying. "My lord and master, do you no longer protect your child? You have never failed to look after me and answer my every need with kindness. I had meant to die at your feet to repay my debt of gratitude. Every night I think that I'll never be far away from you, even if I have a husband and children. But I'll be miles away, at the other end of the earth, of the whole three worlds! I won't know whether you're hurt, sick, dead, or alive. Even if he loves me greatly, even if he tries to please me in every way, a husband is not the same as the mother and father who brought me up. It's like closing my eyes to follow a torch, not knowing whether I'll bash into a stump and break my neck. He's no virgin, and probably has a wife and children, so I'll run into jealousy everywhere. The Thai have sharp tongues. Being a minor wife has hundreds of problems. If his love for me lasts, then I might just survive, but when he's away, his wife will bully me and the servants will trample me down too. I was born to die for nothing."

The parents feared the future would turn out as their daughter was saying, but they suppressed their own sadness and concern. "We've looked at your horoscope. It says that this year you'll have a partner and nothing bad will happen. When you arrive there, it'll be rough, but only a little. From then on, you'll float through the air like a bubble, without a care. You were born with this fate so please stop crying. We'll go over there near evening."

The maids bathed her, powdered her face to look fair, swept her hair into a neat chignon, decorated with waving golden flowers and shimmering golden aubergine blossoms, held by a beautiful jeweled hairpin, and hung with pendants of diamonds and crystal. She wore breast and waist chains glittering with gold and gems, bracelets on both wrists, rings of diamond, jet, and emerald, and an uppercloth of ripe yellow color, full of fragrance.

All their relatives came to accompany Laothong without needing to be told, bringing whatever they had as gifts for the army. When they reached the camp, soldiers turned out in droves to gaze at the young woman with her slim waist, stacked breasts, and complexion glowing like the moon.

"Wow! Really something."

"Immaculate face."

"She jiggles along like a dancer."

"If I got my hands on her, I'd never let go."

They came to Phlai Kaeo and paid respect. The gifts were set down in piles, and Phlai Kaeo invited them to come up and sit on a carpet. He glanced at the daughter, thinking "She's lovely. Very much like my Phim." The parents met his eyes. He picked up a betel tray and talked about something else.

The two parents spoke in the manner of elders. "We've come to thank you for your protection. Other villages were cut to pieces like fish on a slab, but here there was no killing or looting. Since you'll be marching the army down to the Thai city, we've brought whatever poor gifts we can for provisions along the way. We don't have much money or other things to give, only our charming daughter, Laothong, who we offer to be your servant until death. Please don't abandon her. We're afraid of what will happen when she's out of our sight. We'll be far away and have no chance to visit her. If in the future you come up here again, kindly pay a visit to give us peace of mind."

Phlai Kaeo replied with a smile, "I understand what it means to be far apart. If you're offering me the daughter who you love like your own hearts, it must be because you love me. Perhaps it was some merit accumulated from the past that made me be kind to Chomthong. It wasn't because I knew you had a lovely daughter. No woman came to lie with me here. Now I'm happy beyond comparison, even beyond getting heaps of silver and gold, and thousands of men and women. You need have no doubt that I'll look after her in a manner that befits her dignity. I'll not weary of her and let my heart wander away. Whatever wealth I acquire, I'll not share with anyone else as much as with her."

He ordered servants to prepare clothing, silver, gold, cattle, buffaloes, elephants, horses, and people to be given to the parents. The villagers presented their gifts in a joyful spirit. The parents took leave of the army chief, and entrusted their daughter to his care. Laothong was distraught. "When will I ever see you again?" All of them were bathed in tears. The two parents left, struggling to bottle their feelings.

As dusk fell, Phlai Kaeo assembled his officers to discuss the conclusion of the war. Clerks drew up a register of the massive number of captured families. The weapons and equipment abandoned by the enemy were marked with seals as royal property. Fine silver, valuables, elephants, and horses were entered on an inventory. Cattle and buffaloes were distributed to the troops. Trays, tables, salvers, and other household articles were given to whoever won them in battle.

"Don't try to conceal things or get into jealous fights. The ruler of Chiang Thong will be escorted to Ayutthaya to hear the king's order on his fate. We will give evidence in his favor."

The nobles left. Servants fell asleep. Candles were extinguished and darkness fell. Phlai Kaeo went to find Laothong. When he drew back the curtains, she was not there. A servant told him she was with her maids and still in a pitiful state. Phlai Kaeo ordered, "Tell the maids to bring her up here because I want to talk about her future."

Knowing that Phlai Kaeo wanted her to go up to the bedroom, Laothong clung to the two maids, sobbing and trembling with trepidation. "Wan and Wiang, go up first. I'm no good at talking with nobles. I was brought up to this age with no young man ever setting eyes on me. Now the army commander wants me to go and talk! What'll I say? I'm not going to survive, Wan."

"Mistress, why do you think that you won't like him? Your mother and father sent you to be his servant. You must learn how to please him and win his kindness. If you annoy him, he won't be friendly and might be cruel. Our friends and neighbors will suffer the consequences, and your father might too. You're meant to be the savior of the family now. Wipe away the tears smudging your cheeks. Let's put on powder to freshen you up."

The two maids marched her up to the curtain and knelt down to crawl in together. When Laothong hung back, they pulled her in by the hand. She cowered down behind them, in turmoil.

Phlai Kaeo understood she was still nervous. He gazed at her radiant skin and beautiful face and could not help falling in love. "Don't hide in the shadows. Let's talk together calmly. The day the army came to Chomthong, were you frightened? Other villages fled in fear, so how come your village took the risk of staying put?"

Wan and Wiang nudged Laothong to respond. She did not say a word.

The maids smiled at Phlai Kaeo and burbled answers to his questions. "The day the Thai army attacked? We didn't run away in time because we didn't know what was going on!"

"People stayed put to protect their property and families. The headman told us not to flee."

"Perhaps I'd made a lot of merit, and that induced the men not to harm Chomthong. But really, I didn't expect to get a beautiful wife. She's exactly what my heart desires. Why isn't she talking? If she's not willing to love, it doesn't matter. But she shouldn't cry. It dulls her cheeks."

Wan and Wiang nudged Laothong. "Why are you keeping silent? If you do well, we two can depend on you. But if you don't listen to us, you'll end up on your own in Ayutthaya because we'll run away back here."

Laothong had never spoken with a man, let alone in Thai. But she was afraid the two maids might really abandon her, so she forced herself to speak in a tremulous, timid voice with her face shyly turned away. "I agree to be your servant. I'll go to the southern city. But I'm desperately worried about what I'm leaving behind."

Phlai Kaeo could see that further conversation would take a long time. He enchanted a betelnut and passed it to the maids. "Please offer this to Laothong. You both take from the tray. It's late. Please go now and come again tomorrow."

Laothong received the betelnut without raising her face. Fearing he would not let her go unless she ate it, she put it into her mouth. The mantra thrilled her. To this point, she had not once looked at Phlai Kaeo's face. Now she stole a glance at him, broke into a smile, and wanted desperately to go over to him. Phlai Kaeo asked the maids to leave and closed the door of the room. His hands groped around and found Laothong. She sat still and did not cry out.

"Who is this? Nothing comes out of her mouth at all."

She pushed his hand away from her breast in surprise.

He stroked, kissed, and fondled her, then lifted her onto the bed in his arms, and lowered her gently onto the mattress. "Don't get alarmed when I embrace you." Her skin felt velvety soft. Her breasts were pointed like lotuses when the petals are on the point of bursting apart. She was fragrant, sweet, and very lovable.

A storm rumbled. Fierce clouds gathered. Dust swirled in a monsoon wind. Thunder crashed across the universe. Beyond resistance, waters flooded the whole three worlds.

Both were bathed in bliss. He struck a flint and lit a lamp. Laothong lay limp, face down on the bed. Phlai went on gently kissing her, keeping her heart spinning. She was listless, languid, lissome, lovely. He kissed her hair and pressed his face against hers.

"This is the truth, I tell you. I love you very much and I'll follow your desire. If I didn't have my army duty, I wouldn't go back. I feel sorry for you. Leaving your parents will be a source of endless sadness. I feel sorry for them too. But if I were to abandon you in Chomthong, I would never lose you from my thoughts. To gain a wife and then leave her would be a great loss. This is perplexing, because either way a love has to be broken. We can go down together, or you can stay here—it's up to you."

Laothong shyly averted her face. Her passion had not yet subsided. She clung close to Phlai Kaeo's chest, not wanting anything to change.

"My old parents are lovely. They took care of me and I haven't repaid their kindness very much yet. I'll miss them more than I can describe. And I worry about how things will be once we get to the southern city. If you love me and look after me, I'll just about survive. But I'm worried it won't work out with your wife. Out of love I agree to follow wherever you go. Though love makes me an outcaste, I'll face it until I die before your eyes."

"Even though I have a wife, don't worry. It won't be as you think. I look after everyone on an equal level. Eye's jewel, though you'll be alone with no kin, don't be afraid."

He nuzzled both her cheeks, caressed her breasts, and gently lay his cheeks between them, lighting flames of desire that scorched her heart. They kissed and caressed till dawn.

Phlai Kaeo drew the curtain and went outside to receive the nobles. Laothong called the two maids. "I've had this idea. I'm going down to the southern city and who knows when I'll return. Since I'm good at embroidery, I'll make a tapestry and offer it to the wat in Lamphun as a memento. Go and find some good cloth and all the other things."

They ground, mixed, and boiled dye to make the silk a glossy bright purple. The fabric was put in a frame and stretched evenly. Sitting with the two maids on either side to thread the silk, she embroidered a scene with the lord of the demons leading his army into battle under a great bo tree. His soldiers were transforming their bodies into various shapes. Some wore glinting armor and others held clubs across their chests. He rode a lofty elephant with upcurving tusks and carried poison arrows, a glittering short sword, shining crystal discus, mace, trident, throwing knife, bow, dagger, and shields. A tall and powerful lion followed behind. A magnificent horse, decked in ornate harness, high-stepped elegantly across a field. The army's standards fluttered against a pall of clouds obscuring the sun, while the gods of every direction fled away. Behind were the seven mountain ranges, five bands for the oceans, a river of crystal splashing water, mythical animals coming to bathe and drink, lotuses in bloom, bees hovering, and masses of birds and animals.

Laothong sat from morning through nightfall. Phlai Kaeo came to see and was dazzled by the tapestry. "So lovable and so skillful too. Beautiful from head to toe. Her face is just like Phim."

The longer he looked, the more he was carried away by memories of his beloved Phim. Laothong's skill in this embroidery captivated him because Phim had the same skill. He sat close to her but got excited and had to leave. Laothong and her two maids lit lamps and went on embroidering without sleep. At the first streaks of dawn, the tapestry was complete. They cut it from the frame, then bathed and went to see Phlai Kaeo.

Still thinking about Phim, he said, "Your embroidery is very skillful. You're more knowledgeable about the story of the war of the demons than any woman in the capital. Even in Ayutthaya, nobody can match the skill of Phim—oops!—Laothong."

Hearing his slip, Laothong nudged the two maids, and thought before answering very deliberately. "I will offer this tapestry to Wat Chedi Luang in Lamphun. Please come with me. Because I'm going to the southern city, I'll also have my statue made as a memento for my parents, and inscribed with the name *Phim*."

"Oh! Look here. What's making you apprehensive? So you think my wife is called Phim." He smiled and stood up.

They went to Lamphun and arranged for a craftsman to mold the statue. Servants pounded the mortar, and added water steeped with cinnamon tree bark and cattle hide. The statue was exactly like her, beautiful from head to toe. The figure was inscribed with the name Laothong.

The two maids strung a cord to hang the tapestry. Laothong offered a prayer: "Oh lord, may this tapestry I have embroidered completely in one night and one day, and hung as an offering to the holy Buddha image, help me towards nirvana and wealth without decrease. Should I die, may I go to the heavens. May this statue and tapestry remain for a hundred years. If and when Lamphun disappears, let them disappear together."

They returned to the army camp in good spirits. That evening, Phlai Kaeo and Laothong lay together in blissful happiness. After Laothong went to sleep, Phlai Kaeo's thoughts turned to home. "My gentle Phim must be waiting forlornly for me every night and day. As soon as I get the order, I'll go back to enjoy my darling love. How many more days now?"

PHIM CHANGES HER NAME TO WANTHONG

Phim slept alone and lonely in the bridal house, straining for news of the army, but no news came. Every night, she missed Phlai Kaeo so much she never slept soundly. In daytime, she lay engrossed in lifelike dreams, sleeptalking as if possessed by spirits. Saithong tried to console her but Phim had no ears for listening. "Oh, my brilliant Phlai Kaeo, don't you care for me at all?"

She contracted a fever that would not go away. Many doctors came. One said tetanus had entered her heart. Another said the fever was caused by menstruation. A third said the spirit of the house was running in and out of her body. None of their medicine had any effect. Siprajan rolled her eyes and berated them, "You sit around eating and eating. When the patient cries out like a mooing cow, you don't take a look—you just laugh. Get out of my house!"

Siprajan hugged her daughter. "Would you like some rice gruel? Has some spirit taken possession of you? Is it the spirit of my husband? Oh husband, I didn't realize it was you. I'll make an offering of liquor, rice, turtle, and fish. If you help our daughter recover, I'll feed the monks and send the merit to you."

Phim was angry. "What spirit has come? My father gets blamed for so much. Don't bother tending to me, Mother. I'll die within days."

Siprajan's thoughts turned to the abbot and she hurried off to Wat Palelai. "Lord Abbot, Phim has some kind of fever. None of the doctors in Suphan can cure it. Please look at her stars."

Abbot Ju examined the horoscope. "Phim's luck right now is bad, but it can be cured. She must change her name to Wanthong."

Arriving back at the house, Siprajan cried out happily, "She won't die! The abbot says so, for sure."

Siprajan did a soul ceremony, getting some of it right and some wrong.

"Oh, soul! Don't wander into the woods alone.
Don't stray after mole, rhino, bear, lion,
Treeshrew, porcupine, rabbit, kingfisher.
Don't get lost over deer, elephant, and tiger."

She scooped up rice and fish and threw them on Phim. "Away with all diseases and dangers, thorns and splinters!" She tied a black thread round Phim's wrist, extinguished the candles, and changed her name to Wanthong.

Before long, Wanthong began to eat, to sleep soundly, and to put on weight day by day.

Khun Chang heard that Wanthong's fever had gone. "If Phlai Kaeo had taken Chiang Thong, he'd have returned by now. What powers of lore does he have? The enemy probably slit open his liver and left him rolling in the dirt. Well! I'll take this opportunity to plead for Wanthong's hand. I'll tell Siprajan that Phlai Kaeo is dead."

He sent his servants to fetch the neighbors, Granny Kloi and Granny Sai, and entreated them, "I need your help. Whatever money it costs, I'll pay without a thought. Phlai Kaeo went off to war and was stabbed to death. Kindly help by going with me to ask for Wanthong's hand." Granny Kloi and Granny Sai agreed at the thought of getting cash.

Khun Chang whispered orders to a trusted servant. "Hurry over to the wat, collect some bones from the bodies in the graveyard, and put them in a new earthenware pot."

Khun Chang got dressed up smartly. When he lifted up a mirror to look at his head, he was upset by the sight of his bald pate. "It's hopeless! Nothing at the front, nothing at the back. Awful!" He slapped on a couple of handfuls of soot and smudged it over his head. Though he used a small stick to arrange the hairs in rows, they still did not hide the smooth patch. "I've enough money to redeem over a thousand slaves and buy over a hundred elephants or horses, so why can't I have enough hair to cover my head? If only I could buy some, what fun it would be to have a haircut and admire the styling!"

At noon he tied up the pot of bones in paper and walked to Siprajan's house. Servants ran off to tell their mistress, "Khun Chang is waiting at the bottom of the stairway with an oily glint in his eye."

Siprajan invited them in. Khun Chang climbed the stairs with the two old ladies close behind. They sat down, raised their hands and wai-ed repeatedly, one after the other. Siprajan returned the wais but could not keep up. She turned and pushed a betel tray towards them. "Why have so many of you come? What brings Granny Kloi and Granny Sai here?"

Khun Chang screwed up his face and pretended to sob. Wiping away the tears, he brought out the pot. "These are the bones of Phlai Kaeo. The ruler of Chiang Thong sided with Chiang Mai but then switched and pretended to side with Phlai Kaeo. One day at dusk in the forest, he crept up and stabbed Phlai Kaeo. His men returned to the city and were clapped in prison. One of them sent this pot of bones." Khun Chang put on a sorrowful face. "He was so young! He shouldn't have volunteered so boldly and left Phim a lonely widow."

Siprajan burst out, "Phlai Kaeo is dead? Oh no! Wanthong had a fever but didn't die, and now Phlai Kaeo has died before her. They were in the bridal house such a short time." She shouted out to Wanthong, "Mother's jewel, your heart is broken!"

From her room, Wanthong had been listening to Khun Chang. She came out and spoke angrily. "Who's making up this bad news? You cobra, you big trickster, you just bought this pot for ten cowries." She stamped her foot down hard. "A curse on your mother's clan!"

She went back into her room and collapsed crying on the bed. "I don't believe this baldy. His deviousness got my husband sent off to war, and now he turns up with a pot of bones to fool us. Oh my Phlai Kaeo! If you were here, no one would dare get at me like this."

Siprajan was very cross at her daughter's cursing. "Oh good people, please pay no attention to her. Since she had the fever, she's been a bit crazy. Whatever I say, she takes no notice. She won't ever see Phlai Kaeo's corpse now."

Granny Kloi and Granny Sai fluttered their eyes and whispered, "Well, my dear Siprajan, the law has always been that anyone who dares volunteer for war and comes back defeated gets the chop."

"That's the law laid down by the ministry."

"And the troops who come back defeated are clapped in jail."

"And if anyone dies in war, his wife is seized to be a royal widow."

"That'll be tough for Wanthong. Let Khun Chang take her as his wife. He's got bags of money to fix things in the capital."

Siprajan's thoughts whirled in desperation. "Who'll protect us now Phlai Kaeo is dead? Khun Chang can shell out money without a thought, and we can depend on him in the future."

She spoke out loud, "We can't sit still and let her become a widow. If there's a law case, it'll be a bed of thorns. If Chang wants her hand, I'll do the clever thing. But if Phlai Kaeo comes back alive, there'll be trouble."

Granny Kloi and Granny Sai spoke up. "Phlai Kaeo died for sure."

"The men are all in jail."

"Even if he comes back, you can say you didn't know he was still alive. We'd be the ones who might get fined."

"If you consent to the match, make an agreement now. If you delay and they take her off, it'll be the talk of the town."

Siprajan gave her consent. "On the third of the waning moon, come to the house for the ceremony. I agree and won't change my mind."

In her room, Wanthong heard her mother giving her away. She leapt up, shaking in anger, and summoned old Phon. "A curse on your mother, you useless baldy. You're a servant but you don't look after the house. You were supposed to be watching the gate but you let a pack of dogs stray in and they're pissing and shitting all over the place. The mangy dog is making a row barking, and the bitches are howling and whining. Why do you let your mother's ancestors make such a racket?"

Granny Kloi and Granny Sai sat with grim faces. Khun Chang pretended he was deaf and did not know what was going on, until it became too much to bear. "Time's getting on. Let's go." He wai-ed Siprajan, who repeated, "Don't forget what we've agreed."

Wanthong shouted out, "Hey! Where have you got to, Grandma Mi? You don't do your duty morning or evening. Wherever there's chitchat you'll be sitting there wagging your tongue. Your head looks like a scraped coconut, as weird as wild waterfern boiled in coconut milk. You're descended from a bunch of lying fish-owls."

Khun Chang hurried down the stairs. The two ladies followed, grumbling. "We've lost face."

"I don't wish to come here ever again to have my ancestors reviled."

"I wouldn't come for a pile of gold."

Khun Chang said, "It's not like that. Wanthong was speaking in riddles. She told me it's a woman's ploy. She wants my mother Thepthong to pay a call. That's why she talked about my mother's ancestors. I should certainly get her as wife!"

In her room, Wanthong yearned. "Oh my brilliant Phlai Kaeo, how could you really be dead? On the day your life ended, I should have dreamed a little something but there's been no bad omen. They're saying that when a commander dies the men are jailed, but it's beyond poor me to find out. I don't know how things are in Ayutthaya. I've never once been there. The day I went to see my husband off, all I can remember is the Bang Lang Canal. The bo trees! We planted them together so that if anything happened there'd be a sign. If Phlai Kaeo is dead and gone, the middle bo tree will be dead too."

Saithong crept in to find Wanthong with her face bathed in tears. Wanthong flung her arms round her neck. "Oh Saithong, I don't want to live."

Saithong soothed her, "Don't weep. How come you can't find even a little happiness? It's all because this villainous Khun Chang is a rich man and ready to spend money like water, and our old mother has fallen for it. Where can we run off and hide? Your mother-in-law lives far away in Kanburi. Why don't we go to Wat Palelai to see Abbot Ju? He foretells the future well."

Around dusk, they quietly stole down from the house. At the wat, the abbot peered out, shading his eyes. "Oh, Wanthong! I changed your name to make the fever go away. Are you still not well? You look unhappy but you've put on some weight. That's good. Why have you two come?"

"I've been terribly upset because my husband went to war and has not returned. People are spreading bad news that he's dead. Master, please check by the manual. Is what they say true?"

Abbot Ju examined the positions of the sun and moon. "Divining by the three-eyed time, whoever told you this is lying. Your husband won a victory, and has acquired money, goods, and people in large numbers. In a little while, he'll return. Don't worry, and don't believe anyone sowing confusion."

Wanthong and Saithong felt their sorrow disappear. They wiped away their tears in relief and hurried home. Going up into the house, they joyfully told Siprajan everything the abbot had said.

"I don't believe it. How can these divinations based on some tricks with time compare to seeing with your own eyes? Oh, child! Sometimes these predictions are not even a little bit right. Don't be naive and believe him. They'll seize you as a royal widow. The only thing wrong with Khun Chang is his skull. And even though that's bald and shiny, what's inside is good."

"If you talk like this, I'm done for. All you can see is his money. Even if he were a pig or a dog, you'd give me to him. Sixteen years old and already two husbands! If the abbot's advice is wrong, then the bo tree will tell us. Let's go there to see."

"Don't prolong matters, you abomination. It's a long way to check the bo tree and I won't go. If you keep crossing me, I'll give you to Khun Chang today."

Wanthong screamed out loud, "Beat me to death, I don't care. When I'm born again in my next life, I've no desire to enter your womb. Not ever! Not for hundreds and thousands of eras. What kind of mother is this? Please kill me and let me have done with life."

Siprajan jumped up and grabbed a stick. "Your mother's clan! You've got a foul mouth. I'll beat you into dust." She hit Wanthong on the flank with a big thwack. Wanthong shrieked and turned sideways. Siprajan thrashed her with the stick until the welts showed. Wanthong asked for no forgiveness. "My husband's dead so I'll follow him. That vile Khun Chang has no more hair than a pygmy owl. I'll have nothing to do with this shiny skull."

Siprajan pinched Wanthong's lip. "You difficult child! I'll flay your back into stripes. Khun Chang is like a goldmine."

"Even if you beat me until you're worn out, I won't listen, I won't listen. You won't even check the bo tree we planted. Why do I want to live like this? Tomorrow when the sun comes up, I'll take leave of you and die!"

These words made Siprajan afraid that Wanthong really would hang herself. "If you want to see the bo tree, we'll go tomorrow. I carried you in my womb and I don't want to stand in your way."

"Bringing me up was a waste of your efforts. Even if Phlai Kaeo breathes no more, I won't consent to be given to that baldy. How could I sleep with someone like that? It's like tossing me away in a forest. Don't you love your daughter any more?"

"Don't say that. I don't really want to give you to him. I love you like my own eyes. Why should I force you?" She slept in Wanthong's room for fear her daughter would hang herself if left alone.

That afternoon, Khun Chang had stolen over to the house of Siprajan and heard the uproar inside—including the plan to visit the bo trees. He rushed back home, mounted an elephant, and set off across the paddy fields. By dawn he had reached Bang Lang and found the bo trees planted in a line with their foliage green and bushy. He grasped the central tree and wrenched hard. Phlai Kaeo had made a prayer for the local guardian spirits to protect the tree but it was still very young and could not withstand such treatment. The leaves shriveled and fell as if touched by fire. Khun Chang returned home.

Next morning, Siprajan summoned the servants. "Find some fish, rice, betelnut, and pan. Where's the boat? Bring it here. You men do the rowing." She hitched up her lowercloth, stood with legs akimbo, and cursed their mothers' clans loudly.

Wanthong and Siprajan boarded the boat together, "Cast off! What are you hanging about for?" The servants raggedly paddled the boat away. Siprajan scolded, "Can't you keep in time?" The men sang,

> "Lightning strike! We're used to riding buffalo.
> Just wiggle a leg, or waggle a leg, like so.
> This way, that way, the beast knows how to go.
> But paddling a boat is deathly boring, oh!
> We miss the stroke, we don't know how to row."

Siprajan raised her eyes to the heavens and shouted at them. "You're not paddling in time, you clan of slaves! I'll break your necks with this punt pole."

After one night and one day, they arrived at Bang Lang. The servants dived in the water and splashed around rowdily. Wanthong walked straight to the bo trees. Seeing the fallen leaves, she sprinted ahead, beating her chest and screaming out loud. At the tree, she fell prostrate.

"Oh, Phlai Kaeo, you're dead and won't return! I didn't believe it but now I do. Who'll protect me now? Mother is like a stick planted in buffalo dung, never standing up straight. By dying alone, you leave me lonely. Khun Chang will persist in asking for me. I'd rather die and follow you."

Siprajan began to worry why Wanthong had not returned. She rushed frantically in pursuit and found Wanthong lying under the central bo tree, motionless as if on the point of death. Siprajan embraced her body and cried out loud, "Wanthong, oh Wanthong!" No sound came in return. She shouted to the servants to help. They propped Wanthong up, massaged both her legs, and pressed between her eyebrows to open her eyes. Siprajan cried out, "Softly now! Why don't you massage her jaw? Do everything you can, everything." Someone bit Wanthong's big toe, and then she murmured.

Siprajan carried her back to the boat. Wanthong came to and grieved along the waterway. "Oh, my beloved bedmate! You shouldn't have been plucked away to lose your life in Chiang Thong. I was married only a moment and now I'm a widow. I did not even see the flames on your pyre. If only I could have laid one piece of kindling in your honor! I just saw the bones in a pot, and that was too pitiful. Why is life so strewn with obstacles? My father died when I was young. My husband died far away and left me with nobody to rely on. If I go on living, I can't escape shame. Eye's jewel, I yearn for you."

Overcome with pity, Siprajan hugged Wanthong with tears streaming down her face. In her grief, she slipped into pining over her own husband's death. "I wished to die and follow him but I was afraid of ghosts. I was going to jump into the water and drown but I was scared a crocodile would bite me. I wanted to slash my throat but I was afraid it would hurt. I prepared a rope to tie my neck but I feared I'd throttle myself. I worried I might die but still not meet my husband again so I kept putting it off. Now I'll just have to live on into old age."

When the boat moored at the landing, both were still grieving. Saithong heard the sound and rushed down to meet them. Wanthong called out, "The central bo tree has almost no leaves, while the other two still look fine."

Saithong's heart sank. The two of them stayed in the boat, weeping until sunset, when Saithong coaxed her up to the bedroom. "I'm sure

Phlai Kaeo isn't really dead. Abbot Ju has never once been wrong. I fear that oily-headed Khun Chang is up to something evil. After we had the loud argument with Mother and begged her to go to the bo trees, that villain disappeared. The lowlife must have done something to the bo tree."

Wanthong said, "I think you're right but I'm still uncertain." She sobbed on the bed until falling asleep.

Next morning Wanthong went to talk with Saithong. "Whether Phlai Kaeo is really dead or not, we shouldn't be attached to his things. I'll donate his possessions to Wat Palelai to earn merit and send all the merit to him. If he survives and comes back, we can acquire things again. I also want to question the abbot."

She went to find Siprajan and mumbled between sobs. "Now that my husband is dead, I'm going to the wat with his possessions to make merit and send it to him."

"Go. Please go. I've no complaint about you making merit. I intend to pour water and send the merit to him. Why should we keep his belongings? Khun Chang has heaps of money."

Wanthong tossed her head in anger and left. She arranged Phlai Kaeo's things in piles and summoned servants to carry them over to Wat Palelai. Seeing Wanthong, Abbot Ju asked, "What's all this you've brought? Why are you crying?"

"I saw the bo trees where we made the prayers. The leaves have dropped. I can't be sure that Phlai Kaeo isn't dead. I've brought all these possessions to make merit and send to him. If my husband still survives, we can acquire things again."

"Whether it's true or not, your thinking isn't bad. This good cloth can wrap texts and cover Buddha images. The common cloth can be cut into flags to decorate the wat at festivals. We'll keep the gold and silver for making Buddha images. Make a prayer with these gifts. Pray for your husband to come quickly. Ask to meet him tomorrow."

Wanthong laughed through her tears. "Your Lordship, what did you say? If my husband hasn't lost his life, I promise I'll build monks quarters as an offering to the wat."

"Is that right? I'll make certain you're not disappointed. If he doesn't come within this month, come and burn the wat down. Really!"

With their troubles lightened, they returned home and related the abbot's words to their mother.

Siprajan cried out, "I don't believe it. The abbot has his eye on the donation, on everything you carried over there. He's just saying things to please you. I don't believe a word of it."

SIPRAJAN GIVES WANTHONG
TO KHUN CHANG

Khun Chang ordered the craftsmen among his servants to fashion a bridal house in time for the wedding. "A grand house as big as a preaching hall with nine rooms and wooden floors is what I have in mind."

He went to see Siprajan. "I'd like to clear the ground by pulling down Phlai Kaeo's old bridal house and offering it to a wat. My bridal house will be huge, like Lord Indra's golden abode. There'll be nothing comparable anywhere."

"Thank you so much, sir! That suits our standing. Build it without delay! We'll take the old one to a wat."

Siprajan went to sweet-talk her daughter. "I've been thinking that Phlai Kaeo's bridal house should be given away to make merit on his behalf. If by the power of this merit he returns alive, then we can rebuild it even bigger. My darling, what do you say?"

Wanthong fell for the trick. "Just what I've been thinking, Mother. It'll help my lord and master survive."

Once Siprajan had arranged to store the contents of the old house, Khun Chang's servants dismantled every plank and reassembled them for the monks in Wat Klang.

At Cockfight Hill in Kanburi, Thong Prasi thought about her son. "He's been gone a long time. I feel sorry for Phim. Is she well or sadly wasting away with fever? Tomorrow I must go to visit her and see for myself."

She ordered her servants, "Round up the buffaloes with good hooves and hitch them to the carts at dawn tomorrow. Don't be late or you'll be flogged. Thap and Thian, look after the house and don't steal anything when my back's turned."

Next morning they loaded the carts and set off. After two nights they reached Suphan. At Siprajan's house, Thong Prasi was shocked not to see her son's bridal house. She quickly went up inside and sat down with a thump.

Siprajan said tearfully, "There's been a disaster. Phlai Kaeo fell dead in the war and left my daughter a widow. The bridal house has been pulled down and offered to a wat."

As Thong Prasi listened, her eyebrows furrowed and her face puckered in anger. "Here, who came to tell these tales? It's untrue, all of it. If my son had died, some news would have come for sure. What about all those men who went with him? I've not seen a single one return."

"The soldiers that escaped death were all clapped in jail. Khun Chang went to the city and brought back the news. Even then, Wanthong didn't believe it. She got in a boat and rushed off to see the bo trees where you all made a prayer. For some reason, the leaves had fallen."

Glad to hear her mother-in-law had come, Wanthong came out of her room and paid respect. "Thanks to merit, you came quickly or else you might not have seen me alive. Khun Chang has been sowing confusion. He wheedled my mother to give me to him in marriage. I almost hanged myself. I'd have run away but I hadn't the faintest idea where to go. Now that you've come, I feel I've been raised from the dead. Let me come to live in your house in Kanburi."

Siprajan was livid. "Look at her! She talks without shame, making insinuations about her own mother. She deserves a beating! Someone brought the bones, and Khun Chang just helped to deliver them and tell us Phlai Kaeo met disaster on campaign. I'm worried they'll haul you away by the ear and you'll suffer. Khun Chang can get you out of this problem by spreading his money around. If you want to go to Kanburi, fine—off you go. But if I don't beat you, I'm not Siprajan."

Thong Prasi was now angry too. "I'm not listening to this. You believe this dirty old man so easily. Someone just comes to fool you and you happily give away your daughter. If Phlai Kaeo comes back alive, how are you going to deal with it?"

"My dear lady, don't believe in ghosts. He won't come back. Besides, even if he does return victorious, what can we depend on *him* for?"

These words hurt Thong Prasi so much she shook with rage. "You'll see how good he is. I'll pursue this until I hit my head against a wall."

She went down from the house and asked around to find the village headman. "That mischievous old woman believes people who claim my son's dead. She hasn't checked the news but has simply given her daughter to be married. It'll create a big issue. Please come to be a witness."

The headman agreed to go over to Siprajan's house and was invited up. "You shouldn't be too hasty and create confusion. Think carefully before giving your daughter in marriage. It could blow up in a dispute, and we'd have the bother of sending her back to Phlai Kaeo."

"Enough! My daughter has to be married off. Whatever will happen, gold and silver will take care of it. Even if Phlai Kaeo returns from war victorious, what can we depend on *him* for?"

Thong Prasi quivered with anger. "What will be will be. I've made my case. I love my son and I warned him but he wouldn't listen. He was just a youth and he fell in love—so besotted he didn't look where he was going. He pleaded with me so sincerely I was forced to follow his wishes. Now you're going to snatch Wanthong away from him. Well, I'm not a bit disappointed because with her lineage, there's nothing to be sorry about. I'm saying that because you forced me to. Enough!"

She hurried down from the house. Wanthong rushed to follow her but Siprajan grasped a stick and dragged her back. Thong Prasi grabbed Wanthong and tried to pull her away. Siprajan called the servants who came in force and hauled Wanthong up into the house. Thong Prasi returned home with a scowl on her face.

On the eve of the ceremony, Khun Chang ordered his servants to carry the materials for the bridal house to Siprajan's compound.

"Fetch old Khun Chot, the astrologer. He knows the ancient stuff about making offerings." Khun Chot called for incense, candles, six coins, a bowl for offering sacred water, and a banana plant. He cut squares of banana pith for placing offerings to Krung Phali, chief of the spirits, and plaited the leaves into a square tray for a pair of large pig's heads offered to Lord Phum, the spirit of the place. Young coconuts, sweets, bananas, and sugarcane were offered to Lord Indra, Brahma, Vishnu, Yama, and the gods of wind and fire. Khun Chot changed into white upper and lower cloths, pronounced sacred verses calling on the deities for good fortune, and sprinkled enchanted water on the ground to dispel any obstacles and obstructions.

They staked out the plan, buried the offerings, and dug holes for the posts. The post timbers were chosen with a lot of shouting and argument. "That one's wrong. Look at the holes. Hurry, dawn's almost here. Go and fetch Uncle Rak to do the soul ceremony on time." A timber judged to have the best knots was chosen for the main post. Each post was smeared with cow dung, tied with a banana and sugarcane plant, and decorated with lotus leaves and pink cloths inscribed with yantra to ward off dangers. At four in the morning Khun Chot called out, "Bring some little sweets, strong liquor, duck, and chicken, whatever you can afford. Plus scented water, sandal oil, and scents." Khun Chot invited the lady tree spirit from the forest and great Gem Treasurer to ward off fire and danger. A gong was beaten, and people hollered as the main post was raised and inserted in its hole. Other posts were raised, then the beams were placed, floor joists hung, gable ends set, riser posts attached to the roof beams, ridgepole raised, purloins fixed, flooring laid, walls completed, windows and door frames inserted, gable boards raised, rafters attached, and thatch passed up to cover the roof.

Khun Chang cried, "Don't mess it up, young man! You'll have to do that corner again. Tie the top of the thatch neatly on the corner beams! Hurry up! It's getting late."

Once the roof was finished the workmen cried out for food and liquor. Siprajan ordered servants to bring what had been prepared but all soon disappeared. "That's not enough! Bring some more." They finished off two hundred trays and still kept crying for extra.

Siprajan complained. "What a pestilential lot. I've never seen such a set of hungry ghosts. Coat that rotten old mat in flour, fry it in fish oil, and give them five pots of fermented fish sauce as a dip. They're so drunk, anything'll taste good." All five pots were demolished.

Siprajan walked to Wat Palelai to ask the abbot to chant prayers at the house that evening. "Now that Phlai Kaeo has died, I'm marrying Wanthong to Khun Chang."

Abbot Ju replied, "Hold off and listen to me before there's a problem. Do you know for certain he died? I think this will turn out badly."

"Your Lordship, you're losing your mind, talking nonsense."

"Look here, Siprajan. This shouldn't be any business of mine but it is, because I helped to bring Phlai Kaeo up. I fear he'll come back and complain that I knew about this yet still let it happen. It'd be better for you to invite other monks."

Siprajan went to Wat Klang and Wat Phlap to find monks to chant prayers that evening.

Thepthong was busily arranging the dowry, shouting at the servants until the tendons on her neck bulged. "Would you run around and help a bit? Hey, tell Granny Kloi and Granny Sai that it's almost afternoon and the sun's high in the sky. How come they're not dressed yet?" When the whole dowry procession was ready, they set off.

In front came a bottle-drum band, followed by a Chinese ensemble and then a flutist tootling on the Lao pipes. The four main dowry trays were carried by daughters of wealthy families of Suphan, all dressed to the nines. The first, from a Chinese family, walked with her chest thrown forward, looking like a puffed-up Garuda. The second, from a Mon family, had a slim waist but a large bottom with a cleft like a monkey. The third, of a Lao lineage from Vientiane, had bandy legs, sunken eyes, a bulging belly, and flat chest. The fourth, daughter of a Javanese trader, was dark and beautiful like a bright-eyed crow, short and roly-poly but with a fine bottom. These four carried tiered trays with the dowry and offertory cloth for paying respect to the parents and grandparents of the host. Behind came the 101 trays of the secondary dowry, loaded with sweets and fruit. At the rear came a mass of retainers and a music ensemble.

At Siprajan's house, they made a racket shouting and beating gongs. Baldheaded Phon leapt out to close the door and prevent anyone entering. The elders dug out money for him to let them into the house. They led the way up and sat on carpets while the dowry trays were set down in rows. The elders inside the house welcomed them and counted the gifts, then everything was carried into the house. The customary presents were distributed. Food and sweets were provided. The elders returned home.

In the evening Khun Chang bathed, patted sandal powder on his unruly chest hair, and examined himself in a mirror. "I'm fed up with this beard. Why doesn't it run up and sprout on my head? The more I shave it, the heavier it returns, but on top of my head there's not a trace!"

He put on a pricey lowercloth, recently purchased inside the palace, an uppercloth of good wool in a bright color, and a belt worth over eight hundred baht. Descending from the house, he waddled along with his servants following en masse. People came to look at his finery, but when they saw his face and body they laughed, winked, and whispered among themselves.

At Siprajan's house, Phon slammed the door shut. Khun Chang lost his temper. "Who are you making fun of, you damned bald fraud?"

Phon said, "My lord Khun Chang, I was bald since I was a baby, and I'm not making fun of anyone. You're such a rich man, give me some money and I'll open up."

Khun Chang handed over money and went up to the terrace. The monks had already arrived and were sitting holding a sacred thread. Siprajan told her daughter to get dressed. Wanthong refused. Siprajan smacked her back loudly. "You difficult, foulmouthed child!" She tried to wind a cloth round her but Wanthong resisted. Siprajan dragged her by the hand. Wanthong clung tight onto a door bolt. Siprajan put her foot against the wall and tugged, but her hand slipped and she tumbled backwards. Boiling with anger, she called out to the monks, "Chant the prayers now. It's coming to lamp-lighting time. The bride is sick and in pain. She can't come for the water sprinkling. When the chanting is over, please let me have some lustral water to pour inside here."

Khun Chang looked on awkwardly. The monks chanted prayers, sprinkled water, and then left. The groom's party changed their clothes and sat in rows on the verandah to feast. Everyone ate their fill and returned home happily, except Khun Chang who was overjoyed that he did not have to go anywhere. He had sepha recited with a music ensemble.

Next morning, the abbot and monks arrived at the new bridal house, where cooks had prepared food ready and waiting. The monks and novices filed up in order, set down their bowls, and chanted prayers.

Khun Chang picked up a scoop to ladle rice and called out to Siprajan, "Please get Wanthong to come out here so we can give alms together."

Wanthong wailed angrily, "I have no desire to give alms and be shamed in front of pigs, dogs, and servants."

Siprajan groaned. "Khun Chang, please don't take offense. Since she was very ill in a year of the dog, she's been a bit crazy."

"I can see that. She can dig up my ancestors as far back as she likes but I won't take offense."

After the chanting was over, the monks and novices were fed from five big earthen pots. "The abbot knows how to eat. Give him a full helping!" The monks chanted the offertory blessing, and returned to the wat, with novices carrying many hampers.

At dusk, Khun Chang went to sleep in the big bridal house. Overexcited with longing for Wanthong, he paced up and down for three days. He tried hugging a long pillow and imagining it was her. At the dead of night, he sat driven almost mad by fantasies. The mattress was bathed in sweat from his fevered body. He got up and recited a verse, beating claves to keep time.

"Oh little Chim, my own true bride,
say when will I lie by your side,
be gratified, dessert of mine?
When we meet I'll slurp the pot!
I pine, hot tuna boiled in brine.
Oh turtle, come to drink moonshine.
Dear mother fine, please send her quick!"

Siprajan praised his poetry to the skies and tried to pacify her daughter. "Don't delay. You've already been in a bridal house so don't be hesitant."

Wanthong was so pent up that she pounded the walls of the room, shouting, "I don't wish to see that hateful baldy's face! If you want him, have him yourself."

Siprajan could not tolerate her daughter's sarcasm. She grabbed a stick and beat her many times. Wanthong cried out, "I don't love this baldy so you hit me. Though not ashamed before other people, you should be ashamed before the spirits."

"You won't stop arguing, will you?" Siprajan grabbed a rope from the wall, tied Wanthong's hands up to the ceiling, and circled round thrashing her with the stick. "Are you going into the bridal house or not? Answer quickly. I won't untie you until you reply."

"Where are you, Saithong? Help me please or I'll die this time."

Saithong ran up and snatched the stick away. "Mother! Don't hurt yourself attempting the impossible. Let the hard work fall on me. I'll persuade her to go into the bridal house."

She untied Wanthong's hands, led her into the room, and put salve on her back and shoulders. Wanthong lamented over Phlai Kaeo. "If he's dead, there should have been a sign. I'd go to Ayutthaya to find out the truth but I don't know my way around the capital. As a woman, how can I travel through the forest where there are many wild animals? But if I do nothing, I have this threat close at hand. It looks like I'll die. Truly, karma is catching up with me!"

KHUN PHAEN AND WANTHONG QUARREL

In Chomthong after sunrise, a duty officer of the guard rushed into the camp. "I carry the king's orders. Close the campaign and return to Ayutthaya."

Phlai Kaeo was very happy. He had his elephant loaded with food, gold, silver, and other goods. He gave orders for the captured families to be sent on ahead. At an auspicious time to march, elephants and horses swarmed across the plain to the sound of gongs and shouting.

In the forest, a breeze fluttered the flags and wafted a fragrance of flowers. Laothong wept despondently at the thought of her parents. "I won't know whether they're sick or well, dead or alive. Who'll look after them? Nobody is the same as one's own child."

Phlai Kaeo felt sorry for her. He ordered his mahout to slow down so her elephant came alongside, and lifted her into his howdah. Curtains were arranged to conceal them at front and rear. With his arms round her lovingly, he urged her to enjoy the forest. Leaves and flowers sprouted from every branch. Pollen sprinkled down from on high, suffusing the air with scent. As they sat embracing cheek to cheek, love lulled away her tears and longing. He pointed out the tigers, gibbons, lemurs, and langurs. A male monkey grabbed his mate, swung up to the treetops, and hugged her. Phlai Kaeo pointed. "Look at that dirty monkey!" She shyly hid behind him, averting her eyes.

At a river landing, they made rafts and boarded the captive families. Phlai Kaeo and Laothong embarked on a large sleeper boat. The oarsmen pounded ahead for seven days and reached the city as dawn came up. Phlai Kaeo took the three governors and the ruler of Chiang Mai to the official hall inside the palace. Senior officials asked to be told tales of the victory. On a command, they were escorted into the audience hall.

The king entered. A senior noble had his turn. "My liege, pray allow your servant to report. This matter arose when a Chiang Mai army went to besiege Chiang Thong. Your Majesty graciously allowed Phlai Kaeo to attack on your behalf. Through the power of Your Majesty's accumulated merit, victory was won. Families, cattle, and buffaloes were captured, along with pikes, swords, guns, and masses of materiel including clothing. All has been sent to the capital under inventory."

The king clapped his hands loudly. "You Chiang Thong are a rogue with thousands of ruses. You switched sides, back and forth. You didn't honor the water oath of allegiance. Did you believe you have sufficient merit not to depend on anyone?"

The ruler of Chiang Thong stuttered, "My liege, please have mercy! I was not in revolt but acted in fear of danger. If I had not submitted, I would be dead. The Chiang Mai army numbered in tens of thousands. Their commanders had invulnerability and expertise as warriors. Yet on the day that the Thai army arrived, I immediately made a secret agreement with them. We attacked the Chiang Mai forces at the same moment. The enemy did not realize in time and so could not avoid defeat. If you fail to show me favor, my punishment is death. Have mercy."

"I still have doubts about what you say. Heigh, Phlai Kaeo, tell us what you know about this. He looks to me like an evil two-headed bird. Chiang Mai comes so he sides with Chiang Mai. The Thai arrive so he submits to the Thai. He sways this way and that like a stick planted in mud."

"Probably he was maneuvering to save his own skin, but in the end his army charged the enemy camp. Even a very bad action can be erased by a good one."

The king ordered Phramuen Si, a head of the royal pages, to present caskets, sabers, cloth, and other gifts as tokens of royal appreciation. Phlai Kaeo was appointed to the title of Khun Phaen, assigned to guard a remote frontier region in command of five hundred men, and presented with a boat nine fathoms in length.

For action beyond the call of duty, the governors of Kamphaeng, Rahaeng, and Thoen were rewarded with betel boxes and golden flasks. They left immediately by boat along with the ruler of Chiang Thong and arrived home in fifteen days.

Khun Phaen went to board his boat along with Laothong. They left with the oarsmen loudly singing boat songs. A haloed moon shone serenely in a cloudless sky strewn with shining stars, highlighting the fairness of Laothong's face.

Late at night, when a breeze came up, his thoughts turned longingly to Phim. "Is my jewel waiting forlornly? With me so far away, she must have faced many obstacles. There's an old saying: If you sleep on high, lie face down so you'll spy anything that happens, but if you sleep down low, lie face up. A man with a beautiful wife shouldn't entrust her to a mother-in-law. Khun Chang has jealous intentions."

He urged the oarsmen to hurry. In the bright light of dawn, they arrived at Suphan and moored at the landing just as Saithong was coming down there. She went straight back to tell Wanthong that Phlai Kaeo had returned.

Wanthong was overjoyed. She grabbed a cloth to put round her shoulders, opened a window, and saw the boat. "It's him!"

She came down the stairs and walked quickly to the boat, noticing the mattresses, pillows, and curtained partition. Khun Phaen saw her coming and stuck his head out of the curtain to greet her. She raised her hands to wai him but her face clouded over and she struggled to speak. She embraced her husband's feet, sobbing.

Khun Phaen thought, "What's up? She looks thin. Has she been sick with grief because I took so long? She should be happy to see me but she's weeping in utter misery."

With growing suspicion, he asked, "What's the matter, Phim? What's troubling your heart?"

"I feel a thorn is stuck in my breast, making it swell up, fester, and ache. It's hard to speak because my heart is bursting. You protected your wife like a bird that looks after the nest so no eggs fall and no enemy can steal them. But when a nest is left empty, hawk and crow swoop down and scatter it to pieces. Our bridal house has disappeared because a friend has been treacherous. Khun Chang came to tell my mother that the army was defeated and you'd been stabbed by the enemy. He brought some bones to show me. I cried endlessly. I went to see the three bo trees. The leaves of the middle one had withered. I sickened with fever almost to the point of death. The abbot at Wat Palelai said I had to change my name to Wanthong. After that I began to get better. Then that lackey Khun Chang told Mother that I'd be taken into the palace unless I married him. Mother didn't know this was a lousy trick. She got greedy at the thought of wealth. The old house was taken down and sent to Wat Klang. A new bridal house was built and a prayer chanting held. It's seven days now and I haven't gone in there. Mother shouted at me and beat me to a pulp but I've borne it and borne it until today."

She peeled off her white uppercloth, "Look at my back and shoulders. Like flayed meat. I'm deeply, deeply hurt. If you don't believe me, I'm done for."

Khun Phaen felt angry enough for blood to flow from his eyes. "Can a friend be so disloyal? The whole place knows you're my wife but this baldy thinks he can wreck everything. And that old mother thinks she can beat you to her heart's content. What a liberty to pull down a bridal house and simply build a new one over the remains! If I don't repay him, then I'm not a man. If it means the king won't keep me, well that's the way it is. And you, Wanthong, not going into his bridal house for seven nights—you're the best in Ayutthaya! Any other woman would have lost her honor. Hey men! Surround the house!" He drew his sword and brandished it furiously. "I'll slash down the whole of Suphan!"

From behind the boat's curtain, Laothong saw him shaking with rage. Fearing he would kill someone, she opened the curtain and came out to block his path.

"Hold off and think first. There are laws in the land, and no matter where you go you won't escape them. Why not report the matter to the king? If you rashly attack people, later you'll be in trouble. You've heard only one side and don't yet know the rights and wrongs of the matter. How come this fellow had the nerve to seize her even though you two were already married? Was there some kind of consent? She's no iron lady, nor is she a baby child either. And the mother-in-law gave her consent. That's why he had the nerve to do all this."

Wanthong felt a thunderbolt had broken her head into seven pieces. "How come you float your face into the middle of this, raising your voice and flaunting your body like a flying swan! Cutting me off. Telling my husband what to do. Knowing the rights and wrongs of the matter so perfectly. Suspecting something fishy. Flirting and flaunting to get my husband to fall for you. Is this your wife, sir, or is her ladyship some palace consort? Is that why she followed a torch, blundered into a stump, and broke her neck? Or perhaps she's a relative of yours? Or a stray Lao kid you abducted along the way?"

"This wife of mine is from Chomthong. Her parents gave her for me to marry. She's the child of a headman from a big house and her name is Laothong. I was bringing her to wai you, but then things blew up. Please show me some consideration, the two of you. Laothong, wai Phim first. Phim, calm down and don't take offense. If there's any problem, we can talk it over later."

"Enough, sir! I have no desire for a wai from her. I only find out that you have a lover when she shows her face here, spitting out these contemptuous insinuations to hurt me and create confusion. Shouldn't I feel insulted? She's crafty, subtle, and sharp as nails."

Laothong felt as angry as if licked by fire. "I didn't know in time that you were his major wife. I saw that he was wild enough to kill someone. I don't sway around like a stick stuck in mud. If I didn't stop him, who would? You were too worked up and not likely to back down. If a fire's flaring and you carelessly fling on more firewood, it flames up even fiercer. You don't wish to receive my wai but I'm not a hard-headed little thing. I'm just a simple-mannered Lao from the forest. If I'd known the situation here beforehand, I'd have brought good presents like eaglewood and ivory. That's the custom among forest people. Now I'm at a loss because I came empty handed. So let's just greet each other for the time being. There, let me wai you. Don't be angry."

"Tcha! This little upland Lao can weave words full of wiles! If you'd brought wood and ivory, I'd have brought a tusker out to receive you so that Lady Laothong would not have to walk on the ground. I'd have sent up a palanquin so soldiers could take turns carrying you along the way. That would be fitting for the Chomthong family with its rank and its big house. I thank you for stopping him from being aggressive. Because of your ladyship's action, we now have absolute peace and quiet. No, you're no stick stuck swaying around in mud. You're thick clay so firm that a boundary post can be rammed in nine spans deep all day long—until the man falls flat on his face! If that weren't so, how would you dare come? Here at Ayutthaya you'll be a sensation, talked about every day and night. Hundreds of villages and thousands of cities will celebrate this one lady. Nay! Not only the humans who walk this earth, even Lord Indra will probably come down too!"

"In truth, good people are not celebrated and evil people become popular. It's shameful. I thank you for wanting to bring an elephant to receive us because we don't have one but you have plenty in reserve, both real elephants and man elephants!"

"You little forest Lao, I'll beat you and use the blood to bathe my feet. Saithong, come and help me! I'm not letting her get away with it."

Khun Phaen blocked Wanthong. Laothong hid behind him. Saithong rushed up, ready to deliver a slap.

Khun Phaen protested, "Don't make more trouble, Saithong. Wanthong, please restrain yourself."

"Even if Lord Indra comes down to forbid me, I won't listen. If you don't want to keep me, so be it. Just slash me down in this boat. But this little upland Lao, this clever talker, this eater of lizards and frogs, is getting a slap!"

She grasped Laothong's arm. Khun Phaen cried "Don't! Don't!" and blocked her with his hands. Laothong dodged away. The slap came too late and caught Khun Phaen full on.

"What's this? Don't you fear me one little bit? I say 'don't' but it just fans the flames."

"If you want to beat me, then beat me. Strange, you didn't have a temper like this before. Why is the sight of me as hateful as the sight of a tiger? Have you been dosed, my dear husband? Did she cut open your body and eat away all the innards so the potion would seep into your body hair and blacken your bones? Your face is covered with freckles, all over the nose and lips. Before long, you'll be crawling on the ground and she'll ride on your neck like an ox."

"Too much, Wanthong! Even if you don't fear me, at least show me a little respect. For better or worse, I'm your husband, but you don't seem to want me to be. Don't lose the fish by beating the water in front of the trap. If you love yourself and fear shame, calm down."

"I know now you don't love me. You brought her home to slight me. If you bring someone else here, will you expect me to receive her like a public footbath? Before long you'll be like a board used for chopping fish and this little Lao will chop you to shreds. We're finished from today."

Wanthong leapt up onto the jetty. "So no stain is left, I'll scoop up river water to wash the house, scrub it with my feet, even spread some fragrant oil and powder, and leave it to dry as a crust. To get this liar out of my life, I'll even dig his feces out of the ground so there's not a trace left behind. I cut myself off from you completely from today. I won't miss you in even one joint of my little finger. Even if Lord Indra comes down to scold me, don't wait around for me to go back on my word!"

"You're full of yourself, Wanthong. And you want to put the blame on me, don't you? When I arrived, I thought things were fine. I didn't yet know your trickery. You pretended to weep and wail but you were hiding a lot away, you little schemer. You were scared I was about to go and slash Khun Chang. You couldn't stay still because you love your baldheaded husband. To conceal the truth, you shouted at Laothong then quarreled with me. A nettle vine is horribly itchy but not as bad as you. With ringworm, mange, or flukes, the itch can at least be soothed with medicine. But this lowlife is as bad as the worm that bores its way in and gives one the shakes. Even if I looked for a cure all over Suphan, I'd exhaust the medical manuals in one day. You're going to die, Wanthong."

He stamped his foot, drew his sword, and raised it to strike.

Wanthong ran up into the house, threw herself down on the bed, and flailed around in utter despair. "Oh my Phlai Kaeo! It was a waste to have preserved myself untarnished like a brilliant gold ring, like an egg buried in stone. My body was untainted. Even the breeze had no chance to brush me. But as soon as we met again, trouble flared. I can't blame you at all. I'm the one with guilt on my face. Now everything is severed, snapped, cracked, and crumbled into dust. I'm like a swan with a broken wing that falls into mud, loses its glittering color, and becomes like a crow. Oh my lord and master, my partner at the table, partner in bed, friend in sickness, friend in health, this is our first quarrel. You still loved me and meant to live together as before, but jealousy made me so mean, hasty, and stubborn. I should have borne things for half a year and let you beat me to your heart's content. But I've slipped up and you've cast me away. How can I escape Khun Chang now? Only this old and already two husbands! When I'm dead and buried, my name will still be notorious. The pain won't lessen and the shame will never disappear, like a tattoo on the back of a hand. Why should I love this body? Death is finer."

She found a rope, raised her hands, and prostrated three times.

"In this life, I've lost you. In fear of shame, I'll die and wait to meet you again in the next life. Don't let Khun Chang have even a hint."

She climbed up onto a roof beam, tied the rope tightly round her neck, and let her body swing. Saithong came in at that very moment.

She shrieked, took the weight of Wanthong's body, grabbed a knife to cut the rope, and cried out loud, "Mother! Come quick! Wanthong has hanged herself!"

Siprajan jumped up and fell flat on her face. Khun Chang leapt up too with bleary eyes, tripped over his mother-in-law, and crashed down with a thud. Siprajan complained, "You old elephant! You almost broke my spine."

Servants massaged Wanthong but failed to bring her round. Saithong cried out, "Wanthong has really hanged herself, Phlai Kaeo. Come and look."

"I won't miss Wanthong." He ordered servants to harness the elephants and left for his mother's house at Cockfight Hill in Kanburi.

Two days later Thong Prasi saw many people, elephants, and horses approaching and understood her son had returned. "Servants, come quickly to receive him. There are two of them. It must be Wanthong." She hawked and said, "Why ever did he bring Wanthong?"

Khun Phaen dismounted from the elephant, brought Laothong along to prostrate at his mother's feet, and told her the story.

"Oh my son, no need to tell me. Siprajan is full of herself. When she gave Wanthong away to Khun Chang in marriage, I went and made a big commotion and severed relations completely from that day on. We can't keep Wanthong." She turned to speak to Laothong. "Come to live with us. I trust you to look after me in sickness and death, dear child. Whatever we have, poor or plenty, I give to you. Love yourself, protect yourself, and fear gossip."

The many Lao families who had arrived with them went off to build new houses around the village.

Khun Chang spent fifteen days in the bridal house in utter misery. At the slightest sound, he asked "Have you come?" But the only reply was a house lizard's chatter. He lay down, stood up, sat, and went back to lying again—first face up, then face down, then turning on his side. He got up to recite a love poem.

"My love, this bed is cold as ice.
What must I do to eat young rice.
I miss you darling club of wood,
Please say we'll meet or else I die."

Siprajan praised him to the skies. "It's so eloquent, so poetic, I'm enthralled!"

"Oh, Mother dear! Be kind to your tormented son. Spirits of my grandmothers and grandfathers, come and help. I'll give you strong liquor and roasting pigs. Anyone who can persuade her will be richly rewarded."

Siprajan tried to bring Wanthong round. "Today fifteen days are up. Precious child, please go into the bridal house."

"Oh Mother, my husband just came back from war. If he hadn't survived, I'd live with Khun Chang. If you murder me so easily, it will waste all the effort of carrying me in your womb."

"Don't you want a rich husband? Don't you want to sit and eat in comfort until your dying day? Why make so much of his bald head? You're moaning on about Phlai Kaeo but he's gone off with that woman, hasn't he? Khun Chang will give you so much money, you won't be able to sew sacks fast enough to hold it all."

She grabbed Wanthong. They grappled clumsily. Siprajan's hand slipped, and she fell against a wall, ripping her cloth and cracking her head. Wanthong too fell face down with a bang. Siprajan pushed her, rolling her head-over-heels, and beating her remorselessly. "All tears and snot like a toddler. Are you really not going? Well I'm not listening."

Khun Chang blundered up, rubbing sleep from his eyes, opened the door, and waited.

Wanthong shouted, "Hold off, Mother! Oh neighbors, come and look!"

Old Phon thought that robbers had come to spear his pigs. He grabbed a pike, came out to his doorway, and cried out, "To battle! No retreat!"

Siprajan shouted angrily, "Why are you jumping up and down, you hairy-chested old baldy? Nobody's spearing your pigs."

Khun Chang thought she was shouting at him. "Heavens above! I haven't speared anything yet. Why are you slow at sending Wanthong to me?"

Siprajan cried angrily, "You sex maniac!"

She grabbed her daughter again and hauled her up into the new bridal house. Wanthong lost her uppercloth in the struggle. Khun Chang's eyes glazed over. He leapt across, missed Wanthong, and kissed his mother-in-law twice.

Siprajan pushed him away. "You dirty baldy, you ghost's skull!"

"Ay! Damn! Riding your wife's mother is a big mistake!"

He released Siprajan, grabbed Wanthong, and dragged her across the room in high excitement, clumping along on his knees like a turtle. "I'm going to heaven today!"

Wanthong shouted, "Get away from me, you lowlife! Your head's like a dried old coconut!"

Khun Chang pushed her into the mosquito net. Wanthong kicked him in the chest, and he fell off the bed with a thud. Scrambling up, he lay across her stomach. The string of the mosquito net broke. As she squirmed desperately, the net wrapped round her like a coating of egg white. Khun Chang groped around, getting the net totally tangled. "I'm really furious with this net. First thing tomorrow, I'll throw it in the shithouse."

He ripped the net, and peeled it away from her body, leaving only her head in the tangle, giving himself an opening. He jumped up in a frog-like pose, found her little belly with his hands, and rocked.

Wanthong kicked him off and freed herself enough to sit up. Khun Chang stumbled over, grabbed her by the throat, and wrestled her down onto the bed. Wanthong struggled and pounded on the wall.

Wondrously, the sky burst and rain sluiced down in an unbroken babbling stream, bathing the earth. Fish and shrimps jumped happily up from the water. Huge fish slipped over rocks. Catfish swam down and wriggled into the ground, looking for food, scraping their heads and scuffing their barbs on the undergrowth at the riverbank. An eel nosed into a hole but stuck, rose to the surface, and careened about. Two fighting cocks struck, sinking in their rear claws to the hilt.

Khun Chang's body hair bristled in bliss. "I love you enough to swallow you up. Thousands of other women mean nothing to me. I'll give you piles of money. No matter where you go, you can ride on the neck of your loving husband instead of a bull elephant."

Wanthong tossed her head. Her thoughts turned to her husband and she wanted to die. Too ashamed to let anyone see her, she stayed in the room for two days. She was now forced to live with Khun Chang but behind his back she pined for Khun Phaen.

KHUN PHAEN STATES HIS CASE

Two nights after the quarrel, Khun Phaen woke at midnight. The earth was bathed in bright moonlight. Only birds calling through the forest and the relentless trilling of cicadas disturbed the silence. A cool dew lay on the ground and a fresh breeze blew. His thoughts turned to Wanthong.

"I was really rash. Should I have thrown away a loving wife? Khun Chang had already built a bridal house, ready and waiting. The longer I leave her there, the more chance he has to fulfill his desires. Does a tiger dally with a juicy chunk of meat? Tomorrow I'll go to Suphan. If Wanthong is sleeping with him, I'll slash both their throats. Siprajan and Thepthong were involved too, and those old ladies who asked for her hand. I'll treat them like dogs with crooked tails."

He chose twenty skilled men. "Put enough rice in your waist pouches for about four days, and ready the weapons you usually carry. You survived one war so now I trust you to follow my arse."

He made his farewell to Laothong, picked up his sword, and rode away. They reached Suphan after two nights. At sundown, they made a shrine, recited formulas to instill their equipment with power, and enchanted rice and limes.

Close to midnight, under a glittering starlit sky, they arrived at Khun Chang's bridal house. Khun Phaen dismounted and scattered enchanted rice to drive away all the spirits of the place, tied a lighted candle to the first post and split the wood with an adept's knife, intoned a Loosener mantra to spring the bolts and open the windows, and scattered rice mixed with bones of the dead to put everyone inside to sleep. Climbing up to a big window, he jumped down onto the floor inside. In the dim light, he cut down a curtain, opened a mosquito net, and saw Wanthong and Khun Chang asleep in each other's arms. He pushed them apart to see her face, and lifted the cloth covering her chest.

"I didn't realize such a figure would have no heart. You're so beautiful I wanted to swallow you whole, but I should not have put such store in looks. All the promises we made still stand but I was hardly out of the door when you took a lover in full public view."

He kicked them off the bed. "Why should I let you live?" He raised his sword to cut them in two, but a house lizard chattered close by, an omen of warning. "Your fortune is good or else both your heads would be off. But I'll make you pay."

He pulled a cord out from a curtain, wound it tight around their prone bodies, tightened the bonds with splints, and wrapped them in cloth like a corpse for cremation. "That's what you deserve."

With dawn almost brightening the sky, he hurried down from the house, pulled the knife out of the post, and ordered his men to light many torches like a royal procession. He released the mantra, allowing everyone to wake up, and told his men to shout loudly and beat on the walls.

"Is Wanthong there?"

"Are people awake?"

"Lower the stairway to receive Khun Phaen!"

Saithong heard the noise, rushed out, and saw Khun Phaen and many people on horseback. "Now we're in for it! Wanthong is already spoiled and he's come back for her. I must try to calm things down."

She pushed the stairway down and descended nervously. Arriving in front of Khun Phaen, she burst into floods of tears. "How come you abandoned Wanthong so easily? On that day when she hanged herself, you wouldn't even look. Siprajan forced her to marry that baldy. They had a big fight and Siprajan beat Wanthong until her blood flowed. She was spoiled by force just two days ago."

"Saithong, there's no need to say anything else. I understand the trickery. I don't have wealth and good fortune so Siprajan sees no benefit in me. I have to accept this, and bear it somehow. I came to fetch her, and would love her if she weren't spoiled, but now she's tainted. You can't wash this away however hard you try. Even you won't escape his clutches in the end. When he doesn't have her, he'll take you instead because you're the same in flesh and spirit. I thought of bringing charges but it's a waste of time. I'll just slash the whole house! The couple will be hanged, and I'll have fun with those who helped ask for her hand. And what about you, who are also my wife? How come you fell in with them?"

"Don't talk like this. It's like looking in a basket of fish and seeing only the one that's rotten. It's almost light. Come up to the house."

Saithong went up the stairs and into Siprajan's room. "Get up quickly! Khun Phaen is downstairs with lots of men, pikes, horses, and swords. He's in the king's favor now. Someone will be hanged for sure. He named you and Thepthong. I heard him telling his men that he'll rip us to pieces and leave the results for people to see."

Siprajan trembled like a chick. Sweat flowed down her face and dripped from her ears. "My time has come to die!" She buried herself under a mattress. "Saithong, please tell him I fainted down dead several days ago."

"Where will you hide? You think he won't come in and search?"

Saithong pushed on Wanthong's door but found the bolt closed tight. She went to the doorway and called Khun Phaen to come up.

He asked, "Why don't I see my mother-in-law? Why is Wanthong still sleeping so late?" He made a show of shouting loudly and pounding on the walls.

Trussed up tight with rope and cloth, Khun Chang and Wanthong rolled their heads around, trying to breathe. They had no lowercloths and were bound together face to face. Khun Chang got hard and laughed. Wanthong hissed, "You villain! We're tied up like corpses but you're still happy."

Khun Phaen called out, "Wanthong! Aren't you coming out of your room? Don't you get up until midday? Come and talk."

Wanthong recognized her husband's voice and shivered in panic. Khun Chang called out, "Whee!" and tried to roll over on top of her.

"Lie still. Why are you butting me with your knee?"

"You think it's my knee but it's not. Who called you just now? It sounded like a man's voice."

Khun Phaen shouted, "Hey, Khun Chang! Put my wife down. Today you meet your death. I'm coming in to cut your head off." He kicked the wall to make them panic.

Saithong called out, "Mother, he's going to slash Wanthong for sure. Why are you hiding away? How do you think you can escape?"

Siprajan was too scared to come out but also afraid he would slash her daughter to death. She found some string to tie a mattress around her body. "Even if he slashes me, it'll only hit the kapok." She folded a cloth and wrapped it round her head, completely covering her ears and eyes, and thrust her hands inside the mattress. Stumbling forward, she got jammed in the doorway. "Saithong, come and help me!"

Saithong burst out laughing. She wrestled with the mattress but Siprajan slipped and fell down with a thud.

Khun Phaen's men cackled with laughter. "See the masked raider!"

"The horses are bucking about in fear this spirit will eat them!"

Saithong guided Siprajan out onto the terrace. Khun Phaen called out, "What's this wrapped in a mattress? Where's Siprajan? She won't escape being killed." Siprajan thought he did not realize it was her, so she leaned against a wall and said nothing.

Khun Phaen sent for the headman. "When I went to Chiang Thong on royal service, you knew that Wanthong and I were married. On my return, my bridal house was nowhere to be seen. Who does this new house with nine rooms belong to?"

"Khun Chang brought Granny Kloi and Granny Sai to say that you were dead and to arrange a marriage ceremony. Thong Prasi came and had a big argument with Siprajan over whether you'd died. Siprajan wouldn't listen. Before she went home, Thong Prasi informed me."

Khun Phaen pondered the truth of the matter. "Wanthong was intent on waiting until I arrived back from war, but we got into a stupid quarrel. I was too hotheaded—just blundered in and put the blame in the wrong place. Sadly, that allowed Khun Chang to close in. As I still love her, should I think about taking her back? But now that Khun Chang has enjoyed her, it'd be like drinking water and seeing the leeches and everything else. Making a complaint to the king would result in Wanthong being shamed in front of a law court. It wasn't her fault she was spoiled, so why let the king see? But should I think about the loss of face? Khun Chang dared do this because his money makes him arrogant. If I let things go, he'll trample over me again. I have to teach him a lesson."

He told the headman to summon everyone involved. The headman sent a deputy to fetch Thepthong. "Oh, Grandma, things have blown up. Our village has a case as big as the earth on fire."

"A fire? Servants, fetch the machetes and protect the house!" Thepthong got up and bustled about frantically.

"It's not a fire."

"Then it's robbers come to steal. Robbed ten times you don't lose everything like a fire." She sat back down and asked, "What case?"

"The case concerning Wanthong. Her husband has come. He wants to arrest people, take them to the city, and ask the king to execute them. Khun Chang, Wanthong, and Siprajan are tied up already."

"Karma, oh karma, karma! How can we to talk our way out of this? Now almost at death's door, I'm being taken to court because that lackey Khun Chang didn't listen to his mother."

She cried out to Granny Kloi and Granny Sai in a nearby house, "That damned Khun Chang has fixed you good. Khun Phaen has come back to arrest him but he's shifted the blame onto you. Khun Phaen will truss you up like sea crabs."

The two old ladies tumbled down the stairs in panic, and tottered to Thepthong's house with their sagging breasts slapping on their bellies.

Thepthong jerked her head. "Let's go and find out how bad things are. Grab some cloth to cover those droopy dugs. Hurry up now, we have to give evidence."

Seeing people swarming all over the house, the three became even more terrified. As they climbed the stairs, Khun Phaen called out, "Who's come?" Thepthong shrieked and fell down with a bump. Sai and Kloi tumbled after her. A stair rail crashed down on top of them, pinning their necks.

Thepthong called out, "Why put us in the stocks, sir? I'm ready to give evidence though I've never done it before." She raised her head and saw the stair rail. They all got up and looked around for a place to hide. When a house lizard chattered, Kloi and Sai dropped to their knees. Thepthong bumped into a roll of mattress, knocking Siprajan down flat. "Heavens, I've met a ghost!"

Siprajan cried out, "Spare me, sir!" She extricated her trembling body from the mattress. "Sir, please forgive me."

Khun Phaen furiously demanded answers. "Now, you, Wanthong's mother, when I went off to distant Chiang Thong, I entrusted my wife to you yet you gave her to Khun Chang. Perhaps you thought I had only low rank and little of any kind of property so you could act highhandedly and I wouldn't have the standing to pursue you in court. Your new son-in-law is such a big fellow, overflowing with so much property and so many elephants and horses, that you conspired together to treat me with no respect. You think I deserve to be cut to pieces like this just because I'm poor."

Siprajan's mouth went dry with fear. Her skin crawled and her lips trembled. She buried her tearful face in both hands then sat up, wiping away snot like a child. "Yes, yes, sir! Granny Kloi and Granny Sai came to sow confusion by bringing bones and saying that you were dead. They asked for her to marry Khun Chang. I was worried that I couldn't prevent Wanthong being taken as a royal widow, so I consented. For fifteen days Wanthong refused to go into the bridal house. She only gave up and went in two days ago—not time for her to be worn away *that* much. Don't hold it against her. Take her back."

Kloi and Sai could not remain silent. "No! No! Why are you saying this? It was Thepthong who asked us to come and say that you'd been stabbed in the forest. Have mercy on us. She coached us to say it, so we did."

Thepthong reeled around, beating her breast. "It was Khun Chang who told you to say it! I was completely in the dark. Please spare me."

Seeing such frantic confusion, Khun Phaen had to suppress his laughter. "It was wrong from the start. The whole of Suphan knew but you had no fear. In effect, you challenged me to take you to court. With all your money that was no worry. Why are you afraid now? Where's Khun Chang, where is he? Come out here! If you speak rashly, I'll beat you to death. But if you're good, I'll think of you as a friend."

When no answer came, Khun Phaen said, "My anger's rising up to my throat . . . "

Khun Chang called out blearily, "I'm tied up."

Siprajan pushed on the door of the room. "Why are you lying in there, you lowlife? Thepthong, let's haul him out by his ear."

The two shoved on the door but it was locked tight. Khun Phaen held his breath and blew a formula. The door opened with a click. Siprajan and Thepthong went into the room, shrieked, and collapsed, trembling. "Who brought a corpse in here?"

Khun Chang cried, "Mother, don't be scared. It's not a corpse. Help untie me."

Thepthong screamed in greater panic, "This corpse can speak like a live person!"

Siprajan cried, "And I've never seen twin corpses before."

Thepthong shouted, "A Chinaman died just this afternoon, and his dreadful wife made such a performance that she fell down dead too."

Khun Chang hissed, "It's me!"

The two old ladies leapt about frantically and fell down on their backs. Siprajan turned to take a closer look. "What's this? He doesn't have a pigtail."

Thepthong shouted, "There in the middle, that's a pigtail. How come both husband and wife died? Why haven't they been cremated? Who brought them here?"

Khun Chang shouted, "It's me!"

The two ladies jumped in fright, and started praying loudly.

Thepthong cried, "Maybe they're not corpses. The rope is tied too messily for a shroud. Surely it can't be Wanthong and Khun Chang."

Siprajan and Thepthong got down to look, and wanted to die of shame. "Did a robber strip off your clothes and tie you up?" They found a knife to cut away the ropes. The couple sprang apart. Khun Chang had only a handkerchief. He tried to hide his rear, leaving the front bare. Thepthong cried, "Tcha, cover yourself!" Khun Chang rolled over on his stomach. Wanthong covered her face in disgust.

Siprajan passed a cloth to her daughter and spoke to Khun Chang, "Just now Khun Phaen said, if you're good, he'll look on you as a friend; but if you're obstinate, he'll kill you. Go along with what he wants so the case disappears. He's got a new wife close by his side so I don't think he's upset about Wanthong. He's come here to complain that we acted highhandedly. Ask his forgiveness and I think it'll come to nothing."

Khun Phaen shouted a warning, "Why don't you come out to talk? If you're too stubborn, I'll slice you up."

Siprajan shoved Khun Chang in the side with her foot. "Get out there, you thinhead." Khun Chang shook his head. Thepthong thumped him. "You'll turn this house into a coffin, you villain."

Khun Chang pried open a chink in the wall and peered out. "Wanthong, please come out with me. He'll soften up if you come too."

"Forget it! Even if Lord Indra comes down, I'm not going. I'm happy for him to strike me dead right here."

"If you won't come, why should I go out to get killed? If we're slashed dead beside each other, we'll be born again beside each other in heaven."

Thepthong found a block of wood and bashed him in the midriff.

"Don't hit me! I'm going out." He looked around for a way to escape, and started to climb up the wall. Siprajan grabbed one foot, Thepthong the other, and they pulled him back down. His cloth slipped off but he hung onto the end.

Khun Chang picked up a betel tray and went out, raising his hands to his forehead. "Please have some betel, dear Phlai." He prostrated on Khun Phaen's lap and raised Khun Phaen's foot onto his head. "I'm so happy, Your Fragrant Excellency. They said you were dead but you've came back! Your stock of merit was enough to bring victory. Your innards are as beautiful as lotus flowers."

He lifted Khun Phaen's lowercloth, stroked his hands here and there, and then rubbed them on his own head. "As fragrant as scent!" People around shook with laughter.

Khun Phaen pushed him away and quickly drew his cloth closed. Khun Chang went on busily kissing and stroking. Thepthong and Siprajan looked away.

Khun Phaen ground his teeth in anger. "Hey, Khun Chang! What were you thinking, my friend? Wanthong here is my wife. I did not abandon her or sell her to you, yet you knocked down my house, said I was dead, turned up at the house with some bones wrapped in cloth, and dug up a bo tree so it withered. You were bent on being her husband. What were you thinking? Tell me."

The question made Khun Chang's scalp crawl. He embraced Khun Phaen with eyes and mouth closed. Khun Phaen posed the question three times. Khun Chang did not answer.

Khun Phaen's temper rose. "I'll ask Wanthong first. Why are you lying in the room hiding your face? When a guest comes, rich or poor, you should welcome him properly. Here there's no sight of any betel from dawn to dusk. Are you not coming out because you're ashamed to talk about something in front of others?"

Wanthong was so miserable that she truly found it difficult to talk. Terrified he would storm into the room, she darted forward to close the door and shoot the bolt.

Khun Phaen called out, "Do you think I can't get in there? Or are you luring me into a secret place where you'll catch me and eat my liver?"

He drew his sword and raised it aloft. Khun Chang embraced his feet, whimpering. Khun Phaen kicked him away. Khun Chang grabbed at Khun Phaen's cloth. Khun Phaen clutched at the waistband and raised his sword to strike. Thepthong cried out plaintively. Siprajan stumbled on top of Granny Kloi.

Khun Phaen bellowed, "I'll kill both man and wife! Look out for yourselves, all four or five of you! Wanthong, do you love your room so much you won't leave it? Now you're a rich lady, you're afraid your fair face will lose its luster in the wind. On the day I returned, you cut me off completely. I was still naively thinking of how we were before. I didn't know you'd ditched everything. When you cut a banana flower, it hangs on by a strand, but for you, the memory was already faded and forgotten. At the start, I believed you were a genuine ruby but you turned out to be a paste gem. A crow disguised as a swan deceived me because I didn't look at the crest beforehand. You swap heads like an actor in a mask play. If the audience likes dancing, you arrange barrel drums. If they like bawdiness, you give them bawdiness. The time you spend in rehearsal is not wasted. When I was here, nobody came to give you a job, but now that you have a new teacher, your name is mentioned everywhere. People invite you to dance and insist you dance all through the day, not taking off your headdress until nightfall. Today I came to make a booking, and go back to prepare the theatre."

He left the house, mounted his horse, and led his men through the forest back to Cockfight Hill in Kanburi.

Khun Chang took Wanthong to live in his house. She resigned herself to her fate. He provided her with every comfort and was attentive to her every need. They lived happily as husband and wife, looking after his lands and property.

KHUN PHAEN IS PARTED FROM LAOTHONG

One afternoon at the royal audience, the king commanded Phramuen Si, a head of the royal pages, "That Phlai Kaeo who won victory and was made Khun Phaen has been sent to patrol the forests. If we leave him there, he'll not get to know the work of the capital. Bring him to serve in the corps of pages. Also that Khun Chang from Suphan, the one with a bald skull like a Chinaman. Train them and see how they turn out."

On Phramuen Si's orders, a group of palace guards went to Cockfight Hill and conveyed the king's command to Khun Phaen. He promptly informed his mother. "I'm going to the city tomorrow morning to be trained on royal service. Let me leave Laothong in your care."

"Go, and don't worry about your wife. I'll look after her. Put your heart into training. If you do well, you'll get rank to show for it, and that will repay the debt of gratitude to your father. In the old days, they laid down four qualities for a king's servant: he must be gentlefolk with lineage and proper manners; he must study and gain knowledge; he must be mature enough to understand his responsibilities; and he must be quick-witted to distinguish good from bad in the course of his work. You seem to have these qualities. But don't be too sure of yourself and carelessly do something rash. Servants of the king must follow the principles laid down in ancient manuals. One, whatever capability you have, don't hide it from the king. Two, be courageous in any task and determined to bring it to its proper conclusion. Three, don't neglect any royal duty. Four, be honest and reliable, as if following the precepts. Five, adopt a modest attitude and don't stray into boastful arrogance. Six, when close to the king, do not abuse his graciousness by acting as his equal. Seven, never sit on the throne. Eight, at court pay attention to the business at hand and avoid being either too close or too distant. Nine, don't meddle with any palace woman. Ten, show love and loyalty to your royal master and never answer back. May you succeed and be raised to high noble rank!"

Khun Phaen took his mother's blessing then went to Laothong. "Why keep on crying? I'm not abandoning you. Whenever I'm free, I'll come home."

At dawn, Khun Phaen and the guards left for Suphan. When Khun Chang saw them coming, he slammed the door shut and said tremulously to Wanthong, "Khun Phaen is coming up to the house with lots of guards. I think a court case is going to flare up."

The guard cried out, "Hey, you rogue elephant! Have you gone to sleep inside there? We're calling and calling but there's no reply. We have the king's orders to fetch you."

Trembling in terror and dripping with sweat, Khun Chang called out, "I can't even sit up, my dear sir. The doctor says it's a severe fever and I'll die this afternoon. Don't bother me, I beg you."

"Just now I saw you closing the door and hiding away. If you don't come out, we're coming in to get you."

Khun Chang nudged Wanthong, "Bolt the door, my dear wife!"

Khun Phaen blew a Great Loosener formula, and the bolt slid out. The guards crowded into the bedroom. Khun Chang rolled his eyes, stuck out his neck, waggled his head to and fro, and cackled with laughter. "A spirit has possessed me! Do you know me or not, officer?"

"You clown around too much, damn you."

Khun Chang jumped up and down. "If you threaten me, you'll get what you deserve!"

Khun Phaen pretended to be scared by the spirit possessing Khun Chang. He sprang back, deliberately treading on a curtain, and ripping it in two when it fell. He barged into Wanthong, who tumbled flat on her face. Khun Chang suddenly calmed down and went to her aid.

The guard said, "So the spirit possessing you has gone already! You're to be taken for training at court. Why are you putting on this act of being possessed?"

Khun Chang calmed down. "If I'd known from the start there'd be no trouble, why would the spirit have possessed me? I'm not one little bit shy at the prospect of entering royal service."

They left immediately and cut through the forest to Ayutthaya.

They began training together every day. Khun Phaen was easy to teach but Khun Chang was quite hopeless. He crawled into audience like a field turtle. Yet after long practice he gradually became accomplished, and both went on duty together.

One day Khun Phaen and Khun Chang went to Phramuen Si's house to dine and drink liquor with Khun Phet and Khun Ram, two officers of the guard. After they had drunk enough for their eyes to glaze over, they took an oath to be loyal to one another at all times. They sat around, drunkenly shooting their mouths off, until the liquor was finished, when each went merrily home.

In Kanburi, Laothong came down with fever and was at death's door for several days. Doctors were summoned to give her medicines but to no effect. Thong Prasi made many offerings but these did no more than keep death at bay. In despair, she sent a servant to inform her son.

Khun Phaen was very concerned. He examined the horoscope carefully. "On Saturday in the morning at the time of the moon, the fever will be almost fatal but should then abate. Other omens are favorable. The manual indicates she will not die but she'll be miserable without her husband beside her. Even the treatment of ten doctors is not the same as just seeing her husband's face. As I'm on duty today, I must first find someone to take my place."

He approached Khun Chang. "My friend, a servant has come to tell me that my wife is suffering from a high fever. We're gentlemen and sworn friends. Can I ask you to take care of my duties? I'll be grateful until my dying day."

"No problem. Go off as you wish and don't be worried."

Khun Phaen rushed through the forest to Cockfight Hill. Laothong told him, "I've been at the point of death countless times but hung on patiently waiting for you. If you'd delayed your return a few more days, I'd have stopped taking those bitter medicines. Seeing your face I feel the fever has retreated even more than if Lord Indra had come to be my doctor."

Khun Phaen tended her for many days. The fever quickly disappeared and her health gradually improved. Khun Phaen pondered, "I should return to Ayutthaya tomorrow."

On that day at audience, the king asked Khun Chang, "Where's Khun Phaen? Isn't he on duty with you? This fellow usually does his work properly."

The past entered Khun Chang's thoughts like a raging fire. "Khun Phaen has a grudge against me. One day he may bring a case to take Wanthong away from me. Well, I'll have him demolished like chopped fish."

He spoke out. "My liege, I can tell no lie. We were on duty together, and I heard him moaning about his wife every day. Yesterday, he said he would go home. Your humble servant advised him against such a rash move but he just cursed me. Late at night he climbed over the palace wall. I remonstrated with him but he threatened to kill me. I think he went to his wife's house."

The king stamped his foot and bellowed, "This fellow, who turns out to fear nobody, is condemned to execution! Skewer his head on a pole as an example to others!"

But then the king had second thoughts. "He won my favor and so should be spared. But why can't he bear to be apart from his wife? Did she float down from heaven and make him forget he should be fearful? Officers of the guard, go right now and bring this Laothong away from her husband. I don't want to see Khun Phaen. He must stay in Kanburi and patrol the frontier. If there's a war, he can be called back to fight."

That same night, Khun Phaen and Laothong tasted bliss with no thought of what the future held in store. After falling asleep, Laothong dreamed that a big monster entered the room, dragged her from the pillow, put her in an iron cage, and made her suffer greatly. Her husband came after her but fell into a mountainous ravine and also faced enormous hardship. Then a man of great power came and carried both of them to safety. At the end of the dream, she woke in fright and aroused her husband to interpret it.

Khun Phaen knew that the dream meant that they would be forced apart for a long time, but he was reluctant to upset her. "This dream is neither good nor bad. Because of your fever, the elements in your body are unstable. The dream is confused and meaningless."

Khun Phaen woke as the sun rose, and lay listening to a chorus of eerie sounds. Mice clacked. House lizards chattered. Spiders beat their chests. He knew these signs foretold something unusual.

At dawn, the palace guards arrived and came towards the house with sullen faces. Khun Phaen felt as if someone had plucked the life from his body. He went out to meet them. "What business brings you here, sir? Is there a war or other trouble?"

The commander told him. "At audience, Khun Chang told the king that you had climbed out over the wall. This is a capital offense but the king has been merciful because you took Chiang Thong. You're banned from the palace, and we're under orders to take your wife away with us."

Khun Phaen felt feverishly cold. He went inside and embraced Laothong. "We're going to be parted just as if someone had cut us in two with a sword. Khun Chang has killed me this time. I feel like a bird flying in the sky that gets blown by a gale straight into a snare. My feet are trapped and I'm now squirming helplessly until death. The king is lenient with me because of my past service, but you'll be taken away. Oh, when will I see your face again?"

Laothong felt her breast had been slit open by a sharp kris. Sobs escaped from her mouth and tears flooded her eyes. "You have possessed me for less than a year. To leave you is like falling from a golden mountain and rolling along, dead and broken, bones cold as ash. Nowhere under the sun can I escape sorrow. During the waning month, I'll wane like the moon. When it waxes, my confusion and sadness will increase. Oh, what karma made this happen? You two are bent relentlessly on revenge. He'd already grabbed Wanthong, destroyed a bridal house, and stolen everything. He's like a scorpion whose curved tail shows he's never straight. Yet you were too complacent and handed him an opportunity to fulfill his desire."

"My love for you has dragged us to disaster. This is the result of some karma we've made. Do no more bad deeds, and through the merit we've made in the past, there should come a day we overcome this misfortune. If any senior noble wants you as servant, you must consent and ingratiate yourself. The palace guards are impatient to leave. Get your things ready."

They went to see his mother. Laothong wept and wept. "Since I had to leave my parents in Chomthong, I've depended on you. Your generosity has made me happy since the first day I came. When I was sick with fever, you nursed me morning and night. How can I repay your kindness? Will I ever see you again?"

Thong Prasi felt so sorry for her that sad tears streamed down in an endless torrent. "Karma is truly dragging you off. Where will I find someone like you? You absorb everything I teach you and never grumble. But now you'll disappear from every room of this house."

She counted out two hundred and fifty baht. "When it's finished, send for more."

Thong Prasi went out to speak with the guard. "Sir, please be considerate. She's only a forest Lao. If she makes a mistake, please just put her right."

"No problem. Khun Phaen and I are friends."

Laothong prostrated to take leave of her mother-in-law, then turned to her husband. "I feel sorrow for myself, sorrow for you, sorrow for the house, sorrow for your sobbing mother, sorrow for this garden and its fragrant flowers, sorrow for the servants, sorrow for us all."

Khun Phaen said sadly, "I feel sorrow for you, sorrow for our room, sorrow for the bedding and pillows where we sleep." He watched until she disappeared into the forest, then went into the room and lay weeping on the bed.

Along the way, Laothong sobbed unstoppably on the elephant's back. They reached Ayutthaya in two days and one night. Laothong was taken into the palace and presented to the king.

"So this is Khun Phaen's wife. Trim, curvy waist, attractive face, good complexion, nice chin and eyebrows, good-looking. Was it for this that Khun Phaen neglected his work and couldn't be stopped from climbing over the wall?"

He spoke out loud. "Head governess, make sure she doesn't leave the palace. Put her to work embroidering silk."

Laothong was billeted in a building beside the treasury. She sat embroidering every day and grieved for her husband morning and night. She concentrated on her work, ingratiated herself with all the palace governesses, and was intent on acting modestly and avoiding punishment.

KHUN PHAEN FORGES A SWORD

Khun Phaen started awake at midnight with an unsettled heart. He had been sleeping alone for many days and felt aroused thinking of his wife. "Khun Chang had sworn friendship yet treacherously wronged me over my wife. If I can't repay him to my satisfaction, I'd rather die. I'll go and kidnap my Wanthong. If Khun Chang comes after me, I'll kill him. The only thing I fear is that the king will send troops to slash me dead. How can I protect myself now that my spirits are old and losing their powers? I'll forge a sword, buy a horse, and find a spirit son. With these, whatever arises, I need have no fear."

In the murky light before dawn, he packed his kit in a sidebag, put thirty pieces of silver in a waist pouch, stuck a kris enchanted by a teacher in his belt, and left for the upland forests. In search of what he needed, he passed through villages of Karen, Lawa, and Mon, and slept along passes through the mountains.

In preparation for forging a sword, he collected the metals prescribed by the great manual on weaponry. Metal from the peaks of a relic stupa, a palace, and a gateway. Metal fastening for the coffin of a woman who died while with child. Metal binding from a used coffin. Fixing for a gable end. Diamond bolt. Bronze pike. Copper kris. Broken regal sword. Metal goad. Bolt from a gateway. Five-colored metal. Fluid metal. Ore cast at the Phrasaeng mine. Iron from Kamphaeng and Namphi. Gold. Bronze. Genuine silver. Forest copper.

All were collected and combined into an ingot that was heated red hot, beaten, dipped in a solution, left for three days, then beaten again—seven times over. Then on an auspicious day, the fifteenth of a month in which the first waxing fell on a Saturday, wood was cut to make an eye-level shrine, and many offerings prepared.

The metalsmiths dressed handsomely in white lower and upper cloths, made a circle of sacred thread, and waited until an auspicious time of kingly power with the sun at midday in the house of the lion. Khun Phaen worked the bellows to heat the metal bright red. The head smith shaped the sword, one cubit and one fist long, and three and a half fingers wide in the middle. The haft had the face of a chick. The blade was heated and doused three times for tempering, then filed until suddenly it became smooth and glossy, with not a single cat's hair scratch. Catching the sunlight, it flashed green like the wings of an emerald beetle.

The handle was made with victoriflora wood, inscribed with a yantra of the Buddhist wheel of the law, and filled with the hair of a fierce spirit. A sheath was made from pacifier wood, coated with glossy lacquer, and decorated top and bottom with one baht weight of gold.

Khun Phaen picked up the sword and brandished it. The heavens darkened and swirled, bursting in echoing bolts of thunder. Khun Phaen listened, his heart surging to have the good omen of thunder like a gunshot. He named the sword Skystorm.

He placed it on the center of the shrine and intoned a prayer. The sword showed its power by jiggling about. He poured out fifteen pieces of silver for the head smith. "Your craft is supreme." Catching sight of a tree three fists wide, he slashed it to the ground as if it were a banana flower.

He traveled a long time in search of spirits until he came upon the grave of a dead woman. He chanted a mantra and put himself in a trance. The earth trembled and split apart, and the woman's spirit rose through. She had disheveled hair, a lolling tongue, and sunken eyes. Her body spiraled upwards until her huge head towered over him. From a mouth as hollow as a cave, she shrieked in his face, then collapsed to the ground, and asked, "Sir, what revenge do you seek? Do you desire anything from me? I pay respect at your feet."

Khun Phaen replied, "I want the child from your womb according to the manual." He pierced her belly with a chisel and took the child.

He went to another graveyard and found a long oblong burial pit. He put a fresh egg in a leaf basket and chanted mantras to summon the female spirit up into the air. She had hollow eyes, a huge glistening head, sunken chest, short neck, white teeth, long hair, and flashing eyes. Her bloated belly was split open to reveal the intestines. Lolling a tongue as long as a tall tree, she peered at him from sunken eyes and growled, "Why do you come to this graveyard?"

Khun Phaen hurled rice and chanted mantras. "I want to take the child in your womb. I want to raise it according to the manual."

Overwhelmed by the mantras, the spirit fell to the ground, pulled open her belly, took out the child, and offered it to Khun Phaen. The child wailed. Khun Phaen plucked the mother's hair by mantra, cut her tongue, and took the infant as his personal spirit, Goldchild.

Searching further, he found graves in the forest, strung a sacred thread around them, placed liquor, rice, and fish as offerings, stood on one foot, held his hands in wai, and chanted mantras. Spirits from bad deaths rose up through the earth and ran around shouting loudly, poking their tongues, rolling their eyes, and transforming themselves into tigers, elephants, or cobras as large as sugar palm trees. They swarmed inside the ring of sacred thread to feast on the food and liquor. Khun Phaen pronounced mantras and scattered rice at them. They prostrated before him, shaking with fear, and asked, "What is your desire?"

"I wish to make use of your services as warriors. In return I'll feed you with liquor, rice, duck, and chicken."

The spirits laughed happily. Khun Phaen cut all their tongues and hastened home.

Khun Phaen prostrated to his mother. "May I request a hundred and fifty baht to purchase a brave and powerful horse."

Thong Prasi understood that her son would not listen to any opposition. She counted out the money, ordered the servants to prepare supplies, and deputed ten of them to accompany him. Each found a sword or pike and waited for the master. Thong Prasi gave her son a blessing.

They traveled far to the north and far to the east. He saw over one thousand two hundred horses but none matched what he wanted. He looked all over Ayutthaya, the surrounding region, and all the provincial centers, without success.

Eventually he came to Phetburi. In a group of horses being delivered to the king, Khun Phaen saw a foal acting boisterously and knew that he had found what he wanted. The horse was spry and nimble. His features matched the manual completely, as if he were a gift from Lord Indra. Khun Phaen promptly approached the leader of the party, Luang Songphon.

"Is this grey colt yours? Do you want to sell him?"

"That horse, Color of Mist, over there? He's not one of the king's horses under our care."

Luang Songphon told Khun Phaen that he had waited in Mergui for over half a year for the season of the wind to bring horses purchased for the king from lands to the west. A bay, who was said to have mated with a water horse, saw the royal horses crossing a river and tagged along. The bay had a foal called Color of Mist, born on Saturday, the ninth day of a waxing moon, with black eyes and a formidable presence. When they reached Cha-am, the foal bit one of the foreign horses. Luang Songphon angrily ordered his men to chase the foal away, but Color of Mist kept returning to his mother.

"We're fed up with him. If you want to buy him, I'll drop the price. You can take him for seventy-five baht."

Khun Phaen counted out the money at once, and walked towards the colt, proffering some grass he had enchanted with a formula. Once

Color of Mist had chewed and swallowed the grass, he became loyally attached to Khun Phaen.

Khun Phaen stroked his back and put on a saddle, bridle, bit, and pretty crupper, all brand new with attractive gold trimming. After three days travel through the forest, they reached Cockfight Hill just as the sun disappeared behind the hills. He ordered servants to make a stable for the horse, feed him grass, and set a bonfire at the door to ward off mosquitoes.

Khun Phaen was happy at his accomplishment. "I can now think of taking revenge on Khun Chang. I'll seize Wanthong and take her away into the forest. With Goldchild, my beloved son of sacred power, I have a spirit of expert capabilities. With Color of Mist, this exceptional horse, even if I have to flee, none can give chase. And with Skystorm, a sword as sharp and shiny as a diamond, I can sever seven necks in one stroke. Even if an army of five thousand were raised to pursue me, they'd be slashed down into dust."

KHUN PHAEN ENTERS
KHUN CHANG'S HOUSE

Losing Laothong left Khun Phaen gloomy. None of the many young women in his service interested him. He pined for her. He slept alone and lonely through each season of the year. In the hot season, his heart burned like fire. In the rainy season, he grumbled like the sky. In the windy season, a draught blew through his heart, and swaddling himself in a shawl still left him soulful. Not seeing her fair face for over a year made him fret in frustration.

"Dear heart, I'm not used to being apart. I pity the room left chilly without you, the bed and pillows now somber and sad, the lamp languishing unlit, powders and perfumes unused, mirrors cracked or closed, mosquito net frayed and fallen, oil that has lost the fragrance that used to scent your clothes. My heart aches as if pierced with a poisoned arrow."

Too fretful to slip back to sleep, he parted the net and went to look outside. Hearing a coel's clear call, he pulled open the door, but she was not there, only a dipping moon, shining so dazzlingly bright he felt even more wistful. A cool wind rustled banyan leaves, bathed in a chilly dew. "Sadly, you're far away from my sight, though this dew reminds me of your trickling tears. Late at night, you'll lament.

From morning to evening, you'll mourn. Oh, what store of karma made these troubles arise? A friend could do such wrong to a friend. There's a saying: With someone crooked, oppose him in every way, with someone honest, be honest till your dying day. This bad fellow broke the rules of friendship. If I'm condemned to punishment, that's karma. Tomorrow I'll go to Suphan, split open his chest for revenge, and take Wanthong away into the forest."

By first light, he had arranged everything, and went to see his mother. Thong Prasi was pounding betel. She stopped with pestle raised, and looked up. "Where are you going so strangely early in the morning?" Her heart shivered with trepidation.

"I've been mournful for so long I can't stand it any more. I'll take Wanthong off into the forest. If Khun Chang follows, I'll slash him dead."

Thong Prasi tried to calm him down. "I hate him too but aren't there any other women in this town? If she were worth running after, then you should do it, but Wanthong is beautiful in body, not in mind. She's ruined. A diamond broken into two or three pieces never regains its beauty. I warn you that you'll only get hurt."

"If you want to call her bad, then she's bad through and through. But I've thought it over. The day I reached Suphan, her jealousy was proof that she hadn't deserted me. I made the mistake of accusing her, of trying to hurt her, and walking away in anger. She felt so bad that she tried to hang herself. She was still in love with me, still true to how we were. Saithong pointed all this out to me but I wasn't thinking. While I had Laothong sleeping in my room, I forgot Wanthong completely, but then Khun Chang treacherously had me separated from Laothong. Mother, please give me your blessing. I'll succeed, don't you worry. Even if they raise an army of three thousand to chase me down, I'll slash them into dust."

Seeing that opposition was pointless, Thong Prasi gave him a blessing. "May your mastery and martial powers be sufficient for success in your aims. When you find Wanthong, may her heart agree to go with you. Don't be fooled by wiles, or misled by love. Reap success and return to this house."

Khun Phaen went to a prayer room to make offerings of candles and incense. He ground sandal on a stone, and mixed it with oil to anoint himself so anyone seeing his body would be charmed. He put on inner britches of purple with a bird pattern, a lowercloth with bright golden cross-branch design, a short inner shirt with yantra designs, and an outer shirt with floral patterns embroidered in gold. He tied a sash round his waist fixed with a medallion, and put on a plaited ring, a breast chain with amulets interleaved with the hair of spirits, and a bandeau round his forehead. Finding the conjunction of great success he needed, he stood holding Skystorm aloft, and turned away from the direction of the Great Spirit and the Lord of Darkness. Descending the stairway, he mounted Color of Mist and summoned all his spirits. With them following rowdily behind, he left Kanburi and entered the forest.

They crossed Crocodile Stream, slipped by the shimmering pond of Ban Phlap, and arrived at Khun Chang's house. He cut wood to build a shrine, lit candles and incense, summoned up powerful deities, and concentrated his mind to make a prayer. "May the gods be my witness. Grant me the power to destroy Khun Chang, this bad friend, who snatched my wife away for his own pleasure. If I have ever disloyally caused calamity for a friend, do not let me succeed in this endeavor."

He checked the direction his breath flowed easily then urged his horse ahead. Coming to a bank and moat with guards sitting by fires he reined in Color of Mist to take his bearings.

Khun Chang's five female spirits were patrolling the boundary. "Enemy! Let's have fun chasing him away." They soared through the air, bellowing, scattering sand and earth, dangling their heads, twisting their bodies to and fro, lolling their tongues, and pulling fearsome faces. Khun Phaen's spirits responded by swooping at them, hurling rocks and lashing out with nettle vines. The two sides were well matched and the battle was fierce.

Khun Phaen flung herb-coated rice that hurt like hard gravel. The five spirits jeered, and hid themselves to consider the situation. They could see he was young, handsome, and obviously well versed in lore, so they transformed their bodies into lady attendants of the palace and walked out to meet him, flirting, making eyes, touching him and then acting scared. One cocked her head, peered out of the corner of her eye, and asked, "Why are you standing here, blocking the way?"

Khun Phaen knew they were spirits transformed. He stood smiling at them and said, "I'm not a villain or thief. I have business here, and I've run into you by chance. I was feeling upset but I'm a lot better since you came to greet me. Still, love will have to wait a while. I'm Wanthong's husband. Khun Chang took her away. Without her, I've been lovesick and miserable. Now that I've met you five lovely ladies, please help me by opening the door. I'll be grateful to the end of my days." He blew a mantra onto betelnut and invited them, "Come and have a mouthful each."

The spirit ladies hid their faces with coy smiles. One answered, "Khun Chang looks after us. You shouldn't come sweet-talking us to help you. It's trickery, and it won't do. He feeds us well, and we should repay his kindness. You don't love us. You've got crowds of spirits of your own. Yet the first thing you mention is love, and your mantra went extremely deep."

"Now, now. Don't sulk. If you were human I'd take care of you truly well. But as to love, what can I do? I could enjoy only your false bodies. If you'd return to true human form, I'd pleasure you to the full. But now please show me the way to Wanthong."

He scattered more rice, driving the spirits away, chanted a Subduer mantra to send people to sleep, sprung all the locks and bolts, and urged Color of Mist ahead.

All the sentries guarding the house nodded off and lay motionless. Axmen hit the ground already asleep and snoring. People cooking rice and grilling fish dozed off, heads drooping, eyes closed, and mouths mumbling. A fellow who had been chopping ganja nodded off with one hand wiping the sleep from his eyes. Another napped with his head flung backwards while a rice pot boiled over. A drinker waved his cup drunkenly and lowed like a buffalo.

Khun Phaen crossed another moat. "That fine house must be his cousin Sonphraya's, and this must be the house of that toasted turtle with the smooth bald skull. He has some lovely lush plants with beautiful blooms. Tomorrow morning, he'll lie hugging only a pillow and groaning in misery."

When he intoned a mantra, and scattered enchanted rice over the roof, the guardian spirits of the house swarmed out and fled. When he threw limes over the house, all the bolts and locks sprang open.

He climbed up the wall and leapt down onto a terrace tiered with flowers planted by Khun Chang. Even past midnight, the fragrance of pollen wafting on the wind was fresh and pleasing. Gem jasmine, damascene, milkwood, lightleaf, orangegold, and angelbreast were neatly trimmed and artfully arranged. Jasmine, rose, and hiddenlover lured him on with sensuous scents, while a waitinglady stayed him to stare in admiration. Past the pots he found a basin with goldfish slip-sliding along in pairs like loving couples, wheeling around and waving their tails sublimely. Beyond he came upon a yoke, plough, animal bells, coils of rope, horse harness, and elephant equipment.

Peering through a doorway, he saw a slender body sleeping silently, looking lovely, lissome, and fresh. Her eyebrows were fine and softly bowed, her hairline neat and pleasingly shaped. Hair fell loosely down over her shoulders, curling up prettily around her face. The room was neatly arranged with screens, tables, spittoon, bowl, and cup as petite and pretty as their owner's figure.

"This isn't Wanthong. Maybe a sister but I doubt it. Her manner is not that of a poor person. Is she a minor wife of Khun Chang? But why hasn't he put her in a room worthy of her status?"

He examined her face, finding it fair and lovable. "If a man had enjoyed her, she'd have lost that sheen." He stole in close, touched her breast, and chanted a love mantra to excite her.

Kaeo Kiriya started awake in surprise. She slid down from the bed and hid behind a screen, nervously thinking what to do. "Sir, who invited you to stray in here? Your slight figure and fine bearing are not those of a ruffian."

"I'm a skilled soldier. The king bestowed on me the name of Khun Phaen. I came to find Wanthong. I thought you were her so I've already been kissing and caressing you all over. Please excuse me. Don't shyly turn your face away. Tell me honestly what brought you to Khun Chang's house?"

Kaeo Kiriya stayed still and thought, "His slender, slight figure is very lovable. How come Wanthong did not stay with him? He's gained great powers from a good teacher. Khun Chang would be no match. He's walking around all the rooms here at will! If I don't answer his question, he might turn nasty. Fighting him or fleeing away would be as futile as flinging money into the wind."

She said, "This is laughable. You get the wrong person and the wrong room. And now you try to flatter me so contemptuously. I'm not Wanthong. My father is the governor of Sukhothai, an old friend of Khun Chang. He mortgaged me into service here for seventy-five baht because he faced jail for failing to deliver revenue from fines to the treasury. My name is Kaeo Kiriya. You're a freeman. Don't consider consorting with a slave. I shouldn't be so bold as to sit on the same level. Please go and take your revenge in the manner of gentlefolk."

"I feel sorry for you not having a lover yet. Any man who could possess you would hold on tight. I'm after love, not a one-night affair. Only seventy-five baht! I can redeem you, even if it were four hundred. Some merit I made in the past has caused me to meet you by chance."

He snuggled close to her and took out a packet of money to give her. "Heart's delight, don't shy away from me."

Kaeo Kiriya pushed him away to forestall his fondling. "I raise my hands above my head in gratitude for your goodness. But I still think of my father's words of warning: love your back and beware the lash. If you love me truly, please speak to my father in the proper way. I won't give in so don't plead."

"Your skin is as fresh and fragrant as cinnamon. I pledge my love to you, Kaeo Kiriya. Should I deceive you by breaking my word, let me suffer endless misfortune, and let all my fine learning go to waste. Your skin glistens as if gilded with gold."

He took off his belt with all its gear, and hung it over a screen. Lifting her up in his arms, he held her, breast to breast, then laid her down, and covered her gently like a nugget of gold. A breeze blew through blossoms, strewing their pollen and bathing the room with fragrance. The end of her embroidered uppercloth rippled in the wind. A shimmering moon bounded into the sky. Stars sparkling alongside were snuffed out. Flickering fireflies frisked among the trees. The tread of tramping beetles made tall trees tremble.

Kaeo Kiriya clung to him, weak with rapture, softly sobbing and sighing. "I resent the way you force yourself on me. Now you'll leave and steal Wanthong away into the forest, while I'll be counting the nights sadly waiting for your return. Khun Chang will take it out on me. You came to find her not me, yet you leave me tainted and in turmoil."

"I won't forget what's happened. There'll be a time I'll return to couple happily again and chase away your sorrow. Cheer up, and please make plans to recover your freedom."

He hugged her, wiped away her tears, took off a diamond ring, and slipped it on her finger. "Please help me by pointing the way to Wanthong."

"Go straight that way, past two partitions, and into the inner room. The house is lit with lanterns and there are people everywhere. Please give up your plan and don't go at all. If you get caught, you'll die, and I'll wish to die along with you."

"Don't worry, Kaeo Kiriya. Close your room tight, put out the light, and stay still." He crept away, peering ahead for Wanthong's room. Kaeo Kiriya could not stop herself running after him. "You'll soon forget me for sure. Pass the hall and then enter. It's right *there*." ·

"Don't make so much noise. I can find the way." He led her back into the room and soothed her to sleep on her little bed. "Though the sweat trickled down, you still don't slumber."

Holding Skystorm, he walked up to the central hall, newly built by Khun Chang. A sitting area was furnished with folding screens, a hill myna in a fine golden cage, and a framed portrait of a Westerner in profile. He entered a room full of glittering crystal, screens, curtains, and blinds.

"This curtain is Wanthong's handiwork. Her silk embroidery is very precise. Such workmanship can be hers alone."

She had embroidered the Himaphan Forest in all its grandeur with Mount Meru surrounded by seven mountain ranges, Mujalin Lake with all its five streams, and throngs of birds, animals, and celestial creatures. As he admired the scene, he thought of Wanthong—and slashed the curtain to ribbons.

Stepping through into a second partition, he found another curtain. "Exquisite! Your skill is superhuman."

She had embroidered the story of the handsome prince, Phra Lo, enjoying the love of two princesses. "Your efforts aren't wasted, Wanthong, but why did you get lost in lust with Khun Chang?" In rage, he cut down the curtain, ripped it to shreds, and tossed it aside.

He found a third curtain. "Beautiful!" She had embroidered the story of Khawi killing fierce eagles and winning the love of the beautiful Jansuda who was then lured away by the rich ruler of a neighboring city. The story inflamed his rage.

"It's like Khun Chang seizing Wanthong from me. That lord would have no difficulty getting ten thousand women. Khun Chang is a rich man too—loaded." He raised Skystorm and slashed the curtain into shreds. Cutting the mosquito net away from the bed, he saw Khun Chang's stout form lying with his arms around Wanthong.

"Lay bare his neck. I'll slice it to pieces!"

Goldchild intercepted the sword, and then prostrated in apology. Khun Phaen kicked Goldchild off the bed, but the spirit came between them and would not yield. "Hold off! Cool down. Don't kill him, Father. Don't you fear the power of the king?"

"No! I don't. The wrong Khun Chang did me deserves a response this dire. If I kill him secretly who'll catch me?"

"Don't kill him, just make him so hurt and ashamed that blood flows from his eyes. If you slash him dead, the gods may ensure you're arrested."

Khun Phaen calmed down and looked at Wanthong. "You black woman, you feel even less shame for your own body than there's dirt under your fingernails. Is he a good match for your figure? Now you're enthralled by him, you don't look at his head. With a new pleasure, you forget me. I look at your cheeks but they've lost their sheen. I gaze at your breasts but they're flabby. You've lost your old beauty. I can't stand this any more!"

He raised his sword but Goldchild jumped forward, seized the sword, and would not let go. Khun Phaen hurled the weapon away in anger.

"Oh my Wanthong! I didn't think it could come to this—that you could sacrifice your rank and your dignity, like a jewel ending up with a monkey. I'd like to slice your body into a hundred pieces and feed them to crows and vultures in the hills. I'll enjoy slashing Khun Chang too. And Siprajan—all this happened because she looked down on me."

He grabbed Khun Chang's head, combed his straggly hair upwards into a topknot, tied it with cotton, and plucked a track two fingers wide round the base with tweezers. "Damn you, your empty skull makes fleas go hungry." With soot he drew a fish on Khun Chang's skull, a turtle on his neck, and a catfish poking out of the water on one thigh. Standing back, he laughed at his handiwork, then kicked Chang off the bed face down in a heap on the floor and found two pots to tie round his neck.

He sat on the bed beside Wanthong and stroked her softly. "My hand alone should feel your soft flesh this way. I alone should love and cherish you this gently, and touch you with my palms like pressing gold leaf. It's pitiful that your flesh and breasts are sad and wasted. That evil monkey, drunk on riches, has squeezed you sore already."

He drove off his spirits and chanted a mantra to revive her. "Wake up and take a peek at your husband."

Wanthong started awake, and cuddled up to what she thought was Khun Chang. "Let me tell you my horrible nightmare. You built a fire in the mosquito net. The curtain, pillows, and mattress went up in flames, and I was blistered in several places. Please tell me what this dream means."

"This is a good dream, eye's jewel. The burning of the mattress, pillows, and curtain means someone else will bring these things to you. As for feeling upset, it means you'll hate some bad, besotted person. Dreaming you cried out means something loved and lost will return."

Wanthong did not recognize the voice. She felt the smoothness of his chest and the slimness of his waist. "Is Khun Chang this slim? I can't even get my hand round his wrist." In alarm, she groped around, found Khun Chang on the floor, and desperately tried to shake him awake.

Khun Phaen said, "Wanthong, my love, open your eyes and look what's happening. I'm not some bandit so don't jump up and start shouting. Leave him be. You're shaking a sleeping person awake while making a waking one feel unwelcome. It's a pity, I can remember every inch of your face and body but to you I'm a stranger. You feel me with your hands but you have no inkling. You've found yourself a rich husband and forgotten the old house and a poor friend. You fell for the ploys of this pestering Khun Chang, and now you're hugging a log that looks like a person. Go on, wake him up so he can knock me down dead."

Wanthong's heart lurched. "This can only be Khun Phaen. He's so sure of himself and fears nobody. With his powers, he'll create havoc. Stay still and think! What will be will be, according to karma. He may trample me to pieces but I'm not afraid."

She batted over a betel tray and got up with tears in her eyes. "That's enough! You're true to your word in everything—but in reality, never in full measure. You can even spit saliva out of your mouth and swallow it back again. You're *really* good."

"So sharp and so eloquent. Don't stop. Today let's hear each other out. You make lots of insinuations, and you're very self-righteous, but when it comes to keeping one's word, it's you who gives short change. You broke your promise first so I've come after you to balance the account. As soon as you had Khun Chang, you weighed matters up and became very, very light with the truth. How many days has he been allowed to enjoy you in my place? Aren't you sated and satisfied yet? Does he still make you shake, shudder, swelter, and swoon?"

"Say what you like, I'm not afraid. It all comes down to calling me bad, over and over and over again. You're the one who's so self-righteous. Only recently you came after me with a raised stick and a clenched fist. You told that woman to slap me with no respect. I tried to stop Khun Chang making love to me. He's ugly and it was shameful. But my mother forced me into the bridal house so Khun Chang had the opportunity to do the damage. When I've been through this much, don't you come back and carp at me. I'm spoiled because you didn't care. If you'd had some mercy, nothing would have happened. When things are going your way, you soar. You get a good new wife and have no complaints. All lovey dovey. Now Laothong has left you, hasn't she? That's why you blunder up here in a blaze in the night. Starved for water, are you turning to drink mud?"

"So eloquent and so self-righteous! You don't want me to say anything—just stay at home with my eyes closed like an idiot while you do as you will. Just who did I call to slap you, as you say? You were in such a black fury with Laothong that you insulted her to her face. Who wouldn't take offense? Because I had mercy, I didn't slash you dead. I was angry with you, yes, but I didn't break it off. Two nights later, I came to the house and found this wild elephant all over you in bed. If I'd used my kris, by now you'd be ash. Though I was angry, I still loved and missed you so I forgave you. I'm still wavering and thinking of our love but you're twisting everything to blame me. Because your lover pleases you, you invent anything to stab me and sow dissension. In the past you said that you'd rather die than let another man touch you, that you'd keep your love only for me. Why do you now let this fellow feel and fondle you? You even want to rouse him to kill me. Where are his pike and sword? Bring them in! But wait a bit. If he opens his eyes to see me kissing you, then I'll die easily, topped at the neck. It's not every day that a good man dies. In olden times, they said women had three hundred wiles, and they weren't making it up."

Wanthong tossed her head and said, "So, you don't remember your own words. On the day of the quarrel with Laothong, you roared and bellowed on and on, and even threatened to slash me dead. I was so angry I went to hang myself. When Saithong told you about that, you cursed and took Laothong off on your elephant. I'm sleeping with Khun Chang, it's true. But I put up a huge fight first. If my husband had protected me, who could have done this to me? You just cast your net and take whatever fish is in front of the trap—and you have the nerve to say *I* don't keep my word. You're ashamed you made the mistake of becoming my husband. You were as blinded by smut as if you'd fallen into a pit. Because you were dosed with a love potion and mated with a bad woman, it detracts from your manliness. When you lived with me, your complexion turned dark and blotchy as if affected by something in my body. But since you went with Laothong, your skin glistens as if tinged with gold. So why flip-flop back to philander here? It's not right for you to eat leftovers. Don't keep circling round and round. I release you like I'd free a bird. If you want money, I'll give it you. Or is it losing Laothong that's making you gloomy? I'll find a squeeze to cheer you up. Would you prefer a Thai or a Lao? Should the young lady have a chignon or a topknot?"

"Bang! Bang! Full of hidden meanings. As if nobody knew what's behind it. You think I'm poor and penniless so you can just mock and tease me. I have nothing—no gifts to bring you, no means of support. Your husband is a real aristocrat with heaps of money to give whenever you wish. You want to foist some other woman on me so you can cuddle Khun Chang in comfort. Don't bother thinking that I'll give you up. Even a lady from heaven won't make me waver. My love is still sincere and hasn't faded. If I can't have you alive then I'll have you dead. Though you're spoiled and fallen now, I don't care. It's almost dawn and time to go. If you won't come, I'll cut you in two."

"Why are you bullying me? I'm spoiled and fallen because he forced me. I squirmed and screamed enough to break the house apart. I got up to flee but he dragged me back. I ran into my mother, who beat me over and over. Because I'm a woman, I was cornered. Strike me down, I'm not afraid. Whatever I say you don't believe me, so why should I bother to live and put up with this? Don't grind your teeth and growl for nothing. Do it!"

"Are you really so stubborn? Today I'm not listening to you say you won't come." He pulled her over and drew his sword as if to cut her dead, but then he blew a love mantra onto her face. "Don't underestimate me. Quickly. We're in a hurry."

The mantra made Wanthong feel drowsy and the sword made her heart skitter in fright. She stopped struggling. "I'll fetch some things—rings, money, cloth. Why raise your sword to kill me? I'll leave quietly so let go of my hands."

"No more sounding off and waving your hands around? Good. Go and pick out some clothes and come back here." He blew a mantra onto his hands and stroked her back. "I love you, really I do. I teased you only because I was angry."

She walked into another room, unlocked chests, and picked out cloth, rings, and other jewelry. She bundled everything into a little basket, and walked over near Khun Chang's sleeping form. As the mantra was weakening, she began to feel regret.

"Leaving you, I feel like a kite that's lost its wind. Don't wait expecting me still to be alive. How can you sleep and abandon your wife? How can I let you know that Khun Phaen suddenly turned up and would have chopped off my head if I hadn't gone—that I didn't run away because I'm unfaithful?"

She wrote a letter relating everything and fastened it to the wall of the room. She tried again to shake him awake. "Are you under the control of bad spirits? I'll make offerings to them of turtle salad, fish salad, duck, chicken, strong liquor, and sweets. Please let my husband wake up."

One spirit listened with her mouth watering, ravening for duck and chicken. Goldchild called out in a fearful, forbidding tone, "Don't even think about it. I'll lop off your head right now." The spirit knew to fear Goldchild.

Wanthong hugged Khun Chang but he did not respond. "Oh my lord, your merit has really run out." With her heart trembling in fear, she blacked out and fell unconscious.

KHUN PHAEN FLEES WITH WANTHONG

Khun Phaen grew impatient waiting for Wanthong's return. He went into the inner room and found her crying and still groggy from fainting. He enchanted water with a mantra and sprayed it on her face. "Why have you taken so long to pick out your clothes?"

"The back-basket has gone missing, and the hairpins too."

"Don't waste time over them. I'll carve you a hundred."

"Do you think I don't want to leave?" She tossed her head in annoyance and stood up. "Let's go. Run quickly and I'll follow."

"Oh love, I'm not used to this wooden floor. I'm afraid I'll get a splinter or trip over a bowl and be stuck with the shards."

"Why are you so angry, my lord?" She quickly left the bedroom, not raising her face, and walked to Kaeo Kiriya's room. "I say goodbye, dear Kaeo. Look after Khun Chang and console him."

She came to the cages with a pair of hill mynas and a lory. "Your sweet songs lifted my spirits. Oh myna, you mimicked Khun Chang calling me 'Mistress Wanthong,' but now I won't hear you morning or night."

On the terrace she stopped and turned to look back at the house with pangs of regret. She walked to the fish pond, leaned over and slid in her hand to feel the smooth, round, sculpted shapes of the fish as they wheeled and whirled. She glanced her eyes over the pot plants, paired in couples with pretty blooms.

"I say farewell, my fragrant sandalwoods. Stay and flourish, double jasmine and hiddenlover. Oh *lamduan*, I lament having to hurry away. Dear *jampi*, till I see you, how many years? Oh fragrant friends, your flooding scent will sadly lift and fade. Oh flowering friends, your blooms will wither, wilt, and fall. I leave this house to live in a forest where mosquitoes and midges will swarm over me. Tree roots will replace my pillows, and I'll sleep pitifully. The stars will serve as torches, and I'll despair." She descended the stairs streaming tears as if about to die.

Khun Phaen consoled her, "Don't cry. Be my companion in the forest for a month, then I'll bring you back here, and come to fetch you again a month later. With him, you can relish a house, and with me, revel in the forest. You can take turns at being rich and being poor, and find out which is best."

"Oh shut up! I'll go anywhere with you for the long term. Taking me away then bringing me back would bring shame and misery. I won't go, won't go!"

"Can't I tease just a little? Why are you so touchy, Wanthong? I love you and will take you to enjoy. Don't imagine I'd really give you back to anyone."

He led her to the horse, put his arm around her soothingly, and whispered, "This is Color of Mist. Please beg his pardon so he won't feel offended."

Wanthong was too frightened to go close to the horse but raised her hands in wai. "Oh Color of Mist, please allow both of us to ride you."

Khun Phaen stroked the horse's back and gently took Wanthong's hand to pat him. Color of Mist licked the hand, making her squeal in fright.

He gathered her up in his arms and helped her mount. Once in the saddle, Wanthong fearfully clung on tight to Khun Phaen.

"That's nice and close. Give me a little kiss and we'll be off."

With her arms around Khun Phaen, Wanthong's sadness gradually slipped away. They sped across the plain until they were clear of Suphan and Khun Phaen reined the horse to a trot. Reaching the river at Ban Phlap, he worried about crossing at night because of crocodiles but remembered there was a ferry close by. He rode down to the landing and shouted in an intimidating voice, "We're here on orders from the king to investigate whether a herd of elephants has come to the saltlick. Fetch us across without delay!"

Matho Thabom, the ferryman, started awake. "Who's shouting? My boat's stuck in the mud. Maybe it hit a stump and is leaking."

"Get a move on. I'm on royal orders."

Catching the part about a royal order, Matho Thabom stirred himself. He took off all his clothes, waded round to the stern of the boat, and heaved, spattering mud up to his shoulder blades. He got into the boat and began paddling. Seeing a horse and two people at the landing, he levered himself up clumsily. "Is he fooling me? Looks like he's kidnapped a palace lady and spun a tale to get me to bring the boat."

Wanthong shyly shut her eyes. "Oh! Look, this fellow goes too far!"

He had the paddle raised high and his feet placed wide apart. Khun Phaen cried, "Put a cloth on first, boatman! And wash off the mud before you come up here."

Matho Thabom glanced down at his belly. "Who took my cloth?" He sank down on his heels, covered himself with one hand, and groped around for a cloth. "I think you're fooling me. You've kidnapped one of the king's ladies."

Khun Phaen knew that delay would bring disaster. He chanted a formula, leapt down from the horse, and blew it on the boatman's face. From his little finger, he took a ring with a lustrous pearl. "It's nearly sunrise. Please take us across quickly and I'll reward you for your trouble."

Matho Thabom's mouth fell open. He cupped his hands to receive the beautiful ring and quickly wrapped it in a cloth. "I'll sell this to redeem a slave I can hug in bed. I'm in love with Khlai at the end of the village, and Phon with the dangling breasts, the wife of Phan Son. Come along quick. Before long the sun will be up. You must get clear of the village. Once people wake up there'll be trouble, and you'll be the death of me too."

Khun Phaen and Wanthong sat side by side on the central seat. He picked up the reins. "I'm sorry, Color of Mist, you have to swim. We're greatly indebted to you for carrying us at night through the wild forest. I'll take care of you as well as I can, my hardworking friend."

Reaching the other ferry landing, he lifted Wanthong up onto the horse, held her to make sure she would not fall, then dug his heels into Color of Mist, who set off at a thundering gallop. They went like a streak until they reached Ban Yung Thalai.

He scraped a tree trunk with his sword and wrote on it with charcoal: "If that shiny-head follows me, he'll meet disaster. Let them all come. I'll slash them dead with this sword, split open their chests, and chop them into chunks. I'm not afraid of a court case. When they're dead, what can they do? I'll make his three miserable cousins feel a ghost scraping down the nape of their necks. I'll hug Wanthong with my left hand while I slash them to pieces with my right."

He drew Skystorm and wildly slashed and stabbed. His elbow hit the chest of Wanthong who cried out and doubled over. He hugged her. "Oh karma! I'm sorry. I truly was carried away." They mounted and set off.

At Phra Hill he pointed out to her, "From here, Venus looks like a firefly." Peeping through the mist, a red-tinged moon shone on splendid sprays of flowers. A patter of pollen softly suffused the air. He pulled down a branch, picked a posy, put it behind her ear, and gaily inhaled the scent.

"Let me savor the flower. Don't stop me. Just a little taste."

"Hey! Don't touch. My things will bruise."

"I'm touching very softly, just enough to drive away the weariness of the night. I'm never rough. That's an old bruise you got in a row."

"Oh, what's this? Even now, you're making fun of me."

A loud cockcrow announced the approaching dawn. The shrill of cicadas and drone of crickets rang through the forest. A gibbon, hanging from a branch, whooped plaintively at seeing the light of the sun, tinged red like dripping blood. At the sight of people, she swung away, followed by her young, worried their mother was abandoning them.

By the bank of a pond, Khun Phaen saw a lone adjutant stork, wading and bobbing its head. He whispered to her, "What's this? Khun Chang has chased us down already. Look!"

Wanthong's heart skipped a beat. She peered around for a moment but saw only a stork catching crabs.

"Oh, it's a bird, Wanthong. From a distance I thought it was your husband, but now we're close I can see it's a stork. Why has it got no hair on its head? There are people with heads like that too. Why do such birds cruise around catching nice fresh prawns? What if he really had come? If he got too close, I'd hand you back to him. If he sued me in court, I'd give evidence that I didn't take his wife by force but she raced after my horse, begging to come along, so I took pity on her, and let her mount and ride. Next thing, she was begging to sleep with me but I didn't agree to lovemaking."

"Oh right! I'm a bad person. I leave the husband I hate, and run off with the lover I love. You notice only that great adjutant stork, but further on, don't you see that mound with another bird? Is that Laothong following us? Somewhere I heard she went into the palace. You can't have her anymore. That's why you came after me. Oh, are you annoyed? Let me down from the horse. I'm not going."

"Hey! Do you want to jump off? So brave! Aren't you afraid you'll lose your way? Don't give up, my jewel. Now that we've come here together, my love for you has returned. Besides, who would believe me saying such things? When has a rich man's wife ever come like that? If I lost the case, that'd be normal. Whether we live or die is down to fate." He hugged her, kissed her, and stroked her back lovingly. "Calm down. I love you. Don't be angry."

Wanthong scratched, pinched, and squirmed. "Stop making love to me. It's not a fee for the horse ride. You're all sweet talk and playing around. Take your arms off me. I won't fall from the horse."

"You seemed scared before so I was protecting you, but now you're an expert rider, are you?"

He dug in his heels and Color of Mist galloped off, wind whooshing out of his ears. Wanthong clung on tight. "Lightning strike! I'll fall off and die. Please rein him in!"

"I thought you said you weren't afraid of falling off. How come you're hugging me so tight now that you'll leave a mark? We've reached a place to stop and rest."

They had come to Banyan Landing. Pools brimmed with crystal clear water. A stream poured over rapids in a torrent. Overhanging cliffs soared above. Lovely lotus flowers, peeping from behind leaves, loosed their scent into the stream. A thicket of tall trees screened the bank, and the ground was strewn with petals of blooming flowers. A fresh breeze blew cool fragrance through the lofty forest. He lifted Wanthong down from the horse's back, and urged her to change clothes and plunge into the stream.

They splashed around in the water, merrily ducking and diving, laughing and joking. "Look how really clear it is!" He swam close to her, smiling, teasing, and tickling.

"Hey! Why are you squeezing me there? I didn't ask you. Hands off!"

"Well, there's some dirt or something—something black on your breast." He stroked it and laughed. "Oh, it's a mole!" He gaily splashed water on her breasts.

"Hey! Too much! I'm getting angry. And I'm cold. I can't bathe with you." She got out and sat laughing on the bank.

Khun Phaen changed his cloth and said, "It really is cold." Leading her under the shade of the banyan, he cut banana leaves to lay on the ground, and ordered his spirits and Goldchild to keep watch.

He removed his bandeau, raising hands to his forehead to pay respects. He took off his golden beads, waist sash, belt embroidered with letters in gold thread, shirt dyed with powerful herbs, and single inscribed amulet. Carefully he laid out everything, then snuggled up and hugged her blissfully.

"Let's ask forgiveness of this holy banyan together. It's broad daylight and he might not approve."

"Don't get carried away so! It's not the end of the day yet. Where can I flee in this forest? I've abandoned house and home to be your friend to death. My love is plain to see. Aren't you ashamed in front of this banyan's spirit? Even though times are hard, let's make a hut. How can I sleep here? Don't make me miserable."

"We've got nothing. No curtain, no mosquito net, no home. It's like old times at our beginning. Remember going to the cotton field? This lofty forest should make your heart bloom. Have some sympathy for me. Don't be shy of this heavenly banyan."

He hugged her tightly with desire. Thunder rumbled and rain splattered heavily down, drip-drip-dripping through the banyan until the leaves were soaked sopping shiny wet. A breeze rippled through the forest, swaying the tree and setting its branches trembling. The pair found happiness in the shade of the banyan.

The coupling greatly satisfied Wanthong. She tasted the love she had missed while they were apart, and her passion for Khun Phaen was rekindled. She picked a leaf to fan him, swatted away bothersome gnats and mosquitoes, and watched over him until he fell fast asleep from great fatigue. Sitting alone beside him, she became lonely and wistful.

"Look at me now. I came without thinking into this great forest where I'll be prey to its wild animals. Khun Phaen brought me because of love. That's obvious and I can't ignore it. But, goodness, I've never experienced this kind of hardship since the day I was born. Before, I'd never met buzzing bugs and crawling caterpillars; now I know them all. How will things be tomorrow? Even worse?"

She thought back to Khun Chang. "I was happy in that house. He was very protective, let nothing upset me, and cuddled me every morning and evening without fail. Life was easy and sweet. I had a bed and a net to fend off the mosquitoes and flies. When I bathed, there was someone to scrub me and put turmeric on my skin, a fine bright mirror to admire myself, tooth powder to polish my teeth to gleam, perfumes with rich floral aromas, cloths and silks by the thousand. From here on, there'll be only dust and wind, grime and gloom. Before long we'll have to weave leaves to wear."

She picked up a tree root to use as a pillow, then stared at it in utter despair. She felt the ground, finding it rough and rock hard. "I left my home to come and sleep in the wilds where there are no lights, only the moon, no roof, only the shade of a tree. Oh, the misfortune of being born a woman! I should be happy but I cannot be. I dislike shame, but I enjoyed love too much. Because I wasn't strong-willed, I now suffer. It's a waste to have beautiful looks, a pretty name, and a gentle manner if you have a terribly wicked heart. The good in me is the best in the land; the bad, nobody can match."

She heaved a deep sigh and lay sleepy, lonely, and sad. "How did I go astray and go too far? I can't be angry at Khun Phaen. He truly loves me deeply. We'd been apart a long time, and he had another wife. He could have become distant. But out of love he had the nerve to come after me and spirit me off to the forest, with no fear of the uproar of getting dragged to court. He offered his life in exchange for me. I can't quit now. I have to go with him. Whether I die is down to fortune."

She stretched out, slipped her arms around him, and wept. Lying still, her face nestling against his, she fell asleep.

KHUN CHANG FOLLOWS WANTHONG

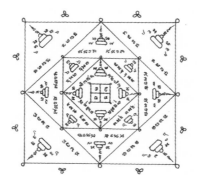

When Khun Phaen's mantra had worn off, Khun Chang revived. His head hurt. He felt where the hair had been pulled out. "It shouldn't be bare like this. My whole body is covered in soot. Eh! Why am I under the bed?"

He got up, saw Wanthong was missing, and shouted out for her at the top of his voice. He found the ruined curtains, gathered a pile of shreds in his arms, and roared, "Khun Phaen must have come and taken her away!"

When he opened a chest and found many rings and pieces of cloth had disappeared, he lost his composure and began sobbing. Looking round, he saw the letter on the wall. He read, "Make haste to follow after me. At cockcrow, Khun Phaen came to the house and entered our room. I tried hard to shake you awake. I resisted him several times but he raised his sword to kill me. I'm just a helpless woman with no one to help me so I had to go with him, not because I'm tired of being here. Don't abandon me to die. Hurry after me at once."

Khun Chang raised the letter reverently above his head and writhed around in distress. "How come I slept through all this? Khun Phaen shaved my head, playing with me like a dog. Those five spirits are a sham. It's a waste to feed them with food and liquor. I'm going to drown the whole lot of them. May they die bad deaths."

He called his cousin, Sonphraya. "Why did you hide away and sleep? Why didn't you bolt the gate?"

"I was in the other house. You didn't even wake up when he was plucking your head bare. Why are you so upset about her going? She doesn't love you so she ran away."

"I'm not besotted with Wanthong. I'm angry because she stole my money. If I catch her, I'll carve her so the blood flows. As for Khun Phaen, I'll chop him into pieces with my sword, reclaim all the property, and bring back Wanthong—Oops! I forgot."

Sonphraya laughed uproariously.

Khun Chang commanded, "Fetch those Karen and Lawa who sell eaglewood from the deep forest. When there are five hundred, we'll march."

The Karen and Lawa arrived carrying crossbows with bolts dipped in powerful poison. Khun Chang gave orders to feed them and pour a hundred liters of liquor for his elephant. Then he hurried over to his mother's house and told her everything.

Thepthong responded, "She's gone off with another man. It's not fitting to chase after her. You can choose from all Suphan. There are plenty as good as her."

"Wanthong is not wicked, Mother. She did her best to wake me but he raised his sword to kill her. She wrote a letter telling me everything. Don't stop me, Mother. Give me your blessing." Thepthong knew she could not restrain him so fell in with his wishes.

Khun Chang tied on a cord hung with auspicious amulets, mercury charms, a sacred thread, a copper testicle from Kamphaeng, a turmeric-colored stone from a duck egg, and a single amulet from Abbot Khong of Wat Khae. In his mouth he put an amulet to make his speech stun. On the back of his neck, where his hair was sparse and curly as a conch, he put a yantra cloth.

He mounted an elephant along with Sonphraya. The men, all merrily drunk with glazed eyes, waited together in front of the stairway. At an auspicious time, they struck gongs and set off into the forest, waving banners, firing guns, and shouting rowdily.

After leaving Suphan, Khun Chang was uncertain which way to go. Coming upon a forest hunter, he asked, "Have you seen two people on horseback? A villain has kidnapped my wife."

"I saw them. I'll tell you about it."

Khun Chang dismounted and poured liquor for the hunter. After quickly sinking nine cups, the hunter dizzily told him, "I saw them crossing the river at cockcrow. They were laughing and flirting. He grabbed her breasts. I couldn't look. The woman had very beautiful, soft arms and they rode in the saddle with legs intertwined. A while ago they went to sleep at Banyan Landing. I'll take you there."

The hunter led the way through the deep forest almost up to Banyan Landing and pointed out the spot.

Goldchild and Khun Phaen's other spirits saw this horde approaching and ran over to wake their master. Khun Phaen grasped his sword and softly stirred Wanthong. "Eye's jewel, please wake up and get dressed. You're about to see the battle of your lover versus your husband. Khun Chang has a huge force with hundreds of men. I have only little me. I'm concerned for you. If you try to get away again, Khun Chang will be furious enough to slit you open and leave your flesh as prey for the crows. But if you go over to him and speak nicely, he should take you back to enjoy and I'll escape into the forest. What do you think? Will you stay or go?"

Wanthong gave him a black, wounded look. "Do you no longer love me? I intend to entrust my life to you. I've no regrets over leaving Khun Chang. With all your powers, aren't you ashamed to run away so easily? Don't imagine I'll return to die in that house. I'd rather fight to the death. If you're afraid, hide in the banyan and hand over Skystorm to me."

"Oh! These words I like! I'll dress you up properly with a shirt, cloth leggings, and a helmet dyed with herbs. I'm just a bit worried that you're not used to riding a horse. You'll have to master the rhythm of spear play, because Khun Chang's timing is expert and his spear is huge. I'm a man. If I die, that's commonplace. But why trouble yourself, my jewel?"

He quickly prepared himself for battle, and intoned a powerful mantra to make Wanthong invisible and ensure no enemy weapon would touch her. He sent his spirits to cut couch grass, then composed his mind and intoned a formula that transformed the grass instantly into dummy spirit soldiers, all equipped with lances and spears.

He spurred Color of Mist away. The spirit soldiers surrounded the enemy at the front and flanks. Khun Chang called out, "Prepare to defend!" His men raised their guns and pulled the triggers but there was no flash, no bang. Khun Phaen rode up in front of Khun Chang and bellowed a mantra. Some men took fright and ran away, abandoning their guns. Others stood stunned, their swords slipping from their grasp.

Khun Chang fired his gun and urged his troops to advance. Gunners and pikemen swarmed towards Color of Mist who wheeled around, kicking and biting. A man tried to catch hold of the horse but Khun Phaen slashed with his sword, sending a head tumbling along the forest floor.

Khun Chang did a war dance on the back of his elephant. "Forward! No retreat! Why be afraid? There's only one of him. Sonphraya, advance the elephant so I can slash him in two like a banana stalk."

Sonphraya said, "Eh? If we blunder over there, we'll get knocked down in the dirt. Don't you think it's a good thing our elephant is far away from him?"

Khun Chang saw this was true and quietly offered no argument, but shouted at his troops, "Forward! Split up and form crow's wings abreast! Shoot him off his horse!"

The Lawa troops poured forward in tight formation like an army of ants. Seeing their numbers, Khun Phaen signaled to his spirit soldiers to join the fight, shouting, yelling, and slashing down Khun Chang's men in piles. The spirits were elastic and nothing pierced them. Khun Chang's men broke and scattered in defeat.

Khun Chang turned his elephant and fled into the thick forest. The howdah got caught on thorns, teetered, broke apart with a crack, and slid down the elephant's side. Khun Chang fell from the elephant with a thud, and ran, bent double, straight into the thorny undergrowth, snagging and grazing his flesh so the blood flowed. His leg tangled in a vine and he fell rolling on the ground. "I'm caught in a trap! Because I love my wife, I lose my life. What a pitiful thought! There's not a scrap of clothing left on me. I came to die for nothing, absolutely nothing."

Realizing the enemy was not following them, Khun Chang's men fanned out through the dense forest, cutting away the thorny rattan until they found their master, looking as if he had been mauled by a tiger. They brought clothes for him, mopped away the blood, washed off mud, and pried out thorns. People went off to find medicines from the forest to treat him.

Khun Phaen rode back to find Wanthong. Close to the shady banyan, he dismounted and walked forward, pretending to have an injured leg. Wanthong rushed out to greet him. He leaned his arm on her shoulder and whispered, "I'm badly wounded and it hurts. Please walk steadily."

Wanthong was shocked. Under his weight, she could hardly walk. At the banyan tree, Khun Phaen collapsed as if on the point of death.

"I was shot at the top of my leg and nearly fell off my horse. Khun Chang had countless men. He followed and stabbed me so hard my innards almost spewed out. His spear play is good. Please staunch the blood for me."

He picked up Wanthong's hand and put it on his belly. "There's blood or something dripping down here. Please staunch it. This damn muscle is twitching. Press it hard."

Wanthong now knew he was fooling. She turned aside, withdrew her hand, and shoved him away. "Too much, my good fellow! You must be tired. What is there to eat?"

"The rice crackers aren't finished yet, my sweet. If you loved me like I love you, you'd overlook your stomach pangs like I do mine. I brought supplies from Kanburi but I forgot them when we left last night. Just looking on your face, my hunger disappears. I'm full to bursting with love for you. I hope you feel the same."

"What a talker! You're very smart, lord of a hundred tricks!"

The sun was about to disappear behind the mountains. Khun Phaen suggested, "My love, let's go and bathe to cool down."

Wanthong tossed her head in annoyance. "My legs ache. All those lies about being shot were very hurtful. I'll go down to the water in a while."

"Don't take long, my love, or you'll shiver with cold on the approach of evening. I know why you're hurt. It's because you went to war no holds barred, fighting with me so urgently in the shade of the banyan. Do you have to lean on me to walk? I'll carry you."

"I dislike this, I really do. I'm not some lame hunchback. When have you ever carried me before?" She got up and strode off in a huff.

Khun Phaen coaxed her to enjoy the stream. A breeze rippled the water. Buds rose elegantly from lotuses. Bees bunched around blossoms, buzzing and bathing themselves in pollen. Wind rustled the leaves and blew ripe petals into the stream, suffusing the water with fragrance like celestial nectar. With her fingernail, Wanthong nipped off a lotus leaf and flower, and fashioned them into a little boat. Khun Phaen pulled up a lotus stalk and coiled it round her like a necklace. Wanthong gathered floating lotus petals and gently blew till they flew in the wind. They watched fish swimming under the limpid water, threading through the lotus stalks. Khun Phaen suggested they play hide-and-seek.

Wanthong cried, "I'll be it. Don't go too far away. I'm scared of crocodiles."

"Hide your face. If you cheat and chase after me without closing your eyes, may you run into a puffer fish or get nipped by a scissortail that sucks all your flesh and blood."

"I've never played with such cursing. You come back and close your eyes while I go and hide. If you peek, may a rat bite your leg and drag you off to devour."

"What's this? Now you're cursing too. I've never heard such cursing either. Let's stop picking at each other." She swam off to hide among the lotus leaves.

"Wanthong, little Wanthong, where are you hiding?" He swam over and grasped her breasts with both hands. Wanthong pried them off. "You're too full of tricks."

"I'm afraid you'll run away so I'm holding on tight."

"It's cold. Let's go up."

"I'll scrub your back. Let's take turns."

She turned her back. He slipped his arms around and softly massaged her breasts.

"Why aren't you scrubbing my back but squeezing there instead?"

"I thought there was a spot of dirt but the bump turns out to be just you."

"Now, now, don't be sarcastic. So this 'bump' doesn't please you? It's not like the time you climbed the palace wall. That heavenly flower has floated away into the palace so you have to admire a grassflower instead. How maddening for you!"

Khun Phaen was stung and embarrassed. He mumbled, "Don't pick at me. There's no woman I love as much as you."

They walked back under the shade of the banyan and tasted bliss together.

After midnight, Khun Phaen woke, chilled by the cold dew, hugged Wanthong, and coaxed her to admire the full moon. Filtering through the banyan leaves, moonlight fell on her breasts, full and firm as the buds of red lotus. Dew drenching the little leaves spattered down in drops like diamonds, collecting on her bosom like a lustration of liquid gold, scenting the air softly like a garland of sweetpassion, as if the banyan itself wished to caress her.

Crickets shrilled a plaintive chorus, lilting in lament like a young girl grieving. He nudged Wanthong to listen to the sound. "I can't hold you close here for too long. That villain Khun Chang will go and make accusations to the king. Things will blow up like a raging fire, and I think a huge force will be dispatched after us. We must leave this banyan and go deep into the forest."

After they had taken leave of the banyan, he harnessed Color of Mist and they rode off through the hills. Wind wafted pollen far and wide, dusting the forest with fragrance. Khun Phaen pointed out flowers to Wanthong.

"There's a smilinglady smiling in the forest fringe, just like you smiled in the cotton field; an elegant spray of hiddenlover, just like us two hiding away as young lovers; a secretscent perfuming the air, like the fragrance of your delicate cheeks when you were sent to me in the bridal house; a lady's fingernail with its tiny petals open, like your fingers fanning and combing for me; and an eveningbloom all over the bank of a lotus pond, like I'm all over you, evening and morning too. There's climbing jasmine twined round miseryplum and parting palm; after only three days, karma parted us in misery. There's a heartache tree hanging with braidflowers; for more than two years, heartache and gloom were hanging over me. Fragrance from that cinnamon tree mingles with the scent of a happyshade; enjoying you today sent me such happiness. The air is bathed in the aroma of roses and waitingladies; little lady, let's wait a little—and enjoy a kiss."

Wanthong cried, "Oh don't stop! Please let me listen to you admiring the forest a little more."

"There's nothing to admire as much as you. It wards off the loneliness of the night." The moon slid down into the forest as the dawn came up.

They came to a valley among the hills where a broad area had been cleared for cultivation and houses clustered at the foot of a hill. Bamboo fences surrounded areas planted with sweet potato, taro, gourd, aubergine, chili, and dry plantain. Some young Lawa women ran away at the sight of people coming on horseback.

Khun Phaen rode over to halt by the terrace of a house. An old woman there wondered anxiously, "What are officials coming to my house for?"

Khun Phaen and Wanthong dismounted and greeted her. "We've come looking for the medicinal herbs and roots said to be in these hills. Where have all your menfolk gone? May we please stay in this village for about five nights, and then we'll move on."

Wanthong gave her a bead wristlet. The old lady was pleased and called the young women to come back. They stood looking shy and peeping furtively. When they too were given beads, they laughed gaily and their shyness disappeared. They promptly arranged a hut and brought sweet potato and taro in gratitude.

Khun Phaen flirted with them. "Later I'll come back and give you necklaces, earrings, bracelets, and rings to put on both hands."

Wanthong teased, "So you're going to be a Lawa son-in-law, are you?" She stretched out her hand for the old lady to read her palm. The old lady went on and on, relating many, many things.

Khun Phaen ordered Goldchild to be on the alert for an army coming.

Khun Chang lay in the forest, aching and whimpering. After nightfall, his men collected wood, lit fires, and made shelters to sleep in the wilds. The injured lay around groaning. Some went off in bands to gallivant around the forest. Late into the night, many cocks crowed in the wilds.

By dawn Khun Chang was nursing revenge. "I'll inform the king and get an army sent to arrest Khun Phaen."

He ordered Sonphraya to harness his elephant and hustle everybody to prepare to leave. Khun Chang lay in his howdah with a fever, feeling the wounds all over his face, and lamenting over Wanthong. "You'll be in a pitiable state. Khun Phaen has a lot against you. Maybe he's killed you already, taken all the gold rings, and left your corpse in the woods."

Sonphraya said, "Why are you so concerned? She ran off because she doesn't love you. Because of her you almost died from thousands of rattan thorns. There are lots of servants at the house. Aren't they as much fun as Wanthong?"

"I'm not in love with her. I'm crying over the property that's been lost. He stole gold rings and cut curtains to shreds. I want revenge. If

I find Khun Phaen I'll slash him and his people to death. All I want back is Wanthong—Oops! Forgot."

"The mouth and the heart seem to have a slight disagreement here."

They reached home just as the sun set. The sight of the house empty of Wanthong made Khun Chang even more dark and desolate. Ruined curtains were still scattered about. Mattresses, pillows, betel boxes, bowls, trays, and salvers lay in disorder.

He grabbed a pike and raised it above his head. "I'll stab myself to death. May it enter easily and may I die well! Have all the goods here put in my coffin."

He threw the pike down, ran to the kitchen, picked up a pestle, bludgeoned some fermented fish, and threw pots all over the place. "May I die and follow my wife."

He went back to his room, found a rope, tied one end to a roof beam, the other round his waist, and swung out into space, shouting "Help! Untie me!"

Sonphraya saw the rope tied to a beam and thought Khun Chang's neck must be broken. He pushed open the door and found Khun Chang hanging by his waist.

"Eh? People usually hang themselves by the neck." He pushed Khun Chang's hands and feet so he spun around, flailing.

At that moment Siprajan arrived and saw Khun Chang swinging from the roof. She asked Sonphraya, "What's going on here? What *is* Khun Chang doing?"

"Haven't you seen this before? Khun Chang is playing spin-the-wheel."

Khun Chang managed to untie his waist. "Khun Phaen has kidnapped Wanthong and stolen gold, silver, cash, and cloth. I chased him down and stabbed several hundred of his forest bandits to death, but my elephant ran amok and plunged into the forest before I could seize Wanthong. I was caught by the undergrowth and bloodied by many thorns. This is the end! I'll see him dead."

Siprajan pursed her lips. "I don't believe you. No one beats you at lying. Khun Phaen is a skilled and experienced fighter. Anyway, what are you thinking of doing?"

"Lightning strike! Why don't you believe me? If you'd seen me in the fight, you'd have admired my fine spear play. I want revenge. I'll ask the king for a great army to hunt down Khun Phaen and kill him. Harness my elephant quickly. I'm going straight to Ayutthaya."

He went to bathe and change clothes. Inside the room, he took up a mirror to look at himself. In the furrow through his hair, new shoots were just sprouting.

"Oh, how long will it take for my hair to grow back? If only I could exchange this head for someone else's! Even if it cost a thousand baht, I wouldn't mind. Oh, who else is like me? No wonder Wanthong is in two minds."

He reached Ayutthaya in one day, left the elephant beside the graveyard of Wat Na Phramen, and crossed to the city by ferry. People addressed him as if he was an old beggar. A child took fright, "Mummy, mummy, what's that coming over there with a red head like a vulture in a paddy field? Will it eat my liver?"

The mother shouted, "You slave, fancy coming to frighten my child, damn you!"

Khun Chang walked on, shaking his head. At the official hall in the palace, a noble friend asked, "Where have you been? You look like you've been mauled by a cat."

"Sir, Khun Phaen has gone too far. He kidnapped Wanthong and stole my property. I went after him but he'd recruited a force of forest bandits, armed to the teeth. I charged with my elephant and scattered them, killing hundreds of them dead like rain. I would have caught Khun Phaen but he galloped away and hid in the forest. I've come to ask our king for an army to arrest him. Sir, please help me. I don't care about the money and other things. If he's caught, all I want is Wanthong."

KHUN CHANG ACCUSES KHUN PHAEN

At audience, the king heard cases concerning the populace and gave judgments of life or death according to the crimes. Looking around, he asked, "Who is that prostrate at the back? Is that you, Khun Chang? Where did you get your chest and shoulders striped with welts, your face and forehead scored with scratches, and your hair hacked about? Did somebody beat you up?"

For a moment, Khun Chang was nonplussed, and he left the royal question hanging without a reply. The king roared, "Khun Chang, who did this to you?"

Khun Chang twitched and trembled until Phramuen Si hit him in the chest. "His Majesty has issued a command. Why do you remain silent?"

Still trembling, Khun Chang addressed the king. "My liege, your humble servant's name is Khun Chang from Bigwall Village. My father's name was Khun Siwichai and my mother is Thepthong. My elder cousin, Phanson, was born before me, son of my aunt. Next came Sonphraya and Ratthaya, and then myself, your humble servant. I had a wife, who died many years ago..."

The king became very angry. "Who asked you to recount your household census details?"

Khun Chang was shocked to his senses, but still got everything muddled. "Wanthong disappeared into the forest on horseback ... many, many forest robbers ... weapons scattered everywhere ... Khun Phaen, son of Thong Prasi ... a great deal of money and valuables ... with Wanthong at a banyan tree ... lacerated by rattan thorns ... a sacred thread around the house ... elephant into the undergrowth ... hundreds died ... a shrine near the gate ... "

The king said, "Everything's topsy-turvy. Phramuen Si, whisper in Khun Chang's ear to speak without panicking."

Phramuen Si followed the king's order. Khun Chang calmed down, and wove a story of fact and fiction.

"The villain put people to sleep, plucked my head, drew patterns on my body in soot, and chopped three beautiful curtains to shreds. Cash and property are missing. He wound a sacred thread around the house and made many offerings to an eye-level shrine. My wife, Wanthong, disappeared. I gave chase and found them at a banyan tree. Khun Phaen had several hundred bandits who ambushed us and killed many of my men. I was caught and lacerated with rattan thorns. He shouted that he would not kill me but let me return to Ayutthaya and tell everything so that the king would come out. He would defeat the king in an elephant duel and seize the city as ruler. These were his vile words. He has built a royal lodge in the forest and a camp fortified with spikes."

King Phanwasa pondered over this story. "I think some is true and some false. Khun Phaen probably took his wife away and Khun Chang chased after him but got beaten. He probably blundered into the rattan in flight but he accuses Khun Phaen of lacerating him. Listening to one side is misleading."

The king gave orders to Phramuen Si and Phramuen Wai, two lieutenants of the royal pages. "Conscript five thousand men. Put Khun Phet on the right wing and Khun Ram on the left. Find out where Khun Phaen is hiding, and whether Khun Chang's words are true or false. See if Khun Phaen fears me or not. Tell him I will adjudicate the dispute between him and Khun Chang. If he comes quietly, he will not be executed or caned, but if he resists, his head will be stuck on a stake in the forest."

Recruiters were dispatched to drag conscripts in by force. Weapons, horses, elephants, and provisions were prepared. The astrologers found an auspicious time to march on the following day at four in the morning.

That night, Khun Phet's wife dreamed that her husband was sliced in two, his chest slit open, and his heart discarded in a forest. In fright, she woke her husband to tell him about the dream.

Khun Phet knew this was a bad dream but did not want her to worry." Your sleeping mind is just racing. Don't be upset. Go back to sleep."

Khun Ram's wife dreamed a tooth broke into three pieces. She woke her husband in alarm. "You're going with the army to arrest Khun Phaen. This strange omen signifies danger."

Khun Ram reassured her, "Because I'm going away, you're having dark and fearful thoughts. Don't be frightened. I'll bring back Khun Phaen."

Next morning, as Khun Phet prepared to leave, his wife had a shocking vision. "Don't go. Just now, I saw you with no head. This fits with my terrible dream!"

Khun Phet's face turned ashen. He knew this was a warning. He had been with an army many times but had never experienced anything like this. "Probably I'll die in the forest, but if I don't go, I'll be in danger from the king." He shooed his wife away and steeled himself to leave.

Khun Ram strung on many amulets and picked up his trusty sword. As he descended from the house, the stairway splintered, and five steps fell to the ground. He knew this was a fatal omen.

The troops were already drawn up ready. At an auspicious time, gongs were beaten, guns fired, and shouts echoed around. Khun Chang rode in a howdah with Sonphraya on the elephant's neck holding a goad and Ratthaya on the rear. Onlookers broke into laughter. "Those bald elephants go very well together!" Khun Chang looked the other way.

Along the march, soldiers seized dried fish, fresh fish, or whatever they could find from every house. They camped at Sam Ko, crossed the river the next morning, and reached Banyan Landing. Khun Chang told Phramuen Si, "This is where I charged and slashed them dead. Survivors ran off into that rattan thicket."

Phramuen Si cackled with laughter. "Oh, really? I can see the rattan thicket has been demolished, but probably by your men trying to rescue you. Where's Khun Phaen? I don't see him."

Khun Chang's men reported that they had found the tracks of a horse. The army followed the trail through the forest. Phramuen Si called out, "Hey, hairy chest! Send some people out to spy."

Khun Chang and Sonphraya climbed a tree to look around. They saw Color of Mist eating grass, Wanthong lying asleep, and Khun Phaen all over her, hugging, kissing, and stroking her breasts. Khun Chang almost fell out of the tree but Sonphraya grabbed him just in time. He shaded his glazed eyes with a hand, shaking and growling with rage.

Khun Phaen's spirits rushed over to intimidate them by leaping around, lolling their tongues, and bellowing menacingly. Khun Chang staggered backwards, slipped out of Sonphraya's grip, and crashed down flat on the ground. He picked himself up and ran over shouting, "I've found Khun Phaen! He's hugging Wanthong tight over there."

Phramuen Si gave orders. "Surround him but stay out of sight."

Khun Phaen's spirits informed their master that they were surrounded. At the sight of so many soldiers, Wanthong clung to him trembling with fear. "How are we going to survive this? If each of them rips you a little, you'll be dust."

"Don't be afraid. If ten times this number had come I'd still win. They're like mosquitoes flying into a flame. Though there's only one of me, I'm as fierce as a lion, and they're a tribe of pigs. First, I'll hide you away in the forest."

He lifted her onto the horse's back, and rode out of the trees and across in front of the troops, blowing a formula to stun. The artillerymen and pikemen stopped stock still. Khun Phaen nudged Wanthong to look.

"Over there's your husband, showing off his fine figure and his bald head. Because I love you, I have to engage this massive force. Whether I live or die will depend on merit. If you were anyone else less dear to me, I'd hand you over without a second thought." He kissed and caressed her gently to mock Khun Chang, and then sped away.

He hid Wanthong under the dense foliage of a banyan and scattered enchanted sand to form a barrier. He cut grass, tied it into the shapes of a thousand dummies, and pronounced an incantation. When the dummies burst into flames, he doused them with sacred water, leaving the dummies changed into sturdy soldiers with weapons in hand. He gave them their orders. "Wait until I give you a signal, then annihilate them!" He spurred his horse out of the trees.

The troops slowly recovered from the stunning mantra. Phramuen Si said, "How come nobody moved a muscle just now?"

Khun Chang said, "I'm furious. He galloped his horse right up close here, kissing my wife, all to mock me."

The troops were ordered to advance. Khun Chang urged them forward from his tusker. "Charge for victory!"

Khun Phaen bellowed a formula, stopping the men frozen in their tracks. Military discipline broke down. The main army became the vanguard. The left and right wings swapped over. The forward strike troops went on the defensive.

Khun Chang banged a hand gong and shouted, "Capture and kill him!" Then he hid himself in the howdah and ordered, "Take my elephant over to seize Wanthong."

Phramuen Si and Phramuen Wai rebuked him loudly. "Don't interfere, Khun Chang. We two are in command of the army."

They rode their elephants out front and waved Khun Phaen over. He galloped across and asked, "Why did you come here with all these troops? Has some enemy appeared somewhere? And why has this fellow been banging a gong? Who picked this scum to lead an army?"

Khun Chang seethed with rage. "Advance and arrest him!"

Phramuen Si silenced Khun Chang and turned to reply to Khun Phaen. "His Majesty commanded us to investigate whether you abducted Khun Chang's wife, associated yourself with bandits, set yourself up as royalty, lacerated Khun Chang with rattan thorns, acted as if you were planning a revolt, and hoped to provoke the king to engage you in an elephant duel. As far as we can see, nothing that Khun Chang told the king has any reliable basis. Even so, we have to take you and Wanthong back for the king to hear the case about your dispute over Wanthong. His Majesty will not pursue the case about the killing of Khun Chang's men. You have no need to fear. Let's go together. Where's Wanthong? Bring her here."

Khun Phaen replied, "There's a lot more in the past but it's no use to tell you. Is she my wife or is she really Khun Chang's? It's totally obvious who is being crooked. When Khun Chang brought troops after me, I had a choice to fight or to die, to act like a man or to run away. Khun Chang's men were gutless cowards. When I attacked, they broke and fled into the forest. Khun Chang got scratched when he was running away, yet he went back and told the king I beat him up. Really it was two sides fighting tit for tat. You say you're on the king's orders to take me and Wanthong back. I'm in a tight corner. I fear royal authority but I've nobody to help me. Sir, please take the army back and report the truth to the king. I'll wait for the king's anger to cool before I come."

Phramuen Si warned Khun Phaen, "The king will be angry that we found you but failed to bring you back under arrest. Your past deeds will be forgotten and the king will side with Khun Chang. Why not come along with us and clear everything up? If you continue to resist, I'll order the troops to seize you."

Khun Phaen shook his head. "If you want to take me back under arrest, I won't die quietly."

Phramuen Si gave an order. "Take him alive! Don't kill him."

The troops swarmed forward with swords flashing and pikes glinting. Khun Phaen bellowed a stunning formula. The troops were stopped in their tracks with their hair standing on end. Khun Phaen spurred Color of Mist away from an engagement. "If I act first, I'll be judged a traitor."

On the left and right wings, Khun Phet and Khun Ram saw that all the guns and troops had fallen silent. Khun Phet thought, "Phaen may have crooked ideas to revolt and seize the country."

He wagged his finger and called out, "Khun Phaen, you're acting insolently. Your lineage is nothing yet you're full of ambition for kingship. You think you can take the territory, but who's going to pay respect to *you*? Everyone knows your merit is insufficient. Your father, Khun Krai, was executed and his head stuck on a stake in the hills. Your property was seized and your mother sneaked away to hide in Kanburi. You went to fight at Chiang Thong, made a reputation, and became Khun Phaen, but then slunk off with ideas of revolt. You gained royal favor but then you turned bad. I can no longer associate with you as a friend. Don't imagine you'll escape alive." He drove his elephant up close.

Khun Phaen was flaming with anger. "You big mouth, slandering someone already dead. You won't remain standing for eternity. Today, I'll give you a bad death, falling from your elephant to roll on the ground. Your wife will be a widow and I'll take her naked as my wife."

He chanted a formula, and summoned his mass of grass-dummy troops who swarmed out of the forest, whooping and shouting. Under the power of mantra, the sky grew overcast and the earth trembled. Khun Phaen swooped down on the vanguard, slashing with his sword. The grass-dummy troops, impervious to bullet or blade, slashed with pike and sword. The troops fought back with necks straining, arms at full stretch, and lungs gasping for breath, but their weapons broke and shattered as if they were slashing stone. Guns were raised and fired but the shot bounced back.

Khun Phaen suddenly came upon Khun Ram face to face. Khun Ram thrust with a long pike but landed only a glancing blow on the shoulder that spun Khun Phaen around. Khun Phaen slashed Khun Ram down from his elephant, leapt from his horse, and slashed again. Khun Ram tumbled forward and died in a pool of blood. "One down, you meddler!"

Khun Phet charged up and thrust his pike into Khun Phaen's chest but it was as impenetrable as iron or diamond. Khun Phaen leapt onto the elephant and swung at Khun Phet's neck, which severed like a plucked flower.

Khun Chang drove his elephant away in panic, straight into a grove of cowitch. He lost his cloth and his helmet. His head burned like a torch. He fell off and the panicked elephant ran away, shitting floods. Naked as his pate, he climbed on a tree stump, caught sight of Phramuen Si's elephant, and scrambled up on its rear. Phramuen Si turned to look, mistook Khun Chang for a tiger, and poked him with the handle of his goad. Khun Chang cried out, "Damn you! It's me!" Phramuen Wai thought it was Khun Phaen and hit him with a pike, cracking his skull and drawing blood. Khun Chang dangled from the elephant, scrambling to climb back up and almost falling to his death. The elephant charged straight into a thicket of rattan.

The troops broke and scattered, shedding the weight of their weapons and baggage. By dusk, the survivors gathered at Sam Ko. Horses and elephants were exhausted. Men were filthy, weak with hunger, hollow-eyed with exhaustion, and low in spirits. Phramuen Si caught sight of Khun Chang beside a bo tree and cried, "How did you get here?"

"I got up on the rear of your elephant and you hit me. Please have mercy! My wife is still in dire straits. She has to put up with lying on the hard ground and eating roots rather than rice, with moonlight instead of lamps."

In fury, Phramuen Si came up and kicked him down on the ground. "Are you still thinking of her, damn you?"

"Hey! You broke my ribs."

"You're vile, Khun Chang. Stop moaning. We just got thrashed because of you."

After the army fled, Khun Phaen galloped away on Color of Mist. He walked down to a stream where beautiful lotuses bloomed, scrubbed away the dust, washed his sword, and went to find Wanthong.

"Did you see what a great army your husband brought here? I killed Khun Phet and also Khun Ram. They used insulting words about me and so brought disaster on themselves. Except those two officers, I didn't go after anyone to kill them."

Wanthong said, "We're starving. The food is all finished."

"Eye's jewel, don't be so troubled. We've been through much hardship already. There's still fruit in the forest. We can make do in a forest sort of way. Why mention these things when it serves no purpose?"

The moon shone brightly through the leaves of the holy golden banyan, highlighting two breasts like heavenly lotus buds. Dew drops plopped gently down from the banyan's leaves. A chill wind brushed Wanthong's body, coaxing the couple to cling together. They gazed at the moon and listened to the crickets' chorus. He covered her, nuzzled her breasts, kissed to raise her passions, and caressed her softly until they slipped into sleep.

The defeated army waited in the forest at Sam Ko for two days until all the survivors had straggled back—in total around five hundred, far fewer than those who had died. They had been stripped of their cloths and weapons and were fiercely resentful.

"All because of that pestilential Khun Chang."

"Parents will collapse in grief by the cartload."

"One time more like this and the whole clan's done for."

"What a scandal because of your woman, Khun Chang!"

"You can't blame me. If people run off and fling things away, they get lost. I'm still upset over my wife. If it were Phramuen Si's wife, I bet he'd run after her, roaring out loud. We saw who did the fighting and who ran away. Khun Phet and Khun Ram were on the left and right wings but I was in the vanguard, wasn't I? When Khun Phaen was slashing around, I stabbed him eight times. When he chopped

Khun Phet and Khun Ram down dead, I turned and saw Phramuen Si driving his elephant to escape, so I fled too."

Phramuen Si said angrily, "You lowlife, you turn everything around. In truth you were at the rear."

Phramuen Si ordered the army to march. As they approached the city, many people came to look. The troops hurried along in shame. As there was no further audience on that day, they all went home. The wives of the fallen flailed around in distress.

Khun Phet's wife beat her chest. "Oh, my lord and master, didn't I tell you not to go because of the bad omens? Now your corpse will decay in the undergrowth, with no cloth as cover, prey to wild animals, left to rot in pustules. Pitiful! Had you died at home, your body could be cremated properly with all the adornments appropriate to your status. Why did you deny me the chance to make your corpse look fine? No umbrellas, only great trees. No pipe, drum, and gong, only the sound of animals in the forest undergrowth. No incense and candles, only the moon and stars. No lofty canopy, only the sky murky with clouds. No curtains, only the surrounding hills. Nothing but the bare ground to support the body in place of a pyre."

In the bright light of dawn, Phramuen Si, Phramuen Wai, and Khun Chang went to the audience hall. A curtain was drawn aside to reveal the royal presence. Nobles prostrated with faces bowed. Those who had returned from the campaign prayed feverishly and fearfully.

The king asked, "Have you brought Khun Phaen?"

Phramuen Si replied. "My life is beneath the royal foot. We marched to the place where Khun Chang said he had found Khun Phaen and Wanthong, but saw no royal lodge. We went further and found Khun Phaen with Wanthong, just the two of them. No forest bandits. I spoke with Khun Phaen who said that Wanthong was truly his wife but Khun Chang had deceitfully seized her. Khun Phet and Khun Ram insulted Khun Phaen, raking up matters about his family from the past and accusing him of revolt. They then attacked, and Khun Phaen slashed them both dead. We set out with five thousand men. Over four thousand five hundred have died. Only four hundred and fifty-five persons have returned to the city."

The king stamped his foot hard enough to bring the audience hall crashing down. "What? The officers and so many troops have been wiped out—elephants, horses, and weapons in thousands? Only one person and you can't defeat him? You shamefully ran off like women. What a toll on the conscription rolls and the rice supplies! You deserve to be flogged and sent down to prison. If you saw some tiger droppings you'd run off into the elephant grass without looking back. There's only one thing you're good at—strutting around and swishing your tails to flirt at the palace back gate, combing your quiffs and making up your faces. You're sex mad! Fighting wars doesn't interest you at all. You're only good at cheating your own men for corrupt gain, and using fancy words to get blood out of a crab. You deserve to have your heads lopped and your clans obliterated. First off, send out arrest warrants to the guard posts in all the regions and cities, all the provinces under our control, all cities of the first, second, third, and fourth classes. Wherever Khun Phaen is found, arrest him but do not kill him. In the order, give his name, appearance, and age so he will be recognized."

KHUN PHAEN GIVES HIMSELF UP

Khun Phaen enjoyed the hills and forest, the absence of any threat, and his intimacy with Wanthong. Though their bed was logs, their life was bliss. No mattress cushioned Wanthong's soft flesh, yet she slept as if on a resplendent golden bed, lulled by the soothing strains of cicadas, the orchestra of the forest. In the lightless night, their lamp was the lustrous moon. The wind wafted soft perfumed pollen and the sweetly scented fragrance of flowers as they drifted to sleep in each other's arms.

One day, Wanthong aroused her husband to interpret a dream. "I reached up into the sky and could pluck the sun like a flower. When I put the sun in my mouth and swallowed, my whole body shone brightly. Then a strong man came along, boldly gouged out my right eye, threw it away, and offered another that was less bright. Please tell me if this dream is good or bad."

"Oh, my heart, you'll have a child. That's the meaning of the sun in the dream. This will chase away our misery!"

But the part of the dream where her eye was gouged out meant great difficulty in the future, and he worried this would make her miserable. He suggested they go looking for rambutan, persimmon, water chestnut, and lotus in the forest.

Wanthong winced at the thought of the hardship a baby would suffer from earth, dust, and wind. "If we were living safely in a house, we'd be only too happy, but how to bring up a child here?"

Khun Phaen understood her apprehension. "We can't stay here any longer. The king may send troops after us again. We have to make for the hills, where we can hide until matters simmer down."

At dusk they rode down beside a flowing stream, drank the cool water, and washed their hair among the blooming flowers. He plucked lotus pods, and pulled up a lotus root that popped out of the earth in naked coils. He stripped the skin, leaving it white and curly, and begged her, "Try this, my love."

"Oh, I've never eaten the root. I'm afraid it'll make my mouth itch and my tongue sting. I'll just eat the seeds."

"Try it. Believe me, it's delicious. You'll be captivated once you know the taste."

"There's only one lotus root and you're giving it to me? Oh no, if you're not having any, nor am I."

"There's more lotuses, don't worry."

"In that case, you dive down to pull them up while I pick the pods. They're easy to pluck."

They flirted happily while collecting the lotuses, both gradually shedding their fatigue. They left the stream and found somewhere to sleep in the forest. At dawn they set off again. Life was hard but they were free from danger.

One day, Khun Phaen realized it was the end of her sixth month. He faced a sad dilemma. They had been forced to live in the forest because it was remote, but medicines for giving birth would be hard to find, and there was no one to turn to for help.

Puzzled by his misery, Wanthong asked him straight out, "What are you thinking? Do you have doubts about our love? Have you had enough of me?"

"Don't have such thoughts. I love you as much as when we were first in love. Because I now know you well, there's not a single reason for doubt. I'll tell you the truth but don't be upset. I keep looking at your growing belly. You'll give birth before long, and there's no one to nurse you. We've got nothing, no place to live, no cradle, no mattress, no pillow, no mosquito net, no curtain, no bedding or anything else for the child. We alone are already starving. The baby will wail for food. These thoughts are what bring tears to my eyes." Desolate enough to die, the couple clung together and wept.

Khun Phaen pondered and said, "Did you ever hear people talk of the governor of Phichit and his wife Busaba? Anyone who is poor can go to them for help. Anyone condemned to death can rely on their mercy. Let's go there. Even if he sends us down to Ayutthaya, the king will probably hold an inquiry. My past reputation is still very good, and I have the powers of my knowledge."

They rode off late in the morning. He kept the horse to a steady gait so as not to cause her belly any discomfort. They took a direct route, stopping every now and then at a stream or pond, digging up taro and sweet potatoes to eat, and resting among the trees. After ten days' travel through hill and forest, they rode into Phichit and reached Wat Jan at dusk. After paying respect to the Buddha image, they stayed in a big hall beside the monks' quarters.

At lamp-lighting time, Khun Phaen daubed enchanted powder on their foreheads as a charm to induce love, made them all invisible, including the horse, and went straight to the residence of the governor.

Phra Phichit and his wife Busaba, who was at the end of the fourth month of pregnancy, were sitting in their residence under a luminous moon, watching their young servants merrily playing chase. Khun Phaen tethered Color of Mist at the gate and released the formula of invisibility. They entered on all fours to pay respect. Prostrate in front of the pair, Khun Phaen intoned a mantra and blew it hard towards them, while believing in his lore and thinking of the virtue of his teachers.

Phra Phichit guessed that this couple came from elsewhere. "Where are you from and where are you bound? Are you man and wife or brother and sister?"

Khun Phaen replied, "This young child's name is Wanthong and mine is Khun Phaen. We have made our way here through the forest." He told the story of Khun Chang's treachery and their flight. "Wanthong's pregnancy is now advanced, and we're concerned something could happen in the wilds. I know that you, sir, are kind to people, so we made our way here. We put our two lives in your hands. Please be merciful."

Phra Phichit and Busaba were touched by this story and also affected by Khun Phaen's expertise in lore, which made them love the couple like children of their own. They called servants to take the horse to tether, and led the couple by the hand up into the residence.

Phra Phichit said, "You have no need to fear. For better or worse, I'll try to ease things."

He ordered servants to prepare a large meal. Busaba gave them fresh clothes. When they had eaten, Phra Phichit arranged for the couple to stay in an apartment beside the central hall. They lived there happily for a month, enjoying the affection, protection, and support of Phra Phichit. But then Khun Phaen began to worry.

"The king is still enraged. He's ordered officials to keep watch on all hideouts. Anyone who catches me must send me to the capital for the offense of killing several thousand people. Phra Phichit has been like a father, having the mercy to look after us and let us live here, but before long this will expose him to punishment. If we lie low but news reaches the capital and an order arrives for me to be sent down, I'll be at a disadvantage."

He conveyed these thoughts to Wanthong. "I'll ask Phra Phichit to order us sent down to the capital. I must confess guilt and think of how to counter Khun Chang's charges. If I give myself up rather than being captured in the forest, the punishment should be light. Besides, I can create obstruction with the power of my knowledge. The king has appointed me and fed me, and I drank the water of allegiance several times. It's unthinkable for me to act otherwise. Let matters fall according to the karma I've made. If I'm destroyed, I won't complain, but I'll find a way for you not to face punishment."

Wanthong agreed. "It's grim but necessary to go and find out whether we'll live or die. I don't cling to life. There's only one thing I'm afraid of—that he'll send me back to Khun Chang. I couldn't stand the shame and I'd much prefer death."

Khun Phaen wiped away her tears. "If the king isn't merciful and has us executed, we must bow our faces and be born again well. In this life we've made some karma. If he sends you back to Khun Chang, I'll not fail to come after you and kill him before he can have you."

They went and explained the decision to Phra Phichit and Busaba. "You've hidden me for many days and I fear it's risky. Other officials may talk and pass on the news. You'll be an associate of criminals and that will bring down the king's anger on you. Sir, it would be better to avoid this risk. Send me down. Just help by explaining in your report that I gave myself up properly, and convey my testimony, including my wife's words, in full. That will help me to beg the king's favor. The rest is up to karma."

Phra Phichit saw the truth in Khun Phaen's words. "At first I thought of requesting the king to allow me to place you in charge of the guard posts on the forest side. But then I realized this was not appropriate. Because you're under charges, the king would say I'm siding with a criminal. But I was extremely concerned about sending you down, so I did nothing. But your thinking is exactly right. Because you came to confess to me, it's clear you had no subversive ideas of revolt. If the old case is examined, matters appear to be greatly in your favor. All you did was take your wife back. Who can say that's seditious? Only your battle with the royal army lays you open to charges of revolt, but they attacked first, giving you no option but to stand your ground. The fact the army couldn't match you but broke and scattered is not your fault. Now, the royal order is very insistent that you must be imprisoned with no clemency. Along the way, things needn't be so strict, but if you're not under restraint when reaching the capital, I'll be in the wrong too.

It's not difficult to make your case in the report. I'll just give evidence that's true in every detail. I think you'll get clemency. After that come and live up here with me."

Busaba hugged Wanthong tearfully. "I love you like a child of my own womb. It's a pity you're being parted from me. By the power of your merit, may you survive. When the case is over, please come back here."

Wanthong put her arms around Busaba. "Though my body leaves, my heart stays here with you. Even though we're criminal suspects, you looked after us lovingly like your own children. May you earn merit. At the capital there'll be no mercy. We'll have bricks and stones from the road in place of pillows, and the bamboo mats and slats of the jail as a mattress. There'll be no one to bring us water, no relatives to send food, and not a gnat's wing of money. They'll demand judicial fees, and if we lose, we'll probably be loaded with heavy fines, and have only our own flesh and blood as money."

Busaba prepared supplies for the journey and gave them two hundred and fifty baht. "A court case is expensive."

Phra Phichit composed his report and placed it in a message cylinder along with the testimony of Wanthong and Khun Phaen. He ordered the guards, "Don't lock them up until you get close to Ayutthaya. If they want to visit somewhere on the way, let them do so."

They went to find Color of Mist. Wanthong said, "We've come to say farewell. You went through hardship with us in the forest, getting eaten by gnats and mosquitoes for many days. You've been our friend in trouble, friend to death, through many travails."

Khun Phaen said, "Farewell, friend in trouble. I'd like to take you with us but I fear you'd be used as a workhorse if we were no more. If I'm released, I'll come to find you at Phichit."

Because he was affected by a mantra, Color of Mist understood. He shook his head from side to side and lowered his face onto the couple's feet.

Khun Phaen asked Phra Phichit to take care of the horse. Phra Phichit replied, "We have plenty of boys to look after him, and plenty of grass, straw, and water. Don't worry about the horse."

They boarded a boat and made their farewells. The boat floated along quickly past villages and towns. Beyond Lopburi in the early evening, they halted at a settlement with lush trees. Khun Phaen picked up Skystorm and disembarked, found a hollow under a big banyan tree, placed the sword inside, chanted a concealing formula, and prayed to the guardian deities to look after his weapon.

As they approached the capital, the warders put the couple in chains. Feeling sorry for Wanthong, Khun Phaen wound a cloth round her and tied a string so she could lift her chains to walk. She accidentally took too large a pace and fell down with a shriek. Khun Phaen picked her up and dusted her off. Tears of sympathy streamed down his face.

Kaeo Kiriya had redeemed herself from Khun Chang with the seventy-five baht that Khun Phaen had given her, and now lived with old friends in Ayutthaya, running a dry goods store. As that day was a holy day, she was on her way to hear a sermon when she saw a big crowd of people. She stood craning her neck from a distance but did not recognize Khun Phaen and Wanthong because their faces were dark and freckled. Khun Phaen looked over and was tempted to greet her but was afraid she would be angry if it was not his old love. Then Kaeo Kiriya heard someone say, "They've got Khun Phaen!" and her doubts disappeared. She pushed her way through the people and sank down to wai them, with tears streaming down.

"Oh pity, pity! You look so different I almost missed you. You disappeared into the forest as if you had died."

Khun Phaen recognized her voice. "I thought it was you, Kaeo Kiriya." She turned her face away, embarrassed because of their misery and poor circumstances. Khun Phaen walked off in his chains, leading Wanthong. Kaeo Kiriya followed along behind.

They approached a guardhouse in the palace. Phramuen Si saw Khun Phaen coming and happily called him over. He broke open the cylinder and read the report. "The king is unbelievably angry, but now I've examined this report that you gave yourselves up to Phra Phichit, I think it'll be all right."

Phramuen Si looked across at Kaeo Kiriya. "You went to the forest with Wanthong alone so where did you get this spare seat from? Oh, friend! Even as a prisoner in extreme hardship, you arrive with something in reserve."

"She's my wife from a long time back. I met her just now on the road."

Phramuen Si gave them a big meal. They chatted away like old times, with no hard feelings.

KHUN PHAEN IS JAILED

Towards eleven in the late morning, nobles went into the audience hall. Phramuen Si made obeisance and reported, "We have Khun Phaen."

Not yet knowing the details, the king stamped his foot in anger. "This trickster believes he has powers and thinks I can't match him. If he's so able, why didn't he fly away instead of coming here with head bowed? Give a reward to whichever city arrested him. Was he locked up on the way here?"

Phramuen Si relayed the contents of Phra Phichit's report—how Khun Phaen and Wanthong had been married, how Khun Chang and Siprajan had conspired together while he was away in Chiang Thong, how Khun Chang maliciously reported that Khun Phaen had climbed the palace wall, and how Khun Phaen abducted Wanthong and killed officers sent after him.

"He knows that the fact he killed officers and men in the forest carries a death penalty. He was not arrested but gave himself up to clear himself. If Your Majesty does not spare him, he begs to surrender his life calmly in grateful recognition of Your Majesty's virtue."

The king's anger cooled. "Bring both Khun Phaen and Wanthong here immediately."

When they arrived, the king was still too angry to look at them. Khun Phaen intoned a mantra and blew it with faith in its lore. The king's mood relaxed and he turned his face towards them. "You stole off into the forest and now come back to give evidence, shifting the blame onto your mother-in-law. Is Wanthong really your wife as you claim?"

Khun Phaen said, "If investigation shows that she is not my wife, I willingly surrender my life."

The king pronounced, "On the killing of Khun Phet and Khun Ram, I absolve you of guilt because you had no thought of revolt. As for the dispute with Khun Chang, I will see this matter contested. The loser will be executed. Release them to contest the case."

Phramuen Si led the couple away, had the chains removed, and ordered a guard to fetch Khun Chang from Suphan.

The guard arrived at Khun Chang's house as Khun Chang was sitting in the hall in the evening breeze, thinking longingly of Wanthong. Since she had left, he slept less than half the night and his stomach felt queasy all day. On the day Wanthong arrived in the capital, he had dreamed he was wading across a huge lake and saw a brilliant blooming lotus, yet the stamens had wilted and the petals were empty. He wanted to pluck it but a bo tree got in his way. He woke with a start, convinced that the dream meant a lover was enjoying Wanthong.

He was reciting verses in lament over Wanthong but was in such turmoil he kept getting lost in the middle and returning to the start. The guard officer got tired of waiting for him to finish and said, "Khun Phaen and Wanthong have been brought in. There'll be a trial in the palace. The king has sent for you. Come without delay."

Knowing Wanthong had been found, Khun Chang felt reborn. He bounced up and down in joy, ran into the house to get dressed, mounted his elephant, and made for Ayutthaya. Reaching the audience hall, he pushed through the crowd to Phramuen Si, and asked, "My dear sir, where is my wife?"

Phramuen Si indicated, "Just there!"

Khun Chang looked round and grabbed hold of her in glee. She shrieked and clawed at his chest. Khun Phaen punched and kicked Khun Chang away, then stood shielding her.

Khun Chang cried loudly, "Oh pity, Wanthong! I've missed you and never forgotten you for one moment. Are you with child? When you left me, I had morning sickness and a craving for tamarind and pickled thornweed. I'm overjoyed to see your face today. Come back to the house at once."

Phramuen Si raged like a roof on fire. "You lowlife! Didn't you say you chased after Wanthong because of the property and wanted to chop off her head? Now that you see her face, your eyes glaze over. Stop driveling! You have to answer a case on royal command."

The court convened and the examination began.

"Khun Chang stated that he asked for Wanthong's hand, and her mother consented. People were aware that they held a prayer chanting and sprinkled holy water."

Khun Phaen objected, "I did not know."

Khun Chang cited witnesses.

"Next issue. Khun Chang stated that he had lived with Wanthong for about two months when she disappeared, taking a large amount of property. He went after her and found her sleeping beside Khun Phaen, who had many forest bandits under his command."

Khun Phaen objected, "Not true."

"Khun Phaen launched a murderous attack in which Khun Phet and Khun Ram died."

Khun Phaen admitted this was true.

"Khun Phaen and his bandits mischievously constructed a royal lodge, attacked Khun Chang, tied him to a tree, and lacerated his body with rattan thorns."

Khun Phaen objected, "Not true."

Khun Chang stated there were no witnesses because the army scattered in defeat, yet cited the marks on his back that were still visible. He rested his case.

Khun Phaen chanted an anus-stuffing mantra and blew it onto Khun Chang's chest. His face reddened. His scalp crawled. Sweat streamed down. His mind swam. "I beg your pardon, I'm not well. My head is spinning and my bowels are churning. Please grant a recess until tomorrow, Your Honor."

Phramuen Si said, "This is a case on royal command. No recess."

"I'm going to shit myself. I'm bursting. Please delay for just one day."

"Overruled. Continue with the questioning."

Khun Chang jumped up, "For life or death, please let me shit."

Khun Phaen said, "Objection, Your Honor. The plaintiff will abscond."

The shit burst out and splashed down. People laughed and scattered. "Smellier than dogshit!" Guards grabbed Khun Chang and pushed him out of the hall. He ran down to the riverbank and jumped into the water. Returning to the hall, he changed his clothes and went to sit beside the defendants. The stench was still unbearable. The judges sat holding their breath as the defense began.

Khun Phaen testified that Siprajan gave Wanthong to him in marriage and they lived together happily as a couple until he left on the Chiang Thong campaign.

Khun Chang responded, "Your Honor, as to this count, I do not know."

Khun Phaen cited several villagers as witnesses.

"When the army returned to Ayutthaya, Khun Phaen found Khun Chang had asked for Phim in marriage and built a bridal house."

Khun Chang objected, "Not true."

Khun Phaen cited several witnesses.

"Khun Phaen came to take Wanthong back but did not remove any property as alleged."

Khun Chang turned with fiery eyes and objected angrily, "Not true!"

"Khun Chang came after Wanthong and wanted to slash Khun Phaen down dead. They exchanged blows with each other in the forest."

Khun Chang denied everything. Khun Phaen said he could present further evidence. He withdrew any further counts and requested to proceed to the witnesses.

Then Wanthong gave evidence. "Mother forced me to marry Khun Chang against my will. When I refused to enter the bridal house, she beat me, as could be heard all over the village. When Khun Phaen went on royal service, Khun Chang came to say that Khun Phaen was dead."

Khun Chang cried out, "Shameless, Wanthong! Now that you've got someone new, you brazenly change your evidence." He jumped up with eyes bulging and tucked up his lowercloth. "I'm going to kick you down, you evil woman."

Wanthong appealed to the judges. "If I give evidence, the villain will beat me. Khun Chang, how much did you pay to ransom me?"

Khun Chang was furious but the guards obstructed him. He jumped up and down and his cloth slipped off. Phramuen Si shouted, "Beautiful! We can see your whole belly, you abomination."

Khun Chang sat down, pulled up his cloth, and grumbled to himself, "It's a pity I can't kick her down. Even if it cost me money, I wouldn't mind."

Phramuen Si ruled that Wanthong's testimony was inadmissible. "This woman is in the middle. She loves her lover so she sides with him. She lives with her husband and so she sides with him."

On the following day at dawn, the three parties went to take evidence from the various witnesses. They walked to the house of Siprajan, who tottered out trembling and took the oath.

Khun Phaen promptly lodged an objection. "She's the mother-in-law of the plaintiff and completely prejudiced. It was she who separated me from Wanthong and gave her to Khun Chang. She likes talking to her son-in-law in private. She had him massage her stomach in the house so much that an unwanted baby popped out. She's such a shriveled old fraud even vultures issue warnings."

Siprajan shook so with anger that her sagging breasts slapped against her chest. "You foul slanderer!"

The judge commanded, "Order in court!"

They passed on to take depositions from all the remaining witnesses. In the afternoon, the judges assembled and listened to the record of evidence. A legal code was produced and consulted. The case was prepared to be presented in royal audience.

The king arrived to preside. "Phramuen Si, how is the case?"

"My life is under the royal foot. Khun Phaen has offered evidence that has been confirmed by the testimony of neutral witnesses. The judges have conferred and found the mother-in-law guilty of acting with folly and negligence in giving away her daughter to two men. She is sentenced to undergo public ridicule. Khun Chang was intent on marrying Khun Phaen's wife and hence stated that Khun Phaen was dead. He rashly dismantled Khun Phaen's bridal house and married Wanthong. Khun Chang must pay a fine, as well as compensation to Khun Phaen for adultery. In addition, Khun Chang, Siprajan, Kloi, and Sai are sentenced to be flogged. Finally, if Khun Phaen does not fear for his own karma and is so disposed, he may have Khun Chang executed. Wanthong is returned to Khun Phaen. By royal decree."

The king asked, "Khun Phaen, will you have Khun Chang executed?"

"I do not want vengeance. Impose only the compensation and fines, as Your Majesty wishes."

The king said, "There'll be vengeance for certain. Close the case and carry out the sentences."

Khun Chang paid for the fines and for commutation fees in place of flogging without difficulty, but Siprajan, Sai, and Kloi counted out money as if their hearts were breaking. "He's a rich man who floats on water like cottonwool, but he lets poor people like us almost die."

Khun Chang went to see Phramuen Si. "Sir, have mercy on one point. Please let me have Wanthong back. I'll repay your kindness with fifteen hundred baht."

Phramuen Si said angrily, "You fool! Nobody can overturn a royal order. Get out."

After the case, Khun Phaen, Wanthong, and Kaeo Kiriya stayed happily in Phramuen Si's house. One night, a breeze wafted the soft refreshing scent of flowers, and Khun Phaen awoke thinking of Laothong.

"You left your hometown to come south, and then were parted from me. I now possess Wanthong and Kaeo Kiriya but I feel concerned for you. If the news of my pardon has reached you in the palace, I expect you're waiting for me to fetch you. Out of consideration for the two wives I love, I could just let you stay hidden. But there's an old saying: Sacrifice money but not morals, sacrifice anything but your word. I'll petition the king but I fear it could turn out badly. He's just pardoned me and it might be an improper imposition if I dare to approach him again."

After sunrise, he went to find Phramuen Si. "The case ended successfully because of your assistance, sir. But now my only concern is Laothong. Please help me appeal to the king to let her out."

"Wouldn't it be better to wait a year? A fire not fully extinguished can flare up easily. She's not far away, and no lover can go in and out of the palace. Waiting a while won't matter."

"I've no doubts about her character. What upsets me is that she herself did nothing wrong but was confined because of me. Now that I'm happily free again, it might seem I'm selfishly satisfied with the wives at my side. Though lightning may strike, please see what you can do to help. I think the king will have mercy."

"If you don't listen then it's up to your fortune."

They went to the palace. Khun Phaen sat outside. Phramuen Si waited for his opportunity to address the king. "My life is under the royal foot. Khun Phaen has requested your humble servant to address Your Majesty. In the past he faced charges but has been pardoned by royal grace. To make amends, he requests to serve the royal foot until the day of his death. Laothong has been confined in the palace for a very long time. May Your Majesty graciously release her."

The king's face turned white with rage. "This fellow dares to presume on my kindness. I waived his punishment of execution for killing my officers. I gave Wanthong back to him. He still dares to pursue Laothong! Because she's in the palace, he fears I'll have her behind his back. This is abominable! Were he to set his mind to do royal service, then we wouldn't talk of Laothong alone—I'd give him another two or three. If I let this pass, he'll think he can get away with anything. Clap him in jail, and apply the full five irons. Weld the rivets in his leg chains too."

Phramuen Si backed out and spoke to Khun Phaen through tears. "I told you but you didn't listen." Guards led Khun Phaen away to the main jail, and put on fetters, chains, and cangue. Phramuen Si went home and told Kaeo Kiriya and Wanthong. "I tried to stop him. As soon as I'd addressed the king, it was like the city was on fire."

Wanthong was choked with sadness. "He should have been less hasty. We just started to be happy and now there's more hardship. Somehow this man never makes life easy. When will he cut loose from this young Lao woman?"

The pair rushed to the jail and finagled their way in. Wanthong collapsed at Khun Phaen's feet. "Husband, you never tell me anything. If you'd consulted me, I'd have stopped you. From now on, we'll all suffer. We have no servants to send you food, and there's nobody I can speak to for patronage. I can come every day, but while I'm giving birth and lying by the fire, there'll be nobody except Kaeo Kiriya. I feel I'm almost dying."

Khun Phaen sorrowed together with the two women. "I misjudged things. In truth, if they doubled these irons, I could still escape but I'd sacrifice my good name. When my father was condemned, he didn't try to escape. Wanthong, you're pregnant and terribly uncomfortable. Let Kaeo Kiriya stay here until you're back on your feet. I'll have to suffer for several days until the guards have some respect for me, then I can ask them to let me visit you. Put yourself under the patronage of Phramuen Si. And be patient. It'll be a long time before I'm released."

Kaeo Kiriya and Wanthong returned home, found betel, tobacco, clothes, mattress, pillow, and mosquito net, and asked Phramuen

Si's servants to take them to the jail. The prison governor had some convicts build a shelter for Kaeo Kiriya outside the jail gate.

At sunset, all the gates were closed and double bolted. Locked in a cangue and the full five irons, Khun Phaen was tormented by stiffness. "I don't have to endure this. Just keeping my promise not to escape will be enough."

He chanted a mantra. The irons slipped off his hands and feet, and the cangue fell. He left the lockup and went to sleep with Kaeo Kiriya in the shelter.

The jailors awoke and took a roll call. All responded except Khun Phaen. The jailors lit torches, went to look, and reported to the governor, "There's only a pile of chains, sir. He's got free of everything, even the cangue."

The cry went up to give chase. They came to the shelter but passed it by. In growing panic, they swarmed around looking behind doors, up on the roof, and in every nook and cranny. The governor had an idea. "His wife's in that shelter, right? Take a torch and have a look."

Finding Khun Phaen with Kaeo Kiriya, the guards dragged him out roughly.

"Why are you lowlife manhandling me? Do you think I'm trying to escape?" He bellowed a mantra. Hands lost their grip. Heads toppled over and banged against the wall. "Leave me alone! Do you think you can lock me up? If so, then try."

They fetched the irons and clad him up to his ears. Khun Phaen chanted another mantra, and everything fell off in a tangled heap. He beckoned to them "Hey, come and try again."

The governor and jailors saw he was truly able. They sank down in silence and raised their hands to wai him repeatedly.

"Forgive us for what we did."

"For your own karma, please be kind."

"If you escape, we'll all have our backs flogged."

Khun Phaen said, "If I wanted to escape, I could simply go off in broad daylight. Just watch this." He held his breath and made his body disappear.

The governor and jailors were horrified. "Sir, we're dead now!"

"Please come back."

"We won't lock you up. Just don't escape."

Khun Phaen relaxed the mantra. In relief, the guards sank down to salute him.

At dawn, the governor went to see the minister of the capital, Phraya Yommarat. "Khun Phaen's expertise is like the power of the wind. All the irons slipped off him. He said he wouldn't escape but we can't trust his word alone. Sir, kindly help."

Phraya Yommarat told them to fetch Khun Phaen. "You've being convicted under the law but you still dare to break the locks and chains. If word gets to the king, he'll punish you with death."

"On my honor I won't escape, but I can't stand being placed in irons."

"Fine, but you must swear an oath that you won't escape."

Khun Phaen prostrated and spoke the oath. "If I escape, may I fall into hell. I'm ready to die in jail unless the king graciously releases me. I'll not think evil, treacherous thoughts from now until my dying day."

Phraya Yommarat told the guards not to put Khun Phaen in irons and warned Khun Phaen not to be seen gadding about.

Khun Phaen now lived happily with Kaeo Kiriya in the shelter. Wanthong visited from time to time, and Khun Phaen sneaked out to see her when the guards were not looking. The jail governor and Phraya Yommarat took no notice.

Since the court case, Khun Chang had been thinking of Wanthong. There were masses of servants in the house but he had no desire to couple with them—and the servants would not consent anyway. He dreamed of Wanthong all the time. He could not eat. He could not sit still. As soon as he dozed off, he started awake like a dancing prawn.

"If this goes on for a year, I'll die."

He called his cousin Sonphraya to play chess. As soon as the pieces were set out, he moved a knight and took Sonphraya's king.

"Oh sir, I beg your pardon. Please take that back."

Khun Chang laughed, "I won't!"

"Not even the abbot could match you! My moves are so clumsy and slow. There's a rumor going round that Khun Phaen asked the king for Laothong, and the king had him clapped in jail. Wanthong is on her own and maybe lonely. We should go for a chat. She should agree to come back without any sulkiness."

Khun Chang promptly ordered his servants to harness an elephant. As dawn streaked the sky, he reached Ayutthaya and commanded his men. "Go along, seven of you. Grab Wanthong and bring her here."

The servants slipped through the city until they were close to the front of Phramuen Si's house. Seeing Wanthong on her way to visit the jail, they surrounded her. "Where are you going? You borrowed four hundred baht from our master, and since then both you and your husband have been hiding. We're taking you away."

Wanthong cried out, "I didn't borrow any money. No, no! Where are you taking me? Oh, townspeople around here, help me! I beg you!"

The people in the neighborhood thought this was something to do with government money.

"Why should we get involved?"

"Not our business."

The servants took her out the city gate and across the river by ferry. Khun Chang was so happy his body quivered. He lifted her up into the howdah. She showered him with abuse, pushing and pulling, tugging his hair, and spitting at him. "Don't expect me to make up with you. As soon as we reach the house, I'll die."

Khun Chang hugged, kissed, and climbed all over her. "Khun Phaen is in jail. How many years till he can come after you? Come home with me and be happy."

Wanthong cursed and abused him through the forest. Nearing dawn, they reached Suphan. Khun Chang carried her up and lay her down on the bed. "Why are you wriggling and whining? The first time, when you were young and not pregnant, you couldn't fight me. Now you're pregnant and clumsy, so why wear yourself out struggling for nothing?"

Khun Chang coupled with her, fulfilling his most eager wishes. She was forced to give her body in tears. At the last light of the sun, she fell asleep. Khun Chang kept on climbing all over her, making love, and blissfully kneading her breasts—as jubilant as if he had chanced upon a gold mine.

THE BIRTH OF PHLAI NGAM

Wanthong's labor was very painful. Her pelvis was distended and her thighs stiff. She saw fireflies flickering before her eyes. Loath to call Khun Chang, she massaged herself until the pain became intolerable and she cried out, "I'm dying! Help me!"

Khun Chang awoke and looked at her belly. "It's coming!" He found a pillow to support her neck and called out frantically to the servants. Women were sent to fetch the midwives, who arrived amid the uproar. They felt her belly and said the child's head was pointing downwards and the face twisted to the right. They made a correction as her time approached. Medicine was pounded, oranges squeezed, and water boiled. Wanthong wept as if her heart would break. As dawn broke and the sun rose, her womb loosened and the infant emerged wailing. Khun Chang took a look and called out, "The kid's a boy!" Both grandmothers came to look and give medicine. Wanthong went to lie by a fire.

To cut a long story short, the child was raised to be of good character. At the age of nine, he looked exactly like his father, Khun Phaen—plump and handsome, with fair skin, a nicely rounded head, and a topknot. Because the child had inherited his father's features, Wanthong told the servants to call him Phlai Ngam.

Khun Chang was resentful. "At first I thought he looked like me but he's Khun Phaen's son for sure, not a shadow of doubt."

Every night he thought about killing the child. One day when Wanthong fell sick, Khun Chang waited until she fell sound asleep, then invited Phlai Ngam to go out for a ride on his shoulders. As they walked through the forest, he prattled away to keep the child's spirits up, distracting him to look at birds and animals. When they reached a remote spot, Khun Chang swung Phlai Ngam down onto the ground, and laid into him with kicks, punches, slaps, and elbow jabs, delivered with loud grunts.

Phlai Ngam cried out but Khun Chang stopped up his mouth with both hands. Phlai Ngam wriggled out of Khun Chang's grasp, shouting, "Mother, help! Father's beating me to death!"

Khun Chang pummeled him mercilessly until he himself was exhausted and soaked in sweat. He straddled the child and gripped his neck. Phlai Ngam squirmed and pleaded, "Don't kill me, dear father. Spare a thought for Mother! Please keep your child to serve you as before." Khun Chang pinched Phlai Ngam's nose, covered his mouth, and dragged him bumping along the ground until the child spluttered and passed out.

Khun Phaen's spirits came to embrace and protect their master's son. Thinking he had crushed the child to death, Khun Chang made a pile of elephant grass, earth, and logs over the body, and sauntered home blithely enjoying the forest.

Khun Phaen's spirits dragged away the logs and blew on the wounds to make them fade away. Phlai Ngam stirred as if waking from sleep. A female spirit said, "We're servants of Khun Phaen. Wait here and we'll tell your mother to fetch you."

The spirits disappeared in a flash. Phlai Ngam wandered around, crying and craning his neck to see his mother. He could not remember the way home through the forest. He watched the sun slanting downwards and smarted about the way his father had tricked him.

"What made him do it? I'll tell Mother to lay charges."

Around him the forest was dark, dense, and still. No branch swayed or twig trembled. Only cicadas droned and crickets shrilled. When a coel called, he called out, "I'm here, Mother. Please come and get me!"

The spirits induced Wanthong to fall asleep in the middle of the day and to dream that she saw Khun Chang piling the logs on her son. She started awake with her breast trembling and looked around for Phlai Ngam. A servant told her he had seen the child following his father into the forest. She suspected the truth. With tears streaming down, she walked into the forest, peering around and calling out forlornly. The dim shapes of bushes in the evening gloom made her heart falter. "Oh Phlai Ngam, my heartstring! Where have you gone?"

There was no sign of him at the mound where he used to play.

"Has he fallen dead—gored by a buffalo or bitten by a poisonous snake? Why has his corpse disappeared?" As the evening turned murkier, her cries grew more desperate. Crows careered around, cackling and cawing. Jackals howled as they sought a lair. The faint sound of a grebe's song floated from afar. Cicadas shrilled like a conch and horn. "Have some spirits hidden him away from sight? I'll offer a pig, liquor, anything."

As dusk fell, the plaintive whoops of gibbons brought on a flood of tears. Several times, she thought she heard a faint sound of someone calling, and felt the hair on her neck stand on end. Coming through a dense thicket, she saw him standing, sobbing, and staring around.

In joy she threw her arms around him. "I'm here now, my love. What happened? Why did you wander away from the house?"

"Father led me in circles to get me lost. Then he hit me, kicked me, pinched my nose, and piled logs on my throat. I almost died. People belonging to someone called Khun Phaen came to help me so I didn't die, but I'm battered and bruised all over."

Wanthong cried as if to die. "Oh, what can be done about our karma in this life? I'll tell you the truth. You're not his child and that's why he hates you. Your father's name is Khun Phaen. He and Khun Chang are enemies from the past. Khun Phaen is in jail and we have nobody to depend on. Khun Chang can be so rough because we're poor. We can't lay charges against him for the same reason. If you don't hide away, you'll be in danger. You'll be safe with Granny Thong Prasi in Kanburi, but it's a day and a half to get there and you may get lost in the forest."

"Oh Mother, if I go away, when will we see each other again? But if I stay here, I'll die. I'm ready to face death or whatever the future holds."

"Oh eye's sparkling jewel, you've never been on a track through the forest. Maybe in the past we made some karma by forcing animals apart, and now you must be parted from me."

As darkness gathered and dew glistened on the ground, she decided to hide her son for that night in Wat Khao. The abbot was helpful. "Leave the matter to me. If your husband comes looking, I'll deal with him. I've never heard of anyone trying to kill a poor fledgling stepchild under their care."

Wanthong quickly returned home. The sight of Khun Chang was so hateful that she turned her back and ran into her room. Seeing the empty bed deepened her sorrow. "Oh my son, here's where you slept until you were ten. I'll miss the sweet sound of your voice."

Khun Chang was drunk. Hearing Wanthong crying, he lit a lamp and went to sit beside her on the bed. Feigning innocence, he inquired jokily, "Is there a thorn hurting you? I'll help pull it out." To cheer her, he sang a line from a drama, "What agony is making you so aggrieved?"

Wanthong tossed her head in anger. Khun Chang struck a dance pose and approached to grab her. She pushed him away, scratching and pinching. "Why are you pestering me? My son's disappeared. Don't try to cover things up. Why did you take him into the forest and not bring him back?"

"Who said I took him? I was drinking and I passed out. I've told you before not to let him go down from the house. He's loaded with bracelets and bangles. Probably he ran into an opium taker who beat him to pulp and stole the bangles. It's karma."

For show, he stumbled out of the room, cursed the servants, and went down to the river to make enquiries. On return, he poured more liquor and lapsed into a drunken stupor, putting on an act of crying like nobody had ever cried before. "Oh, friend for life of your father!" He lay spread-eagled on his back, mumbling thickly, until he dozed off.

Wanthong sewed a little waist pouch and put in some sweets, fruit, and a gold ring. "Going to live in his grandmother's house will have its difficulties. Should he ever go hungry, he'll have some spending money." She sat lost in tearful thought, waiting for sunrise.

At the wat, monks helped to treat Phlai Ngam's wounds. After all went to sleep and quiet reigned, the crowing of a cock chilled Phlai Ngam's heart to the core. Because mother and son were thinking of each other, he kept dreaming that he saw her coming to him. When a coel sang loud and clear, he thought it was her and shouted in reply at the top of his voice. Then he came to his senses and lay quietly sighing and sobbing until the wat bell rang with a merry clang.

Near dawn when a heavy dew fell and the sky was streaked with red, Wanthong came down from the house carrying some clothing and the waist pouch. She sauntered along as if making for the landing, then quickly cut through a sugar palm grove to Wat Khao. She saw her little child waiting and looking pitiable. Not wanting to waste time talking, she took leave of the abbot and led him off.

"The way to Kanburi is right here. Remember it well. Follow the cart track to the open plain, then cut into the forest by the flat clearing. Let your grandmother teach you how to read and write."

She tied his topknot, gave him the waist pouch and gold ring, and entrusted him to the gods.

"O lord spirits of the forest, I pay my respect. Please subdue the tigers, buffaloes, and other wild animals. O spirits of the hills, please guide him to his grandmother without losing the way. And Father Khun Phaen, master of lore, begetter of our eternal eye's jewel, help your son to reach Kanburi."

She sobbed with tears falling as if her breast was an aching abscess. "I carried you in my womb and brought you up till you were over ten years old but now we lose each other. You're used to eating and sleeping close by my side. In the forest, you'll be alone and lonely. Who'll coil your topknot and shave your hairline? For countless years you won't see your mother's face—as distant and unseen as a moon that's set. Oh, I'm so bad I don't deserve to have been born. I had a husband but the husband was forced away. I have a child but the child is parted from me. Such troubled karma!"

Phlai Ngam prostrated before her. "When I'm grown, I'll come back to find you, but at present our karma is to part. May I have the power of merit to travel and find my father. I won't forget my mother's goodness, and I'll return. You love your child and your child knows he's loved. Among thousands and millions, no one else is the same. You raised and guided me with loving care. I leave home and I leave you, but only in body."

"Blessings on you, little Phlai. When you grow bigger, be ordained to study. A gentleman's handwriting shows his rank. You must make the effort to practice regularly."

She led him down to the cart stop. Parting was tearing at their hearts. Son looked at mother, and mother at son, both feeling so overwhelmed they could weep blood. After they sobbed their farewells, he steeled himself and walked away from her along the track.

Son turned to look back and saw mother still gazing after him. Mother looked towards son with great yearning. The path twisted, each slipped from the other's sight, and their hearts lurched.

Phlai Ngam walked along the cart track across the plain towards the hills. Left and right, he saw shelters beside the cotton fields, bright flashes of chili and yellow eggplant, and green magpies that ate them and flew off cawing. Spotting bantams scratching for bamboo seeds, he sprinted zigzag after them. Coming across a big bevy of peacocks, he chased them to whoosh up into the sky, honking in alarm.

When he grew sleepy, his spirits slumped. His thoughts strayed to his mother and he started to sob. The sun slowly slid down the sky, and his heart sank too. Close to dusk, he chased a pack of little jackals, but their howls made his hair stand on end. He reached the upland forests bordering Kanburi and found an abandoned wat beside a hill with the doors of the ancient ordination hall still standing. He prostrated to pay respect to the one remaining Buddha image and slept there.

At dawn, he ate his fill of the sweets and walked through the hills, meeting hill people hefting goods on poles, and boys herding buffaloes. He asked them about Thong Prasi's house.

"She's in the fields over there. At her house, there's a big gooseberry tree with unusually sweet fruit. We often steal them but if she catches you she'll grab your prick and pinch it hard. She's awful, like an ogress. If she catches any kid playing there, she'll slap him round the head with her droopy breasts. Why are you asking after her? Granny droopy dugs will bash you to death."

"Please take me to see this sweet gooseberry tree. I'll climb up and steal enough for all of us to eat."

"Let's go!"

When they arrived, the boys pointed out Thong Prasi's house and went to hide. Phlai Ngam began to feel uneasy. He crept forward and surveyed the place from a distance. It seemed quiet with no sign of the fearsome old lady. He slipped inside the fence, heard a squeaking sound, and knew that someone was upstairs spinning cotton. He climbed up the tree and beckoned to the kids, who picked up the fruit while whispering and winking to one another.

Thong Prasi had been miserable since Khun Phaen was jailed. Over the years, she had become shrunken and somber. Her ears pricked up at the sound of gooseberry fruit falling. She looked through a chink in the wall, and saw the boys. Picking up a cudgel, she descended the stairs. The boys ran away. Hearing a sound in the tree, she looked up to see a lad with a topknot.

"You little forest thief! Stop hiding up there like a squatting god. Come down and let your back have a taste of my cudgel!"

Phlai Ngam was frozen with fear like a timid mouse. "I'm your grandson, the one who lives at Wanthong's house in Suphan."

"Really! Come down here and 'Grandmother' will give you some stick."

Phlai Ngam was rooted to the spot, but thought, "Why should I be afraid of my grandmother?" He jumped down and prostrated at her feet.

Thong Prasi thwacked his back. "I'll tie you up rather than having you fined for theft. Where do you come from? A Thai lad or Chinese? You thieves keep breaking the branches on the gooseberry tree."

He tried to dodge the blows while wai-ing her. "I'm hurt badly already. Have mercy on your grandson. I'm the child of Khun Phaen. My mother's name is Wanthong. I came to find my grandmother called Thong Prasi. Don't keep beating me. I'll tell you the whole sad story."

Thong Prasi saw it was true and threw away the cudgel. She hugged him and scolded herself for thrashing her own grandson. "Oh, poor you!" She took him up into the house, shouted to the servants to bring water, washed him, and treated the wounds. They sat on a fine reed mat and he told her the story of Khun Chang's attempt to kill him.

"I couldn't stay in Suphan so I came here. Let me depend on your merit and kindness like a pauper."

Thong Prasi beat her breast. "That hairy-faced animal, Khun Chang! I'd like to lay charges and have him punished till his ears wilt." She reeled off a flood of curses. "You're in your grandmother's house now so don't be afraid. If that troublemaker comes to claim you're his child, he'll get slapped around the skull by my droopy dugs."

She called a servant in the kitchen, "Bring some thick curry, rice, and fish for him to eat."

In the late afternoon, the workers came back from the fields. They lit smoky fires to ward off the mosquitoes and midges, as was the custom upcountry among the paddy fields. At dusk, a gong was struck and Thong Prasi called people to the house for a soul ceremony. She brought out a pile of bracelets and bangles, saying, "These belonged to your father from childhood, and now we'll put them on our poor grandson because you're flesh of our flesh and dearly beloved. You're exactly like Khun Phaen, handsome and brilliant."

She called the servants up to the house. They all bowed to pay their respect and chanted for the benefit of Phlai Ngam's soul.

"Soul of Phlai Ngam, beloved, come
behold these brilliant golden trays,
scented sandal and garland sprays.
Soul, don't stray to forest, hill, and lea
with lion, monkey, sambar, tiger.
Don't wander, all alone and lonely.
Come to Grandma's home, be merry,
and prosper in safety a hundred years."

They lit a candle, passed it round the circle, then extinguished the flame and wafted the smoke towards Phlai Ngam. Lao girls played fiddle and flute, and sang for the soul of their master. Thong Prasi handed out money.

Phlai Ngam asked her, "I don't know my father at all. Would you please take me to see him?"

"He's been in prison for ten years now. Tomorrow I'll take you. He'll be delighted."

At dawn, Thong Prasi ordered the servants to harness an elephant with a big howdah and pack fish, rice, clothing, torches, gourds, sugar, medicine, betel, pan, and lime paste for Khun Phaen. In two and a half days they reached Ayutthaya and found Khun Phaen at the shelter by the prison gate.

Since his imprisonment, Khun Phaen had let himself go, wasted away, and now looked a mess. To overcome poverty, he wove rattan baskets and Kaeo Kiriya painted them with lacquer. Many were hung for sale around their shelter.

He welcomed his mother inside. Spotting Phlai Ngam, he asked, "Whose child is this? He looks lovable."

Thong Prasi explained, "This is your son. Come on, wai your father." She told the story about their enemy.

Khun Phaen hugged and kissed his son, while his own tears came in floods. "Khun Chang gets his way so often. Because I've given my word that I won't escape, he thinks I can't cut his head off. This evening I must go to his house and chop his head so the blood flows. A man dies where he dies."

Thong Prasi said, "My son, I beg to oppose you. Why go on creating karma by bad deeds? Think of your own child who has come to see you. I'll bring him up, educate him, and have him presented at court so the king may calm down and relax your punishment. In a time of bad fortune, you must act humbly. There's an ancient saying that mortal humans can rebound from hardship seven times. All these difficulties will pass."

Khun Phaen prostrated to his mother in tears. "I have only my mother's kindness to warm my heart. Please teach Phlai Ngam. All the manuals of my father and my teachers are kept in the cupboard."

He stroked his son's back. "No pursuit surpasses the pursuit of knowledge. When you grow up, you'll reap the benefit. We're in trouble, eye's jewel, and you must tread carefully. We've no kinsfolk to support us, only the kindness of your grandmother. I'm relying on her to raise you. However much she scolds you, don't answer back." He hugged Phlai Ngam to his chest. "Oh, what karma did we create in the past? I've just seen my child's face and now we'll be parted again. I've nothing to give you except these beads. They'll make you invulnerable to pikes and guns."

Tears streamed down Phlai Ngam's face as he accepted the beads. "I want to live with you and help draw water, pound rice, make the fire, and find vegetables every day. I'll try to study by and by."

Khun Phaen was overwhelmed. "Where would you find another tiny fellow who knows how to speak like this? You cannot stay here to look after me. This jail is like hell on earth. Luckily, Phraya Yommarat allows me to stay in this shelter, and the guards leave me alone and don't put me in irons. Phramuen Si provides my food every day. His goodness overflows the sky. If you can study I'll put you under his patronage, and he'll present you to the king so you'll be a man of rank in the future."

"Sir, I'll study hard."

They chatted until almost dusk. On parting, both father and son felt their souls skip with yearning as they passed from each other's sight.

Phlai Ngam studied assiduously with Thong Prasi as his teacher. He mastered both old Khmer and Thai, and studied texts on Buddhism and lore. He practiced how to become invisible, stabbed himself repeatedly until a sharp blade was blunted because of his invulnerability. He memorized formulas to unlock chains, to stun people, and to conceal himself. He learned how to read omens from the clouds and from the breath in his nostrils, how to summon spirits, and how to animate grass dummies as warriors. Thong Prasi taught her grandson to be expert.

When Phlai Ngam reached adolescence, he was an attractive lad with a robust body, fair complexion, smiling disposition, and reserved manner. His eyes were round, black, keen, and handsomely bright. Everyone liked him.

Thong Prasi looked for an auspicious time. "You're thirteen now, my dear grandson. On Friday the tenth of the waxing month, we'll shave your topknot."

The day before, she made curried noodles and boiled pigs' trotters. Neighbors brought betelnut and pan, and helped to sweep the floor and lay mats, carpets, and rugs. Silver and gold pots were brought out of storage, conches filled to the brim with sacred water, a half-moon dais prepared for the monks, and gongs and drums readied in accordance with custom.

Monks from the nearby Wat of Cockfight Hill sat chanting prayers until dusk. When they sprinkled water, young men jostled the young Lawa women who pinched them back and there was a lot of noisy pushing and grappling.

Thong Prasi sent her grandson to change his clothes and prostrate before the abbot.

"Whose child is this little one?"

Thong Prasi told him the story. "Currently Khun Phaen is still in jail. When we've shaved this lad's topknot, I'll take him to present at court. Master, please look at his father's horoscope. Will his bad fortune disappear?"

"Phaen is hopeless. After all the knowledge I taught him, he ran off to jail. What fun! I told that loverboy his weakness for women would get him into trouble."

The abbot laughed, reclined comfortably, and examined Phlai Ngam. "This grandson of yours is going to be a loverboy beyond belief. But at eighteen years old, he'll become an official with a title and a young wife, a northerner from a long lineage. This lass will bring disaster. Khun Phaen will be released at the end of the second month in a year of the pig. From then on, he'll have a bed for sleeping and a chair for sitting as an official."

The monks went back to the wat. A music ensemble played. Thong Prasi's family and friends had sought the very best masters of *sepha*. Mi, a firecracker maker, excelled at fight scenes, reciting as his throat swelled with sound. Old people liked to hear him and declared he knew everything. Rongsi was good at being funny. He clacked the claves while clowning around and rolling his eyes. Thang made the quarreling scenes very amusing, while Phet had lots of tricks, and dragged the choruses out as long as a long gun. Ma from the retinue of Phraya Non was good at bawdy improvisation. Thongyu knew how to recite the Lao characters and sing background music in a drone.

At dawn, Phlai Ngam's topknot was shaved. At nightfall, he went to his grandmother's bedside. "Tomorrow, I'll leave to visit father. I'll enter the service of the Lord of Life and gain enough favor to ask pardon for father's punishment."

Thong Prasi was happy to give her consent. "I'll have you sent to see your father, and then delivered to Phramuen Si. From there you must depend on your merit and fortune. Remember everything I've taught you, and you'll rise steadily in rank."

Next morning, Thong Prasi packed silver and clothing in a chest along with various foods, and loaded everything in an elephant's howdah. At an auspicious time with no obstacles, Phlai Ngam mounted and jogged off along the road, crossing the plain to the capital without an overnight stay. At the jail, he paid respect to his father and said, "I would like Phramuen Si to present me at court."

Khun Phaen was pleased. "Those of the Phlai lineage are destined to be fearless warriors. Please make an effort to maintain the family name, my dear son. I'll take you to Phramuen Si."

He grilled Phlai Ngam on what he had learned and made him recite passages. His expectations were fulfilled, and he went on teaching his son other devices and stratagems until dusk. When the gong and drum sounded at nightfall, Khun Phaen made them both invisible and led the way to Phramuen Si's house.

Phramuen Si called, "Come on in, my friend. Who's this young fellow?"

"This is the son of Wanthong who was heavily pregnant when we came from the forest. I wish to place him under your care, sir. Ever since my conviction, I've had nowhere else to turn, and you've kindly given me such support. I have to depend on your merit because now I have none. His grandmother has taught him the disciplines, and he seemed well versed when I drilled him. If there's an opportunity that you deem propitious, please kindly find a way to present him at court."

"He looks like the true son of a seasoned soldier. Don't worry about him becoming a servant of the Lord of Life. When there's a war, he should do well. Leave the matter with me. He can lodge in this house.

Khun Phaen, you know I love you as a friend even though you're poor. It's beyond me to help you because your punishment is by royal command. There has to be an opening before we can expect relief."

Khun Phaen raised his hands in wai. "Though I'm in jail, it cheers me just to prostrate to you every single night. As for my son, Phlai Ngam, his future is now in your hands." He went down from the house in the bright moonlight and returned to his usual sleeping place at the prison gate.

Phramuen Si summoned Phlai Ngam for instruction. "To be a king's servant, you must study. In the big cupboard, there are many volumes of royal laws and decrees, the penal codes, the royal household law, and royal court judgments. You must learn the royal language, consult the sayings of the learned King Ruang, and study the responsibilities of various ministries. Once you know all of this, you'll be ready. You have good family on both your mother's and father's side. Don't go astray."

Phlai Ngam was sharp, good at figures, and diligent. He did not make friends and go gadding about. Every morning and night, he accompanied his patron into the palace and sat outside the audience hall, listening to the king's words. He gradually acquired an all-round knowledge of court affairs. He matured into a smart-looking youth, and many young women were interested in meeting him, but he knew nothing about courtship. If he turned round and saw a young woman, he would run away and hide.

Phramuen Si found an opportunity to present Phlai Ngam at court. When they arrived outside the audience hall, palace attendants took their gold salver with incense, candles, and flowers and carried it inside. Phlai Ngam came and sat by the salver, following exactly the procedure that Phramuen Si had told him. Other courtiers arrived, walking grandly along flourishing their fingernails, and entered the hall at four o'clock.

Phramuen Si made obeisance. "My liege, these flowers, incense, and golden candles belong to Phlai Ngam, the son of Khun Phaen and grandson of Thong Prasi. He is properly educated and well-mannered.

May I request that he endeavor to be a servant of the dust beneath the royal foot." Phramuen Si prostrated three times and waited attentively for the king's words.

King Phanwasa looked at Phlai Ngam's face. He felt pity and was about to pronounce a pardon for Khun Phaen but karma intervened, and his mind veered away, trying to recall a verse from a drama. He forgot to pronounce the pardon, and instead returned inside.

Phlai Ngam was now a royal page. He attended audience every morning and evening without missing a day, and gradually grew in confidence. The nobles were all kind to him. He placed himself under the patronage of the two heads of the pages and acted humbly towards all.

PHLAI NGAM VOLUNTEERS

A missive from Chiang Mai arrived at the palace in Ayutthaya. Chaophraya Jakri, minister of the north, read it and immediately knew it meant war.

Some months earlier, the King of Chiang Mai had learned of the exceptional beauty of Princess Soithong, the fifteen-year-old daughter of the King of Lanchang. He sent a mission to ask for her hand but the King of Lanchang refused on grounds his daughter was still too young. Realizing that this rebuff would provoke anger and perhaps an attack from Chiang Mai, the King of Lanchang promptly offered his daughter to the King of Ayutthaya to gain his protection.

The offer was gladly accepted, and a detachment of five hundred troops led by the military commander Phra Thainam was sent to escort the Lanchang princess down to Ayutthaya. A spy relayed this news to the King of Chiang Mai, who immediately sent an army to ambush the princess's party en route and bring the princess to Chiang Mai. Phra Thainam and his five hundred men were clapped in jail. The King of Chiang Mai knew that Ayutthaya would be enraged by this action. His nobles advised him to send a deliberately provocative message to Ayutthaya in the hope it would provoke the king into dispatching an army in anger without proper preparation.

On learning of this missive, so many nobles crowded into the audience hall that it looked about to burst. Horn and conch sounded. Palace guards drove away people waiting around the doors to see what would happen.

Chaophraya Jakri had the floor. "My life is under the royal foot. Chiang Mai has sent a royal missive. Phra Thainam has been captured but not killed."

The king flew into a rage. "Mm! These arrogant, uppity Lao of Chiang Mai. What do they have to say?"

Chaophraya Jakri read the missive. "An envoy was dispatched to Lanchang to request the hand of the gracious Princess Soithong in the expectation that she would be consecrated in marriage as a wife of the first rank, though, since she is still young and unfit to possess with joy, she would not be kept at the royal side. In the past the Thai city was honest, but now has become woefully besotted with power. Phra Thainam was sent to trespass on our territory and seize Princess Soithong, but our army defeated this force and took the princess. I invite the King of Ayutthaya to a duel by single combat on elephant back. Whoever wins will have Princess Soithong to partner and caress. In the meantime, Phra Thainam will remain in prison as surety. We await your response. At the end of three months, all five hundred Thai will be killed. Whether you stake your glory to be known forever, or shirk coming from fear, is up to you."

The king was choked with fury. He brandished a sword above his head and stamped his foot so the hall shook. Courtiers shrank back or took refuge behind the pillars of the hall. Palace ladies huddled together in alarm. The king again roared like thunder.

"The ruler of this piffling country makes bold to fight with *me*! It's like a lone young deer coming to confront a lion. This fellow is deluded and ignorant. His whole dynasty will be wiped out. He makes up stories that he was granted the princess's hand, but it's known that envoys came to present the princess to *me*. Why allow this man to remain a burden on the earth? In three days, I'll lead an army to Chiang Mai. Conscript untold numbers of troops from the dependent cities. Squeeze them to the last man. Don't spare this Chiang Mai rabble. Lay waste to their city and leave it deserted! Raze its walls and fortifications!"

Senior nobles nudged Chaophraya Jakri to reply. "If Your Majesty is thinking of war, we see there is good cause. But I crave Your Majesty's pardon for saying that it will weigh upon the royal advance to enlightenment. For a matter as small as this, it is not fitting that the king should go to battle with the Lao of the forests. Are there no military officers for such purpose? Your royal dignity may be impaired, while Chiang Mai will gain in glory by proclaiming this is a duel between the kings of the world. It is not fitting to bring the sky down to the earth. What if the king were to lose all the capital's troops? I beg Your Majesty to preserve his honor by making use of his servants."

The king asked, "Who will volunteer to go?"

The high officials all remained silent and prostrate with their heads bowed. The king angrily stamped his foot. "When I want something important, you just sit in stunned silence. You're all chatter and no substance—good only at cheating your own men out of money by using your clever tongues. Your property and rank are a burden on the realm."

The king went into the inner palace. The nobles went home feeling tarnished and fearful from hearing the king's words.

Phlai Ngam had been living with Phramuen Si for over a year. When he heard the news of war, he saw this was a chance for Phramuen Si to propose him as a volunteer and bring up the matter of his father. "Oh Lord Buddha, may I not be disappointed."

At dusk, Phramuen Si was unhappily telling his wife and children about the king's anger over the army. When an opportunity came, Phlai Ngam chanted a mantra to gain mercy, made obeisance, and asked, "What's happening? I hear the whole capital is in uproar."

Phramuen Si said, "Oh, Phlai Ngam, we're not used to war. Today the king posed a question to everybody. Total silence. No volunteer. The king was thunderously angry. He'll come to audience tomorrow but we're at a loss. If nobody volunteers, death and chaos will follow. Everyone's face is black with gloom."

Phlai Ngam knew this situation suited his aim. "Please make a petition on my behalf. I'll volunteer to crush Chiang Mai and capture its ruler. None of what I've studied from teachers with great effort has yet been put to use. Let me volunteer to fight so my name may be known throughout the world as the descendant of a valiant military line."

"I cannot agree. You're still a very young child. I've never seen what powers of lore you've acquired from study. Oh Son, warfare is a deep matter. You can't fight with fine words alone. If you were like your father, than I could have faith in you. If I petition the king and it turns out well, we'll gain face. But if it goes badly, we'll be flogged. All your efforts at study will go to waste. Think carefully. I'm not standing in your way because of prejudice. I just fear you'll not survive."

"You oppose me because you don't yet know my ability. I've been the student of teachers with authentic knowledge and unparalleled powers of divination. If you want evidence, I'll let you see with your own eyes."

He raised his hands to pay respect to his teachers and summon their powers, then chanted a formula. In full view of everyone there, his body disappeared.

Phramuen Si took a moment to recover himself, and then laughed heartily. "Oh, that's good! You'll do well. You're no blight on the lineage. Release the formula so we can talk."

Phlai Ngam reappeared and then turned himself into a tiger, posed to pounce. Phramuen Si's wife and children fled in fright. Phramuen Si understood the artifice and was bent over with laughter.

Phlai Ngam returned to human form. Phramuen Si patted him on the back. "You'll succeed for sure, my son. The king should be pleased. All the officers and nobles will gain face because you alone get them off the hook."

Next morning, Phramuen Si boarded a palanquin and Phlai Ngam walked behind him to the official hall. The ministers brightened up when they heard that Phlai Ngam would volunteer and was skilled in lore. Chaophraya Jakri said, "Excellent! He's good-looking like his father, Khun Phaen, and also has the same brave heart. There are signs this can work."

He turned to Phlai Ngam. "If you're as expert as he says, we'll help raise you to have rank and a reputation known everywhere. If you take Chiang Mai, you'll acquire many families, cattle, and property to make you comfortable."

They entered the audience hall. The king arrived, his face pale with anger. "Why are you quiet? I'm waiting to hear who will volunteer. Or is there nobody? Perhaps some slaves will volunteer, and I can get rid of you lot and appoint them in your stead."

Phramuen Si made obeisance. "My liege, I have found a volunteer. Phlai Ngam is the son of the mighty Khun Phaen and has studied to be expert in knowledge. I myself had my doubts so I tested him and he is indeed accomplished."

The king said brightly, "Aha! Where is he? Summon him quickly so I can see if I like his face."

Phramuen Si turned to pass on the summons. Phlai Ngam crawled past the minor royal pages, prostrated before the throne, and chanted a mantra to gain the king's mercy.

The king roared, "Phlai Ngam, bold young fellow! If you can fix these Lao, you'll be rewarded with money and rank. I see your face is handsome and your character is like your father's. Tell me whether you can do this or not!"

Phlai Ngam raised his hands above his head. "My liege, my life is beneath the dust. May I volunteer, under the protection of your royal power, to capture the impetuous ruler of Chiang Mai. May I request a royal pardon for my father so he may accompany me and give assistance in countering the stratagems of the enemy. If I fail against Chiang Mai, may I offer the lives of all living members of my lineage."

"Oh, you present yourself well! It's a pity that Khun Phaen has festered in jail for many years. It was wrong of me to forget him. Look here, you nobles, he's suffered for fifteen years because not one of you liked him enough. If he were rich rather than poor, all you fellows would have been asking on his behalf every single day. Nobody thought of him for this war because you're jealous that your own knowledge doesn't equal his, and because he attacked you when you went with Khun Chang, and you all ran off in fright, heads nodding like flowers. Have Khun Phaen released and brought here."

Phraya Yommarat, minister of the capital, had Khun Phaen fetched from the jail. "Phlai Ngam petitioned the king, who has graciously granted you a pardon. It's a pity your hair is all the way down to the ground and your appearance is pitiful, but go into the audience without delay."

The king beckoned Khun Phaen to approach. "You have suffered a bad fate for many years, but today that's over because your son requested you as his companion-in-arms and advisor. I found you trustworthy in the past. Nobody can counter your skills. It was wrong of me to keep you in jail—out of forgetfulness, not anger. How many thousand troops do you want? I'll have them conscripted day and night."

"My liege, the call-up will be troublesome and create delay. May I request only enough conscripts to transport food supplies and cook. For battle troops, may I request some convicts from the jail. There are thirty-five men, all tough, invulnerable, capable, and brave. They have studied every kind of knowledge about warfare from various teachers."

The king found this amusing. "The Chiang Mai territory is large and populous. You want to take just these few men? Even though they're able and proficient, and will fight to their utmost, I think you'll be defeated. The day after tomorrow, bring these men to display their skills for us to see. Phraya Yommarat, release all thirty-five to him without delay."

The king returned inside in good humor. The nobles greeted Khun Phaen and offered him moral support, blessings, and advice. "Your bad fortune and unhappiness are now over."

Khun Phaen gave a list of the convicts to Phraya Yommarat, who sent an officer to secure their release. The convicts were brought over and drawn up for inspection. Each gave testimony on his background in turn.

"My name is Phuk. I was convicted for robbery, forcing the victims to dance a forest dance, and making one dance naked single-handed."

"Next!"

"Mi. I robbed Old Khiao, and stabbed Chang while she was pissing. She grimaced and fell down flat, slobbering."

"Next!"

"Pan. I robbed Bang Plakot, tied Uncle Jai and Granny Rot by the neck, and singed off all their hair."

"Jan Samphantueng, in the gang that robbed Khun Siwichai. I shoved a stick up his arse so he died."

"Khong Khrao. Last year I robbed Ban Bang Phasi, taking buffaloes and property."

"Siat. I robbed a Lawa village, then murdered Uncle Pan from Ban Tan-en."

"Thong. I killed a Lao, stole an almsbowl and shoulder cloth from a novice, thumped an old monk, and had a wrestle with the abbot."

"Chang Dam. I burgled a tax collector and took all his money and property—good stuff and no small amount, including jewels."

"Bua Hua Kalok, convicted for robbing Monk Khok, hitting old Duk with the flat nose, and stabbing Uncle Sai, the duck vendor."

"Taengmo. I robbed Chi Dak Khanon, taking all I could carry, and killed the owner of the goods."

"In Suea Luang from Chainat town. I've robbed and killed about a hundred persons and stolen countless buffaloes."

"Mon Mue-dang, a northerner. I've stolen just about everything including mortars and pestles, and robbed boats."

"Mak Saklek. I robbed Kua the Chinese and his slit-eyed wife named Sao."

"Kung. I stabbed Mao's husband and seized her as my wife."

"Song. I killed a Mon and stole cloth."

"Krang. I couldn't find a wife so I robbed boats."

"Kling. I barricaded roads, stole buffaloes, and robbed boats from the north."

"Phao. I poisoned the great Chinese noble and cleaned out his house."

"Jua. I burgled Muen Thon, picking him clean."

"Maeo. I went to Ban Phitphian to rob and steal. Under questioning, I put the blame on someone else."

"Man. I robbed Abbot Phao, but did not stab him as accused. The sheriff's examination found it was an old wound."

"Jan, convicted of robbing Chinaman Kao, burning his shop, and hitting the head of a child with the back of a big machete."

"Sa Noklek. I barricaded roads to rob cattle around Khorat, and stabbed Chua down in the dirt."

"Mak Nuat. I was convicted of daylight robbery in Doembang."

"Koet Kradukdam, convicted of burgling the Department of Elephants with mahout Man, and robbing a forest Lawa. I'm invulnerable with copper testicles and a twisted scrotum."

The thirty-five pardoned convicts were all daring, strong, invulnerable to sword and spear, capable of withstanding anything. They had been imprisoned a long time. After the inspection, Phraya Yommarat ordered his retainers to distribute fruit and cloth. The men threw their old cloths away, often just sacking. "It didn't cover my arse. I shamed my wife."

Phramuen Si rode his horse home, followed by Khun Phaen, Phlai Ngam, and the thirty-five men. He arranged places for all to stay and had food prepared. The thirty-five made merry in high spirits.

When Khun Phaen was released from jail, Kaeo Kiriya donated all their pots, pitchers, and piles of raggedy cloth to other convicts and cheerfully set off after her husband. Phramuen Si welcomed her. "Live with us. Don't worry that your husband is going off to war."

He invited Khun Phaen and Phlai Ngam to sit in a circle and called the minor wives to serve the three of them food. Khun Phaen made a request to Phramuen Si. "Now that this lad has volunteered, I'm concerned over my mother. She's getting older and ricketier every day. Living in Kanburi, she'll be miserable thinking about her son and grandson. If we could bring her to live together, we'd have some peace of mind even though we go off to war."

Phramuen Si replied, "Happy to be of service. I'll have her fetched tomorrow."

King Phanwasa summoned Laothong. "You've suffered for over ten years. I can see you're not happy here. No more embroidery. Leave quickly."

Laothong went to make her farewells to the senior palace women. Her close friends exclaimed that she had had a stroke of luck. Others whispered, "She found a loophole."

She packed chests with betelnut sets, trays, water bowls, and jewelry, then went out of a palace gate and spotted Khun Phaen. "Who's that? He looks similar but thinner, and his hair is down to the ground."

Khun Phaen almost failed to recognize Laothong but called out happily, "Don't you know me? Why don't you come over?"

Laothong remembered the voice. Going closer to him, she recognized his face and clasped his feet, brimming with tears. "I just heard the king gave you a pardon, so I came to find you. You look so strange that I didn't recognize you. Oh, my dear lord and husband, it's as if you'd died and been born again. Ever since I was confined in the palace, I've cried without missing a day. I couldn't eat a mouthful without being forced to swallow tears of sorrow. At night, I'd sleep thinking of love. I embroidered silk endlessly, and the suffering has lasted an age."

The crowd of people walking past stopped to look at them and tut-tutted to one another. "Oh, good lady, in every respect you look like a palace lady, but falling in love with someone who's lost his mind is not befitting. Aren't you ashamed?"

Someone else said, "Hey! You crazy fart. When a tiger falls on hard times, nobody pays him attention. That's the mighty Phaen who has just been released."

Khun Phaen took Laothong into the house and piled up her belongings in a room. They all talked together, getting on well without jealousy.

Khun Phaen and Phlai Ngam went to Suphan to pay respect to the abbot of Wat Palelai. The abbot could not recognize Khun Phaen at first, then laughed heartily. "Oh, I thought it was some madman. What was up? Didn't you have faith in your knowledge, or was it fun lying in jail? You can unlock manacles, disappear, and be invulnerable, yet you still got yourself locked up in chains. Why didn't you use the knowledge I'd taught you?"

"I was not lacking in power, but I'd sworn an oath to Phraya Yommarat and would not go back on my word. I'm going to attack Chiang Mai. My hair is as messy as a lunatic. Please cut it for me."

The abbot picked up scissors and comb, but however hard he tried to cut, the hair resisted. When Khun Phaen enchanted some water and wet his hair, the cutting was quickly done. The abbot had a fire made to bathe Khun Phaen's body. Khun Phaen clasped his hands in prayer while the flames whooshed up to cover his head. His body was not burned but looked as beautiful as a freshly blooming lotus. The abbot anointed him with water and gave his blessing. "Be victorious over Chiang Mai without fail!"

Word had spread around the city that the knowledge of the volunteers would be put to the test. Everybody came in a raucous, excited crowd—Thai, Chinese, Mon, Burmese, and Lao—dragging their children and grandchildren by the hand. As they squashed through the gate, young lads groped at young girls and larked about. Guards whipped as hard as they could. Any offender caught was clapped in a cangue.

The noisy crowd of all ages sat jammed together. Guards carrying canes kept strict order. A circle of leather cord divided the nobles from the ordinary people. The king came to preside and commanded Khun Phaen to bring the first man on.

Bua Hua Kalok lay face up, chanted a mantra, and had someone hack at him with an axe while he lay there winking without suffering any injury.

Khong Khrao sat down, entered meditation, and was struck with a pike full in his chest many times without even bruising. He sat nodding his head and laughing until the handle of the pike gave way.

Mon lay down naked while people tried to saw him in half, but the teeth of the saw bent and broke. Chang Dam jumped three fathoms high. Siat had seven pikes thrown at him but they just slid off and fell to the ground. Thong stood still while a gun was fired and he caught the shot. Jan lifted an ox. Bua transformed himself into several people. Jua showed he could withstand fire.

All thirty-five displayed their disciplines. The king presented rewards of twenty-five baht in cash, a set of cloth, and bonuses according to whether their skill was of first or second class.

"There's still Phlai Ngam, the volunteer. Is he really able or just boastful?"

"His body doesn't look big but his heart is huge."

"Hey, Phaen! Show us a contest with your son."

The crowd swarmed to their feet to watch the father and son test each other's skills. Phlai Ngam asked forgiveness from his father, then picked up a spear. Khun Phaen stood with a sword in each hand. Drums pounded out a rhythm. The pair strutted and struck through several rounds, trading maneuvers of equal proficiency, with neither giving ground or backing away. Phlai Ngam looked the more agile but Khun Phaen had the style and strength.

Phlai Ngam walked away as if retreating, put his spear down on the ground, clasped his hands, and chanted a mantra. A blaze exploded in the middle of the arena in an echoing whoosh of licking flames. Watchers ran away in alarm.

Khun Phaen chanted a mantra, and rain poured down, dousing the fire in a flash. From the audience, the sound of "Aaah!" echoed around.

"Superb skills!"

"This father and son are the real thing!"

"Unmatched!"

Khun Phaen intoned another formula and instantly turned into a huge snake as large as a tree trunk, rearing up and swaying, with a hood and eyes as red as red lead. Two thousand attendant snakes swarmed around, spreading their hoods, slithering everywhere. Women ran off shrieking in all directions.

Phlai Ngam promptly hurled an amulet that turned into a big bird that chased after the snake, clutching with its talons and pecking with its beak. The bird lifted the snake in its bill and flew away. All the attendant snakes disappeared without trace.

Phlai Ngam enchanted a lump of earth and the bird was transformed into an elephant in musth, swaying from side to side and trumpeting. Khun Phaen stepped on the end of a tusk and climbed astride the beast's neck. The elephant squirmed violently but Khun Phaen hacked at the beast's forehead with a goad until it collapsed onto the ground and disappeared.

Phlai Ngam uttered a formula to transform his body into a buffalo. Khun Phaen disappeared and became a tiger. He bounded over with curved fangs bared, and then drew back, enticing the buffalo towards the king's throne. The tiger slapped with its paws and the buffalo went to gore with its horns.

Then both transformed again in the same instant. The father became a squawking parrot and the son a magpie. They flew up to a tree, perched beside each other, and displayed their ability to speak several human languages. The audience loved it.

"What powers of lore!"

"No enemy will be able to stand up to them!"

The king laughed merrily and loudly clapped his hands. "These two fellows are all right! No slouches. Equal in their powers. We've heard that Chiang Mai fellow boast about his might but I'd like to see him fight with my fellows! Before a day is out, he'll flee into the forest. Is this the end of your repertoire?"

The parrot and magpie replied, "My liege, we have not exhausted our teachers' manuals."

The two relaxed the mantras, returned to human form, and prostrated at the front of the courtyard. The king distributed food, cloth, and money, then summoned an astrologer and commanded him to calculate an auspicious time for the army to march.

"As the seventh of the waxing moon has a remainder of five, an auspicious time to open a campaign is 4:09 in the morning. This time is free of obstructions. Victory is assured."

The king commanded that the army be ready on the auspicious day. The nobles got up in a tumult, weak from hunger, and rushed off home. All the spectators voiced their praise.

"Best in the capital!"

"They can transform their bodies like gods."

"Nothing like this was seen in my parents' time."

"I've watched lots of fighters in my life but what we saw today was a feast for the eyes."

"It was worth being born for this."

Next morning Khun Phaen heard that his mother Thong Prasi had come from Kanburi and was at their house by Wat Takrai. Phramuen Si kindly ordered his servants to help carry their belongings over.

Thong Prasi was very happy to see her son. "Oh, meeting is like being born again. I thank you, Kaeo Kiriya, for staying by your husband. You must be sisters with Laothong. Don't dislike each other and cause trouble."

She turned to Khun Phaen. "Now that I've seen you I'm even more distressed. Even though you didn't die in jail, you look so thin and wasted. From now on, may you have only joy for a hundred years, no suffering for a thousand, and remain happy until you enter nirvana."

The belongings were carried up and piled on the terrace. A bamboo shelter was built for the soldiers to sleep. The old house was rickety and about to collapse so they worked until dusk, shoring it up with timber.

The heads of the Department of Rolls busily sent out call-up papers to unit heads in nearby villages. If anyone absconded, their wives and children were tied up and dragged in as hostages. Pleas for remission were ignored. All of the seventy required were found. Their wives and children rushed around asking people to donate as much rice as they could.

Khun Phaen took his men out to a graveyard, where they built a shrine, spread a white cloth as a canopy, placed offerings of pig's head, duck, chicken, and liquor, lit incense and offertory candles, made a sacred area circled with thread, and chanted mantras to convoke the gods. "Lord Indra, Lord Brahma, Lord Yama, Lord of Fire, Lord of the Winds, the mighty guardian spirits of the place, the spirits of the forest, Lord Vishnu the discus bearer, Siva the sun, Lord Ganesh, the supreme Three Jewels, our eternal fathers and mothers, our teachers and ruler, please give your blessings and disseminate your powers into all these weapons and amulets." The weapons jiggled as if someone was turning them over.

They placed a powerful image in a bronze bowl, added fragrant oil, chanted a formula, and blew down on the bowl three times. When the image floated up, they applied the oil to make themselves invulnerable, capable of invisibility, and able to stun others.

Khun Phaen then issued a summons. "Spirits of those who died by lightning and plague, all the various spirits who live in cavities and coffins, spirits who died in childbirth or from hanging themselves, all hasten here!"

Unable to resist these powerful formulas, spirits arrived in droves to feast on the offerings. When they had finished, Khun Phaen requested, "Please volunteer to accompany us to war."

"We'll go, sir!"

Back at the house, weapons, cloths, medicines, water carriers, bags, and waist pouches for food were distributed. The porters searched for wood to make carrying poles, and stripped bamboo to weave into baskets, panniers, and cases. Thong Prasi bustled around arranging food supplies. Kaeo Kiriya and Laothong packed goods for their husband, chatting together harmoniously for fear he might be upset. Phramuen Si arranged everything for Phlai Ngam.

In the morning, they went to audience. Chaophraya Jakri addressed the king. "My liege, these flowers, incense, and golden candles are offered by Khun Phaen and Phlai Ngam, who have come to take leave of the dust beneath the royal foot, and go to war in response to a royal command."

The king presented them with insignia of rank, cloth, sabers with gold-tooled hafts, cash to be used for the war, horses for each of them with saddle and bridle, and a set of cloth for each of the soldiers.

They led the horses out through the palace gate. Young women crowded around to look. "Oh sir, this young and going to war already."

"So slight I can't take my eyes away."

"Such a pretty body, I'd not go to sleep at all."

"I'd love to go to war with you but the action would make my clothes filthy."

Widows fluttered their eyes at Khun Phaen. He still looked brisk, galloping along with his legs in the stirrups powerfully urging the horse ahead.

"I'd like to jump up in his saddle for a ride."

Khun Phaen arrived home and went to say farewell to Thong Prasi. "Please look after the house and take care of Laothong and Kaeo Kiriya. If there's any problem, consult Phramuen Si. He and I are true friends. If the house collapses, I've left enough money to fix it."

"Don't worry about things here. Those wives of yours, leave them to me. It's good we can rely on Phramuen Si. Set your mind to the task, my dear son. Young Phlai Ngam, don't be so brave in battle that you're careless. Look after your troops well. Then they'll fight as if following you to death. Also, be grateful to the king. May you succeed through your powers and lore."

Khun Phaen went to say farewell to his two wives. "Laothong and Kaeo Kiriya, please try to get on well. If there's dissension at home, it may be a bad omen for those who go to war. On this trip, I'm likely to meet your parents as we'll pass close to Sukhothai and Chomthong. Do you two have anything to send?"

Laothong and Kaeo Kiriya struggled to suppress their sorrow in fear that crying would be a bad omen for the journey.

"Don't worry about us. We'll get on and love each other."

"We'll do whatever Mother wants us to."

"If you meet our parents, just say their daughter is well."

Then the husband and wives talked with the love and intimacy of parting.

At dawn the army assembled at Wat Mai Chai Chumphon, an auspicious place laid out according to the manuals. The area was packed with people. Khun Phaen and his son made inspections. Thong Prasi, Laothong, and Kaeo Kiriya arranged the food supplies. Phramuen Si arrived with his major wife, all his minor wives, his children, and his mass of staff to help organize the baggage. Big items were put on elephants while the food supplies were loaded on oxen, and light materials needed along the way were carried by the conscript porters. The astrologer paced out the sun's shadow to determine the exact time for the column to move off.

Kaeo Kiriya had been rushing around since morning arranging the food. Her belly was now swollen beyond tolerance. The pains came and she screamed. Thong Prasi frantically called Khun Phaen, and rushed over to support her shoulders. Khun Phaen quickly made some loosening water. Immediately after swallowing, she gave birth to a boy, right on the auspicious time for the army to march. Thong Prasi lifted the child, hugged him close to her body, and gave him the name Phlai Chumphon Ronnarong. She summoned a boat to take them home.

Khun Phaen looked at the sky, saw it was bright and clear, and ordered them to beat the gong. The army marched out to Three Bo Trees Plain with all the troops hollering and the monks chanting a prayer of victory.

Some men hefted a sack of ganja on a shoulder pole, and a hookah in their sidebag. Some had a bamboo cylinder of liquor hanging from their pike. Whenever they felt tired, they took a quiet swig. At a river junction, they came upon a liquor boat and quickly paddled over to grab some pitchers. Some went off to catch girls. Others took a whole field of cabbages from a Chinaman and pulled his pigtail when he protested. Seeing the troops coming, guards at the customs post rang a gong to assemble their men, and raised lances and swords to defend themselves, but the soldiers bounded away.

When they halted, the local headman arranged for them to sleep at the wat, and had villagers carry over food, firewood, torches, and candles. In the heat of the following day, they reached the village of Dap Kong Thanu. Khun Phaen called Phlai Ngam to walk over to a big banyan tree. "My sword, Skystorm, has been buried here since the time the governor of Phichit sent us down. This sword has the power to win battles."

Phlai Ngam dug into the earth and found the sword. As he passed it to his father, the blade glinted. Phlai Ngam exclaimed, "It's been buried for fifteen years yet has no rust! How can that be?"

"Hundreds and thousands of swords cannot compete with this one. Many metals were collected. Auspicious times were found for each stage. Herbal waters and spirit oil were used for anointing. The haft was filled with a diamond, jet, yantra, and mantra. A damned spirit was inserted for protection. Once made, it was activated in seven graveyards. How could it ever get rusty? This Skystorm is superb. Even the king's regal sword is not equal to mine."

At dusk, Khun Phaen gave orders to stop and rest. The soldiers lit a circle of bonfires. Exhausted ones collapsed into sleep. Some looked for a log to chop ganja and sat smoking a hookah until their heads fell backwards. Opium users stretched a cloth to screen themselves from view, lay next to a fire, and busily filled their pipes. Mates offered to exchange their sword, pike, or washing bowl for some opium dregs but the owners refused to sell, fearing they would die when their stock was gone.

PHLAI NGAM ROMANCES SIMALA

As Phlai Ngam slept, troubled by the lustiness of youth, the gods sent him a premonition. He dreamed that a young woman, just come of youthful age, faultlessly beautiful with fair skin and breasts like plump lotuses, walked towards him with an alluring smile. When he greeted her, she turned to flee and disappeared. Dozily he reached out and hugged his father, saying, "Don't you have any mercy?" Khun Phaen woke up and pushed his son's hands away. "What are you doing?"

"I dreamed I saw an extremely beautiful young woman but she ran off. I got carried away. Sorry. Forgive me."

"There's an ancient saying about dreams like these: The dreamer gets a good wife. Maybe a governor's daughter, huh?"

He walked over and told the men, "Today we'll reach Phichit before evening." They ate and set off on the march, not stopping in the heat though covered in sweat. When Phichit came in sight, they turned into Wat Jan.

On that same night, Simala, the daughter of the Phichit governor, dreamed she saw a lovely lone lotus flower poking prettily above the surface of a lake. She picked the flower, sniffed it, and snuggled it close to her breast. Opening her eyes, she groped around but the lotus had disappeared. She woke her Mon servant, Moei, to interpret the dream.

"Mistress, this is a good dream. The lotus can only be a husband. If not tomorrow, then the day after he should turn up here. I've interpreted dreams like this for many people."

"What nonsense, you lousy Mon! That's a silly, indecent interpretation. If anyone turns up, even a god, with the cheek to court me, it'll be in vain. I have no desire for a man."

"Don't say that, mistress. You haven't met him yet so wait until then."

Next morning, Simala went off to see to household affairs as usual, but could not escape feeling uneasy on account of her dream.

After resting in the wat until late afternoon, Khun Phaen called his son to go to the governor's residence. They walked along followed by a crowd of men carrying a betel tray and flask as marks of rank. When they went into a market for a look around, the woman vendors smacked their lips in appreciation. "Just perfect! Figures good enough to eat."

The widows fancied Khun Phaen. "I think we would be just right for each other." The young women thought Phlai Ngam was a dish. One wriggled her shoulders to make her uppercloth fall from her breasts and jiggled her eyebrows as she turned her body away.

The shops were well-stocked with patterned cloth, crockery, silk, brassware, glassware, and sundry goods. The shop girls were youthful, well-built, and forceful in the manner of people from the capital. They used yellow turmeric, shaved their hairlines, put on perfume that wafted along the street, and powdered their faces like people in Ayutthaya. Phlai Ngam thought one with a girlish figure and a fair complexion looked like the lady in his dream. He went for a closer look and found she was not as slender, and her breasts drooped a bit, and she really was different in all sorts of ways. They left the market and went to the governor's residence.

Phra Phichit was disturbed to see a crowd arriving. "Why are so many officials coming here? The one at the front looks like a noble."

Then he recognized Khun Phaen, rushed down to greet him, and dragged him by the hand up to the residence, shouting to his wife, Busaba, "Khun Phaen has come!"

Busaba came out wreathed in smiles. "Since you left, we didn't know who to ask for news. We had no idea whether you were living or dead. Seeing you again is like being given a jewel because we love you like our own beloved child. And Wanthong? When you left here, she was heavily pregnant. Was the birth easy or painful? Was it a son or daughter? You haven't brought her?"

Khun Phaen told the story of the trial, his imprisonment, Khun Chang's seizure of Wanthong, Phlai Ngam's birth, Khun Chang's attempted murder, and Phlai Ngam's petition for his father's release. "We came here on our way to attack Chiang Mai. I thought of your kindness during my hard times so I called by to pay my respect."

Phra Phichit lavished praise on Phlai Ngam. "He's good-looking and brave, a military type exactly like his father. I was desperately disappointed that Busaba's child was a girl. If the child were a man, I'd send him along with you."

He called to his daughter, "Simala, why are you sitting in there? Come out to meet these people."

Simala peeped out. "Are these some relatives I don't know about?" She slowly pushed a door open and looked through the gap. The young man with a fair face thrilled her. Moei came up, nudged her teasingly, and giggled. "What's the matter? I predicted this already."

"Hush, you lowlife! What nonsense you speak. If you say anything else, I'll give you a tongue lashing." She glared at her before turning her face aside to conceal a smile. When Phra Phichit called her again, she walked in, keeping her face bashfully lowered, and sat hidden behind her mother. When she raised her hands to wai the visitors, her heart leapt and she quickly lowered her face. Looking from the corner of his eye, Phlai Ngam returned her wai. Their eyes met and he felt a tremor of excitement.

"This is the one in my dream, I'm sure. Oh, how lovely! Even ladies in the capital can't compare. Like a full moon shining pure, clear, and brilliant. She has the beauty and poise of true gentlefolk. When she smiles, her eyes make her even prettier. Is this the one destined to be my partner? When our eyes met, I felt she was cutting out my heart to take away. I've seen thousands of other young women but none that captivates me like this. If I could make love with her for just one breath, I could face death without a thought."

Seeing Phlai Ngam looking intently at her, Simala turned away and shifted behind her mother. After a while, she glanced at him again. "So this is Phlai Ngam, sitting with his father and looking made from the same mold. He has a bright face and cheeks like nutmeg. His lips look as if painted with rouge. His black teeth gleam prettily when he smiles. Hair as cute as a lotus pod. Eyebrows curved like a bow. The black pupils of his eyes gleaming like jet. A strong chest and slim waist. Everything looks perfect. If he came to lie with me for one night, I'd gobble him up."

They looked at each other without any shyness and with the same intent. Then she came to her senses, felt shy in front of him, and went up into the residence. From inside, she looked through a chink. Love was arousing her and befuddling her like madness. She could not tear her eyes away. "This man is no waste of time! Handsome to perfection."

She slipped away to hide in her room. Moei followed with a big smile on her face. "Today you don't look well. Has some evil spirit alarmed you? If so, I'll make some offerings to appease him. O spirit, do you come from the city or the provinces? Please don't haunt her. Wait a bit until sunset, then I'll swat the mosquitoes and make offerings here inside the net."

Simala thumped Moei's head. "Stop going on, you evil Mon! Making offerings to a spirit in a mosquito net!"

They teased each other until evening when her mother called Simala to help with the food. As she carried in the meal, her heart was thumping. She put everything down without raising her head to look at Phlai Ngam. Phra Phichit invited them to eat. Phlai Ngam gazed at Simala with only an empty bowl in his hand. Swallowing rice felt like thorns in his throat. He glanced at Phra Phichit and his father to see if they had noticed his confusion.

Phra Phichit knew what was happening and pretended to complain. "What's up? You don't seem to be enjoying the food. We northerners can't match the skills down there. Is the taste of our cooking too mild?"

Then he invited the two of them, "Spend the night here. It's more comfortable. Don't stand on ceremony. Come and sleep as you please in that hall."

When the meal was over, he told Simala to arrange the bedding. "Get out those two little velvet mattresses and the soft double mats."

Khun Phaen asked Phra Phichit, "Is Color of Mist well, sir?"

"The horse is well but very old and his hide is wrinkled. He gets plenty of grass and water, morning and evening, and I go to see him on my rounds."

Khun Phaen called his son to go to the stables. Khun Phaen enchanted grass and fed it to Color of Mist so the horse could understand the words spoken to him perfectly. He tapped a hoof on the ground, jiggled with joy, and licked and sniffed Khun Phaen all over. Khun Phaen hugged the horse with tears flowing. "I've only just been released from jail because my son asked for a pardon. Phlai Ngam, here, is the son of Wanthong who you carried into the forest with me."

Color of Mist looked round for Wanthong and seemed sad at not seeing her.

Khun Phaen said, "I'm going on campaign. I'd like to take you with us because you were of assistance in the past. Will you come or has your strength gone?"

Color of Mist pranced around, stretched his legs, and whinnied as if saying, "I'll go, have no doubt." Khun Phaen understood perfectly and was pleased. He picked a handful of grass shoots and enchanted them with a formula to restore the horse's former strength. He decked

the horse in a fine harness and put him through his paces. His speed
and agility were perfect in every way. Even a young horse could not
compare. He ordered the stable hand, "Make sure he's well fed. I'll ride
him tomorrow at dawn."

He told his son, "I fear if we're slow it'll look negligent. Besides,
tomorrow is a very auspicious day with no obstructions and a ninth
constellation on a Saturday."

Phlai Ngam did not want to leave Simala but dared not confess this
to his father, so he tried to manage the situation with subterfuge. "The
troops are still tired. Let them rest until their fatigue has gone."

"Look here, Phlai Ngam, we can hang around here enjoying
ourselves and not bothering about the king's orders, but what place is
the same as one's own home?"

"Nowhere," replied Phlai Ngam, "but I want to enchant our devices
one more time. The power is still weak. Let's rest the troops and
enchant the gear."

"Tomorrow is both a day of great power for enchanting the gear and
an auspicious day for setting off. It's better to enchant the equipment
in a forest because the crowds of people in town get in the way of
composing the mind."

"In town there are graveyards that are quiet enough."

Khun Phaen knew Phlai Ngam was hiding something. "Why are
you concerned about staying in this town? You're not listening to
anything I say."

Phlai Ngam was afraid of his father and did not argue. They went
into the residence and talked with Phra Phichit about warring, routes
for travel, and various matters until Phra Phichit said, "You two are
leaving in the morning. Please get some rest."

Phlai Ngam quickly responded, "Somehow today I'm not well. I
feel very tired and my back's stiff. I'll make it an early night to get my
strength back ready for the march tomorrow morning."

Khun Phaen thought to himself, "What a loverboy! He thinks I
don't know. Karma, karma! How's this going to turn out? Will he set
us adults at odds with one another?"

He decided to play a trick. He closed his eyes and lay perfectly still. Phlai Ngam pretended to fall asleep but his heart was on fire, his stomach churning, and his patience gone. "Oh, my plump-breasted Simala! Right now are you fast asleep or is your heart feeling love? Do you realize my heart is bursting? By the look of it, you'll have mercy on me but you're staying quiet because you're a woman. Tomorrow I have to go away and there's nobody to act as a go-between. If I delay asking for your hand until the way back, I think I'll die. Now that everyone's asleep, I'll sneak in on you. If you don't have mercy on me, then let fate take its course."

A bright shining moon and the gleam of the dew cloyed his heart. The crow of a cock signaled time was pressing. He listened to his father, went over for a closer look, and called out a question. Knowing his son's game, Khun Phaen did not answer. Phlai Ngam slowly got up and walked out. Khun Phaen followed him. "What did you come out here for?"

"I'm going out to pee on the terrace. All today I've been aching to pee. I've got groin ache and it's killing me. I was going to wake you for some medicine."

"No use, Phlai. This kind of groin ache is terrible. Even if hundreds of doctors treat you, it won't go away."

He pulled his son back into the room. Phlai Ngam lay boiling with frustration and resentment. "So he wasn't asleep, he was just waiting to catch me. No problem!"

He chanted a sleeping mantra, composed his mind, and blew the mantra onto Khun Phaen, who promptly fell fast asleep.

Phlai Ngam crept out of the room into the bright moonlight, where a breeze wafted pollen and a fresh fragrance of flowers. He came to an apartment and hid in the shadows. "Is this the one?" He decided to chant a mantra to put everyone to sleep, and another to spring the locks.

Hanging lanterns shed light on a powder set, comb stand, washing bowl, two betel sets, footed trays, chests, cloth all neatly folded, a looking glass with Brahma's face carved from ivory, hairpins by a big clear mirror hung with flower tassels, and an embroidered curtain. Everything was neat, tasteful, and attractive. Her bed was magnificently gilded with feet shaped like lions and prettily carved paneling. The mosquito net was in yellow silk with a pattern of scattered flowers and a frilled opening—the sort of net used by gentlefolk. A horsetail whisk hung beside. He opened the net and stared at her sleeping form, his heart racing.

Caught by the lamplight, her pretty face seemed to smile in sleep. He gently embraced her and planted a kiss. Her fragrance made his heart leap and tumble over. When he touched her breasts, he trembled in utter confusion. He picked her up then put her down, growing ever more tormented. He was young and had never been with a woman. He worried that if he woke her up, she would cry out and run away. But he released the sleeping mantra and coughed to wake her.

Simala opened her eyes, saw Phlai Ngam at the end of the bed, and thought she must be dreaming. She bantered with him, "What's this? You dare come in here! This will cause shame and embarrassment."

When Phlai Ngam came close and embraced her, she realized it was a real person, uttered a scream, and fainted.

Sleeping on the balcony, Moei recognized her mistress's cry. She went into the room and saw Phlai Ngam lifting Simala onto his lap. Realizing what had happened, she took a washbowl over to him. "Take this cloth, soak it, and wipe her face until she revives. Then console and comfort her, make her happy. If you force her, she'll die in the blink of an eye."

Moei walked off, closed the door of the room, and sat out front to keep guard. Phra Phichit was woken by his daughter's cry and called out, "What's up? I thought I heard Simala's voice."

Moei replied at once, "My mistress called me to help swat mosquitoes inside the net. By mistake I swatted a house lizard down onto her tummy. That's why she cried out."

"You lousy Mon. Next thing, she'll have ringworm."

Khun Phaen also started awake and listened with apprehension. "Young Phlai's gone off, that's for sure. The accursed child's probably in her mosquito net. I think this'll be a mess tomorrow." He lay awake, racking his brains for a solution.

Simala slowly came to and found Phlai Ngam wrapped round her whole body, with one hand bathing her face. Her heart skittered with fear. She slowly slid down from his lap and turned her back to him.

For a moment, Phlai Ngam did not know what to say because he was uncertain how she felt. He gradually gathered up courage, picked up her fishtail fan, and softly fanned her.

"Lie still and I'll fan you. Just now I was so worried. If you'd died, I'd have died too. I prayed to the gods for help. They are kind towards us because they can see the love I have for you. Since our eyes met when I first arrived, I've felt like a fish caught in a trap. I'm burning with love and craving. If you're not willing, I'll die. I'm so sick and sad and lovelorn. Please give me some care as a cure. Turn your face towards me and say something to give me heart."

Listening to this, Simala fell ever deeper in love but feminine manners required her to resist. "I'd like to know who gave you permission to come here. You're a gentleman but you have no consideration for my parents at all. We've only just met, not even a day, and you come to kill me with an excuse about love. If you truly love me, why not inform my parents and ask for my hand? You've already gone too far and now you beg me to talk. Who would agree to it?"

"What a pity you speak like this, eye's jewel. I dare come with no fear of death because I love you more than life itself. For sure, I'll ask for your hand. Your father should be agreeable because he's long been a friend of my father. Didn't you see how he was teasing me like a son during the meal? But I have to leave with the army tomorrow. If I part from you lovelorn, my misery will persist and I'll probably die before we have a chance to be lovers. Let me entrust this body of mine to you in this room of yours."

Simala was torn. Phlai Ngam seemed sincere, but she risked shame for inviting a man into her room. It would be difficult to delay his advances, and love was tugging at her heart. She got up and turned to give Phlai Ngam a disdainful look.

"So young men from Ayutthaya are like this—smart with tongues as sharp as thorns. Whatever you say, they have an answer. You come up to Phichit and fall for a young woman but can't ask for her hand because you're going off on military service. You wait till the parents are asleep and slip into her room. If I'm not friendly, you say you'll die. You think country bumpkins are the same everywhere. If any young woman is softhearted enough, you enjoy her, go off to war, and she could wait a hundred years for your return. She's spoiled and ruined because she fell for the deceitful romantic trickery of an Ayutthaya man. I thank you for helping tend my sickness. Now go, please go. It's near dawn. If my parents find out, this will blow up in confusion, and you won't get what you want."

"Don't imagine I'm leaving. I'll die in this room. I'm not deceiving you. I'll possess and protect you as your partner until death. Be kind to me. Now that I've felt you like this, I'm not fleeing away."

He moved close against her. She tried to fend him off. "If you're sincere, give me your word that you'll definitely be honest with me into the future. If I believe you, then I'll agree to be lovers. But if you're lying, don't waste time on more pleading."

"Is that true, my jewel? I'll give you my word on oath. Let the gods come to hear me. If I should abandon you and not look after you in the future, may I descend alive into the deepest hell. There! I've given you my word on oath. Please accept my love."

"I can see you love me. I'll probably consent to be lovers, but now I'm still shaking with fever. Please wait for some time and I'll follow your will."

Phlai Ngam understood feminine "fever." With no delay, he hugged her tightly, kissed her, and slipped his hand inside her uppercloth. She pushed and pulled until they collapsed on the bed.

He was young and had just been taught to mount a horse. The filly—never ridden before—bucked and swirled at full force. When he cracked the whip, the filly slowed to an unsteady trot, and the rider clung on with legs trembling in fear of falling off such a bumpy ride. Then the filly got stirred up and stampeded, panting heavily. He went to whip her hard but had to slow down. The track was not yet as smooth as a stiff chopstick. The rider was unskilled and kept losing the timing, gripping onto the mane to steady the pace. Then the horse calmed and the rider found a rhythm. With strength undiminished, the filly pranced and reared in fine tempo. Once she knew the way, she was as good as a trained steed. Now that they knew each other, there was no limit to their energy, no need for him to urge her onward, just follow the rhythm until the sweat soaked down to her hooves and he unharnessed her.

Simala was swept away by passion. She snuggled close and used her cloth to swab the sweat that soaked his skin. She fanned him and, fearing he was fatigued, asked, "Are you famished? I'll find something."

Phlai Ngam wrapped himself around her. "Just holding your soft flesh, I'm divinely full. No need to talk of food. I floated up to heaven and saw a palace flash before my eyes." They fondled and whispered secretly together until they slipped off to sleep.

Pink glimmers lit the sky and the crow of a wild cock hastened the break of day. Simala woke first and sighed at the thought they had to part. She washed her face, powdered, and combed her hair, then shook him. "Wake up. The sun's almost up. If you linger here with me, we'll be shamed."

Phlai Ngam awoke, intent only on kissing and caressing, loath to leave, saddened at having to be severed from her. Listlessly he got up and washed his face. Simala took him to her powder table. Phlai sat down again with a deep sigh and lifted her onto his lap. "I'll miss you so much. I don't want to go."

"Think about this. You're going far away. The parents don't know about us. Suppose someone asks for my hand after you've gone? I might have to go against my father's word."

"I'll get my father to ask for your hand. If at least we were betrothed it would prevent anyone else from getting involved. If father doesn't agree, I won't go to war. Don't worry, my jewel. Though I go away, you'll not go missing from my mind. As soon as the war ends, I'll hurry back here. Don't cry. If anyone sees you today, they'll think something's up."

He helped wipe her tears, kissed her on the left cheek and then the right, and walked away. Simala went back to her bed and lay with her face buried in the pillow.

Phlai Ngam crept along the wall in the shadows, intending to lie back down in the sitting hall. He was shocked to see his father awake.

"Where have you been?"

"I had a belly ache. I went downstairs to the privy."

"Which privy in this city has a powdering service? Your face is covered in it. Don't try to deceive me. We came to stay in Phra Phichit's house. His kindness has been enormous. Yet you've had the bad manners to take liberties with his daughter. If we didn't have this little matter of the army, I'd take you under the house for a thrashing. What do you have to say for yourself for causing this mess?"

Phlai Ngam thought for a moment and saw a happy opportunity. "It's true, I did wrong, but only because my heart was overflowing with love beyond endurance. I gave her my word that I'd get you to ask for her hand. Leave the proper marriage until the way back. Father, please consent so I can go to war with a still heart."

Khun Phaen watched his son's distress, thinking quietly to himself. "To abandon her would be unjust. He got besotted and befuddled. If I don't help, there'll be trouble down the road. If you stumble on a stairway, you must leap and trust to your luck."

He pretended to be angry at Phlai Ngam. "A young heart is never satisfied. Phra Phichit loves his daughter like his own heart but you ravish her like some villain. Now we have to find a solution that doesn't make him lose face. If you ever abandon Simala, I'll kill you."

Phlai prostrated and wai-ed his father in delight. "I won't disappoint you on this."

Simala lay listlessly, hugging her pillow and heaving heavy sighs until mid morning. Moei noticed her mistress was not to be seen, and crept in to wake her. Moei flopped down beside her with a thump to shake her up, and feigned a sigh.

"What a pity! I'm so poor and can't find anything to put in my mouth. I dreamed that a god came last night and departed just before daylight. On his way, he'll want betel and tobacco. I haven't even a hundred cowries. Where can I get offerings for the god? When you get up, you must give me an advance because I'm very worried about this god. It was nice of him to fly down and if my mistress has no mercy, he'll be disappointed."

Simala got up and thumped her. "Don't you have anything better to do than poke your nose in others' affairs? Don't talk so much, you loudmouth. Sit here and help for a moment."

They sliced betelnuts, made rolls of pan leaves, stitched leaf baskets to hold tobacco, and added snacks to eat along the way. Everything was placed in a basket and covered with a cloth. "Take this carefully."

Moei received it. "Offerings to the god who came to visit you . . ."

Phra Phichit and Busaba finished giving orders to feed the troops and went to find the two commanders. Busaba called out, "What's up with Simala? Khun Phaen is leaving this morning. It's already late and she hasn't brought food."

Moei came out. "Dust got in my mistress's eye while she was washing her face. It's still stinging badly."

"You're just a chatterbox. You only grin and think about food, you lousy Mon. Why don't you give her eye drops of turmeric water?"

Phlai Ngam was amused. "This girl is quite something. She came to lend a hand last night when Simala fainted, and now she helps by fibbing to her parents."

He sat quietly waiting for an opportunity, and then said to Busaba, "Opening the eye underwater and fluttering the eyelid makes the irritation disappear."

Busaba laughed. "You're very considerate. Moei, tell Simala what Phlai Ngam said."

Then she turned to Khun Phaen. "I'm eternally annoyed with myself that I have no son."

Khun Phaen saw the opening, picked up the thread, and ran with it. "I depended on you when I was in dire straits and you showed kindness in countless ways. I've often thought about how to repay your kindness but couldn't see any means until I came here. As the two of you have no son, I'll offer young Phlai Ngam here to be at your service, to repay the kindness I've received from you both. How do you feel, sir?"

Phra Phichit was delighted. "No need to go through the formalities. In truth, to my mind they're perfectly suited. But I have some apprehension that my daughter, being provincial, is just a simple straightforward girl, not up to city people. If in the future my daughter doesn't please you, don't cause any shame."

"I've given considerable thought to this point. Only after I'd extracted a promise from Phlai Ngam did I speak to you. As for Simala, even in the capital no match for her can be found, either in appearance or manners. Even were young Phlai Ngam to become a high noble, she could entertain anyone as guest. As long as I'm alive, I'll make sure no shame will attach to you."

"If that's so, we can trust each other. But Busaba will say I'm too easy. Simala is her child so you must ask how she feels."

Busaba was sitting listening with a smile on her face. "I was eager to tell you how pleased I was. Because I love you like my own flesh, I can't oppose your request, but I'm still a bit concerned about Phlai Ngam. He has business far away in the Lao country. There are plenty of young women there. If he falls for the daughter of some lord, whatever we've said today will be meaningless. I may be called an addlebrained oaf who doesn't know how to judge a man, and I'm not saying that I want to break it off, but if I'm to give my only child to him, some means have to be found to make matters secure."

Phlai Ngam said, "If you parents can all agree, have no doubts about me. I'll not go astray and be unfaithful. I know of your kindness in the past because my parents told me. Allow me to be a golden shoe to support your foot."

Khun Phaen added, "If they are betrothed, his thoughts will be here—in body somewhere else but in heart with his partner. This would be prudent. Today is a very auspicious day. Please accept this gift of betrothal. All the business of fixing a day and making a bridal house, I'll leave to you, sir."

Phra Phichit accepted the gift. "If matters go smoothly, the war should be over around the second month so the marriage can be around the fourth month."

Everyone was pleased with this arrangement. As food was ready, they sat round in a circle to eat, chatting merrily until Khun Phaen and Phlai Ngam took their leave.

On their way to Wat Jan, Moei intercepted them. After Khun Phaen had walked past, she coughed as a signal to Phlai, who slipped off the road into the trees and asked, "Why did you come here?"

"This basket of goods is for sale to Phlai Ngam."

He smiled and said, "I'll take it without even asking how expensive it is." He gave her fifteen baht and whispered, "Keep her happy morning and night until I return and I'll give you more cash in reward." He hurried after his father and helped to organize the troops at Wat Jan.

The column was drawn up and the troops moved off. Villagers and townsfolk rushed up to watch. As they passed a wat, monks sprinkled them with sacred water.

Phlai Ngam rode his horse behind Khun Phaen. He was very sleepy and swayed in the saddle, feeling both very lusty and very miserable.

"Oh Simala, you must be grieving sadly, just as I'm thinking of you. If you know that I've asked for your hand and your parents agreed, then I think that'll overcome your fears. Sit and count the days until the ceremony. When you have a chance, give some thought to decorating our house. Who will you talk to about it? Moei's just a servant and will probably suggest you buy everything new, but a lot of your old stuff is fine. The bed is a bit narrow for sleeping but that's good for love. Your powder and makeup things are peerless. I'll build a big new bridal house where we can put both your things and mine. I've got lots of weapons, charms, amulets, and yantra cloths. But perhaps you don't like these for fear of spirits. No problem. I'll keep them somewhere else. We'll have a carpet and a pair of pillows where I can hug and caress you morning and night. Who needs furniture anyway? With just a soft mat, a pillow, and our love, we should be happy every night and day."

His sleepy mind began to wander. He imagined she was there and began to talk with her. "Suppose you have a child in the future. I've seen the belly pains and the screaming. They say midwives tend to be careless and have killed many people by just yanking. I'll stand over them with a stick. If they get up to their tricks, I'll thrash them like this." He swung his horsewhip and hit the rear of his father's mount.

The horse reared up. Khun Phaen almost fell off. When he got the mount back under control, he turned round, his face red with anger. "Did you mean to do that?"

"Honestly, I was dozing and dreaming of Simala. She was giving birth, groaning with pain, and I thought the old midwife was taking the easy way by pulling the child carelessly, so I struck at her, but I hit the horse. I didn't mean it. Father, please forgive me."

Khun Phaen pondered to himself. "He's lost in dreams about Simala because he's just known love for the first time and sees everything from the good side. Oh son, you don't yet know the bad taste when love changes and takes flight. The worst pain in the world can't equal the pain and woe of love. When young people are lovers, they feel that they could swallow each other up. They live together and spend all the time in lovemaking with no thought they'll ever part. Oh Wanthong, you've probably forgotten me after so long. Now you'll be carried away by Khun Chang. Or do you still think of me, your long-lost friend in hardship, like I think of you, day and night, all the time?"

The army left Phichit, skirting lakes that teemed with fish, crocodiles, and birds. A golden pelican floated in the current, its food sack hanging from its beak, open to scoop the water. Darters plunged down to catch fish. Egrets stood staring intently. Flocks of hawks hovered above, swooping down to eat fish from the lake. Baldheaded adjutant birds waded on long legs, looking for a catch. Painted storks and openbills scooped up shellfish.

A carpet of red lotus—some blooming, some turning to seedpods—stretched away as far as the eye could see. Clusters of star lotus dazzled in the streaky light of dawn. Bees flew around with a sleepy hum, probing into the flowers for their sweet taste. A light breeze blew the water into ripples that glistened gloriously in the light.

Leaving the lake, they turned to cut through the forest, then followed a path on the riverbank to Phitsanulok, where they went to Wat Mahathat to pay their respect to the Buddha images, Phra Chinnarat and Phra Chinnasi, and ask for victory and well-being.

After a rest, they marched to Sawankhalok in one day. Local officials welcomed them and looked after them as instructed in their sealed orders. They stayed three days, then marched across the upland to the hills. Cliffs with shadowing overhangs towered above. A funnel of water crashed down through a ravine. The mountain sides rippled in hollows, promontories, spurs, and caverns. In the valley, the stream ran through a deep gorge of crumbled rocks, gouged with pools and shallow caves. Stalactites began as uneven bulges and narrowed down to points dripping with water, some looking sharp and glistening with many colors. Stalagmites stuck up like barbs, some rounded, some knobbly. In the distance, the gorge opened out to a distant view of nothing but mountain peaks.

They walked into the hills with their refreshing shade. The squawking of quails and cooing of doves echoed through the trees. Parrots sat eating on an orange jasmine. Peacocks spread their tails. Weaverbirds babbled softly. Plain black drongos perched on a pine. Bulbuls whispered lovingly. Junglefowl dashed around, cackling boisterously and scratching for bamboo seeds. A partridge strutted around its mate in a courtship dance.

As the sun descended to hide behind the hills and the wind dropped, they came out onto a plateau where new grass shoots were sprouting after a recent forest fire. A powerful tigress loped along. Timorous deer watched with bodies stooped, or ran off helter-skelter to hide. A sole young gaur forged through the forest. Wild buffaloes chased one another through the trees. A cow elephant noisily tugged at clumps of bamboo. Sambar peered out from bushes before coming out to taste a saltlick.

They cut across the Rahaeng region and through Thoen district without entering the towns. After fourteen days' travel through forest and hill, they were within two days of Chiang Mai. They halted at Turtle Mound Lake and made a camp.

Khun Phaen called Phlai Ngam over to talk. "If we rush to attack, they may just cut off the heads of Phra Thainam and the other prisoners. We should sneak into the city and find some way to bring them out first. Just the two of us will go. We must disguise ourselves as Lao locals."

After decking themselves with charms and bandeaus infused with power, they stood with eyes closed, praying according to an ancient teacher's manual, and examined their breath. As it flowed from the right nostril, they set off on the right foot. They cut through marsh and bushes rather than keeping to a road, and hid in a wood.

A Lao farmer and his son were returning from planting vegetables. The son was dreamily playing a fiddle, and the father the Lao pipes.

Khun Phaen whispered to his son. "Don't you see? The Lao with the fiddle has no head. He's reached the time of his death."

They unsheathed their swords and hitched up their lowercloths. When the Lao approached, they burst upon them and lopped off their heads, then picked up the heads, stuck them firmly on the necks, and recited mantras while Khun Phaen scattered rice. The spirits of the Lao rose up and made obeisance at their feet. Khun Phaen commanded them, "Help lead us into the city!"

They stripped off the Laos' upper and lower cloths and put them on. They cut off their hair with a sword, and attached it as hair pieces, wrapped with the Laos' pink headcloths.

When they arrived back at Turtle Mound Lake at dusk, the soldiers stayed hidden until Khun Phaen called out, "Why is nobody moving?" and the soldiers rushed out to salute.

"Sir, with those clothes and the long hair, you really look just like a Lao."

"We hid to take a good look at you, and you were truly unrecognizable!"

Khun Phaen gave orders to break camp. They marched through the forest at night, sleeping during the day. After two nights and two days, they reached a broad lake and made a camp with a boundary of stakes. Elephants and horses were fed grass and water. Howdahs and saddles were arranged side by side for the two army commanders to rest.

KHUN PHAEN RESCUES PHRA THAINAM

In prison in Chiang Mai for half a year, Phra Thainam was almost mad from misery, starvation, and discomfort. "This is like falling into hell while still alive. Hey Ta-Lo, come and cheer me up a bit. They've left us here to die. It's odd the king hasn't sent troops to rescue us."

"Sir, that could turn out well or badly. If they sent anyone except Khun Phaen, it'd just be hastening our own deaths. But when we left, Khun Phaen was still in jail. None of the other Thai nobles could match the Lao."

"I agree. Oh, may the gods induce the king to send Khun Phaen!"

As the sun sank from sight, warders made their tour of inspection, putting chains and cangues on everyone. The prisoners slept sitting with backs against the wall and heads lolling forward over the cangue.

Phra Thainam dreamed that a Brahman descended from the sky, walked into the jail, and poured water from a conch over his head. All the chains fell away. The Brahman repeated the trick with all the other prisoners, then disappeared in a flash. Phra Thainam promptly woke up with a start, but found his body was still in chains. He roused Ta-Lo, who interpreted the dream: "Some able person is coming soon. We're going to get out of here alive!"

Next morning, the prisoners were assigned to work duty. "Ta-Lo and Ta-Rak, you're cutting grass. Find sickles and shoulder poles."

Thinking of Phra Thainam's dream, Ta-Lo sang and danced along merrily. The warders took them through a market where they grabbed betelnut and bananas from vendors, who cursed and tried to fend them off. They ran off with their chains clanking along the road, across a bridge over the river and down to a meadow. While they cut grass, the warders laid out cloth behind some bushes and went to sleep.

Khun Phaen and Phlai Ngam disguised themselves as Lao and walked into the city. Young girls eyed up Phlai Ngam but he walked along looking straight ahead. Old ladies shouted to him, "Where are you going, young fellow?"

"Why not relax here a while? I'll give you betelnut and good tobacco."

The spirit of the Lao farmer, who had come along with them, replied in Lao. "Dear ladies, please forgive me. I've got business in the city. I'll come a-courting on the way back this evening."

One vendor offered a flower to Phlai Ngam. He took it and gave her hand a squeeze. She brushed his hand away, feeling excited. "Where do you live? I'll come to sleep with you."

A widow selling betelnut called out to him loudly, "You good-looking young fellow, try my betel and pan."

A younger vendor, cut in. "He's not interested in a widow with a body like yours. Aren't you ashamed to be bothering him?"

"Don't interfere. You've never made love so what do you know? You young girls have got as much inner rhythm as a corpse. When it comes to the tricks, watch out for us widows. A young chap like this is a pushover. Just tug his string and he'll tremble."

The spirit of the Lao farmer made enquiries for them. "There's talk that some Thai have been imprisoned in the city. I've never seen the face of a Thai fellow. Where are they being kept?"

"They're locked up in the jail beside the stables. The men are taken to cut grass. Go to the meadow."

They hurried to the meadow, and spotted the Thai and the sleeping guards. Ta-Lo looked up at the Lao villagers approaching. "Where do this couple of good-looking fellows come from?" Then he recognized the face. "That's Khun Phaen for sure!" He rushed to clasp Khun Phaen's feet, shaking with tears.

Khun Phaen said, "Don't make too much noise or the warders will wake up."

Ta-Lo and Ta-Rak wiped their tears. "Pa Phaen, it's been torture."

"Jailed and manacled."

"My back's got over a hundred stripes."

"Phra Thainam is locked up day and night."

"He's been thinking of killing himself."

"By the power of merit, you've come in time, sir."

"Who's this young fellow, Pa?"

"This fellow is my first born son with Wanthong. Though his body is still that of a boy, his heart is huge. I was released from jail because he had the nerve to volunteer to the king. Tell Phra Thainam and all the men we'll come around eleven o'clock tonight. Where's a good place to hide during the day?" Ta-Lo directed them to a ruined wat.

In the evening, the warders took the prisoners back through a market. The vendors heard the clank of chains coming and closed their awnings or held tight onto covers over their wares. Ta-Lo and Ta-Rak scooped up eels and fish. The vendors tried to slap them away. Ta-Lo laughed uproariously. "What shall I order today?" He grabbed oranges, bananas, and papayas. One vendor tried to hit them with a pole but he grabbed it and she fell over in a heap.

"Why are the prisoners so rowdy today?"

"I'll petition for their backs to be flogged to ribbons."

Ta-Lo said, "If you want to lay charges, go ahead. You don't scare me, funny face."

Back at the jail, they steamed rice and grilled fish. At sunset, warders counted the prisoners, checked the manacles, threaded them all on a big chain, set lanterns at three places, and double-bolted the doors.

Ta-Lo crawled to Phra Thainam and whispered, "Sir, your dream has come true. Khun Phaen is here with his son. Everyone is to get ready. They're coming tonight."

Phra Thainam felt he had been anointed with celestial water. He ordered Ta-Lo to pass the message along the chain. Nobody slept.

Khun Phaen found an auspicious time late at night when the sky was starless and the waning moon had set. The pair removed their Lao clothes and put on bandeaus infused with power, and shirts enchanted with yantra and dyed with herbal medicine. Detecting their breath was stronger through the left nostril, they stepped off on the left foot, chanting a formula to stun others into not seeing them.

At the jail, Khun Phaen chanted one mantra to put everyone to sleep and another Loosener mantra to spring the locks. The two hurried in. When Khun Phaen scattered enchanted rice, the manacles fell off everyone, and the prisoners stood up on shaky legs. Phra Thainam came out and saluted Khun Phaen. Many men wanted revenge on their guards. "They pushed us around, cursed us, and flogged me almost to death."

They cut the three warders to pieces. Ta-Lo smashed down a wall and swung his sword to despatch the governor. Ta-Rak wanted revenge on the officer in charge of bonfires. "He flayed my back into chopped meat. Why should this villain be left alive?"

The prisoners rampaged around, lopping off the heads of those they hated, leaving others dreaming, mumbling, and snoring, spattered with gore like a graveyard.

Once outside the jail, Ta-Lo told Khun Phaen, "We've been trussed up so tight that many people's legs are weak or lame. We can't run or fight well. We must steal horses for everybody. I'll go because I know the stables."

Khun Phaen said, "Slow down, old fellow. I don't think you can do it on your own. You'll run into some Lao and the whole city will be in uproar."

He ordered Ta-Lo to lead the way and all the rest to follow. At the stables, he scattered rice and chanted formulas. The guards and their wives fell asleep, hugging one another and snoring loudly. The Thai swarmed in and went around poking into everything, stripping people of their lowercloths, snatching purses, stealing waist pouches, and picking up anything that caught their fancy.

Khun Phaen shouted, "Hey! Don't waste time!"

They all came to untie the horses and harness them. Ta-Lo chose good steeds for the four commanders. They mounted and trotted away to a crossroads where Khun Phaen cut a post from a coral tree and wrote a message in charcoal.

Ta-Mo said, "Pa, in the hills the Lao keep some thirty elephants. We have a battle to win. It'd be good to have elephants to ride."

"Good idea. Here Ta-Lo, take a hundred men to seize the elephants along with their howdahs and gear."

They cut through the forest, stormed the camp, trussed up the elephant handlers, and seized everything they could carry—harness, howdahs, stirrup ropes, tooled saddles, and goads. They mounted the necks and charged back through the forest. Khun Phaen laughed heartily and ordered everyone to march. Late at night under bright stars with dew falling, they arrived in the area of the lake.

The thirty-five soldiers heard a racket coming through the forest and thought it was Lao from the city. They rushed to get kitted out and stage an ambush at a place where the road passed through a defile.

When Phra Thainam rode his horse into the defile, a volunteer gave the order of attack, and leapt onto Ta-Lo's elephant, hitting Ta-Lo hard enough for blood to ooze like sap. Ta-Lo swung his goad and knocked the volunteer down from the mount. Picking himself up, he hurled his sword at Phra Thainam, hitting him square. Phra Thainam's shirt ripped and he lost his balance, but he dug in his heels and galloped off.

Many of the released prisoners ran off in fright, abandoning their swords. Thinking it was a Lao ambush, Khun Phaen spurred his horse into the thick of it with Phlai Ngam on his heels, slashing left and right. A group of the volunteers swarmed over the pair. Khun Phaen bellowed a stunning mantra. Swords slipped from hands and dropped onto the grass. Two men thrust at Khun Phaen's chest, but their pikes broke. Khun Phaen stabbed back with a dagger, but the skin was not pierced. Another slashed at Phlai Ngam, but it was like striking stone—the sword did not even penetrate his outer shirt and crumpled to pieces.

The volunteers were perplexed. "How come they're invulnerable, beyond our powers?"

One volunteer suddenly caught sight of Khun Phaen. "Is it you, Pa?"

In shock, they dropped their swords and prostrated to Khun Phaen.

"We didn't know it was you, Pa."

"Please forgive us."

"We thought it was the Chiang Mai army."

"I stabbed you several times. I'm guilty of a capital offense."

Khun Phaen was pleased rather than angry. "It's good you're this brave."

They milled around getting to know one another then trooped back to the camp by the lake.

As the early streaks of dawn touched the mountaintops, Lao officials went to unlock the prisoners. They found the warders lying tumbled over one another with heads off, eyes rolled up, and faces blanched. Chains, cangues, and manacles were scattered around. The prisoners had disappeared.

"These chains and cangues are still intact. How did they slip out of them?"

At the stables, the Lao overseer awoke and drowsily looked around, seeing that pillows, mosquito nets, and baskets had disappeared. His wife asked, "Eh? Who took your lowercloth?"

"Where've all *your* clothes gone?"

She grabbed a rattan mat. He found a sack to wrap round himself. In both stables, there were no horses. The ostlers rushed around, some of them naked and dangling.

"They've all gone from my stable."

"We're dead!"

They ran off in panic and met the prison officers. Then the elephant keepers appeared, and they all shared their stories. On the way to the palace, they came across a post in the middle of their path. Seeing the Thai writing, they uprooted the post and carried it along with them.

Nobles and high officials were discussing government business in the main hall when they saw an unruly crowd coming, some wearing sacks and mats, others naked.

"Who are these outcastes? Were they robbed? Are they madmen?"

The warders replied, "Late last night, some able people came. They put us to sleep, killed the governor and many warders, unlocked chains by mantra, and released the Thai and Lanchang people. Sirs, please have mercy."

The elephant keepers added, "They tied us up and stole around thirty big elephants along with their gear."

The ostlers explained through trembling mouths, "Almost five hundred horses are missing. We found this wooden post with a boastful message that they're going to destroy Chiang Mai."

A Lao lord said, "Those damn Thai!" He picked up the message and led the whole crowd to the audience hall.

The king was presiding when they arrived. An interpreter was summoned to read the message. "Because you seized Princess Soithong and imprisoned several Thai, the eminent monarch of the Thai city has sent me, a diabolical soldier, along with my son and thirty-five seasoned soldiers, to destroy your city. Will you wait there for us to come and defeat you? Or will you come out to the lotus lake? If you love life and care for your colleagues, deliver Princess Soithong to us, and bow to show your fear."

The King of Chiang Mai blazed with anger like the sky on fire. "These arrogant, leprous Thai! Their bragging is provocative and insulting. There's only a handful of them! Those who broke out of jail aren't capable of putting up a fight. We can round them up and chop them down in less than an eye blink."

The minister of the army promptly addressed the king. "If he weren't able, he wouldn't issue such a challenge. But thirty-five men can't do much and the five hundred prisoners are half-starved. Like a herd of deer once attacked by a tiger, they won't come back for more. Send out a rider to look. If they're still at the big lake, take an army and crush them to dust."

The king ordered the commanders to have the army ready before four o'clock the next morning. The minister of the army sat in the official hall issuing call-up notices for troops, and allocating elephants, horses, and weaponry. Five thousand battle-hardened cavalrymen equipped with bows, spears, and throwing knives were assigned to the vanguard under the command of Saentri Phetkla, a man with invulnerability and skill in the arts of war.

His body was tattooed with a tigress, bear, disciples of the Buddha, and devices for stunning enemies. He had a jet gem embedded in his head, golden needles in each shoulder, a large diamond in his forehead, a lump of fluid metal in his chest, and herbal amber and cat's eye in his back. Since birth he had never been touched by a weapon and did not carry even the scratch from a thorn. He never slept with his wife and never bathed, but applied a paste of medicinal herbs. The only exception was prior to battle when he filled a bath with river water, put in charms and herbs, used a formula to make the water boil as if over fire, scooped some water over his head, took out the charms and herbs, then stepped in, washed himself, and looked for an omen in the water. Phetkla stared at it, knowing the meaning exactly. The omen in the water was red. He was fated to die.

"Even so, my skill as a valiant warrior will still be known."

He dressed brilliantly, decked himself with charms, and daubed enchanted powder on his forehead. Picking up his lance, he leapt on the back of his magnificent horse, and ordered three cheers to begin the march.

Thao Krungkan, deputed to command the main army, pressed forward with the preparation of the troops. The men bound auspicious threads around their heads, and made themselves invulnerable against weapons by chanting formulas, daubing themselves with herbs, wearing yantra designs, drinking enchanted liquor, or carrying fangs, tusks, animal eyes, or hide embedded with diamond or jet.

The left wing, right wing, and rearguard were each arrayed with a thousand men, all battle-hardened and fully armed. The king presented his commander with a royal elephant in musth with tusks hooped in gold, long tail, large ears, and auspicious dual frontal humps on his head. A mahout brought this elephant beside a platform for Thao Krungkan to mount. He concentrated his mind and saw a strange omen in the shape of a man with no head. On a second look, the arms and neck were not attached to the body. As he urged the elephant forward, a bird chick fell dead before his eyes, a barn owl skimmed over his head, and a vulture alighted on his parasol. "Oh, my life is going to be crushed to dust! But asking the king to delay would bring shame for the troops. No one born as a man can escape death."

The army moved off. The flags drooped instead of waving. Even the sound of cheering did not echo.

At the lake, the Thai saw a pall of dust cloaking the sky. Khun Phaen sat quietly with eyes closed, examining the path of his breath. "The Lao are bringing an army of ten thousand."

He commanded men to mark out a moat on the ground and pile up cut reeds as an embankment across the end of the lake, as crow's wings on either side, and as models of battle towers. When Khun Phaen scattered enchanted rice, the reeds turned into hardwood and the marked ground became a deep moat stretching across from lake to forest. The fortifications could withstand even large cannon.

Khun Phaen announced, "As expected, the Lao have brought a large force. Gather all the Lanchang men together inside a circle of sacred thread. Only the Thai will ride out to engage them. Phlai Ngam will lead the thirty-five volunteers as the vanguard. I'll lead the main army in support. Even if there are thousands of Lao troops, we'll kill them all. Be resolute, don't fear, have courage."

Khun Phaen and his son decked themselves in imposing devices, and gave orders for the army to move off.

When the two armies came face to face, Saentri Phetkla saw the Thai army was just a handful. "It's like winged termites flying into a flame. Do they think they can survive? Take them, men!" He spurred his horse to lead his troops into the attack.

They surrounded the Thai vanguard, slashing with swords and stabbing with spears. Phlai Ngam and the thirty-five swirled around like windmills, parrying the blows, batting the spears away, and stabbing back, sending Lao troops tumbling dead from their horses. Other Lao stepped over the bodies, and kept coming forward, surrounding them in such numbers that the Thai began to feel weary in the shoulder.

Phlai Ngam hurled himself into the fray, slashing like lightning with his yantra-inscribed sword. Though the Lao were decked in charms and herbal medicine, they were scattered dead on the ground by this weapon. Others backed away in fright, like a pack of dogs in face of a tiger.

"Our swords don't pierce his flesh."

"I slash him but it doesn't go through his shirt!"

Seeing his troops wavering in confusion, Saentri Phetkla charged to the front, slapping his feet into his horse's flanks and bellowing loudly until he came face-to-face with Phlai Ngam.

"Here, my good officer, what's your name? You're just a youth—slight, tiny. You're a pupil of what teacher? A member of whose lineage? Pray tell me."

"I'm a soldier of Ayutthaya. My name is Phlai Ngam following the custom of our lineage, which extends over many generations. I'm a student of my father. And you, sir! What's your name? It's presumptuous to ask an elder who is not yet dead though very old, but what teacher did you study with?"

"You southerners didn't know when you rushed up here. I come from a royal lineage of great soldiers. In Lanna nobody stands against me. My teacher was the famous Si Kaeo Fa from Red Cow Cave on Gold Hill. You're very good-looking, young lad. Your figure is pretty, like a girl's. You're younger than my grandchildren. You shouldn't fight with a grandfather. Go back and tell your father to come and do battle with me, to be a treat for the troops, an example of soldiery."

"You're old like a grandfather buffalo while I'm young like a tiger cub. Through my handiwork, Lao have died in droves. Let me see whether your mouth is mightier than your skill. Forgive me, don't bother my father. Can you even triumph over his son? Perhaps you're so tired you'd rather sully your name?"

Saentri Phetkla's eyes blazed red like gleaming lacquer. "This fellow really won't listen. Boasting he can fight *me!*"

He galloped over to the middle of the battlefield, flourished his lance, and prepared to charge. Phlai Ngam grasped his sword in a two-handed grip and urged his horse to approach with a nimble rhythm. They circled, feinting and slashing this way and that, maneuvering deftly around each other without giving ground. As Phetkla had the longer weapon, Phlai Ngam kept his distance, darting in to slash and dodging away. When Phetkla chased after him, Phlai Ngam allowed him to approach near enough to thrust, then side-stepped so the blow missed, and Phetkla tumbled headlong. Phlai Ngam delivered a slashing blow but it bounced off Phetkla's shoulder as the flesh was as tough as stone. Phetkla raised his lance high and hacked but Phlai Ngam's body was like rock.

Saentri Phetkla pondered to himself, "This Thai lad is really able, much stronger than he looks. I don't think there's any chance of victory using weapons. I must use the inner way of mantra."

He rode his horse to halt some distance away, closed his eyes, chanted, and blew a formula for summoning the Great Waters. Water gushed down in a stream, flooding the whole area, while wind whipped the water into sloshing waves. Horses were lifted off the ground and swept away by the swirling torrent. The Thai soldiers scrambled to swim off and scale trees in total confusion, desperately appealing to their commanders to counter the mantra.

Phlai Ngam chanted and blew a formula that drained the water dry, and blew another mantra summoning the Fire Element. Instantly, the whole plain burst into flames that licked towards the Lao troops, who spurred their horses away in all directions, calling out to their leaders for help.

Phetkla calmed his body and chanted a formula summoning the Great Precipitation. Clouds blanketed the sky, and torrential rains drenched the lofty forest, flooding the ground and extinguishing the fire. The volunteers huddled together under the shelter of trees, shivering from cold, injured almost fatally by hits from huge hailstones.

Phlai Ngam chanted a formula summoning the wind from inside his body as the Wind Element. A howling gale gusted so hard that the raindrops were scattered into thin air. Phlai Ngam hurled a lump of gravel into the sky, making it rain drops of sand and grit that splattered down on the Lao troops, who frantically ran to hide in the bushes, stripping off their cloths to cover their heads.

Saentri Phetkla joined his fingers above his head and blew. A mesh appeared in the sky, blocking the sand drops from falling. Phetkla commanded his soldiers to dismount. "It's no good attacking them on horseback. Better to engage them at close quarters on foot. Select only long weapons—pikes, javelins, and spears. We are over a thousand and they're very few. If we use our strength of numbers to stab them, even though they're invulnerable, their bones will break."

The Lao soldiers formed up in groups and surrounded the Thai, then fell on them, thrusting, stabbing, and hitting. The volunteers slashed back, cutting Lao open from shoulder to hip, lopping heads, and felling bodies in splatters of red blood. The Lao rearguard came up alongside to join the fight, swarming over the Thai in waves. The volunteers hacked relentlessly but the more Lao that died, the more kept on coming. The volunteers' shoulders drooped and they could hardly raise their arms. Wearily they called to their commander.

"Phlai Ngam, sir, we've slashed them to the end of our strength but for every one dead, another five or six turn up."

Phlai Ngam pulled out three handfuls of tamarind leaves and enchanted them to become millions of wasps which turned the sky as black as night and stung only the Lao, over and over again. The Lao doubled over and dropped their weapons, frantically slapping with their hands. Some dived into water to get away but were stung again the moment they surfaced. Horses galloped off wildly with their faces smothered in stings. Officers and men fled in defeat. With his eyes closed by the stings, Phetkla spurred his horse away from the fray.

Thao Krungkan saw the flight and immediately urged his elephant to lead the main Lao army forward. Khun Phaen saw Krungkan's move and drove his elephant out to confront him.

"Is this a royal army? Countless elephants and horses! What country are you going off to fight?"

Krungkan was cut to the quick by this insult. Knowing this must be Khun Phaen, he responded in kind. "Doesn't Ayutthaya have any horses and elephants? Is that why you come to steal from Chiang Mai? My army has come to round up forest bandits. If you return the goods, you'll survive."

Khun Phaen laughed. "Though you try to hide the wrongdoing, there's no smoke without fire. Lanchang sent the princess to the Thai capital but your king abducted her. It's your king who's the forest bandit. Trading your life for this lady is senseless. If you love yourself and fear death, send the princess back, and live!"

Krungkan was taken aback to hear his king had acted badly, but responded in kind. "Your words go too far. The King of Lanchang has always been a two-faced villain. He offered the Princess Soithong to Chiang Mai, then shifted his ground and offered her to the Thai, so we bear a grudge. Come for an elephant duel to settle this matter. If I lose to you, Princess Soithong will be handed over. If you're defeated, she must stay in Chiang Mai."

He commanded his troops to surround the Thai detachment and not let anyone escape. Khun Phaen called out to his troops, "Make a defensive formation. Cover me on both wings. Hold the rearguard. I'll duel with him on elephants."

He rode his mount forward, blowing a formula onto the elephant's forehead and tusks to make his whole head and body invulnerable. The two elephants closed and their tusks clashed. The Lao elephant had been fed a great deal of liquor and was mad with intoxication. The Thai mount was in musth, clear-eyed and fearless. When he tossed his tusks, the Lao elephant veered away, raising his head. The Thai elephant got in under his neck. The Thai soldier manning the side strap stabbed hard. The Lao elephant's head was thrown upwards and his haunches dropped. Khun Phaen urged the Thai elephant forward to press his advantage. The Lao elephant could not hold his ground. The Thai elephant repeatedly smashed into him hard, forcing the Lao elephant to retreat further and further, crazed with liquor and in great pain.

Khun Phaen saw he had the advantage. He flourished his lance and slashed downwards on Krungkan, who collapsed on the elephant's neck, yet his flesh was only bruised not pierced. He raised himself up. Khun Phaen closed and slashed again. Krungkan lost his footing and fell dangling, head downwards, from the stirrup strap. Khun Phaen slashed again and Krungkan plummeted to the ground.

Khun Phaen drove his elephant forward, crying, "Take him!" The elephant trumpeted loudly, coiled up his trunk, and smashed down with his tusks, hitting and stabbing until Krungkan lay flat, then tossed the body into the air so it fell back down onto the points. Krungkan's head shattered and his guts spewed out.

The Lao began to lose their stomach for the fight and melt away into the forest.

When the wasp stings wore off, Saentri Phetkla opened his eyes and saw the Lao army broken and scattered. He mounted and rode back to the battle, calling out to Khun Phaen, "Don't think that I fled. My horse's eyes were stung by the wasps, and I could not stop it dragging me off, but I've come back so we may try out our strength. If I defeat you and leave you dead, my name will be known all over the earth."

"You're still wagging your tongue to challenge me. I saw your prowess against the infant. You had to raise a white flag and disappear off into the forest. Here we have the leader of the Lao army staggering up, intent on saving face! This time your life is up."

Phetkla was fiery-eyed with fury. He rode straight into battle at the head of his troops without chanting any mantra. Khun Phaen bellowed a stunning formula, rooting Phetkla to the spot, then raised his pike and slashed down on Phetkla's head and shoulder. The Lao collapsed down on his saddle.

Ta-Lo said, "Pa, allow me." He rushed over and struck him with an axe. Ta-Rak said, "Me too." He poked a stave in Phetkla's stomach, knocking him down from the horse. Another volunteer thrust with a spear but the metal buckled without piercing. He threw away the spear and hacked with a machete, while a colleague slashed at Phetkla with a sword, but it was like hitting copper or stabbing rock. The weapons crumpled and broke off at the handles. Not even a single bone was broken.

Ta-Lo said, "This fellow Phetkla is shockingly able."

Khun Phaen called, "Hey, someone get a spear and stab his arse. Even though he's invulnerable, if you shove it up to his throat, he should die."

Ta-Lo and Ta-Rak hitched up their lowercloths and wrenched off Phetkla's clothes. Two men brought a spear and pushed it through the anus up his whole body. Many people helped give a heave. Phetkla's face blanched. Blood leaked from the hole down to the ground like the slaughter of an ox.

The surviving Lao troops fled into the forest. Post horses raced to Chiang Mai to inform the nobles. "The troops have been massacred, sir. I don't know how many have escaped with their lives."

The nobles rushed to the audience hall and reported to the king. Though shocked, he gave orders to organize the defense of the capital. "Set up camps around the city. Close the gates securely and reinforce them with wooden barricades. Place defensive guns all around the boundary. Organize ranks of flintlocks. At the central gate, place big cannons. On the walls, suspend logs to drop on enemy assailants. Prepare hot gravel and sand on the ramparts. Summon people from every village around. Set rosters to keep watch. Dig out the ponds, wells, and streams of every house and fill them with water. Have any farm that has food bring everything to deposit here."

The nobles left at once to organize recruitment. Cannons were dragged into position to defend the gates. Braziers were placed along the walls. Villagers flocked in, carrying and dragging their children and grandchildren. In every house, betel boxes, bowls, footed trays, and salvers were buried in the earth. Widows and old folk wrapped valuables in cloth and hid them in the cleft of their bottoms, under the chili and salt, in chignons, in pillows, in mats, or pasted with dammar under the hulls of boats. Not one little thing was left to be seized.

Women who knew their menfolk had already died gave way to weeping. With everyone swept inside the walls, the city was crowded and chaotic. The palace was in uproar. Royal family members wept and beat their chests red in desperation. Some hid their possessions under the palace buildings.

The king spoke with the royal kin and consorts to calm them. "Our few warriors took this little battle too lightly. They fought rashly and were defeated. But, wait till you see my skill. We'll crush them to dust under our feet. Why weep and make a bad omen? Can an army of nobles rival me, a king?"

He walked out to give orders to his officers. "Chiang Mai is our main camp. If they storm the city, don't go out to repel them but stay secure here. We have a lot of food. They have nothing to eat. Go and burn down all the rice granaries in the villages outside. We'll sit and watch them until their supplies are finished, then go out and put them to the sword."

THE CAPTURE OF THE KING OF CHIANG MAI

Khun Phaen spoke to Phlai Ngam, "Since we don't have supplies to feed the troops, we should attack Chiang Mai immediately before they can get organized. Within two days."

Phlai Ngam agreed. After a bright moon rose, they ordered the volunteers to cut wood to build an eye-level shrine, made a circle of sacred thread, enchanted yantra, and arranged offerings of duck, chicken, turtle, pig, and liquor. Khun Phaen strung a sacred thread around his head, enchanted rice, inserted an adept's knife in his belt, lit candles on the shrine, and chanted a formula to summon all the spirits to partake of the offerings.

The spirits of every saltlick, lair, and tree, and the ancestor spirits in every hill, cave, and stream, were touched by the mantra. They arrived in hundreds of thousands and thronged around the shrine, invisible to everyone except Khun Phaen. After watching them showing off their tricks and transforming themselves into various fierce animals, he scattered enchanted rice and blew a mantra to make them docile.

"I beg you, spirits of great power, to come with us to attack the protective guardian spirits of Chiang Mai. As the king does not rule with righteousness, his city is fated to fall. I invite all of you to eat these offerings."

The spirits happily volunteered, feasted on the food and liquor, and swarmed away through the forest. They surrounded the city of

Chiang Mai, creating as much commotion as if the earth had been hit by thunderbolts and the city would overturn and crumble.

The principal guardian spirits of Chiang Mai, who resided in the shrines of the city and received offerings from the king, recruited their colleagues from every locality, including spirits under the ground in graveyards, to repel this horde. They flung awesome weapons. They tossed horses and elephants. They hurled flowers as big as logs. The forest spirits were knocked head over heels but the Thai spirits hurtled up as reinforcements, striking with clumps of camphorweed, and turning the forest spirits back into the battle.

The city's major guardian spirits fled in disarray. The minor spirits followed, carrying their children in their arms or dragging them off by the hand into the woods. The whole city echoed with the sound of their cries. The city's protective aura was weakened.

That night the king and all the city population had the same dream about the Thai army attacking and driving everyone into the wilds. In every household, they were amazed to find all had had the same omen. Everybody trembled in fear.

The king worried that the city would be in trouble. "All because I acted badly and dragged an enemy up here." But he recovered his royal will and again had aggressive thoughts. "I'm already sixty-five, and I won't rule this city much longer. I refuse to lose face and suffer the contempt of the Thai. When one of tiger lineage dies, the stripes remain so people know the valor of the lineage. If I feared them, I'd send them Soithong, but I'd rather fight to the death so my reputation may be known eternally throughout heaven and earth."

He walked out to give orders. "We take the city of Chiang Mai as the home where we die!"

Queen Apson sought out the king, prostrated with clasped hands, and addressed him with tears flowing. "Sire, by your grace, I'm speaking honestly, not out of jealousy. The reason the enemy attacks our city is Soithong. Why keep her here? There are countless cuddlesome consorts more beautiful than her. If you send her to their army commander, Chiang Mai will escape destruction, and you'll be like a god relieving your people's hardship. Please sire, spare the people of the realm this suffering."

The queen's plea softened his heart, but in a flash his rage returned. "My dear, the King of Lanchang deliberately crossed me. On top of that, the loathsome Ayutthayans came to attack our city. If they'd asked for the princess properly, I'd have given her. But they showed no respect and used force first—stealing horses, seizing elephants, slaughtering people, writing a message with an insulting challenge. Even a monk wouldn't tolerate this. It's past the time for sending them the princess now. When karma wills it, anyone born a man must die."

Queen Apson was shocked that her husband was so stubborn. She rushed away and hugged her daughter, Soifa. "The king wouldn't listen. There'll be only tears and suffering as slaves of the Thai. You'll be their war prisoner. Fate led the king astray."

At dawn, Khun Phaen ordered the army to march. They reached the outskirts of Chiang Mai in half a day. Men collected stacks of reeds and Khun Phaen scattered enchanted rice to transform them into a camp for protection against the city's cannon.

At midnight, Khun Phaen looked up at the stars just at the time the Pleiades entered Taurus. The sky was clear, the moon had set, and the Milky Way shone. According to the manual, it was an auspicious time. Khun Phaen and Phlai Ngam decked themselves with protective devices and looked for favorable omens to march. On the road, they chanted a formula to stun others and conceal themselves. Nobody greeted them with a single word.

As they passed the embankment, many Lao soldiers were tumbled over one another in drowsy sleep. At the gate, they mounted on the neck of Goldchild, who leapt over the city wall in a flash. Khun Phaen blew another Subduer mantra to put people to sleep all around the city. They went to the palace and sent a spirit ahead to turn the locks and slide the bolts.

Once inside, they made themselves invisible and went on a tour to see what palace people were like, starting at the residence of the consort mothers. Some were gossiping about the enemy, some beating their breasts and sobbing, some praying to the spirits, and some sewing waist pouches to stuff with their gold and jewelry. Everywhere there was panic. Yet playful ones were still pairing off without a care, beautifying themselves for amusement, seeking out an old lover to fondle her cheeks and nuzzle her breasts, flirting with someone in the manner of a male lover with a clever line in chat, throwing fits of spiteful jealousy, and quarreling cattily.

One asked, "If we finish up in Ayutthaya, explain how we can get on well." An outlandish lady replied, "Easy. Use your body not your mouth. People like us should not take a commoner as husband. It'd be like tiptoeing over chicken dung. Meet a noble. Snuggle close and please him with cuddle and caress. Fan him, massage him, comb his hair—do it well, and he'll fall for you in a trice. It's a better way to burrow into his heart than love potions. He'll chuck his ladyship away. The more doddery and broken-toothed, the more they love a young girl. Just beware of the young lads. They're likely to enjoy a taste and then abandon you. If you can't help yourself, just don't go too far. If your stomach swells up, your price will drop."

When Khun Phaen scattered enchanted rice, the court ladies tumbled over with heads nodding. One lady washing herself fell headlong into the bowl. Another trimming her hairline dropped off holding a cotton bud. Those doing embroidery slipped into drowsy sleep with the silk in their hands. Those spinning cotton dropped the spindle and hugged the wheel.

Khun Phaen commanded Goldchild and the other spirits to go to the palace hall and put the king, his queen, daughter, and attendants to sleep. Because the guardian spirits of the city had been chased into the forest, Goldchild could enter and sit on the king, who blacked out and lay motionless.

Khun Phaen and his son strode into a gilded chamber crammed with palace maidens collapsed on top of one another. All were fittingly beautiful to be royal consorts. They slept on fine mattresses and pillows under silk mosquito nets, fragrant and splendid. These were the attendants for every duty.

They entered a second chamber, brightly lit by torches. Ladies of superlative beauty lay sleeping on velvet spreads under scented silk coverlets, some revealing naked white breasts. Their little mosquito nets had openings fringed with tassels. These were clearly the ladies of more seniority.

The pair entered a third chamber and saw petite palace ladies, all just of age, with superb figures in bloom and fair, sleek complexions like celestial maidens. They wore uppercloths of colored silk, bracelets on their wrists, supple chains around their waists, and earrings hanging from both ears. They were slightly built with thin waists and perfect breasts, firm like swelling lotus buds. A flower tucked between them would not slip through.

Walking behind his father, Phlai Ngam slipped his hand among their budding breasts. Khun Phaen thumped his back. "This is royal property! Don't touch! If you get carried away, we'll fail. These ladies are forbidden to others. What's more, to be expert in warfare, you shouldn't dally with women."

"I just had a peek and a little feel while they're asleep. They're pretty. I'm not getting carried away."

"Hey, we only have to sacrifice one night. When the war's over, you're welcome to all the ladies you want."

They arrived at a gilded bedchamber and blew a mantra to unlock the door. The room was fit for a king. The walls were carved in a floating pattern, the ceiling painted in golden stripes, and a glittering crystal chandelier hung from a chain. In front of the royal bed were many young palace ladies, the batch on forward duty, with superb slight figures and breasts nestled tightly together in beautiful pairs. They had gold bangles on their upper arms, rings on little fingers, soft chains wound round their tender ten fingers, and dangling ruby earrings. Their faces were as delicate as nutmeg.

Beside the bed was a group of musicians, all beautiful, graceful, and fair—as alike as dolls in costume. The xylophone player slept tumbled over the gong player, the singer on the lutist, the fiddler on the claves player, and the drummer on top—all lost to this world.

The pair went to a room on the left, drew aside the magnificent golden curtains, and saw two ladies asleep. Caught by the lamplight, their skin glowed soft, luminous, and as fair as new cotton. The elder one had the supreme elegance of nobility. Her complexion was still clear and fine, but her bosom was no longer full. They saw she was the mother, and the other young beauty was the royal daughter, just of age with a body as radiant as a shimmering star, and breasts like heavenly lotuses peeping above the water, so inviting to pluck. Phlai Ngam stared unblinking. His father whispered to him to restrain himself.

Her radiant face had no wrinkle or blemish. Elegant eyebrows curved softly and sweetly. Eyes were strikingly pretty, even in sleep. Lips gleamed as if freshly painted. Neck and chin were nicely rounded. Her hair was drawn into a chignon held by a gold cloisonné hairpin. She wore earrings sparkling with diamonds, a breast chain studded with jewels of many colors, gold bracelets, and rings set with glittering gems.

Phlai Ngam's heart was thumping with desire to couple with her. He approached, torn by indecision, wanting a little touch yet scared of his father. He trickily pretended to see something and nudged his father to look. When his father turned away as hoped, he made a grab but knocked over some worship offerings with a crash.

"Don't create trouble, damn you! She's a royal princess."

Phlai Ngam mumbled an excuse. When his father walked off, he leapt back beside the bed and stood with his mind in turmoil and his hands itching, the two towers thrusting upwards inviting his caress.

"Oh, lightning strike! I don't care if Father scolds me."

Khun Phaen turned and walked back. Phlai Ngam was so mesmerized, he did not notice his father was standing right beside him as he laid his hand down on the princess. Khun Phaen rapped him on the head. "I should deal with you right now."

"I was about to go off for a pee. Why did you turn up here like a ghost?"

"You're good at quick thinking. This is like your peeing at Phichit." Khun Phaen grabbed his son's hand and dragged him away.

They walked towards the master bed and wrenched the curtain aside. Even in sleep, the king looked imposing. He was fair and had a full, rounded figure befitting the head of the city's royal dynasty. Phlai Ngam walked in on his left, and Khun Phaen on his right. They picked up the swords placed there so he would have no weapons to attack them.

Khun Phaen stepped up on the golden bed and bellowed a mantra. The king started awake, saw the pair, and felt a shiver of deep fear. In the manner of a king, he resolved to fight and grasped around for his weapons, but found none. He was about to plead for his life, but felt ashamed and changed his mind. He raised himself and sat, mute and unmoving, resigned to a probable death.

Khun Phaen bellowed, "Ha! You're an evil fellow. You seized the princess promised to Ayutthaya. You had the Thai escort flogged and imprisoned. You sent a provocative missive with a challenge to an elephant duel. You don't act humbly like a vassal state but are arrogant and devious in every way. His Majesty the King of Ayutthaya has not come himself to crush your city, but has sent us—just middle-ranking soldiers—to put an end to your life. Do you agree to die or will you have a change of heart?"

With no weapon and no chance of escape, the king decided to stifle his pride. "Now, you two gallant soldiers, I did make mistakes, but I haven't had a whiff of Soithong. If you have the mercy to spare my life, I offer myself, my precious daughter and beloved wife, my capital and its people to your king."

"Are your words wholly honest, or are you accepting defeat because you're in a tight spot, but will later go astray perhaps?"

"I won't renege. The word of a king is as solid as a tusker. If in future I crookedly retract like a turtle's head, may I lose my life and be consigned to suffer in hell for a whole era. If my courtiers, wife, or daughter press me to break my word, I won't listen."

This pledge overcame Khun Phaen's doubts. "If you keep your oath, leave the matter of your offense to me. I'll plead your case with the king."

They gave him back his swords, walked down from the palace, and whispered orders to their spirits and Goldchild.

"Stay here and keep watch on the king. His wife and daughter will come to plead with him. If he holds firm, just stay here quietly. If he breaks his word, hurry to tell me."

He lifted the sleeping mantra. The pair made themselves invisible, exited the gate through a keyhole, and returned to the Thai army.

When Khun Phaen and Phlai Ngam walked smiling into the camp, the men crowded around to hear the story, then celebrated that the campaign was over.

The Thai soldiers began gathering up goods and rounding up people. One soldier caught a Lao, pulled his hair, and demanded, "Tell me where your silver and gold is kept or I'll set fire to your arse!"

The Lao said, "Hold off! I can't stand heat. Take the money."

Another got hold of an old lady who cried out, "You can dig the money out of those jars of fermented fish." He whooped and hollered in joy.

One dragged off a Lao girl and mounted her. "If you'd like to sleep, I'll sing you a lullaby. It's ages since I enjoyed a roll. I won't abandon you to be alone."

"I won't consent. This lullaby singer is an evil spirit with a head as high as the roof."

"Oh damn! You're giving me such a hard time the rain's dried up."

Every Thai got some money. Some also carted off cloth, or hauled away buffaloes and oxen.

At dawn the King of Chiang Mai went to the residence of the queen and told her the story. She wailed, "My lord and master, you wouldn't listen. I knew for sure there would be danger from the moment the Thai brought an army to our city. They put everyone to sleep, released prisoners, stole horses and elephants, and killed people with only thirty-five of them! Our five commanders were defeated and the corpses were piled up like logs. Even our spirit army fled away. But you were too stubborn. How can we avoid disaster now? Though we may not die, we'll become vagabonds. Our people will suffer terrible hardship."

"Why do you keep going on like this? I wasn't besotted by Soithong. I was angry at Lanchang. If I'd really fallen for her, how come I haven't made love to her in half a year? I knew Ayutthaya would send an army. It's like a gambling game. You play to see who'll win. But I lost, and now you keep sticking a knife in me. We've come to this point because of fate."

The king went to give orders for standing down the troops and building a lodge to accommodate the Thai. His officers fetched the guns, decommissioned them, and put them in store. They opened the city gates and sent the villagers home. Twenty lodges were built, enclosed by a high fence, with stables for elephants and horses. A deputation went to deliver an invitation to the Thai commander. The troops came to the lodges and were billeted according to rank.

Royal kitchens prepared a feast to feed the Thai army. The king invited Khun Phaen and his son to eat at a head table. The volunteers got merrily drunk. Some enchanted liquor to give invulnerability and then bit bowls to display their lore. Others challenged their friends to slash and stab them. One leapt up and announced, "I'll try out my strength riding *that* Lao girl!"

She cried out, "I'm going to die!" and ran off, white-eyed.

One soldier drew his sword and flashed it around. The Lao stared pitifully. Khun Phaen reprimanded his men. "Don't make so much noise. You're showing off so people will talk. Is that a good thing to do?"

The soldiers became embarrassed. Silence fell and nobody spoke.

Ladies were summoned to sing, dance, and let the guests gaze on their fair and lovely faces. Ta-Rak pointed to a girl with breasts like sidebags, chubby cheeks, earrings, and a good singing voice. "If the boss didn't forbid it, I'd put it in her for several rounds."

Forgetting his body was old, Ta-Lo ran to clutch her but tripped over a water bowl. Ta-Plok got up and danced with a Lao girl, hugging her round the neck. His friends roared with laughter, and got up to strike poses from the mask play and sing boat songs.

As there was no room left for them to dance, the Lao girls sat down.

THE ARMY RETURNS HOME

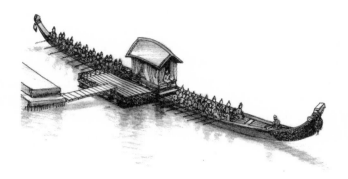

Khun Phaen, Phra Thainam, and Phlai Ngam prepared a missive to inform Ayutthaya of the victory. The missive was affixed with a seal, placed in a bamboo cylinder closed with wax, and given to Nai Jan with orders to deliver it to Ayutthaya and wait to hear a reply.

Nai Jan mounted a horse, slung a sidebag over his shoulder, and galloped away. Lao bowed and saluted to him along the way. He passed through Thoen, and in seven days arrived at Kamphaeng. While he drank liquor, local officials seized a boat from a Mon salt seller, who fell into the water with a splash, losing her cloth, and shrieking, "Oh, my cunt! Lord fuck me! I'm drowning!" with her naked bottom in the air. They gave her two baht and loaded the boat with rice. Oarsmen paddled off, singing boat songs. Officers sat under the boat canopy, pouring liquor in turns. Rowing strongly, they reached the city in seven days. Nai Jan washed, dressed, and went straight to the official hall to inform the minister, who hurried to the morning audience to present the report.

On hearing of the victory, King Phanwasa felt as if Lord Indra had invited him to his heavenly palace. "Oh, I have been sick at heart for over a year, and today this sickness is lifted. For earning my appreciation, both father and son will be rewarded equally. Minister, send an order to recall the army. As for the old ruler of Chiang Mai, according to law and practice, he should be executed, all his family and property seized, and the people swept down as war prisoners. Because the king submits and pledges loyalty, I'll grant him his life, but sweep him and his family down here for all countries to see as an example. As for the beautiful Princess Soithong of Lanchang and his own daughter Soifa, have them brought here to be ladies of the palace. Send royal barges to collect the princesses, and two canopy boats to fetch Khun Phaen. Let them travel by canopy boat so word spreads to every bend in the river that they defeated Chiang Mai. Put the ruler of Chiang Mai and his family in boats behind. Let people enjoy the sight."

Nai Jan was ordered to hurry back. He made the oarsmen holler, shout, and sing boat songs while he poured liquor. Coming across a Chinese liquor seller, they seized several flasks from his boat. At a river junction with fish nets, they slowed the boat to grab some fish. Further on they went into a sugar plantation and carried off sticks of cane.

In fifteen days they came to Rahaeng where the governor arranged dried rice, betel, popped rice, and sweets for his waist pouch, and provided post horses as it was royal business. At Thoen, they were fed with snakeskin, liquor, elephant meat, fishcakes, and boiled eggs. Once full, they mounted and went off, hollering, drunk on the liquor and dribbling spittle. They blurrily saw elephants the size of pigs, "Let's fight!" Any Lao they came across walking alone, they dragged along to sing and dance. Nai Jan arrived at Chiang Mai, saluted Khun Phaen, and handed over the message cylinder.

Khun Phaen cracked it open, drew out the missive, and read the contents to his men. Some sang, while others played flutes and banged drums in joy that the army was returning home.

Khun Phaen deputed Phlai Ngam to inform the King of Chiang Mai that they would leave for Ayutthaya in fifteen days. Phlai Ngam relayed the message. "All the cityfolk are to be swept down, including you, your wife, and consorts. You will go down to the capital under guard. Ancient traditions must be upheld. The king grants you only your life. You'll have to face discomfort but we'll help plead with the king to restore the city to you."

The king walked back into his palace and gave the news to Queen Apson. "We'll probably end up in the Thai city and not return. There'll be piles of dead along the way. Oh, a heap of karma made me act badly!"

The cityfolk packed food and belongings to take with them. They sawed bamboo cylinders and stuffed them with fermented fish, chili, salt, fish sauce, and grilled deer meat. They sewed waist pouches and filled them with crisped rice. They packed betel and pan, mortar and pestle, fermented and dried fish, rice pots, curry pots, and skillets. Newlyweds, still madly sweet on each other, went into their rooms and wept. Men who had just asked for their partner's hand and built a bridal house, were allowed by the parents to stay together. Playboy musicians packed their pipes, flute, drum, claves, lute, and fiddle so they would have means to beg alms for food.

Some hid gold, dried food, and ornaments in their lowercloths. Crude objects too difficult to carry were hidden away in the hollows of big trees. Other things were secreted in ponds, wells, and water pipes, or buried as fake corpses at the wat. The air was filled with the noise of lovelorn weeping, and the whimpering and whining of little children.

Close to the time the army would leave, everyone was herded up. The roads were crammed with people carrying goods on poles. The king had himself, his queen, his daughter, Princess Soithong, and each of his consorts mounted on an elephant. Khun Phaen, Phlai Ngam, Phra Thainam, and other officers also rode tuskers. Behind them, soldiers riding elephants and horses overflowed the road. At an auspicious time, the army set off. Soldiers cheered in unison. The air crackled with gunfire.

As the elephants left through the east gate, the King of Chiang Mai turned to look back at the golden spire of the royal palace. "Oh, I grieve for the palace where we have lived since the time of our ancestors. Now it will disintegrate day by day until it collapses, abandoned and overgrown like a graveyard. I grieve for our favorite trees in the gardens, for the lotus ponds that will run dry, for the audience hall as empty as an open field, and for the Evening Pavilion overrun by elephant grass, brambles, and forest weeds. Walls and fortifications will crumble and collapse. The earth and sky will turn yellow throughout the Lao country."

Queen Apson felt her breast had been slashed open by a kris dipped in acid. "Oh, while I lived in Chiang Mai, I enjoyed only happiness and good company. Wherever I went around the city, I was carried so pleasantly in an elegant palanquin, trailed by throngs of female court officials and surrounded by lovely consorts from the palace. Now I'll end up in the Thai city and have to walk among ordinary people. I won't even have good cloth to wrap around my waist. While living in our city, the royal victuals were so refined following the traditions of the queens of Chiang Mai. Now I'll probably face starvation."

They marched out of Chiang Mai city, driven along by the Thai soldiers. The Lao cityfolk, fearful and subdued, carried goods on shoulder poles, hoisted young infants aloft, and dragged older children by the hand. The old, lame, weak, and crippled were carried clumsily in litters. Gentlefolk who had no elephants mounted themselves on cattle and buffaloes. The Thai soldiers carried canes for herding people along. Anyone trying to hide or slip away was whipped back into line.

Ta-Rak shouted, "Look, that's old Ai-Thi from the market. When we went to beg alms, he flogged me and almost broke my back. Now it's my turn for revenge! I'll flog him so hard the forest echoes with his cries. There'll be only horns and skin left to give his master."

At Chomthong, the headman and his wife heard the approach of the army and rushed off to welcome their son-in-law. The young women of Chomthong carried many presents along.

The two old folk greeted them and handed over gifts, asking questions one after another. Khun Phaen gave them many kinds of cloth, bowls of gold and silver, cartwheels, elephants, horses, cattle, buffaloes, cloth, betel boxes in good-quality lacquerware, pikes, swords, guns, spears, lances, rolled mats, and pillows embroidered with gold thread. His parents-in-law roared with laughter, showing their red mouths.

"We heard you won victory and took the city. Our son-in-law has given us so many things!"

Towards evening, the old couple made their farewells. Khun Phaen and his son reciprocated. "We leave at the crack of dawn."

In the camp, the cityfolk were weak and pinched with hunger. Some just dropped their burdens and sprawled on the ground. A division head called out orders to erect a circle of stakes and set bonfires.

As soon as night fell, the Thai soldiers went searching around. Where they saw young girls lying, they squeezed in beside them, or hauled them off among the howdahs and harness. When they felt a sagging breast, they immediately withdrew their hand, but if they touched a firm one, they gripped and held on tight. Some Lao girls ignored them and pretended to sleep. Some refused to play and cried out loud when they were grabbed.

The division head called out, "What's all that racket?"

"Don't be alarmed. It's not a tiger with a long tail, just a two-legged beast with a teeny tail."

The tiger was abashed, and got out of there. But other tigers rambled about. As soon as one unit was quiet, the next unit started up before there was time to fall asleep. Ta-Lo said, "Oh, you lot start early in the evening! This makes old folk like me unable to restrain ourselves. Young Toe, why are you lying there? Come and massage me for a bit."

Toe, who was rather deaf, replied sharply, "Tomorrow I can't walk, my legs are so stiff. All of us have busted legs. If you can get me an elephant to ride, I'll love you."

Ta-Lo was angry. "See here, I dislike you, you deaf bat, enough to throw up, to vomit, to heave."

"Leaves?" Toe cried, "I'd like leaves in a curry."

Friends laughed, "Oh Ta-Lo, don't bother her. Whatever you say, she hears it wrong."

Ta-Lo laughed. "I'm dragging her off anyway." He got out of the mosquito net, walked over, and grabbed Toe's hand.

She screwed up her face. "I'm very hungry. Stop tugging me. I'm not willing."

"Get up in there." He went into the mosquito net and mounted her.

She shrieked and wriggled. Her lowercloth was ripped to pieces. Just when Ta-Lo was getting into position, she stood up. He said, "You're really uncontrollable. It's worse than herding buffaloes."

He gripped her neck with both hands. She kicked at Ta-Lo's throat, knocking him down. But finally she could not match his strength. Ta-Lo said, "Wonderful, like jelly." Friends laughed, and Ta-Lo stabbed away until he reached the end of his strength and dozed off.

In the pitch dark of midnight, six women picked up their valuables and sneaked away along a path but ran into a group of soldiers sitting on the road.

"Tie this one up and put her in my mosquito net. It's our bonus payment. Why should we catch people for nothing. Let's give them a pounding through to dawn. Is this a moneybag or what tied round her belly?"

He tugged an end, the string came loose, and her cloth slipped down.

"Damnit, hair up to her ears."

"Make her dance the forest dance."

"That would be a sight!"

In the morning they delivered the women back to the army officers.

In fourteen and a half days of quick march, they reached the city of Phichit and camped at Wat Jan.

Phra Phichit and Busaba had learned from a missive that Khun Phaen had taken Chiang Mai. Royal barges had come up several days earlier, and were moored in a row along the river. On the day the army arrived, local officials brought the news. The governor and his wife decided to go to Wat Jan.

Khun Phaen and Phlai Ngam saw them approaching in the distance and happily rushed to receive them. "We've just arrived and things are still chaotic. We meant to come and prostrate at your feet, but the place is overflowing with men and women, children and adults, commoners and royalty. If we're a bit slack, things get out of hand. Also we have to take care of two princesses, Soifa and Soithong. There's no other eye or ear we can trust. We'd thought of coming to see you tomorrow, but you've made the effort to come out here. Have you been well? And how is Simala?"

"Both of us and our beloved daughter have been healthy and happy throughout. But we've been very concerned about you every day and waiting to give you every support. There are masses of people! How can two of you possibly look after them? We have local city officials who'll come to help."

Phra Phichit sent for the deputy governor, magistrate, and all the local officials. "Good sirs, there's a lot of work to be done here. If any incident happens in our city, we'll all be held responsible. Bear that in mind."

They discussed the division of work. The garrison commander would take care of the Thai army and Lanchang men. The chief overseer would look after the feeding of elephants, horses, cattle, and buffaloes. The city officer was to guard the cityfolk, watch the roads, barricade the entrances, and set bonfires. The palace officer would build pavilions for royalty. The treasury officer would keep guard on all goods, including money. The land officer was to coordinate the distribution of food and other supplies. Boats were requisitioned to transport the army. In three days, they would all start out for the capital.

After Phlai Ngam had left, Simala had hidden away for almost a month until her parents began to suspect something was wrong. Her servant, Moei, whispered warnings to her mistress. "Your father and mother will guess. You must dress up, put on a happy face, and be sociable. It won't be long. He'll come as hoped and put you out of your misery."

Simala tried to be as cheerful as before. Only when going back to her room would she sigh and sob, pray, and make offerings to the gods for his protection. She counted the days waiting for Phlai Ngam till they became many months. When she heard the news that the army had returned, she summoned Moei. "Find an opportunity to slip over there. If Phlai Ngam asks you, tell him that I've got a fever. Then listen to what he says. Don't make anyone suspicious."

"Mistress, don't worry. If I don't get Phlai for you, you can bawl me out. But please leave this until tomorrow."

Next morning Khun Phaen summoned servants to carry gifts to the governor's residence. They were received by Phra Phichit and Busaba in the sitting hall. Phlai had only Simala on his mind and looked all around for her.

Khun Phaen paid his respect. "We've brought a few little things—some Lao bowls, soft mats, triangular cushions, footed trays, salvers—everyday things from Chiang Mai. Also betel baskets, water bowls with drinking cups, tea, and sugar juice. Just some presents from the forest. And this valuable ruby ring is for dear Simala."

Phra Phichit said, "How kind of you to take the trouble. It's worthwhile to love you." He called out, "Hey Moei! Tell Simala to come out here. Khun Phaen is here with Phlai Ngam. He's been kind enough to bring some gifts."

Simala had already recognized the voices and wanted to dash out, but she thought twice because of feminine modesty, and because the adults did not know the truth. "If Phlai Ngam made an error and something slipped out, it could ruin things. I must stifle my feelings and put off the meeting. At night he'll probably come to the house."

Spying through a gap in the wall, she saw him looking plump and healthy but very sunburned. He sat hidden behind his father with his eyes staring at the wall of her room. She could not tear her eyes away. She said to Moei quickly, "Tell them I'm sick."

Moei put on a straight face, walked out of the room, and said to Phra Phichit, "Simala has had a throbbing headache since midnight, and woke feeling weak and feverish. She sent me to prostrate at their feet on her behalf."

Phra Phichit thought he understood perfectly—his daughter must be shy about coming out because of her betrothal to Phlai Ngam. He turned to smile at Khun Phaen. "We shouldn't force her. Now that the war is successfully over, we should discuss the marriage. I want to see a roof over our beloved daughter's head. We parents are getting older, and who knows whether we'll fall dead tomorrow. Please look for an auspicious date, then we can find the timber to build a house."

Khun Phaen replied, "I came here meaning to talk about the same thing. After we've taken the army home, we'll come back soon to have the wedding here. I calculated yesterday. On Tuesday the first waning in the fourth month, their fates coincide perfectly."

Phra Phichit consulted with Busaba and replied, "The fourth month is good for the ceremony. The house should be finished in time."

Then he said to Khun Phaen. "Why stay at the wat? There are several days before you leave. Why not come and stay here with us?"

Khun Phaen thought quietly to himself. "Phlai has been apart from her. After dark he'll fumble around to find her. If the matter doesn't stay secret like the last time, it'll bring shame and ruin to both sides."

He replied. "I'm in great difficulty, because the army we brought back is much bigger than on the outward journey. Then there are Soithong, Soifa, the ruler of Chiang Mai, and his wives and children. On top of this, we have to guard the Lao cityfolk. If we don't stay close by, I fear others will report that we two neglected royal service and went to stay in creature comfort in your house. I've had enough problems already. I don't want the slightest hint of any more risk."

They took leave and walked down from the house. Phlai Ngam trailed behind, mutely furious at his father.

"Pitiful! He knows in his heart that I love her and have already had her as man and wife. I could put him to sleep with a mantra again but he still wants to obstruct me. What a joke! Never mind. Don't imagine I'm going to let him treat me like a monkey in a cage. After nightfall I'll go to see her."

He walked along, acting unconcerned. At some distance from the governor's residence, he saw Moei sitting smiling at the side of the road. He secretly signaled her to follow.

At Wat Jan, Khun Phaen was soon embroiled in conversation with local officials. Phlai Ngam sneaked away and found a hiding place under a large tree. Moei walked up behind, sank down, and raised her hands in greeting. Phlai Ngam smiled and said, "I hoped to run into you. We have an urgent matter, as you know. This morning I was hoping to see her face, but no sign. Is she angry for some reason? Before I left, I entrusted you to look after her. You didn't keep your promise. What do you have to say for yourself?"

Moei tossed her head and said, "Oh Buddha! Why are you angry at me? Don't you see my mistress's position? She doesn't want to meet you in front of people so she said she had a fever and wouldn't appear. She's not fibbing or pretending or going back on her word. After the day you led the army off, she was unwell for several months. I had to look after her and jolly her along. I'm glad you came back. Maybe you brought some medicine with you. I hurried over to hear what orders you'd give for nursing her. I fear you don't remember your promises. You've brought piles of gifts for the noble folk but you seem to ignore a poor servant girl."

He took out some money. "Your mouth is as big as your whole body! Here, for Moei as reward. I have some very good herbal medicine, but if taken in daytime the patient dies. A little after dark, I'll come to the house. You work out how to let me in. This medicine should cure her fever by tomorrow." They agreed on a signal. Moei took leave.

At sunset, Wat Jan was swarming with troops. Phlai Ngam went around giving orders, inspecting this division and that division, as he did every day. In one of the monks' quarters, he saw the light of torches where the volunteers were playing chess, and many monks and novices had squeezed in to watch, making a great racket.

"I must fool Father into thinking I'm here. I'll pretend to join the chess game until he's gone to sleep." He went into the room. "Hey! Let me make some moves." The soldiers made room for their commander to sit.

Khun Phaen waited for Phlai Ngam and then went out to look for him. Seeing the light in the monks' quarters, he hurried over, heard the commotion, and knew his son was in there enjoying a game of chess, so went back to sleep.

Nearing midnight, Phlai Ngam left the chess circle, doused himself in fragrant water, dressed in an uppercloth of colored wool given by the king, and put a new ruby ring on his finger. At the governor's residence, he chanted a mantra to spring the bolts on the outer gate. Moei heard the sound, went down, and led him up to the house, threading her way through people scattered asleep. She took him to her mistress's apartment and then deftly made herself scarce.

Phlai Ngam tiptoed softly inside, sat beside Simala on the bed, and gently kissed and caressed her. "I'm here. Don't be miserable any more. I've been thinking of you constantly. My intention hasn't wavered for a single day. At times to eat, I've had no taste for food. At times to sleep, I've dreamed of you. Had I not been afraid of the king, I'd have turned up here long ago. I hear you haven't been well. I've been worried since this morning when I looked everywhere but couldn't see you. I resolved, life or death, to find you tonight. I've come at this late hour because I had to wait until my father was fast asleep. Life's blossom, please turn your face this way for me to see."

Listening to his sweet talk, Simala felt aroused with love. She raised herself and turned to prostrate on his lap. "I thought you'd still be very tired and would want to rest first. You won a victory and took a city. I've heard of Soifa's reputation. Didn't you grab something for yourself? There must be lots of good-looking girls among the war prisoners. Am I to think that you hate girls so much you ignored them? Or could you restrain yourself like a monk? Don't try to fool me. Why bother with the daughter of the Phichit governor? Like a grassflower, she looks fine when you have nothing else, but once you have a real flower, you don't need her. Maybe you've come here out of pity, but soon you'll be bored and think of a reason to go back to the army."

"Look here! This taunting is pitiful. I give you my word that I haven't courted any other woman in the whole three worlds. Though I've been looking at Lao, I've been seeing only the sight of Simala, the ruler of my heart. As for Princess Soifa, she's been offered to the King of Ayutthaya. So has Princess Soithong, both of them. I've made the effort to control myself, as if I'd shaved my head, put on the triple robe, become a monk, and been religiously chanting prayers every morning and evening to share the merit with you. But instead of the merit, I've brought a ring. Now it's the end of lent, and I'll disrobe tonight. You must make up your mind to be merciful."

Simala could not stop herself laughing. He grabbed hold of her immediately. A great storm blew in with a crash. The sky exploded and rain sluiced down, though out of season and late at night. Thunder rumbled across the world, breaking with a great crack and gradually fading away. Meeting after a long time, both joined in joy, whirled around by the full force of love.

Simala had prepared some food. They fondled until the moon slipped from the sky and a coel called loud and clear. "It's almost morning. I have to go, my love. I'll come to you every night. After we've taken the army to Ayutthaya, I'll hurry back to you here. When we've had the marriage ceremony, we won't be apart a single night."

With Moei leading the way, he left the residence and cut quickly through to Wat Jan while it was still pitch dark. He avoided his father, pulled covers over his head, and slept.

In the morning, Khun Phaen saw Phlai Ngam still fast asleep and thought his son had enjoyed himself playing chess. That evening, Phlai Ngam again showed his face at the chess game, then late at night went to Simala. On the last night, the lovers got carried away talking, fell asleep, and did not wake in time. Only when dawn streaked the sky did Phlai Ngam rouse himself and leave.

Busaba had woken early to prepare food as the army would march at dawn. When she opened a window to wash her face, she saw Phlai Ngam walking away and promptly roused her husband.

"Sir! Phlai Ngam went down from this house just now. There's an ancient saying: When a dog shits, it makes a mess. His tracks will lead straight to our dear daughter. We parents are dishonored without knowing it."

Understanding the situation straightaway, Phra Phichit replied, "I thought something was wrong. After the army left, she seemed sick and very upset. He probably got to her and she's spoiled. But it's wrong to get angry and punish our daughter. This is a very important fellow. He knows invisibility, stunning, concealment, and all kinds of love tricks. Even if there were diamond walls, seven layers thick, he'd only have to chant and blow to blast them open. If he loves anybody, he just puffs some mantra and she falls for him without fail, yet he's asked for Simala's hand in marriage. He got impatient and showed no respect but if we get into a shouting match, it'll create a scandal and hurt Khun Phaen. If word gets around that Simala has had a lover, it'll shame her. Let it pass. Don't bring matters into the open."

The couple quickly got dressed, summoned their servants, and walked to Wat Jan.

Many boats that had come up from Ayutthaya were milling around the moorings. The flotilla was arranged: Phra Thainam's boat leading the way, with the volunteers' craft on both flanks; the royal barges with their female servants behind; the two fine canopy boats for the army commanders; craft carrying goods due to the king; the ruler of Chiang Mai; and more boats of the volunteers at the tail.

There were not enough craft for the cityfolk, elephants, horses, cattle, weapons, and large quantity of military equipment. All had to be left in the keeping of Phichit.

When everything was loaded, Khun Phaen and his son went to take their leave of Phra Phichit and Busaba. On a signal of three gunshots, the flotilla set off. Drum, flute, and gong played in sweet harmony. The oarsmen sang boat songs with strong voices. As the boats passed through Phichit, townsfolk massed to watch, standing packed together on the landings, chattering away to one another. "Never seen a water procession like this. My oh my!"

At each stop along their way, the governor came to offer gifts to the princesses, and local officials laid on entertainment with barrel drums, horn, conch, and flute. Villagers swarmed on both banks to catch a glimpse of the procession. The soldiers disembarked to go to the market and flirt with women. One swished his lowercloth to show off his fine limbs to a southern lady but she turned her face away, saying, "You villains with black legs and northern beads, babbling away and eyeing us up, with your dirty hair like clowns in a mask play." She looked over, saw his balls dangling, and ran slap into the shop of an old Mon lady.

"Oh mother, oh lord! You spilled a bowl of shrimp paste. You tousled-headed shit eater, why don't you look. Opening your lowercloth is shameful."

At Ayutthaya, the king summoned his ministers. "Deck out our city to look so splendid that the Chiang Mai people fear our power. Have all the traders moor their junks and rafts along the banks of the river to look busy. On both sides of the roads, have rows of shops crammed together. Make sure all the troops are on duty. Let them see the might of the Thai city and be as shocked as if they'd met the Prince of Death."

As the flotilla approached Ayutthaya, people crowded around to get a look, climbing down the riverbanks with wailing babes strapped on their waists, pushing and shoving, dropping betel and pan all around. The boats moored at the landings below the city walls. People packed every gate and landing, watching openmouthed. A jetty broke and spilled many people into the water. Shouts rang out in celebration of the victory.

"The might of our king defeated Chiang Mai!"

"What city will oppose this power!"

"Look, there are the boats of the army commanders!"

Some uninformed people asked, "Which is the boat of Phlai Ngam?"

"That one, the big one with the golden canopy. Old Khun Phaen, the father, is in the boat in front. Phlai Ngam's boat is behind. Look, he's slender, lightly built, and fair."

Seeing Phlai Ngam's good looks, the women were in turmoil.

"So slight but so much power!"

"If I got him, I'd hug him tight."

Another who used to be intimate with other women began to think she had made a mistake in the past.

One lady exaggerated. "See! Phlai is making eyes at me. Is he just trying to get me excited, or is he serious? He's only just got back and he wants a wife!"

"He wouldn't ask for the hand of people like us. He'd just flirt around, have a free one, and leave us ruined."

When Khun Phaen looked up from his canopy boat, he saw only widows and shy old maids who would be happy with either son or father.

THE PRINCESSES ARE PRESENTED

Khun Phaen took his son into the official hall and made obeisance to Chaophraya Jakri, minister of the north. "The flotilla has brought the princesses and the ruler of Chiang Mai to the capital."

Chaophraya Jakri turned with a smile, "You made no mistake in volunteering. Both father and son are wise, brave, and valiant beyond estimation. The whole realm views you as supreme soldiers. You should be richly rewarded for your achievement."

He summoned Phraya Yommarat, minister of the capital. "Sir, as the Chiang Mai ruler's case has not yet been heard by the king, place him under arrest until such time as there's a royal order."

Minister Yommarat assigned royal punishers and executioners to be ready to slash him dead. Seeing them, the ruler of Chiang Mai thought he would not survive. His mind was numb and his body streamed with sweat. The guards brought chains and cangue. In despair, he bowed his head and kept silent.

Khun Phaen whispered to the ministers, "Please arrange matters with the king so that the lord of Chiang Mai escapes the lash and is reprieved. I'll provide thirty beautiful Lao girls as reward for your lordships' assistance."

The ministers laughed so hard that they bent over double, bashing their heads together and bumping their bottoms.

One spoke out loud for any bystanders to hear, "So you say that royal horse is dead?"

Khun Phaen replied, "Indeed, sir."

"I'll tell His Majesty."

As it was close to the time of the king's appearance, they bustled off. Chaophraya Jakri told Khun Phaen to wait outside the audience hall until summoned.

Chaophraya Jakri entered and addressed the king. "My liege, Khun Phaen and Phlai Ngam have returned with the villainous lord of Chiang Mai, and two golden royal barges under close guard. They bring royal levies of gold, silver, and other goods as follows: cash, 70 chests in total; Lao families, 5,000 in total; able-bodied young men, 1,150; large cannons, 200; small guns, 3,000; spears with feather plumes, 1,000 exactly; swords belonging to the war prisoners themselves, 1,200; swords from the main arsenal, almost 500; elephants, 305; horses, 800; cattle in great numbers. There are no injuries among our men owing to the meritorious power of Your Majesty. The villainous ruler of Chiang Mai has been placed in all five irons according to procedure. We await Your Majesty's wishes."

The King of Ayutthaya was jubilant. "This fellow used to be very boastful and disrespectful but now his head has shrunk! Khun Phaen and his son deserve praise and royal appreciation. Bring them immediately. And that thick-faced Thainam too."

Khun Phaen and Phlai Ngam happily hastened to enter the audience hall, but Phra Thainam lagged behind, trembling with fear.

The king spoke. "Now, Khun Phaen and Phlai Ngam! I sent you off to this war with only thirty-five soldiers. Chiang Mai city has over a hundred thousand troops. Tell us what happened."

Khun Phaen made obeisance. "Owing to the power of Your Majesty, monarch of the three worlds, victory was gained and the city taken." He narrated how they released Phra Thainam, fought off an attack, and then infiltrated the palace to capture the king. "He gave his word that he would beg to be a servant under the dust of the royal foot, and offer his life and throne if required. Since that day, he has not wavered."

"This lineage of Khun Krai does not fail! Both his son and grandson are skillful and clever. As for this old fellow, I won't execute him. Even though he acted arrogantly, it would be wrong to call it a revolt. His city is of primary rank and outside the dominion of Ayutthaya. If I executed him after he has submitted and offered tribute, who would trust Ayutthaya in the future? But if he acts improperly again, he should be punished with his life. Khun Phaen is appointed governor of Kanburi with insignia of rank—casket, saber, umbrella, flask, golden betel box—and royal gifts of an elephant howdah and palanquin for use in war, along with twelve hundred baht in cash. As for you, Phlai Ngam, you're still young and should be retained for service close at hand. You become Muen Wai Woranat, lieutenant of the royal pages, and will receive royal gifts of insignia, cash, and cloth. Now, this fellow has no house. Minister Yommarat! Send a requisition to the district officer to acquire land close to the palace, and build a house of five units with a kitchen and fence around the compound. Make it befitting with his appointment."

Turning to Phra Thainam, the king looking angry enough to slaughter him. "You did a fine job! It was a waste to promote you to high rank. I didn't know you came from a tribe of cowards. The Lao trussed you up like a monkey. Pah! A heart like a woman! For causing your master to lose face, you are reduced to commoner status and assigned to work as a gatekeeper."

The king sent for the ruler of Chiang Mai. Guards lifted him by both upper arms and carried him in. He prostrated, dripping with sweat and shivering in every pore.

"Heigh, you blackguard! Your actions have displeased me. You seized a princess, imprisoned Thai troops, and even sent a missive with a challenge to war. What should be the punishment for such arrogance? Answer right now."

"The errors committed deserve punishment with my life. But if, by your grace, I receive royal pardon, I will be a faithful servant of the foot of Your Majesty until death. Let me present the great territory of Chiang Mai, and let me depend on the bo-tree shelter of your accumulated merit from now on."

"Now that you show proper fear, I will pardon you and send you back to rule Chiang Mai. Make sure you keep your word." The king commanded a lodging be prepared to accommodate him as an official guest, and ordered officials to take him away to swear loyalty and drink the waters of allegiance.

For the thirty-five soldiers, the king ordered rewards of cash and cloth. "They are exempt from royal service, city work, farmed taxes, customs levies, and market dues. They will be called up in future if an army threatens. Place them under Phra Wai. As for the Lanchang troops who escorted Princess Soithong, requisition silver and cloth for them, and send them home."

The king left the audience hall. The minister of the palace arranged palanquins to carry the two princesses into the inner palace, and hastened to arrange a residence and attendants so that they could stay comfortably while awaiting the king's orders.

After sunset, the moon's chariot glided aloft, stars glittered in the sky, and moonlight bathed the earth in a cool glow. The king's thoughts turned to the two princesses.

"Word has already spread that Soithong is the supreme beauty of Lanchang, desired by everyone in the three worlds. Then there's young Princess Soifa, the illustrious daughter of the ruler of Chiang Mai. How splendid is she?"

He gave orders to the head royal governess who went to prepare the two princesses. Their faces were powdered to have complexions like moonlight, and their hair coiled into chignons, fastened with hairpins of sparkling crystal filigree, and embellished with beautiful flowers. They were dressed in lowercloths woven with dazzling gold, uppercloths of silk, glittering tasseled earrings, gold bangles, and rings on every finger of both hands.

The head governess made obeisance with clasped hands. "Princess Soithong is the one prostrating on the right, while Princess Soifa is on the left."

The king looked at them. Both were attractive but the manner of each was different. Soithong seemed quiet and reserved, with a youthful beauty and friendly manners befitting a young lady. "So this was why she became so famous and Chiang Mai tried to seize her."

By contrast, Soifa had an affected manner. "Her poise and bearing are good, but she looks sulky. She has the slenderness and elegance of a racing boat, but a clumsy oarsman would risk capsizing." He looked at her thin lips and rounded chin. "She'll be talkative for sure. If she were a horse, you'd be wary of mounting her; if an elephant, the type that must be pleased or else a careless rider could get hurt. Soithong has both rank and good manners but Soifa looks frightening."

The king whispered to the governess. "Do they look as if they'll please me? Soithong's manner seems good but Soifa has the bearing of a drama actress. I could keep her as an inner elephant and have a trial ride, but on second thoughts, I'm not so sure. I fear I'm getting old."

"I think your appraisal is correct. Princess Soithong merits praise and the king's desire but Soifa looks coquettish and unsuitable. I'm afraid she'll displease Your Majesty like a bucking horse that needs to be controlled. Though her figure with no sagging flabbiness will appeal to you, she will not make you bloom with joy. If she is to enter royal service, the level of lady attendant seems adequate. May Your Majesty, ruler of the three worlds, make the appropriate decision."

The king smiled. "I'm bored with difficult women. But if I make her an attendant, she'll feel it's a loss of face since she's the daughter of a ruler. Better to have her married off. Now then! Phlai Ngam still has no wife. If we leave him unattached, he might seize upon some low person. This solution will both settle the issue of Soifa and give face to Phra Wai. How do you feel, governess? If Phra Wai has Soifa, will it benefit me?"

"It is fitting and will strengthen his loyalty."

The king turned to Princess Soithong and bestowed upon her a gold cloisonné betel box, sixteen hundred baht, golden bowl, wasp-nest ring, snake ring, tasseled diamond earrings, bodice with ornamental glass, and cloth. He also gave gifts to her ladies-in-waiting.

He turned to Princess Soifa. "Although your father made me angry, I have pardoned him. He'll return home, and I'll be father to young Soifa. In future I'll arrange a good marriage for you so that you have face and nobody can cavil about me."

The head royal governess led Soifa away.

Next morning at dawn, the courtiers gathered for audience. The ruler of Chiang Mai prostrated to King Phanwasa. "May I serve the royal foot until death. If in future I break my word and incur your anger, have me executed. As guarantee that I will not lapse, may I offer my daughter."

The king smiled. "I'm very grateful that you bestow on me your beloved child. But when I saw her face, I made up my mind to ask for Soifa to be given to Phlai Ngam. They're very compatible. She is enchanting, while Phlai Ngam excels in knowledge. They'll make a happy couple. Don't be disappointed about his low rank. I love Phlai Ngam like my own son, and he is now lieutenant of the royal pages, so you may consider the two of us connected."

The ruler of Chiang Mai's heart sank in mortification over the honor of his solar lineage. He thought to himself, "Oh what a pity. She shouldn't descend to mixing with menials." But out of necessity, he prostrated in gratitude. "If the king wishes to grant her to Phra Wai, that is the royal privilege. He is a shrewd, talented fellow of military lineage, and should remain in royal service. I'll depend on him from now on."

The ruler of Chiang Mai returned to his lodging and related the royal order to his wife. She was happy about going home but sad about her daughter. She sent a servant to fetch her.

The father embraced her. "We will return home, but you will stay here. The king wishes to present you to Phra Wai. I'm beyond grief, my jewel."

Soifa felt she would writhe to death. "Oh my lord and master, you'll leave your child and flee away? Since I'm being presented in order to save lives, I've no thought of deviating from your wish. Even if you had me fetch water or carry a palanquin, I would not refuse. I'm unhappy about only one matter—having a husband. My lord, I'm not used to such a thing! How can I manage a household in the Thai style when I don't know the customs? I'll be mocked and shamed before the people of Ayutthaya. And the person who is to be my husband does not love me. If he mistreats me, where can I flee? I'll be on my own among the Thai. I'll probably die."

Her father consoled her with a caress. "It's our karma, my darling. You're like a patron to your father, our kinsfolk, and the common people who suffer as war prisoners. Without you, all would probably die here. I wasn't happy to consent but opposing the king's command would have seemed insulting. Besides, as you are presented to Phra Wai by the king, I don't think he'll shame you by beating or cursing. Anyway, I'll give you some people to help protect you, and your mother will select some attendants."

Queen Apson called Soifa into the main apartment. "Don't cry, dear child. Nobody born as a human being can escape sorrow. When a time for happiness is over, sorrow begins. When a time for sorrow passes, then happiness returns again. Your good deed will earn great merit and benefit you in the future. Though your partner is from far away and speaks a different language, he's a good person. When I was in the bloom of youth, I lived far away in the city of Chiang Tung. Your grandfather went to ask for my hand, and I saw your father's face only on the wedding day. We've now lived together for a long time without any falling out. The matter of lovemaking depends on the love in the heart. When you're together with him, you'll be moved by the passion inside. When you lie beside him on the pillow for the very first time, don't be fearful or you'll make him tense and angry. Men by nature are like elephants. If the mahout knows how to treat them, they're hard-working. But at times when they're in musth, the mahout must know how to make allowances for the sake of harmony. A woman must defer to her husband in fear he may use force. As long as that husband still protects her, it doesn't matter if other people laugh. But if a husband leaves the wife lonely and forlorn, it's like the end of her life, her name, her flesh and blood. Women deserted by their husbands are smirked at by people wherever they go. Finding a new husband is very difficult because you've lost the specialness of your virginity. The most important thing for a wife in pleasing her husband is her own body. The next is food. If she can cook to please his palate, he won't abandon her even when she's old and no longer pretty. Your father has about three hundred consorts. He gets these girls and goes gaga over them, but as soon as he's bored, he misses me every time. Though they're beautiful, they're dumb as corpses. If you do as I tell you, it's better than a love charm."

In the late afternoon, they prepared to send Soifa into the palace. The queen took off a nine-peak ring and gave it to her daughter. "Even sold very cheap, it'll fetch eight hundred baht. Keep it to pawn in the palace when you face difficulty."

She selected girls for her daughter's retinue—a chief nursemaid and four others who were just of age with good appearance. She instructed the chief nursemaid, "Don't consider yourself a servant but think of her as your younger sister from the same womb. Try to look after each other."

"It's almost time they close the gate, mother's jewel. Hurry back into the palace. May you be eternally happy. May danger and evil not cross your path."

Soifa prostrated at the feet of her mother and father with tears flowing. The palace matrons warned it was getting dark. Her father and mother watched until Soifa disappeared into the palace, then Queen Apson wept so much that all her attendants gave way to grief. After they recovered, the king gave orders to prepare for departure in two days' time.

The Lao caulked boats and rafts, collected goods together in piles, and went to buy clothes and food. Hearing that the Lao would leave, traders arrived in crowds and happily sold goods at double the normal price. Lao ladies in royal service packed as much powder and oil as could be carried. All of those returning home were beaming, but those who had to stay in Ayutthaya were red-eyed and glum. The King of Chiang Mai took pity on them and handed out many gratuities. "Bear up! Stay here with Soifa and next year I'll arrange to bring you home."

A royal order came for the palace ladies and the goods sent to the capital to be returned. On the homeward journey, they were to call at Phichit to collect the elephants, horses, carts, servants, and people left there. Officials would go along to check items against a manifest.

Near dawn, the moon slid below the tree line, the morning star still shone brightly, and the city sounded with cockcrows and birdsong. At an auspicious moment when the sun's rays appeared, the ruler of Chiang Mai ordered his boat to leave the jetty. As they passed in front of the main palace, the king sat quietly in the stern with tears flowing at the thought of his daughter. When his boat passed the elephant enclosure, he was disheartened at the sight of rows of elephants tied to posts.

"You bull elephants followed the herd and got lured into a trap. Now you stand at these posts with trunks resting on tusks, eyes looking at nothing in gloom, and tears flooding your faces. You no longer charge around in the wilds with courage and fear of no one. Oh elephants, you were carried away by the pride in your own strength and got lured into the lasso. Lust led you into the trap, and now you're tied up all the time. Pursuing Soithong was a mistake that brought enormous misfortune. I lost my home, lost my city, and gained torment. My beloved child cannot return with me."

When they arrived at Phichit, the governor and local officials, informed by an order under seal, came out to receive them. They handed over all the various goods that had to be returned by royal command according to the manifest. Prisoners and goods required by the king were dispatched down to Ayutthaya. Arrangements were completed in a few days, and a report sent on what had taken place.

When they reached Lampang, the governor and nobles all came out in welcome. The ruler of Chiang Mai ordered a halt to recover from fatigue, and sent a detachment ahead to inform Chiang Mai people that their city had been restored to their king and queen.

On an auspicious day, the people of Chiang Mai came out in procession to welcome their ruler at Lamphun and invite him to return and rule the city. The king and queen mounted golden palanquins. On both sides of the route, royal balustrades and umbrellas were set up at intervals, and house owners sat in rows to receive the king's blessing as he passed.

"Hail! May you have victory and good fortune, O lord!"

"May the king be forever happy!"

When they arrived at the palace, the holy patriarch invited the king and queen to sit under arches of banana plants while monks chanted in unison. The holy patriarch took a water bowl, pronounced a mantra to concentrate power, and then poured the water to dispel misfortune to the strains of loud and joyful music.

In the late afternoon, many royal relatives, officials, courtiers, and palace staff gathered in the audience hall. They invited the King and Queen of Chiang Mai to be seated on royal thrones, gave blessings to strengthen the royal souls, and tied sacred thread on each of their wrists according to custom. After the ceremony, the best boxers from all around staged a contest in the palace courtyard. The hubbub continued until evening, when the celebration ended and everybody returned home.

THE MARRIAGE OF PHRA WAI

At the evening audience, King Phanwasa turned to Khun Phaen. "I've given Phra Wai rank, title, and a complete retinue. To be a noble and have no wife is a waste. I'll make sure he has at least one. I'll give him Soifa. That befits his rank and the royal favor he's won."

Khun Phaen prostrated three times. "Your Majesty's kindness is boundless, but I cannot lie. During the campaign, Phra Wai met Simala, the daughter of Phra Phichit. The ceremony was postponed until the fourth month but they have already been betrothed."

"However many wives he has is fitting. If he had ten, it would be even better. Send an order for Phra Phichit to come here together with his daughter, and I'll marry her to Wai."

On receiving the order, Phra Phichit hastened down to Ayutthaya with his wife and daughter. Khun Phaen relayed what had happened. "I told the king about Simala, but the king said he could have more. I don't like that but I dare not oppose the king's wishes. Sir, please have mercy and don't blame my son for being unfaithful."

Phra Phichit said, "The king's power is great. We are his servants and must follow his wishes."

Phra Phichit, Busaba, and Simala went to stay in Phra Wai's new house provided by the king.

Early on the day before the marriage, Phramuen Si arrived to prepare the house. Carpets, mats, and felt rugs were spread. Cushions were placed for reclining. Sets of crystal were arrayed on half-moon tables. Lamps with oil wicks were readied in rows to be lit at nightfall.

Phra Phichit said to Phramuen Si, "Today there's to be a water sprinkling ceremony. Please find about ten young women, all palace ladies, to form the bride's party on this occasion."

Phramuen Si said, "No problem. My house is full of young women."

Phra Wai chose nine good-looking pages to bring along as the groom's party. They attracted a lot of attention passing along the street to Phra Wai's house, where they listened to the monks chant prayers and deliver a sermon.

In Suphan, Wanthong heard news of the marriage. "As a parent, I must go to give some help and have the honor of making myself known to the nobles."

She went to tell Khun Chang. "The news is all over town that Phlai Ngam is getting married. If I don't go, it might cause some offense and make the common people gossip."

"I don't object. He's an officer of the pages and we can depend on such a noble in the future. Don't go empty-handed. Take some money and some food to help them out. I'll follow later by elephant. Precious, I'd like to ask one favor. If you meet Khun Phaen, don't talk with this sex-mad fellow, and if he takes any liberties, give him an earful."

"Don't order me around. I'm not going to sit talking with him."

She went into her room, unlocked a trunk, and picked out some good quality lowercloths and rings for the two brides, and four or five gold bars for Phra Wai. She arranged to take gourds, rice, and fresh palm fruit. "Also those good pumpkins I planted. Cut and pack them."

Everything was loaded on a big boat. They reached the city, moored by Wat Takrai, and went up to the big house of Phra Wai, who welcomed his mother with clasped hands.

Ten pretty young women had been found for the bride's party. In the late afternoon, Phra Phichit and Busaba told them to bathe and get dressed. Each had brought a citrus thorn hidden in their cloth to protect themselves against importunate young men. They huddled around the bride as she walked over to sit and listen to a sermon. A monk took a sacred thread to connect Simala and Phra Wai. When a big gong was struck, the young men and women crowded tightly together while monks sprinkled water, pouring five or six bowls on the side with the women. Thorns were stabbed into bellies, making people yelp. An old lady came into the middle. The pages banged into her. "Oh! I'm going to foul myself. I can't stand it!" She got out of the way, leaving Phra Wai and Simala next to each other.

The abbot laughed and sprinkled more water.

"No more, Master Jan!"

"Enough already!"

The abbot gave an offertory blessing and the monks departed. All the women bustled off into an apartment. As the mother-in-law, Busaba prepared sandalwood fans as gifts for those in the party of the groom, and gold caselets for those in the party of the bride.

The groom's party went to change clothes and gathered in the central hall where footed trays with food in silver bowls were set out with spittoons, water bowls, and salvers placed neatly alongside. When they had finished eating, the tables were carried back inside and betel trays appeared. A music ensemble played, loud and rousing at first, then sweetly plaintive and lamenting. Listening to a wistful melody, Phra Wai drifted off to sleep.

At audience next morning, the king thought about Phra Wai's marriage. "Why delay over this matter of Soifa? Send her to him today. Let it be a dazzling spectacle in view of all the nobles."

He ordered a treasury official to requisition twenty sets of cloth along with combs, mirrors, powder sets, rings, betel trays, and four hundred baht. "Have her ride over there in a palanquin with patterned curtains. Head governess, escort her to the house."

The governess took Soifa off to a beautiful palanquin. Young ladies and sentinelles carried the royal presents behind.

Phra Wai's house was packed with people. Monks had already chanted prayers and the novices had readied almsbowls in a row. Two golden ladles were brought and placed in the middle of the verandah. Wanthong called the servants to fill a bowl with white rice. Phramuen Si went into the apartment to tell Simala, "Come out to give alms, my dear child."

Simala shyly hid behind a curtain looking listless. Wanthong called out, "Please pluck up some courage and just go out there. I'll accompany you."

Simala followed her mother-in-law out to the terrace with heart fluttering. Phra Wai had scooped a ladle of rice and was waiting. He proffered the ladle towards Simala. When their eyes met, she gently lowered her face and was shyly reluctant to take a hold. Wanthong took her elbow and guided Simala to clasp Phra Wai's hand firmly and tip the rice into a monk's bowl.

Just at that moment, the palanquin arrived. Soifa parted the curtains and looked out, seeing the husband and wife giving alms together. She felt a stab of annoyance but gritted her teeth. Phra Wai called his father to welcome the palace ladies into the house.

Cooks rushed around setting out food trays, spittoons, and water jugs. Khun Phaen had the task of looking after the royal party. Phramuen Si took care of the nobles. Phra Phichit saw to feeding the monks and novices. When the monks had eaten and their pupils had packed the remains, they were presented with robes and hampers of everyday articles, and returned to the wat.

Earlier that day, Khun Chang had left Suphan on a bull elephant with a crowd of servants trailing behind. On arrival, he went up to the central hall where all the nobles and pages were gathered. Phra Wai welcomed him, offered him a betel tray, and chatted politely. Khun Chang stooped in feigned deference, saying, "My dear lord, you glow with such youth and plumpness, befitting your merit. Your skin looks as radiant as if painted with gold."

Khun Chang crawled in to pay respect to Phramuen Si, who said, "You didn't appear for your duty round but were intent on drinking liquor. I'll have you tied by the neck and dragged off one of these days."

Khun Phaen called out to Khun Chang. "My, you're truly fat, my old friend, like a great pig."

Khun Chang crawled closer, stroked his knee, and said unctuously, "We were once friends but it went wrong because of ill fortune. Don't prolong the enmity but remember we once loved each other."

Khun Phaen said, "Don't worry, Khun Chang. I'll invite you to our house to dine sometime."

Khun Chang went in to pay respect to Thong Prasi. "What a pity you're getting a little old."

Thong Prasi replied cordially, "Mm, Mm." She shaded her eyes to peer at him. "Oh, Khun Chang! Why is your head so bald? How are Thepthong and Siprajan? I'm full of aches and pains. I keep breaking wind, coughing, and wheezing so I haven't been to visit friends in Suphan."

Khun Chang replied, "Mother Thepthong is still active and her eyesight is good but Siprajan is old and very rickety."

He took his leave of Thong Prasi and came to the central hall. Acquaintances greeted him and he chattered away. Servants brought in sets of food on tiered trays along with brandy, anise, and triple-strength liquor. Khun Chang soon became thoroughly drunk. Some nobles played up to him. "Sir, please sing us a passage from a drama." Khun Chang set his face like a dancer and called out to the ensemble for music. The more people egged him on, the more playful he became, leaping up and miming a mask play.

Khun Phaen got up in embarrassment to stop him. "Drink moderately. When drunk you lose your dignity."

"I'm not drunk. The liquor's no good. Bring the anise over and I'll do a somersault."

He struck a pose, clicking his tongue and hopping from one leg to the other like a mask-play dancer, but fell over flat and got his lowercloth in a twist. Still he shouted, "I want the triple-strength!"

Phra Wai came over. "You've had enough to drink. Go and sleep it off."

"I'm not drunk! Shame on you, Phra Wai, for embarrassing me in front of guests. You forget I'm your elder."

The nobles cheered him. "What a glutton!"

Getting more excited, Khun Chang squatted on his haunches to upend a liquor jar, picked up a trumpet-mouth spittoon, put it on his head, and staggered around with his hands on his bottom, his face pushed forward, and his eyes half-closed. Phra Wai rebuked him, but Khun Chang did not hear. He staggered around and fell over.

Wanthong heard laughter and came to look. So ashamed she wanted to disappear into the earth, she shouted, "You awful man! How can you do this without any shame?"

Khun Chang looked at her through half-closed eyes. "I'm not ashamed." He leapt up and danced around wildly. "Hey, mother of this Wai! Come and be an angel, and I'll be Lord Hanuman. The tail that used to hang past my feet has shrunk to nothing. I used to be the lord of many lands." He stuck out his tongue, scratched his leg, and grabbed at Wanthong.

She pushed him away. Phra Wai cursed him, "You arrogant fellow! Calling me 'this Wai.' Were I not thinking of my mother, I'd elbow you half to death."

Khun Chang stood drunkenly scratching his bottom. "Pah! You think a lot of yourself as an officer of the pages, don't you? You forget my kindness, you ungrateful creature. Who raised you when you were little?"

Phra Wai was so angry that his body shook. "This baldy wants to hurt me with insults, slandering my good name as a noble. Enough! What will be will be."

He clenched his fist and hit Khun Chang in the mouth. Wanthong shrieked and ran between them. Khun Chang tumbled down head over heels. Nobles came and roughly pulled him upright. Phra Wai cursed him mercilessly.

Wanthong cried, "Wai, don't get upset at a drunk. He's not fully himself so he was speaking nonsense. Restrain yourself and you'll gain merit. Have some consideration for your mother."

"Oh, Mother, he always acts so shamelessly. If I wasn't thinking of you, I'd finish him off."

Khun Phaen wagged his finger at Wanthong. "Your husband insulted my son, yet you didn't tell him off. When he got hit, you danced around like a puppet. My son is shamed in front of these people, but you don't care."

Wanthong tossed her head angrily. "You talk like a little thumb-sucking child. You accuse me of loving my husband and hating my son. Do you think I approve of what Chang just did? He shouldn't have insulted Wai but he only did it because he was drunk. He got hit because he deserved it."

Khun Chang began to recover from his daze. He got up, hitching up his lowercloth so far it exposed his bottom. He wagged his finger and said, "Hey, you evil, over-excited fellow, do you remember when you were tiny? I dragged you by the hair, and buried you under logs. If you don't believe me, feel the scar on the back of your head. I thought you died. I didn't know you'd come back to rough me up."

Phra Wai trembled with rage. "Let me tell everybody what happened. This monstrosity tried to break my neck. Because of merit, I was able to escape and survive." He called his men. "Take him! Don't spare his life!"

His young retainers crowded around, punching and kicking Khun Chang until some nobles came between them to stop it.

Wanthong ran over to embrace Khun Chang. He was motionless and seemed not to be breathing. She wept and wailed, "Oh, my lord! You came here because you love your wife but they pounded you as mercilessly as a fish. Maybe your merit is all used up."

She had him carried into the middle of the house. Some people tried massaging him, but his eyes did not open.

Wanthong lamented. "Oh, little bo tree shelter of your darling wife, you're dead and I think I'll be too. We lived together fifteen or sixteen years without a single word to distress me. When I gave birth, you sat gently supporting my back. When I had fever and couldn't eat, you sat beside me and fed me. When you saw I couldn't sleep, neither would you. In the hot season you fanned me. In the cool season, you covered me with a blanket and hugged me to sleep. There's no man on the surface of the earth who loved his wife as much as you. Though your looks are not fine, your heart shines like the moon. Karma made you follow your wife here to die."

When her grief eased, she felt his body and found it was still soft, and his pulse still beating. She ordered servants to bring hot water and wipe his whole body. Suddenly, he let out a groan and began breathing strongly. Fiery-eyed with fury, he gritted his teeth and bellowed, "Even if my body dies, my bones will talk. Don't think you can kick me around with no consequences. If the king ceases to keep me, no matter." He called his servants and hauled Wanthong out of the house by her hand. "You go home first. I'll go to attend on the Lord of Life."

Wanthong warned him through tears. "If you bring up the matter with the king, aren't you worried you could be in the wrong? Phra Wai is in the king's favor. Stop and think carefully."

"I'm not drunk now, my jewel, so don't oppose me." He sent her off to Suphan and hurried to the palace.

Now that the quarrel had passed, Phra Wai brightened up. All the nobles took their leave. The palace governess said, "His Majesty the King entrusted me to bring Soifa to you."

Phra Wai prostrated to pay respect to the king, and ordered presents of cloth for the governess's party. They took leave and returned to the palace.

Phra Wai arranged for the house to be divided. Soifa occupied two apartments with a sitting room, bedroom, bathroom, and curtains and screens to conceal them from view. Now that the wedding was over, Phra Wai distributed cash and foreign white cloth to the royal cooks so that nobody would gossip and criticize. Even the house servants received gifts.

Phra Phichit and Busaba came to see Phra Wai. "There's a great deal of government business at home. If I leave it to the officials for too long, some disaster will happen. We've come to say farewell but our concern for Simala remains. Since birth, she's not been apart from us. Now she'll be very far away in this southern city with no kinsfolk around. Also, you now have two wives. I think there'll be jealousy for sure. There's an old saying that you shouldn't have four houses or two wives. You have to be as even-handed as a pair of weigh scales."

"Don't worry about Simala. Though I'm young and foolish and make mistakes, I'll repay your kindness as I have promised."

"May you earn merit. We two will take our leave."

They went to see their daughter. Simala clasped her father's feet in tears. "Who will I turn to in times of trouble? However much my husband loves me, it's not the same as parents. If he's not fair, things will change and I'll be unhappy every night."

Busaba consoled her. "Don't cry. Your father and I made sure your husband swore an oath to be steadfast. Yet I still fear jealousy will cause trouble and shame. According to ancient practice, having two wives is forbidden. Since you were little, I've taught you that nothing is more important than forbearance. Take care because you're the poorer of the two wives and people will make comparisons. If anyone riles you, ignore them and bear with it. Don't complain to your husband. Obey him without stubbornness for half a year and you should be able to ride on his neck from then on. One other thing, minister to his needs. Anyone good at lovemaking does very well. Make the midday meal without fail. As long as he always has a full stomach, you'll have no need to fear your husband will leave you."

The parents embraced their daughter and went down to their boat. Phra Wai, Simala, and Khun Phaen followed to send them off.

That night, stars twinkled and a brilliant moon shone. Cicadas and crickets trilled a melody. Fireflies flickered. Bees flitted, fondling the flowers, and fluffing up soft clouds of pollen. Phra Wai was befuddled thinking about the two women.

337

"Simala will be lying there thinking despondently that my love for her has faded. Soifa will be feeling lonely since she's never yet been intimate with a man. But if I go to her first, I'll have Simala on my mind."

He dithered and agonized back and forth while time passed. Eventually he bathed and went into Simala's room. With the lamplight catching her sleeping face, she looked as radiant as if lustrated with gold. Overcome with passion, he lay down close and embraced her.

Simala raised herself from the pillow and cast him a sharp, hooded look. "Why do you come here over halfway through the night? Before you left, did you take leave from her nicely, or did you sneak off while she was asleep?"

"Don't be so catty, precious. Just now I was sitting in the central hall, when a scented breeze aroused me so I came to find you. Picking at me for no reason is hurtful. I've come to fine you a kiss on each cheek."

"Don't play around. As they say, a bandit who's been caught but not thrashed will admit to nothing. You turn up here because you think she won't know. Don't pretend you have to be here. My looks can't please you as much. Where there's good talking, go bill and coo. Where there's good kissing, go wallow till the taste fades."

"You're so eloquent, Simala, good at being cutting. I surrender. I can't compete with your fine words." He spread his arms and hugged her against his body.

"I'm not willing, sir. Don't bully me."

"Let me hug you a little. Don't try to escape."

"I'm hot, sir. Please release me."

"Don't push me away. You'll bruise your hand."

"Don't play around or I'll pinch you hard."

"Oh love, aren't you worried about breaking a fingernail."

"Oh sir, your hands are making me shy."

"Who is there to be shy of in the dark?"

Nose pressed to cheek. Hand grasping hand. Leg pressed on leg so she could not move. Belly against belly. Breast hugged against breast. Like a pair of fighting cocks of great skill, strutting up and down on the leash in all directions, then each pecking, picking, and parrying back. The lower one sprang into an attacking stance. The upper one closed and clashed, banging together. The lower ducked, kicked, bucked, smacked. The upper rode every blow without fail. After the long, white, sharp, serum-loaded spur stabbed, spilling blood, they slept.

In the dead of night, a cool dew descended like strands of hair. Flowers opened their petals and new leaves budded. Bees supped pollen from blooming lotuses. Phra Wai lay thinking of Soifa.

"Right now, is she asleep or is she lying awake and waiting? Perhaps she feels I pay her no attention. It would be a pity if she feels slighted. In a moment I'll go to find how she performs. Is she truly good, like a Thai, or somehow different?"

He turned to look at Simala sleeping soundly and carefully slid away. Coming to the room of Soifa, he gently sat down on the bed. In the light of the lamp, her delicate complexion shone. Her lips seemed on the point of breaking into a sweet smile. Her neck fell in three circlets. Her two breasts were like golden lotuses. He was beyond the point of restraining his body. He lifted her onto his lap and kissed her.

When Soifa opened her eyes and saw Phra Wai, she panicked and drew away as she had never tasted love with a man. When he touched her, she flinched like a fledgling, got up from the bed, and tried to escape. Phra Wai grabbed hold of her.

"Ow, don't hurt me! You're squeezing so tight my fingers have lost any feeling already. Let me go."

"There was no need to come outside the net. If my darling isn't merciful, I'll stay here hugging you until dawn, letting the mosquitoes torment you. By morning your body will be covered in bumps. Please come into the net for relief. What's this black thing on your breast?" He groped with his hand and laughed. "Oh, it's a speck of dust." He pretended to look closely, then caressed and kissed. "Oh, here's a beauty spot too."

Soifa turned away and tossed her head. "I didn't invite you to sit inspecting me. Even though a mosquito bites my cheek, don't bother brushing it off. I don't care about my own flesh and blood. I'll sit and let the mosquitoes feed until morning."

"But I feel sorry for your cheeks, so fair and firm and smiling. I wish to defend their softness and fragrance." He kissed her gently on both cheeks. "Only my nose is touching and that doesn't hurt, but the bites of these mosquitoes are sharp. If my devout darling intends to make a charitable donation of her flesh and blood to the mosquitoes, I won't interfere with her wishes. But I can't allow your cheeks and breasts to be given as alms."

"Why not? If the owner of the cheeks and breasts wants to give them away, who are you to object? Don't hinder my charity. Let them be sliced up for the crows."

"I feel sorry for these breasts, so full, soft, and round." Pretending to be shocked, he cradled them gently.

"Take your hands off. The king presented me to you as a servant. He didn't order me to be your wife. I won't consent so cease this fondling. I'll serve only as a slave."

She tried to squirm her way free. Phra Wai held onto her breasts and squeezed. Passion stirred passion. Battle commenced.

She backed. He nudged. She trotted. He thrust. She recoiled. He pressed. She broke. He drove. She started and writhed. He thrust at full force. She responded with the style of a fine-bred filly, only just harnessed for training, mouth still soft, unruly, and not yet used to a rider. He gave the filly her head for a while to watch her performance, till she slackened and slowed, lowering her haunches and turning her neck aside. He covered her, slapping her side so she sprang. Easy, easy. Her bucking slowed to a graceful rhythm. Once she knew the way, she was as good as a trained steed. Now that they knew each other, there was no limit to their energy, no need for him to urge her onwards, just follow the rhythm, until the sweat soaked down to her hooves, and he unharnessed her.

Sated as if they had soared to heaven, they slept soundly.

KHUN CHANG IS FOUND GUILTY

Next morning at the royal audience, Khun Chang addressed the king. "My liege, just now, this excitable fellow, Phra Wai, almost beat me to death. Over a hundred of his men hit me again and again. What's more, he said provocatively, 'I'm not afraid even of your master.' Many witnessed this event. If this is untrue, may I offer my life."

The king quietly pondered Khun Chang's statement. "It may be true that they beat him up, but the provocative reference to his master is probably invented to create a big issue. When this fellow is full of liquor, he becomes insulting. Probably this was just a quarrel that got out of hand. But if I don't conduct an interrogation, Phra Wai will think he can get away with anything because the king loves him."

He sent for Phra Wai. "At your marriage, why did you highhandedly commit violence on Khun Chang—kicking, beating, and even making a provocative reference to his 'master'? Exactly who is the 'master' that you claim you don't fear?"

"My liege, everything that Khun Chang has said is concocted to put himself in a good light. He got drunk and tugged my mother around in front of people. I couldn't tolerate that so we quarreled. He began spewing out insults and addressed me improperly. I was greatly shamed. Then he dredged up matters from the past—about how he tried to beat me to death in a forest."

The king turned to Khun Chang. "Phra Wai claims this incident is the original reason for your quarrel. And he denies the allegation about making a grave insult. So, what is the truth?"

"Everything Phra Wai told Your Majesty is false. If I had tried to beat him to death, there would be evidence. He deliberately got me drunk, lured me to speak under the influence, and now wants to smear me with wrongdoing. His provocative reference to Your Majesty is a grave matter."

The king slapped his thigh. "I'll get to the bottom of this. Those of you nobles who went to the wedding yesterday and saw what happened, speak out. Don't take sides."

A noble responded. "Khun Chang was blind drunk. He even stripped off his clothes quite shamelessly. When Phra Wai told him off, tempers flared and they had an exchange of blows. Khun Chang blurted about matters in the past and Phra Wai summoned his men to beat Khun Chang. As for the improper comment about his master, none of us heard that."

The king appraised the testimony in his mind. "If there really was an improper reference, it's punishable by death. If it's not true, the accuser is liable to the same penalty. If testimony shows that Khun Chang did try beating him to death, he must be executed, but some allowance may be made on grounds he was totally drunk and not fully sensible when he spoke. I need to interrogate Phra Wai for clarification."

The king asked, "Phra Wai, why has the matter of Khun Chang trying to beat you to death come out only now? Where did it happen? Does anyone know about this?"

"My liege, I was only a little boy. No one was around to be a witness. It's beyond my ability to prove it. Should I be found in the wrong in an ordeal by water, let me offer my life to Your Majesty."

"What Wai says sounds right. Khun Chang, if you confess, I'll be lenient. Tell everything without lying or withholding information."

Khun Chang was dripping with sweat. "My liege, Phra Wai's words are untrue. He invented this incident to smother the charges I made.

All the nobles are siding with Phra Wai because they are colleagues. I've no allies so I'm at a loss."

The king carefully reviewed the evidence. "Khun Chang's account is suspicious on every point. If I ordered officials to use the cane, we'd sort truth from falsehood in no time. But at present, Phra Wai is in royal favor, and the common people talk about that. If I side with Phra Wai and punish Khun Chang, there'll be doubt. The case must be examined by due process to let people see who's telling the truth and who's not. That way I'll escape criticism."

The king said, "Khun Chang, I think your case is a pack of lies. If I went by the book, your head would be cut off. You've lied about the improper comment and wrongly defamed Phra Wai. On the matter of defaming him, the two of you must reach a settlement. On the improper comment, you're found guilty and condemned to death, yet I grant a pardon."

The king gave orders to the four chief judges. "As there is no evidence to decide on the charge that Khun Chang once tried to beat Phra Wai to death, arrange for the two of them to undergo ordeal by water. Have both of them enter confinement tomorrow for seven nights until the day of the ordeal. Keep them under guard in the palace."

On the day of the ordeal, crowds of people rushed to watch. Young girls saw their friends on the way and jumped up to join them. Gay ladies in the palace called out to their partners, "We're going to see the ordeal by water, loves."

"Yes, yes, let's all go down to the jetty, Mae Arun."

A pair cuddling together came out of the mosquito net and hid the sac in a basket of kapok. Amphan said, "I'm coming too, loves. Come along, Mae Yisun, don't delay."

"Can't you wait just a little?" She parted her hair so hurriedly that the stick broke. She swiped on a black pencil, dashed a comb through her hair, and raced after the others.

Rafts swarmed all over the surface of the river. Guards boarded boats and went to lay buoys and stand with guns to ward away people.

Others went upstream to push away anything floating dead in the water. The banks were packed with people. Close to three o'clock, the king came down to the river and ordered that the two submerge at sunset.

The chief judges decided, "Following the ancient manual of judicial procedure, Phra Wai should take the upstream side as he is now the plaintiff, and is of higher rank. Khun Chang must take the downstream side."

The two were brought out from confinement and led along under heavy guard. They washed head and body, faced off against each other, and went down into the water. When a gong sounded, guards pushed their necks down and paid out the rope. Immediately Khun Chang shot back up again. The onlookers jeered and booed. Guards put a large chain around his neck and prepared to hustle him away. Khun Chang called out, "Please have mercy, sire. This fellow Phra Wai blew some mantra onto me. Giving him the upstream side allowed him to do this."

The king exclaimed, "Damn this loudmouth! He loses but tries to turn it round by dribbling on about Wai using lore. Such a great, slippery-tongued liar should be thrashed to dust. But what he says about the defendant being upstream is fair. Let him go upstream and submerge again. If he loses a second time, take him away for the chop he deserves."

The gong sounded. They submerged again. Onlookers crowded around in excitement. Boats jostled to get a view. Because Khun Chang was in the wrong, he imagined snakes were twining round his body, and he shot above the surface shaking with panic. Khun Phaen jumped into the water and lifted Phra Wai out. The city guards clapped Khun Chang in irons.

The king stamped his foot in anger. "He was crooked and mendacious even with me. He seemed to imagine there was no authority. He issued challenges and offered his life, but now he's proved to be in the wrong twice over. Don't leave him to pollute the earth. Cleave open his breast as an example to deter others. He took Wai off to kill in a forest. Go and impale him in that same forest!"

The king returned by palanquin to the inner palace. The minister issued orders. "Don't trust someone who's been condemned to death. Have warders put him in all five irons immediately. Chains, yoke, cangue—have no mercy."

Four warders dragged Khun Chang off. He tripped over the chains, fell, and would not get up. He pretended to be winded in the stomach and wailed loudly. The warders punched him and beat him with canes. "Die, see if we care! If we're in the wrong, we'll just pay a small fine to disown responsibility."

Khun Chang leapt up and pretended to be crazy, gaping his mouth open, lolling his tongue, and rolling up his eyes. He threw off his lowercloth and ran dangling. He picked up a lump of dogshit and threw it at the onlookers. He danced around wildly, knocking onlookers with the cangue.

Warders threatened him, "You mongrel! I'll cure your madness with this cane."

"You abominable wretch, throwing shit at people and letting it all hang out."

Women averted their faces and ran away. "He's done for."

"Worse than a beggar."

Young men ragged him, "Why don't you tie it tuck-tail style?"

Khun Chang's servants ran over to pick up his cloth and wrap it round him. The warders dragged him to the jail and applied the five irons. Khun Chang was suspended from the waist with his head lolling over the cangue. He called out to the warders, "Please loosen the chains so I can breathe. I'll give you fifty baht for the reduction fees."

"Fine. Keep quiet until the inspection, then we'll loosen them a bit."

A servant went to inform Wanthong in Suphan. Once she had recovered from the shock, she unlocked a trunk, took out some bars of gold, scooped cash into several baskets, prepared some food including venison and half a pitcher of honey, and sent servants off to buy catfish.

At the jail, she went up to find the chief governor and gave him presents. "Sir, have some mercy on me. I've had no experience of how things are in jail. May I send food to Khun Chang?"

The governor summoned a warder. "Take this good lady to see her husband."

After they passed the gate into the prison, Wanthong appealed to the warder, "Please release him to come down and eat here."

"You may go in to see him, Wanthong, but there's no release for a punishment like this."

Wanthong steeled herself to enter the jail. She saw people with thin bodies like creatures in hell. They stank like corpses and had scabies, boils, running sores, and hairy lice crawling on their skulls. Seeing Wanthong coming, they begged her for food. When she threw them bananas, the prisoners fought over them and ate them unpeeled.

Khun Chang saw her and wailed out loud, covered in snot and tears like a calf. "Go and hand out bribes wherever you can! Don't let me die in chains. Put money in big, big sacks and go to buy some liquor for me. Also food, knick knacks, pork, and Vietnamese sausage."

Wanthong was angry. "You brainless idiot! Drinking liquor is what got you into these chains, and you're still drooling after more."

"Scold me as much as you like, but pay the jail fees and reduction charges. Whatever expense is needed, pay it, my dear."

"Don't babble. We have loads of money. I'll take it to distribute among the officers, don't worry."

Khun Chang grasped a bowl of rice and put a handful in his mouth but his throat was too dry. He put down the bowl and sobbed. Wanthong fed him spoonfuls of lizard curry to ease his dry throat, and then spicy meat, eels, and chicken curry. Khun Chang managed to finish everything. He draped himself round his wife's neck and pleaded, "My dear, hurry off with the money and bribe someone to petition the king for a pardon."

Wanthong said, "I can't do it myself. To extract a thorn, you must use another thorn to pry it out. I'll plead with Wai to see to it."

"Truly, my dear? If I'm pardoned and stay alive, you can ride me instead of an ox!"

"My kinsfolk never ride on their husband's neck. Don't worry. I won't abandon you, no matter what."

She distributed money to the prison governor and warders of all ranks, gave alms to the convicts, and hurried off to Phra Wai's house. She threw herself into her son's arms and cried on his shoulder. Phra Wai asked, "What's troubling you, Mother? Has one of the grandparents died?"

"I can't see anyone to turn to for help except you. Khun Chang is like a sagging breast that weighs on my chest. For better or worse, he became my husband. If I stand by and let him die, the shame will follow me. Dear son, please have mercy on your mother. Ask the king to spare Khun Chang's life. He should not refuse you. Khun Chang did wrong in the past but please don't bear a grudge."

"Why do you come pleading to me, Mother? I didn't make accusations against Khun Chang. He tried to get me on a capital charge, but I got off because there were witnesses. Don't you remember the time he nearly killed me? The king is angry. What can I get from asking for a pardon? It'll be like throwing myself on a fire. Hopeless, Mother!"

Wanthong embraced Phra Wai, racked with tears. "What you say is true. When Khun Chang almost killed you, I was on the point of death myself. To have a loving husband is not as important as having a child. A husband can just go down three steps and disappear. For your mother's sake, help him get out of this, like releasing fish or turtles to make merit. When you were little, Khun Chang found some little servants for you and gave you gold bracelets and chains. At new year, he dressed you up and took you to the wat grounds, with your crowd of little servants tailing along, and a wet nurse to carry you in her arms. When Khun Chang loves someone, there's nobody like him. He gives everything except the moon and the stars. He may be bad but he's also good, very good. Don't bear a grudge. Please let him live. It'll be like repaying the debt of gratitude to your mother."

Phra Wai was softened by his mother's plea. "If I let Khun Chang die, she'll sicken with sadness and might even hang herself. Then the karma will really be mine. Though Khun Chang is as bad as a pig or dog, he's my mother's husband. If I do nothing, people will gossip."

He said, "Though it's probably hopeless, I'll try to make the king take pity on me. But if Khun Chang is fated to die, it's beyond my power."

"Oh, my dear son, please secure this pardon. I'll give you a hundred and fifty baht as payment for the petition."

"What's this you're saying, Mother? Do you think I'm a chicken that can be tempted with rice? You think your poor son will make the plea because your rich husband has lots of money, because with this money I can build a house of five rooms with wooden walls and keep lots of wives and servants, all because of a bribe from my mother!"

"Oh my beloved son, don't get angry. I spoke without thinking. Don't delay. Asking for this pardon is like helping your mother go to heaven. You'll gain merit that will last a whole era."

Phra Wai hurried to audience. When the regular government business was over, he prostrated three times. "My liege, allow me to seek a royal pardon. Khun Chang has been condemned to death. My mother is so distressed she is almost at the point of death herself. Since I was born, I have not yet repaid my debt of gratitude to her in full measure. Please pardon Khun Chang. It will be equivalent to saving my mother's life."

The king pondered. "If I don't spare his life, Wanthong will die of grief, and her son will feel resentful and shamed among his fellow nobles. I was hoping to rely on him for service. He's a strong fighter, a true offspring of a valiant military lineage. I shouldn't make him dispirited."

The king spoke out. "Phra Wai, I greatly detest this mother of yours. She didn't think of your reputation when she took this dreadful Chang as her husband. If he dropped dead, she could make up with your father, yet you're whining at me to pardon this evil-minded fellow who'd even beat his stepson to death. The life you're asking for will be a burden on the earth."

"My liege, dust under the royal foot, lord of all power and creation. I wanted revenge on Khun Chang, but my mother forbade me. To let her grieve to death would be the same as ignoring my debt of gratitude to her. May Your Majesty have mercy for me, his loyal servant."

"I'm not happy about giving a reprieve, but because you want to repay your debt of gratitude, I grant the pardon. Release Khun Chang immediately."

At the jail, warders cut away Khun Chang's chains, broke the cangue, and carried his limp body outside. Seeing Phra Wai at the gate, he crawled forward until his head rested on his thigh. Phra Wai was too embarrassed to speak. He had his servants make a litter to carry Khun Chang. Crowds came to watch along the way.

At Phra Wai's residence, Wanthong was overjoyed to see them. "You survived because of him, didn't you?"

"Oh, yes! I offer myself as his servant until my dying day."

After eating, Khun Chang went to see Phra Wai. "May you be eternally happy. May your good name rise higher and higher and be known throughout the land so we can depend on you like the shelter of a great bo tree."

Phra Wai acknowledged the blessing. Khun Chang took out money. "I hope fifteen hundred baht will repay your kindness, Phra Wai."

"Keep it! At present I've enough for my needs. It's not good to give money like this. It'd be like taking a bribe from my mother."

Wanthong knew his character. She scooped the money into a basket and passed it to a servant. As evening was approaching, they took their leave and boarded a boat to return to Suphan. On arrival, Khun Chang sent his brother to fetch sacred water and pour it over him. Monks were asked to come and chant for three days to dispel bad fortune.

KHUN CHANG PETITIONS THE KING

After winning the case against Khun Chang, Phra Wai lived contentedly with his two wives but missed his mother. "It's shameful that she hasn't got over the falling out with Father. He's now become a noble but she's stuck beside that ugly, ill-intentioned man. I'm furious that she made me beg for his life. I must make this fury disappear by repaying Khun Chang in some way. I'll pry her away from that evil fellow and bring her to live here with Father."

He waited restlessly, counting the tolling of the palace gong, until late in the night. He checked that the time was free of any obstruction or inauspiciousness. The sky was clear, stars sparkled brightly, and a brilliant haloed moon shone. He made offerings of liquor, rice, and fish to the spirits, applied a potion of turmeric and herbs to his body, put a yantra on his chest, tied a sacred thread around his head, blew a mantra upwards into the darkness to urge his spirits to go along, picked up a sword, and set out for Khun Chang's house.

The gates were securely bolted and bonfires shed light as bright as daytime. After chanting a Great Subduer mantra to drop everyone to sleep, and sending his spirits to pull bolts and remove battens, he walked into the compound without being challenged. At the house of Khun Chang, he lit a candle and scattered enchanted rice, forcing all the spirits to abandon the house. He used a formula to open the windows, and climbed up to a frame for plants with blooming flowers and branches intertwined. Fragrance billowed. Twigs trembled. Pollen wafted. Servants lay asleep, tumbled over one another. Light danced off many mirrors and screens.

He walked ahead, glancing around to admire the curtains, blinds, screens, half-moon tables, and abundance of crystal. He opened a mosquito net and saw the face of his mother, fast asleep on the bed beside Khun Chang, embracing as a couple. Phlai Ngam felt hurt enough for his heart to burst. He drew his sword and raised it to chop Khun Chang dead, but feared he might hit Wanthong.

He drove his spirits away and blew a formula to wake her. Sheathing his sword, he stood motionless while Wanthong regained her senses and opened her eyes. Thinking the intruder was a robber, she clutched her husband and cried out at the top of her voice.

"Why are you shouting, Mother? I'm not a thief."

He clasped her feet. Wanthong buried her head in his shoulder. "Why did you come at this time, my son? There are guards everywhere, bolts on the doors, and bonfires all round. Did your father send you? If Khun Chang wakes up there'll be trouble, and I fear something bad will come of this. What's on your mind? Please tell me and then go home."

"I've no wish to get myself into trouble, but I've come anyway because I love my mother. At present I'm comfortable with my rank, money, two lovely wives, servants at my bidding, and all Father's relatives around. The only thing missing is Mother. You're alive but might as well be dead and gone. I came here to take you back to the house. If any bad consequences arise, that's a matter of fate. Why stay with this lowlife? He's like a fly that buzzes around garbage and then bothers a sweetly fragrant lotus. You brought me up until I was seven, but then we were separated by fate. If you care for your child, come home without delay."

"Oh Phlai Ngam, mother's beloved, I'm not wallowing in wealth. Among all these elephants, horses, and servants, there's nothing I love like you. It's not true that I'm happy. I have to bear the karma I've made. When your father went to jail, Khun Chang dragged me off. Don't harbor suspicions that I ran away with him. When your father came back from Chiang Mai, he didn't make any petition to the king. You're not a child so listen to my words. Please go back and think this over with your father. Make a case to the king. He should rule in your favor because of your rank and valor. Don't talk about abducting me. I'm not willing to go that way."

Phra Wai thought his mother was resisting because she loved Khun Chang more than his father. "I'm taking you home, no matter what. If you won't go nicely, that's up to you. Whatever the sin and karma, come what may. I'll cut off your head and take that, leaving only the body to remain here. Don't be slow to answer. It's almost light and we must hurry away."

Seeing her son gritting his teeth and waving his sword, Wanthong feared he would slash her dead. "Don't do something rash. I fear all this abducting back and forth will cause trouble, but if you think matters won't get out of hand, then I'll go along with you."

They reached the house in Ayutthaya as dawn streaked the sky.

As Khun Chang lay asleep, snoring loudly, a strange dream crept over him. His whole body was leprous. A doctor treated him with a medicine of mercury which ate away his lungs, liver, kidney, intestines, and appendix. His teeth broke and fell out of his mouth. In fright, he awoke and fumbled for Wanthong, calling out, "Help me, my dear!"

He opened his eyes and found she was not there. His cloth slipped from his body. He shouted for her but no word came in reply. He frantically summoned servants, who ran up to find their master standing stark naked with his legs splayed. They all sank down aghast, hidden behind a door.

"Why are you dangling like that, master? With nothing on, you look frightful."

Khun Chang peered down at his body and quickly covered himself with his two hands. "Who took my cloth? Someone fetch me one." A servant went in, passed him a cloth, and ran out, averting her face.

Khun Chang asked, "Where's Wanthong gone? Find what's happened to her, and ask her to come here without any fuss."

The servants searched the house from top to bottom and returned to tell him that Wanthong was not to be found.

Khun Chang's shiny bald skull was bathed in sweat. "Truly she can do all kinds of everything. The first time she disappeared, Khun Phaen seized her. This time, who's she gone with? I didn't think this would happen now that she's old. Well, what will be will be. If I don't get her back, then I'm not Khun Chang."

A man arrived at the house and called out to Khun Chang. "I'm a servant of Phra Wai. He sent me to pay his respect and tell you that last night he suddenly had a stomachache and was on the point of death so he sent me here to give the news. I ran into his mother when she came out to relieve herself. I called to wake you in the house, but to save time we hurried off in the middle of the night. She nursed Phra Wai to allay the fever. He gives you his word that she'll return as soon as he's cured."

Khun Chang was angry enough for blood to spurt from his eyes, but he hid his rage and said, "It's all for the good. At present this fatal and remorseless fever is all over the capital. If there's anything you need, don't be shy to ask."

He banged the window shut. With stomach seething, he lay down on a pillow and sighed. "Can this be, Wanthong? Because I lost the case to Phra Wai, he's acting high and mighty. Like father, like mother, like son. The father won a victory in Chiang Mai, and now carries himself like the Lord of the Lions. His son became Phra Wai and now thinks he can bully me without respect. What can I do?"

Fetching a slate, he drafted a charge at some length, then put it down on paper and set off for Ayutthaya. That day the king had gone lotus viewing. When Khun Chang arrived at the palace, he found a place to wait below the royal landing. Close to nightfall, the king returned, speeding along with a full boatload of oarsmen and the usual flotilla following noisily behind. Khun Chang waded doggedly out with the letter held above his head. The coxswain thought his bald head was a water monster spirit and hit it with a coconut shell. Some pages on fanning duty fell out of the boat, shouting, "A big tiger is swimming towards us!"

Khun Chang hung on to the boat and said, "It's not a tiger, it's just my bald head. Let me present a petition. I'm angry beyond endurance."

King Phanwasa was furious. "This villain is inhuman. This is not the way or the place to do it. Someone take his petition. Give him thirty strokes, then let him go."

In the middle of that night, Khun Phaen awoke with a start. The moon was shining brightly and a breeze wafted the fragrance of flowers. His thoughts turned to his old partner. "It's a pity Wanthong has been far apart and lacking in love. Twice she was separated from me. It was bad of me to get lost in love with two others and abandon her to sorrow. Now that Wai has been to fetch her, I must make love to her."

He dressed, doused himself in fragrant water, and walked to Wanthong's room in his son's apartment. Finding her fast asleep, he sat beside her, touched her lovingly, and said "Wake up. I've come to see you."

Wanthong was awake and knew who it was but feigned sleep, unable to find a reply because both love and anger choked her heart, both longing and disquiet churned her soul.

Khun Phaen asked, "Are you angry that I abandoned you? My love for you hasn't lessened even a little. Truly I've been in the wrong but why lie still and hold a grudge?" He lay close beside her, kissing and fondling to kindle her love.

Wanthong rose from the bed. "Are you annoyed that I won't talk? What's right or wrong, you please think for yourself. This body of mine is completely tainted. It seems Wanthong is two-minded—wherever you go, that's what you hear. The truth is, though I went to stay in another house, I always thought of returning to you because I love my child and my husband very much. I went away then because I had to. I was angry because my partner didn't love me. When he had others to enjoy, he ignored me completely. It was a waste to have gone through hardship together in the forest. But I'm saying too much. I'll annoy you. Have a care for me, and don't make me ashamed again."

"Truly I was in the wrong, Wanthong, but it's not true that I was carried away by other loves. When I was in jail, I grieved for you every day and night. I thought of escaping and coming to get you back but I feared that would pile up another problem. On return from Chiang Mai I meant to come for you but Wai's case caused more delay. Nobody else in this land has been wronged and tormented as much as you and me. I thought of appealing to King Phanwasa but I knew it would take a long time. So I sent our son to fetch you. I'll cherish you just like the times when we were in the wilds. I beg forgiveness. My love for you is still a passionate love. Don't make me die of despair."

He hugged her to his chest and gently cradled her breasts. "Heavenly flesh, fulfill a man's feelings."

"I don't wish to disappoint your love. If I'd expelled you from my heart already, I wouldn't have come here. Though my body went away, my heart still counted you as my husband. But I worry the sin will weigh on me when I die. One woman, two husbands! Unless this can be wiped away, I won't fall in with your wishes. You're not a young man so don't be so tormented. If you love me, shield me from shame. Petition the king. Stop pleading to sleep together. I'm having none of that. You'll get too used to it."

"Were it anyone else, I'd give up, but it's you so I'm not listening."

He hugged her close, kissing and caressing, his body twining around hers. Wanthong blocked him and would not consent. He pulled her close, urging her to intimacy. She twisted to obstruct him. A breeze wafted the fragrance of flowers. Bees caressed plants in the deep forest, but the flowers wilted, the stalks withered, and the pollen wept. Thunder rumbled and crashed but the shower shied from the flowers and splashed around the ocean shore. After the heartquake, they slept.

Late at night, only a rustle of dry leaves disturbed the silence. Wanthong dreamed she was transported into a wild forest where she wandered, twisting and turning, until she was lost. A fierce tiger, crouched watching at the edge of her path, pounced on her, picked her up in its jaws, and dragged her away into the forest. She woke in fright with a shriek and related the dream to Khun Phaen.

He knew the omen was serious. He made an astrological calculation which confirmed his fears, but he did not want to tell her. "A dream like this doesn't foretell trouble. It came because you're very unsettled. Tomorrow I'll perform a ceremony to make sure nothing bad happens. Don't be worried."

When the sun touched the hilltops and streaks of dawn brightened the sky, the king thought about Khun Chang. "Is there anyone as vile as this vilest of men? Hardly a night has passed since his last charge, and now he presents another, even standing in water out of his depth. Last time it was about Wanthong. What's it about this time?"

On entering the morning audience, the king asked, "Who's brought his charge?" Phramuen Si presented it to the king. Once he knew the content, the king lost his temper. "What is so urgent about this? Don't these people know that Wanthong isn't the only woman in the world? At the time of the old case, I sent Wanthong to be with Phaen. Why did she rush off to live with Chang? Phramuen Si, fetch Wanthong, Khun Phaen, and Phra Wai immediately!"

On learning of the summons, Khun Phaen called Wanthong into an inner room, put beeswax on her lips, and made her eat a betelnut treated by mantra to overcome various difficulties. He enchanted a mixture of spirit oil and sandal oil, and daubed enchanted powder on her forehead so anyone she met would love her.

When they arrived in the audience hall, the king's mood improved because of the force of the powerful lore.

"Look here, Wanthong, when you came from the forest, I ordered you to live with Khun Phaen. Why didn't you stay with him instead of rushing off to live with Chang again? And now have you begun to hate Chang's awful head and danced back to Khun Phaen? You seem to switch and swap husbands, back and forth."

With face bowed, hands clasped above her head, and hair standing on end, Wanthong addressed the king. "My liege, when Khun Phaen was imprisoned and I was heavily pregnant, Khun Chang came and said that Your Majesty had given an order granting me to him. I didn't want to go but he used force. The neighbors feared they would be in the wrong if they intervened. It was beyond my power to resist. My life is under the royal foot."

The king raged at Khun Chang. "You obscene monkey! Tugging a woman back and forth. It turns out I'm not the Lord of Life. You think I'm just a lord in a mask play with no authority. You should be thrashed with a pair of canes down your whole spine."

The king asked Wanthong, "How were you able to come back now? Did you run away from Chang, or did someone fetch you?"

The question alarmed Wanthong. "My liege, I returned now because Phra Wai fetched me, but I did not sneak off to be unfaithful. Khun Phaen hasn't made love with me. May Your Majesty have mercy."

"Phra Wai has acted arrogantly. It seems the country has no master. People don't pay attention to the law but do whatever they like. If they slash and kill one another, it'll be a danger to the populace. That angers me. I gave Wanthong to Phaen but Chang dragged her off, citing my name and shouting threats to frighten her. He deserves to be knocked unconscious right here, thrashed countless times, and have a ripe coconut stuffed in his mouth. You, Phra Wai, have also committed a serious crime. Why didn't you fetch her in daytime? Chang has laid two charges—that you abducted your mother, and that you did so on behalf of his father. These are serious crimes and a major blemish on your record. If you wanted your mother, you should have made a case in the proper way. There are courts and codes of law. You should be whipped painfully with a lash and fined on par with an adulterer."

The king turned to Wanthong. "This whole affair arose because of a woman, and grew through jealousy and rivalry. To have fruit and flowers on a single branch, many big roots have to be pruned away. Wanthong is like a taproot. If its base is cut, the leaves will wither. Who she should have as partner must be decided today. Heigh! Wanthong, make a final decision right here and now. Your having two husbands angers me. If you love the second one, go and live with Chang. If you love the old one, go to the side of Khun Phaen. Don't spin round in circles and earn people's contempt!"

Wanthong was petrified. Khun Chang looked across, winking and raising his eyebrows. Phra Wai signaled to his mother by pursing his lips towards his father. Wanthong's head spun in confusion. At a loss, she remained silent.

The king asked, "Do you love neither? Then say so. If you want to be with your son, there's no objection. Whatever you wish I will command, and from now onwards that will be final!"

Wanthong's mind went blank. Because she had reached the years for which she was born, fate clouded her reason. "How can I say I love Khun Chang when in truth I don't love him even a little? I love Khun Phaen and my son. If I say the wrong thing, the king will rage and have no mercy. Be neutral. Let the king dispose at will."

She bowed her head and said, "My love for Khun Phaen is a great love because we shared such hardship going into the forest together. We lacked everything but loved and cherished each other. All the time I lived with Khun Chang, he said not one harsh word, heaped money on me and me alone, and placed servants at my beck and call as if they were my own. Phra Wai is my own flesh and blood. I brought him up and love him as much as my husband." As she spoke, her body began to tremble in terror.

The king erupted in anger like gunpowder sparked by flame. "Oh Wanthong, how can you be like this? You cannot say which one you love! Your heart wants both of them so you can switch back and forth. You have a reserve deeper than the fathomless ocean—so deep that filling it with bricks, rocks, rafts, masts, weeds, and great junks makes no difference. You're base, evil, and black of heart like a jet gem in a pile of feces. You have a beautiful appearance and a sweet sounding name, yet your heart is not as loyal as a strand of hair. Even animals know what they want and mate only in season. You're baser than base, a town tramp, lustful, insatiable. Anything new, you'll take. Hundreds or thousands, you'd not be satisfied. Even a harlot has only one man at a time. Nobody has so many sniffing around as you. Why should you stay a burden on my land? Wai, don't count her as your mother. Khun Chang and Khun Phaen, I'll find wives for both of you. There are plenty of suitable beauties. This scourge, this slut, is not suitable for loving. Cut her out of your hearts. Heigh! Execute her immediately! Cleave open her chest with an axe without mercy. Don't let her blood touch my land. Collect it on banana leaves for feeding to dogs. If it touches the earth, the evil will linger. Execute her for all men and women to see!"

THE DEATH OF WANTHONG

Phraya Yommarat gave orders for Wanthong to be led away to the execution ground. Phra Wai and Khun Phaen rushed after her, brimming with tears of grief. Thong Prasi hurried after them on wobbly legs, her body trembling, her tears flowing. News was sent to Laothong, Kaeo Kiriya, Soifa, and Simala, who arrived in a state of shock, beating their chests and blubbering like chicks.

Khun Chang tripped over a brick and fell headfirst into a pile of dogshit, but got up and dashed ahead with a swarm of flies buzzing around the stench. A servant called, "Master, wipe off the dogshit first, I beg you."

"You villain, where is there any dogshit on me?"

"All over your face and the top of your head. You're swarming with flies."

Khun Chang would not listen. "Leave me be!"

They arrived at the execution ground. Wanthong sank down at the end of her strength. Kaeo Kiriya, Laothong, Soifa, and Simala went off to gather flowers for begging forgiveness. A wall of onlookers surrounded them. Khun Chang pushed his way through. People started away from him. "You stink to death of dogshit, sir!"

He stumbled up to Wanthong. Phra Wai leapt up angrily, hit Khun Chang and put a lock on his head, getting both hands dirtied.

Phraya Yommarat said, "Don't, Phra Wai. Why beat this lost fellow?" He grabbed Khun Chang to drag him away. "You villain! My hands are covered in dogshit. If I'd known, I wouldn't have stopped Phra Wai."

Khun Phaen rushed across and hit Khun Chang, who fell down, banging his head on Thong Prasi. She cried out angrily, "Oh, this is impossible!" Khun Chang ran off.

Wanthong hugged her beloved son. "Today I must be parted from you forever. By evening I'll be dead and covered with earth. From birth, your life hasn't been like others'. Sadly you were severed from me at seven and blew away to float on the wind. All I could do was yearn, fearing I wouldn't even see your dead body, but now you've come to cremate your mother's corpse. It was worthwhile carrying you in my womb, trekking across hill, swamp, and stream. With you in my belly as companion, I could put up with the hardship of the wilds, the heat of the sun, rain, leeches, gnat bites, and thorns. Then I gave birth safely and felt relieved. I rocked you, lullabied you, and tended you for seven happy years. But Khun Chang wickedly kidnapped you and we had to be parted again for a long time. It's like struggling to find a way out of a deep forest, seeing the moon shining brightly in the sky, and thinking you'll be happy forever, then the lightning strikes and you fall, buried deep in the earth. You have only half a day to set eyes on me. After that there'll be nothing but cinders and ash. Go home, my son. Don't wait for evening. When they sever my neck it'll be a pitiful sight. Look on my face while I'm still alive so that is what you'll see when you think of your mother."

Her mind swam and she collapsed onto the earth, lying motionless with arms around her beloved son.

Phra Wai massaged her until she revived. "You raised me and taught me, fed me, bathed me, suckled me, washed my hair and coiled my topknot, worried over me when I was sick, strung up a net so I wouldn't be bothered by flies, bugs, and mosquitoes. But then I had to flee to Kanburi to survive. Nobody has been poor in quite the same way as me, starved of the sight of both father and mother. When I was grown, I came to the city and found Father in jail and so poor he had nothing, not even a lowercloth. I applied myself to study, went to war, won victory, and gained wealth, servants, a house, rank, and happiness. The only thing missing was Mother so I went to fetch you. I meant to make you happy. I didn't know I was leading you to your death—like a child killing his own mother."

Phra Wai turned and said, "Hey, executioner! Chop me instead. Let me die in her place."

Khun Phaen sat listening quietly. She turned to clasp his feet. He buried his face in her back. "It was a waste for us to have gone through such suffering, scratching the earth to feed like birds. We crossed streams, crags, ravines. I destroyed an army of thousands to protect you, and we weren't apart for a single day. If they'd killed us both in the forest, I wouldn't have felt as bad as I feel now. But we survived, came to Ayutthaya, and won the trial. I felt happy that our troubles were over and all the effort was worthwhile. But ill fate caught up with me and I was put in jail. When you gave birth, I didn't know whether the child was boy or girl, alive or dead. When I got out of jail I meant to come after you, but on return from Chiang Mai, I found comfort and forgot you for almost a year. Then our son fetched you and I felt our troubles were behind us. In many battles, I was never defeated. My reputation spread throughout the land. What's happening now is pitiful. I've protected the lives of tens and hundreds of thousands. Only my greatest love I can't protect, because the king has passed judgment. If he would pardon your life, I'd deliver him whatever cities he desires. Stay here. I'll go to petition the king."

"Don't! Don't be rash! The time you begged for Laothong, you were clapped in irons. This time you'll be condemned to die too. Hell is a dark place and I fear it. If you live on, you can make merit and send it to me."

Khun Phaen could say nothing more. Feeling hopeless and helpless, he collapsed flat on the ground. The crowds of onlookers could not smother their own sadness. The only sound heard was weeping and wailing, like a forest blasted by a fierce gale that blows leaves, twigs, and branches into trembling turmoil.

Kaeo Kiriya knelt down with a salver of flowers and betel. "I beg your forgiveness. We gave ourselves to the same husband. If there's any matter that has angered you, I beg you to pardon me so it will not be added to my karma."

"I hold nothing against you, Kaeo Kiriya. If I offended you in any way, please forgive me."

Laothong went forward. "If I've wronged you in the past, please absolve me of blame from today."

Wanthong replied, "I abused you a great deal. I beg your forgiveness too."

Soifa and Simala made their tearful apologies in turn. Wanthong called for flowers, and went to pay respect to Thong Prasi. "I take leave of you today. If I've made you angry in any way, let the karma lapse."

Thong Prasi raised her trembling hands in acceptance and fell down faint in the dust. When she recovered, she said, "Don't abandon merit. Be intent on prayer, dear daughter. Find some flowers for your mother, dear Wai. It's better to remember the goodness of the Buddha. Why are you crying, Phaen? Go and find a bowl to pour water on the ground. Simala fetch some rice to make offerings to the spirits. It's nearly nightfall." Thong Prasi mumbled and grumbled on.

Khun Chang sat some distance away on his own, blubbering and babbling. "Oh Wanthong, you'll die because this stupid mole went to petition the king. In truth, I'm not the reason. The king asked you who you loved but you were two-minded and couldn't think straight. If you loved Chang and Chang alone, it would be sweet bliss. You could stay in a house with huge pillars and live a life of ease. But you're going to die in full public view. Where will I find another like you? I'll donate my house and possessions to the monks, be ordained, and grieve from nightfall until cockcrow for a thousand lives, with not one day's relief. Just my own five fingers, until death."

Thong Prasi heard him raving. "Why are you weeping, you baldheaded, cockle-skulled lowlife?"

Phra Wai dragged Khun Chang away by his ear. Khun Chang squirmed and screamed. "I truly love her absolutely, Phra Wai, sir." Phra Wai elbowed him down to the ground. "You slave, get lost."

Khun Chang loped off, barging into some onlookers who kicked him on his way. "I love my wife. I weep for her. And he elbows me for nothing. I won't let this pass."

Phra Wai called out, "Hey baldy! Go and press more charges somewhere."

Khun Phaen called out, "Stop it, Wai!" He tugged his son back.

Phra Wai said, "Father, I'm going to petition the king to pardon her. I don't care about the consequences. When she is this close to death, I must repay my debt of gratitude."

Khun Phaen scratched her horoscope on the ground. "There's a lot of obstruction. Someone with this position cannot survive. Even if you appeal to the king and he grants the pardon, she won't escape death. See her face. She looks white and close to death already. It's nearly time, almost four o'clock."

Phra Wai looked at the horoscope. "I can see it all—bad fate, life, and death. But I must still repay her kindness. I'll appeal for her. Then it depends on her own karma. Father, please stay and protect her. Don't let them kill her first."

He went up to Phraya Yommarat. "Sir, please hold off the punishment. I'm going to attend on King Phanwasa to beg a reprieve."

"Go! Don't delay. If you take too long, I'll fear the king's authority too much to hold off."

Phra Wai rushed to the palace and sat waiting for the audience, chanting mantras to inspire love and reciting prayers for the king's anger to recede. Watching Phra Wai enter and prostrate, the king felt concern for him on account of the lore. "Why have you come? Have they executed your mother yet?"

Phra Wai saw that his lore was working and that the king was not badly disposed. "My liege, most excellent in all worlds, my life is beneath the royal foot. Your Majesty raised me to be a lieutenant of the pages. Every morning and night your goodness is over my head. Your humble servant's mother is a very bad woman who has gone astray as a result of excessive carnal desire. Your Majesty has rightly shown her no favor. If this were a sister, aunt, or grandmother, I'd leave her to die without pity, but this is the mother who suffered to carry me in her womb. Because of her, I was born and live long. I appeal to Your Majesty to bestow on me a favor so word may spread that I repaid the debt of gratitude to my mother. I beg Your Majesty to pardon her life and instead have her thrashed and confined in pitiful circumstances as is appropriate to her improper conduct."

The king felt compassionate. "I have sympathy for you, Phra Wai. You gained royal favor and I've not yet exhausted my gratitude. I'll lift your mother's punishment as a reward." He instructed an official to convey his order to Phraya Yommarat. "Hurry before the sword falls."

Phra Wai and the official each mounted a horse and galloped along the road, waving a white flag as a signal. Seeing them coming, Phraya Yommarat was confused. Because the fruit of Wanthong's karma was to be executed, he misconstrued what was happening. "Phra Wai went away on foot and now someone is coming on horseback, flying a white flag. When Phra Wai made his petition, the king must have been angry that she hadn't been executed yet. I'll be in the wrong. Quick, carry out the sentence!"

The guards dragged Wanthong over. Khun Phaen rushed across and threw himself on top of her. The executioner chopped down, hitting Khun Phaen, but the sword bent and crumpled. Guards hauled Khun Phaen away. The executioner raised his sword, glinting in the light, and struck down, severing Wanthong's neck.

Phra Wai galloped up, leapt down from his horse, and embraced the feet of his mother's motionless body. Khun Phaen collapsed down flat, as if he would never rise again. Khun Chang fell rolling on the ground at a distance away. Thong Prasi flailed in agony. Kaeo Kiriya crumpled, dropping her son. The packed crowd of onlookers was in turmoil.

Phra Wai turned on his father in a fury. "I left you to look after her but you let this happen. I'm blaming you. You won't miss her because you have a fine flock of other wives. You're so skilled in lore that you face thousands of Lao without fear. You have stunning mantras, powerful enough to immobilize people in droves. Why didn't you blow one to stun this executioner? She died because you didn't help her. Or have you lost your powers?"

He turned to Phraya Yommarat. "The king granted a pardon, but just now my mother died. What happened to your promise to wait? Have you some reason for revenge on me? Maybe you loathe me but why take it out on my mother? You had her killed to show off your attention to duty. On top of that, they chopped at my father too. What was he being punished for? Was there a royal command to execute him too? I'm your sworn enemy until my dying day."

In fear, Phraya Yommarat bowed to ask forgiveness. Phra Wai turned to see the executioner and rushed upon him, knocking him down flat on the ground and drawing his sword. Crowds of people ran off in turmoil. Phra Wai kicked Khun Chang down and put a foot on his neck. Khun Phaen rushed over and pulled Phra Wai away. "Don't lose your temper. She had to die as fruit of her karma. It was beyond my powers."

Phra Wai angrily pushed his hand away and growled, "I'm going to slash him." Khun Phaen wrested the weapon out of his hand. Phra Wai collapsed down beside his mother's body.

"Listen to your father. It's natural that all of us born in any shape and form must die. Even the earth, sky, and oceans are annihilated in the era-destroying fire. There's no point wallowing in tears. Your mother's body is still lying there. Think about putting her to rest, my son."

Smothering his sadness, Phra Wai turned to give orders to servants. "Bring white cloth and wrap the body without delay. Cut planks to make a coffin, line it with banana fronds, and have it carried for burial in the graveyard. Assign people to guard the body closely."

All returned home in tears. The house was as chilly as a graveyard. The neighbors and townsfolk shared the sadness.

When dawn lit the sky, Khun Phaen sent a servant to Suphan to tell Siprajan that Wanthong was dead. The servant met Saithong, who collapsed in grief at the news. Siprajan came out and saw Saithong. "Hey you, what did you do to her?"

The servant cried out, "Mistress Wanthong has died."

Siprajan misheard him to say "is to die." She feverishly prayed to the spirits and the Buddha. "Lord, let her survive. When did she get sick? Well, well! Khun Chang is too embarrassed to tell me until she's almost dead."

She blundered off to Khun Chang's house and climbed up to the central hall. Khun Chang, who had returned the night before, sat bent over, weeping.

Siprajan saw his face. "What's up? So bleary eyed."

Khun Chang said, "Wanthong shouldn't have died. It happened because Phlai Ngam abducted her and the king became enraged. I didn't lay charges with the king. He knew and had her executed. That's the truth."

Siprajan realized her daughter was dead. She collapsed flat on her back and lay still. Khun Chang tended to her but she did not move. He sent his servants to fetch doctors who massaged, applied smelling salts, and squeezed her jaw, but it was a long time before she recovered her senses.

After Khun Chang had her sent home on a litter, she continued to wail on and on. "Oh my Wanthong! You shouldn't have gone to the city and let them execute you. If I'd known it'd come to this, I wouldn't have allowed any man to enjoy you as husband. I'd have had the abbot ordain you as a nun, and not let myself be carried away by piles of money. When Phlai Ngam was a little child, I thought of him tenderly as a grandson. I didn't know he'd grow up so heartless that he could be the cause of his mother's death. Oh, I'll be lonely in my dotage! Why should I live to suffer?"

Saithong took leave of Siprajan and went by boat to the capital. On arrival she asked, "Where's Wanthong's body?"

Khun Phaen said, "Buried at Wat Takrai." He told someone to take her there. She descended from the house in tears, and pushed herself along in a daze. At the graveyard, her sobbing worsened and she collapsed down in a sad heap. "Oh dear Wanthong, why did you come to lie in this earth, to make a little tunnel and flee away by yourself? It was a waste to have loved you from long ago. We shared one house, one heart, one husband. We faced good and bad in happiness and harmony. Now you've abandoned me to sorrow. I'll die and follow so we can go together."

Phra Wai's thoughts turned to the cremation. "Let's make it very grand. I must approach King Phanwasa." He dressed and went to attend on the king.

At audience, the king noticed Phra Wai. "How was it with your mother yesterday? You gained my favor but didn't return. What did your father say?"

"I wasn't in time. When I arrived, they'd severed her head down onto the ground." He sobbed fitfully in front of the royal throne.

The king felt as if thunder had struck the palace. For some time, he was too stunned to say anything. "I feel great pity for Phra Wai. You secured your mother's reprieve but she did not escape punishment. That was her fate. I'll provide money and materials for an appropriate cremation. Let it be a lively affair lasting many days and nights with mask plays, dramas, Mon dances, boxing, wrestling, and shadow plays after nightfall. I'll provide a casket for the body, a bier, decorations, all kinds of entertainments, and fireworks."

"The royal kindness is great beyond estimation. Your humble servant is happy as no other. The word will spread through every land that Your Majesty bestowed such favor on the head of his servant. Though I was unable to fulfill my wish and my mother has passed away, let me repay her kindness. I request leave to enter the monkhood for seven days."

"I'm pleased with you, Wai. You show filial devotion in recognition of her goodness with a full heart."

Phra Wai prostrated and took leave.

The requirements for the cremation were carried to the wat. Relatives gathered. Siprajan arrived. Close to sundown, the body was dug up, cleansed, and placed in a casket provided by the king. Flute and drum played. Monks were invited to chant. Phlai Chumphon scattered puffed rice in front of the procession. The relatives, all wearing white lowercloths, followed behind in mourning. The body was taken into a crematory pavilion and raised onto a bier.

The site was fashioned as a mountain, so artfully painted and ornamented that many thought it was really rock. There were steep slopes, cliffs, ravines, streams, a ledge for a hermit's abode, gods and goddesses, a tiger and bear biting at each other, a gamboling deer stalked by a hunter wearing a mule's head as disguise, a forest dweller goggling his eyes and pulling faces like a ghost, and gaur eating grass. Between the rock cliffs was a clearing made from paper stuck on a board and fashioned as ponds and islands. Above, birds posed with outspread wings.

The base for the casket was fashioned in the shape of a lotus. Above, were three sharp peaks made with gold and glass filigree. Fragrant garlands of threaded flowers hung down, along with glittering crystal pendants. Standing screens were painted with scenes from legendary tales. Brightly shining mirrors were placed on the arches above the pillars. Crystal lanterns were lined up along with rows of candles. Handsome mats were laid on the floor. After sunset, performers came to advertise their particular shows, all shouting at the same time in a noisy hubbub.

Next morning after sunrise, the shows began, competing against one another merrily. There were mask plays, dramas, Mon dances, singers, puppets, a troupe of clowns including a hunchback, a Chinese opera with actors made up magnificently, and an old couple exchanging flirtatious repartee, making people laugh uproariously.

Throngs of people walked around to watch. Gentlefolk, ordinary people, and paupers jostled shoulder to shoulder. Young country girls with powdered faces kept bumping into people and making others laugh. Unruly drunks staggered around, raising their fists to challenge passersby for a fight. Playboys with their hair cut handsomely short *en brosse* prowled around, preening themselves and courting girls by throwing flowers.

In the afternoon sunlight came the throwing of alms. People climbed up to trees of plenty, removed the cloth covers, picked off the limes containing money, and hurled them in all directions. The waiting crowds scrambled to catch the limes, chasing, hitting, and elbowing one another.

At dusk, fireworks were lit for entertainment. Candle-showers whizzed and rockets popped from tall towers. Shadow players were called over to set up their screens. The puppets looked grotesque with curly hair, curved noses, and jutting necks like suffering ghosts.

Relatives went to sit with the body. Thong Prasi and Siprajan got into an argument. Thong Prasi said, "I've never seen anything like it. All because you colluded with that Chang."

"He's a rich man. For better or worse, we've depended on him in many ways."

"My dear, that was a mistake. Because you depended on Chang, your child was chopped dead."

"What rubbish! It was your child that caused the calamity."

Phra Wai called on his grandmothers to desist. The pair brimmed over with tears.

Khun Chang arrived in a boat packed with monk's robes, alms offerings, and items of worship. He went up to find the abbot. "I've come for Wanthong's cremation, and I've brought all the requirements along. But the host has been my enemy for many years. I fear he'll attack me and make a scene. Please speak to him and settle the matter."

The abbot sighed. "A cremation ceremony is for making merit. Why quarrel and create trouble? Leave the matter to me. As the other party was my pupil, I can talk to him."

He sought out Phra Wai at the hall for the ceremony. "Today you're making merit. It would be better to put an end to your quarrel with Khun Chang as a good deed to make merit for your mother. He's here but is afraid to come in. He asked for compassion and said he'd remember your kindness until death."

"I wish to make merit without any trouble. Whatever gave rise to my mother's misfortune, let the matter stop right here. Please tell Khun Chang I'll not make any obstruction."

The abbot reported the news to Khun Chang, who went to greet Phra Wai, then made merit by presenting dedicatory robes and giving alms.

After three days of ceremonies, the decorations were taken down. Phra Wai went to the graveyard, sat in a meditation pose, composed his mind, blew a formula onto sesame oil to make it boil, then applied the oil to his body, clothes, and head. He climbed up onto the pyre and had the body lifted and laid on top of him. Relatives brought incense, candles, flowers and carved pieces of sandalwood. The fire was lit. Flames blazed up. An ensemble played with flute and drum. Firecrackers were lit by fuse.

The firewood and coffin were consumed. Phra Wai came back out. The circle of people watching were impressed that he was invulnerable even to fire.

After monks had shaved his head, Phra Wai went into the ordination hall and a monk initiated him into the monkhood. Khun Chang rushed up to Phra Wai and said, "I want to be ordained as a novice for Wanthong. I'd be ordained as a monk but that's impossible, because I can't go without eating and I don't have the thirty-two attributes. Please initiate me."

Phra Wai said, "That's up to you, goggle eyes. I can't do it."

Khun Chang rushed to pay respect to Abbot Nu. "Please help me, Your Lordship. Please shave my head."

"You're always a laugh, disciple. I don't have a shaving knife."

Khun Chang dashed into the wat and asked to borrow a knife. An elder replied, "There's only a dirty old rusty one in the spittoon."

Khun Chang ran back to the abbot. "It's hopeless, Abbot Nu. A machete or a sickle will have to do."

The abbot picked up a huge cleaver. "There's only this blunt blade. Well, I'll give it a try."

He sharpened it on a stone. "The rust hasn't all gone, disciple." Only two strokes were needed to leave the pate totally bare. He had Khun Chang lie on his back and he scraped away the whole tangled mat on Khun Chang's cheeks and chest. "It goes all the way down to the ankles. I don't think I can shave all that."

Khun Chang went to bathe and returned holding his robes. He rolled his eyes and cried "*Uka*," then mumbled, "Please recite and I'll follow, Abbot Nu. I don't know the formula."

The abbot made an appropriate recitation. Khun Chang put on the upper robe very hastily, getting the cloth tangled round his body. Carrying a walking stick, he paced away with face down, trying to hold in the bulges and look composed.

Thong Prasi and Siprajan shakily lowered themselves down and raised their clasped hands. "May we invite you to give a sermon, Novice Chang?"

"Willingly." He lurched up to the pulpit, sat cross-legged, and began. "This year and month are the hibernal season. Two rains retreats have passed. The present is the semolina era when cocks crow. The religion will be complete at five thousand. There's still a remnant of three hours."

Holding her hands clasped, Thong Prasi said, "Pitiful. Please give a sermon that makes sense, damn you."

Novice Chang recited something that sounded like Pali and proceeded to expound on its meaning. "There were thirty women. What all their names were, I don't know. The one with the swollen eyes and stubby legs was the first. Each had six children. They built a house by a cowitch tree."

With her hands still clasped, Thong Prasi spat and said, "This sermon isn't worth hearing, you muddlehead."

Khun Chang spluttered loudly, "Whoever spits on a sermon will turn into a suffering ghost."

Siprajan prostrated and said, "Yes, yes. May you give sermons more wonderful and hauntingly beautiful than I have ever heard!" People around laughed out loud.

Novice Chang turned the leaves of a Pali text and pretended to read. "The lotus lady was the wife of Sang Sinlapachai. Suwannahong flew to Lanka. Nang Montho was the wife of the conch shell. There are many true tales from the past. Follow whatever you can, O disciples."

Someone asked, "Does anyone know what this is about?"

Novice Chang rolled up the text and came down from the pulpit. A boy spoke to his friends a bit too loudly, "The awful old gourd is leaving. Phew!"

Novice Chang turned back angrily, "Mm! What did you say about me, you slave child?"

"I was praising the fine sermon but your ear didn't catch it."

Novice Chang laughed. "Hey, go and fetch some sweets."

The boy shouted in glee. Thong Prasi said, "I'd rather feed dogs than make merit. The boy made a fool of you, you tenderhead."

When Wanthong's cremation was over, Phra Wai stayed in the monkhood for seven days. After disrobing, he went to attend on the king. "My liege, allow me to offer Your Majesty the merit from my time in the monkhood to repay my debt of gratitude to my mother."

The king smiled, joined his hands together, and said, "May you be blessed." After a moment's thought, he added, "How is your father, Khun Phaen? I had him govern Kanburi. Why is he still skulking here? Go and tell him, Wai."

Phra Wai returned home and relayed the news to Khun Phaen, who promptly started making preparations to leave. At dusk, he went to talk to Thong Prasi. "I've been worried for some time that the king would have me go to Kanburi. When Wai went to audience this morning, the king commanded exactly that. I feel sorry for you as you're getting much older. I wish to ask you to come with me."

Thong Prasi thought quietly and then said, "If I go along with you, I'll be very anxious about Wai. Being here on his own, he'll be lonely and in low spirits—orphaned in every way. My heart is split between my concerns for son and for grandson, but I think I must stay with Wai." She sighed wearily from indecision, then added, "Have a care for an old person, Kaeo Kiriya. Please let me have Phlai Chumphon. When I feel heavyhearted, looking at the face of my little grandson will help dispel the gloom."

These words threw Kaeo Kiriya into confusion. She would miss her dear son, but she was loath to displease her mother-in-law. "As you wish. If you want him, then let it be so."

At dawn on the next auspicious day, Khun Phaen brought Kaeo Kiriya and Laothong to take leave of his mother. Thong Prasi was pounding betelnut. She dropped the pestle with a bang, stared in a daze of grief, and mumbled blessings through her tears. "May none of you three suffer sickness. May your ages stretch to ten thousand years. May you be eternally hale and healthy. May you have a thousand children, one a day. Little Chumphon, come over here. Why are you crying to go with your mother? Don't you fear the animals in the forest? Stay with grandmother. I'll give you a doll, and buy you sweets to eat."

Kaeo Kiriya was flooded with tears. Khun Phaen hugged her gently in consolation. "Where will all this weeping and wailing get you? The journey isn't so long. Whenever you think of him, then come." Kaeo Kiriya stifled her sorrows, and passed her son to the grandmother.

Khun Phaen brought Skystorm, handed it to Phra Wai, and gave him a blessing. They mounted elephants and headed into the forest. A jumble of cases and baskets swayed back and forth along the way. Animals fled away in all directions. A great tiger crouched, intent on catching a young gaur. When it pounced and sunk its teeth, the gaur bellowed, but the tiger took fright at the approach of the people and loped away towards the deep forest. The gaur, almost mortally wounded, ran off to hide.

They made their way with all good speed
sun dipping and dropping, colors pale,
A mother gibbon swung from a tree,
He thought of his wife, doubly distressed,
Oh Wanthong, these are woods we knew
to play in a stream, cool-skinned bride.
Wanthong, my love, how can this be,
Some karma made in time's domain
So surely, the abbot saw it all.
As predicted, so indeed it happened.
Along the way, as the elephants drove,
Three nights he slept in a forest clearing
Mounts unroped, goods handed down,
raised men to cut timber, and speedily
At Kanburi, they made a happy household.
The home hummed in joy and merriment,

through grass and reed, by hill and dale,
cock and quail flying to find a nest.
whooped plaintively, piercing his breast.
"You'd be in this forest, had you not died.
when I took you from Khun Chang's side,
Deep inside, this sight compounds my pain.
never to see your bright beauty again?
did foreordain this unfortunate end.
I still recall what omens did portend.
Death did descend, unrelenting."
he strove to still his spirit's seething.
before riding on into Kanburi.
officials of the town met them merrily,
build a residency with every ornament.
On matters manifold, he gave fair judgment.
content and cheerful each night and day.

GLOSSARY

adept's knife—A knife that has been made with special materials, inscribed with yantra, and instilled with power by an adept. It is used in spirit ceremonies and carried for invulnerability.

Ayutthaya—Capital of Siam from 1351 to 1767.

Beguiler—A mantra to induce love.

betel (nut)—Areca nut, chewed as a mild stimulant, often wrapped in pan leaves and smeared with lime.

betel box—A small chest with compartments for carrying betelnut, pan, and tobacco; often carried by nobles as a sign of rank.

cangue—A yoke, board, or frame fitted around the neck as a form of restraint and punishment.

canopy boat—A long boat with prow and stern curved up, and an area amidships sheltered by a canopy, usually roofed with woven bamboo.

Chaophraya—The highest rank in the official nobility.

chicken-flapping—A popular entertainment in which singers improvise verses in a challenge-response style, while dancing with exaggerated elbow movements like chickens flapping their wings.

cowry—A small shell used as currency, worth 1/800th of a baht.

eaglewood—A tree, *Aquilaria agallocha/crassna*, with a resinous wood, highly prized as an aromatic, especially in China.

eye-level shrine—A temporary shrine for making offerings to the spirits, having four posts and holding a shelf at around eye level, with a white cloth stretched over the top (for the spirits to land).

forenoon meal—The one daily meal that monks take, normally during the hour before noon.

ganja—Marijuana.

Garuda—A mythical bird with a human body and the head, wings, and talons of an eagle; the mount of the god Vishnu.

gaur—*Bos gaurus*, a massive wild buffalo of dark grey or black color, weighing around a ton when fully grown.

grassflower—Not an actual plant but a metaphor for a plain woman.

hookah—A water pipe for smoking tobacco or ganja.

howdah—A seat on an elephant's back.

Iron Spear and Great Spirit—Two methods for determining auspicious and inauspicious directions.

jampi—*Michelia alba*, white champaka, a tree from the Magnolia family with very fragrant flowers and a name that translates as "remembered for years."

jataka—"Birth story," the previous lives of the Buddha recounted as moral tales.

Karen—General name for several ethnic groups that mainly live in the hills separating Siam and Burma.

karma—The accumulation of good or bad deeds.

Khaek—Term for foreigners of Malay, Indian, or Arabian origin.

Khun—Title for holders of low rank in the official nobility.

kris—Malay word for a dagger with a distinctive wavy blade.

lamduan—*Melodorum fruticosum*, a tree beloved of poets more for the mournful sound of its name rather than its beauty.

Lanchang—A Lao polity, once with capital at Luang Prabang, but in *KCKP* at Vientiane.

Lanna—A Tai polity with capital at Chiang Mai; absorbed into Siam in the late nineteenth century.

Lao—Language and ethnicity closely related to Thai. The term was applied by Ayutthaya and Bangkok to both Lanchang and Lanna.

Lawa—Name of a Mon-Burmese ethnic group, often used as a catch-all descriptor of non-Thai groups.

Loosener—A mantra for opening locks, easing childbirth, and bringing other forms of release.

lowercloth—Any cloth worn on the lower body by either men or women, usually a simple oblong wrapped around and tucked in at the waist.

Mahachat—The "great jataka," which tells how the Buddha in his previous life as Phra Vessantara achieved the "perfection of giving" by giving away his kingdom, possessions, wife, and children and thus was reborn as the Buddha.

mahout—A keeper of elephants.

mantra—A formula, prayer, or spell.

mask play—A traditional form of drama with actors wearing masks, mostly telling stories from the Ramakian (the Thai version of the Ramayana), popular at court but also in a raucous and stirring folk form.

Mon—A language and ethnic group related to Khmer, mostly found in southern Burma.

Mount Meru—The mountain at the center in the world in Thai Buddhist cosmology.

musth—A frenzied state of some male animals, including elephants.

naga—A mythical snake or serpent, modeled on a cobra.

Nai—Title for a commoner male.

novice—An apprentice monk. Traditionally it was customary for all young men to become a novice for a short period, in part for basic education.

Pali—An ancient Indian language used for the main texts of Buddhism.

pan—Leaf of the betel vine, used for wrapping betelnut for chewing.

patriarch—The head of the monkhood of a city or territory.

Phraya—A senior rank in the official nobility.

precept—Rule of conduct in Theravada Buddhism.

Rahu—A demon-god, believed to cause eclipses by swallowing the sun or moon.

sathu—Pali word uttered to show appreciation at sermons, etc.

sentinelle—An invented term for the female guards in the inner palace.

sepha—A genre of tales in verse form (like *KCKP*) and their performance by oral recitation.

sidebag—A simple cloth bag with a shoulder strap.

Songkran—Thai new year falling in mid-April.

stupa—Monument to enshrine a relic of the Buddha or ashes after cremation.

Subduer—A mantra for immobilizing people or putting them to sleep.

wai—Gesture of greeting and respect made by joining the palms in front of the chest or face.

waist pouch—A tubular pouch tied around the waist.

wat—Buddhist temple or monastery.

water of allegiance—A ceremony of swearing allegiance to the king by drinking sacred water.

yantra—A graphic device made by an adept, combining several powerful symbols, usually to provide protection.

ILLUSTRATIONS

PAGE

viii   Rich man's house

1   Sugar palms

9   Monks clowning

25   Building sand stupas

37   Bathing jetty

53   Monks' quarters

62   Eye-level shrine

76   Dowry boats

85   Camp in the forest

100   Betel tray

109   Abbot examining horoscope

120   Dowry procession

129   Canopy boat

141   Nobles at court

151   Palace ladies embroidering

158   Swords

163   Basin with fish

177   Banyan tree

185   Yantra

196   Elephant and howdah

207   Lotus seedpod

215   The full five irons

227   Soul ceremony

242   Porter with panniers

259   Looking glass

278   Shirt with yantra

294   Musicians asleep

304   Royal barge

319   Palace governesses

329   Monks chanting

341   Ordeal by water

350   A lord in a masked play

360   Incense, candles, and flowers